Lily Quinn

• VOLUME 2 •

NATALIE & ERIC SEVERINE

LOOSE LEAF
STORIES

Cover art by Gwynn Tavares
Edited by J. Cameron McClain,
Amber Presley and Miss Valentine

———

This is a work of erotic fiction.
It is not intended for minors.
All characters, organizations, places and events portrayed in this book
are either the product of the authors' imagination or are used fictitiously.

———

Find more of our books at LLStories.com

LILY QUINN BOOK #6

Raising THE DEAD

Chapter ONE

The old firehouse was a mess, with bulging garbage bags lying heaped up beside stacks of white sheetrock. A dozen paint buckets and stout wooden beams waited to be measured and cut down into new wall studs. My favorite stud, though, was busily tearing out the old drywall. Max had ripped his shirt on an exposed nail and now worked stripped to the waist. The crumbling wall left chalky streaks across his sweaty skin.

Not quite as sexy as grease smudges, I decided, but damned close.

"Too bad this place doesn't still have the fireman's pole," I said. "I could put it to good use."

Max lifted a sledgehammer and smiled at me. Even his dimples had somehow managed to get dusty from the work of renovating the outdated fire station.

"I could install one, if you really want," he offered.

Max Ferguson was my best friend in the world and if I said *yes*, he absolutely would put in a pole for me. For a moment, I seriously contemplated what dancing on one might do for his new garage's business. Once it opened... which was going to take a while if Max insisted on doing it all himself.

"You know, I could have given you money to hire a building crew, too," I said. "This place has been out of commission since the invention of the telephone. It's going to take forever to get fixed up."

Max hefted the sledgehammer and went to work smashing out the remains of the wall. He spoke between blows.

"No way," Max said. "I'm not... even comfortable... borrowing the startup money... from you. I can do this... myself."

"You're stubborn."

Max laughed. "You're one to talk, Lil."

"So did that waitress ever call you? Courtney?"

If she were sitting where I was now, watching shirtless Max at work, she definitely would have.

"Uh, yeah," said Max. He bashed out another chunk of wall.

"Did you guys go out?"

"Once," Max grunted. He stopped to lean on the sledgehammer.

"Just once?" I asked, frowning. "But I gave her your phone number weeks ago."

"I uh... can't really date much right now," said Max. He wiped his arms across his sweaty face, leaving more pale streaks of dust along his skin. "I've been pretty busy here most days. And I can't exactly afford dinners out until I get the garage finished and attract some customers. I have to get this place open before my bank account runs completely dry."

"I could–" I started.

"Not a chance, Lil."

Max picked up the hammer again and returned to work. If the handle on that thing were shorter, Max would have been a perfect Thor. He was certainly built like the hot blond god of thunder.

When Max finished renovating the old firehouse, it was going to make a great mechanic's shop. The garage was sized for fire engines and more than large enough to house several cars. There was room for a pair of tool benches and a lift for jacking up the vehicles Max would be working on.

Upstairs, there were even a couple of bunkrooms and a bathroom for the firefighters who had worked overnight back when the building served its original purpose. Each was meant for a dozen people, but Max was busily knocking the walls out between the rooms. When he was done, he would have a nicely-sized apartment and a short commute downstairs to the garage. It was going to be a pretty sweet setup.

What could Max do if I told him not to pay me back for buying the firehouse? Spank me? I wasn't sure, but the least I could do was help out. Max was already obligingly shirtless... All I had to do was get his pants off, power up a little and then those old walls would be toast.

But then my cell phone vibrated in my pocket. Shitty timing, phone. Max saw me pull it out and set down his sledgehammer. I waved in silent thanks as I checked the number on the screen. It was Stefano Rossi. Frowning, I put the phone to my ear.

"Hey, Stefano," I said.

"Can you speak safely?" the other hunter asked me without preamble.

I glanced at Max and pressed a finger to my lips. He nodded.

"Yeah," I told Stefano. "Sure. What's up? You never call me."

"A new bounty's been posted by the College. My spell card caught it ten minutes ago. The target's name is Richard Sung."

My frown deepened. To say that the wizards who hire me are secretive would be a hell of an understatement. There's exactly one building on their big estate that I'm allowed to enter and I don't even get free run of that. There are a handful of College sorcerers who work as bounty hunters, like Stefano. They're not only just as secretive as the rest of the wizards, but competitive, too.

"And why are you telling me about this?" I asked.

"I'm up in Quebec," said Stefano. "I can't get back to the city just now."

"Are you on vacation or something?"

"No, I'm tracking a werewolf. The one that infected Dominic, we think."

That made sense. Quebec was a long way off, but hunting down and capturing werewolves was practically a religion for Stefano. After what one of them did to his mother – and what that forced *him* to do to her – Stefano was entitled to chase down any demon-wolf he wanted.

"When you find that furry bastard, punch him in the nuts for me," I said. "And then again for Dominic."

"I doubt that opportunity will arise. But if it does... sure."

I laughed. "Alright. But why tip me off about this Sung guy?"

Stefano was silent for a moment. I heard wind whistling over the phone and the creaking of trees.

"Richard Sung killed two College magi," Stefano said at last. "One of them was a... friend. Bianca Taren."

I knew that tone of voice all too well.

"By *friend*, you mean *lover*, don't you?" I asked.

There was another pause and then Stefano sighed. "A friend. With benefits. We studied summoning theory under Vincent Myrdon when we were younger and... spent a lot of time together. But Bianca wasn't really interested in anything serious. She just wanted to have a good time."

"Sounds like I would have liked her," I said. "But I don't recognize the name."

"Bianca and Orson Clark weren't hunters. They were College magi."

Other than beating the rest of the bounty hunters to the punch and collecting my gold from Dorian, I didn't have much excuse to get to know the rest of the wizards of the College. Most of them quietly studied and worked their magic well outside the sphere of human awareness.

"Lilith, I want Richard Sung dealt with promptly and properly," Stefano said. "Can you do it?"

I was strangely flattered by his request. Stefano had called me to avenge the death of his friend and catch her killer. Not one of the other mages. Me.

"Sure. I'll take care of it," I told him. "But you can save me a trip out to the College if you tell me what they know."

"Orson was killed two days ago, and then Bianca was shot late last night."

"Shot? Like... with a gun?" I asked.

"Yes. Both of them. At close range with some kind of revolver, the College thinks, since there were no bullets or casings. But they can't be sure, since ejected shells can be removed and the slugs were dug out of the walls. No fingerprints, either."

"Then how does the College know it was this Sung guy?"

"Both Bianca and Orson were in their sanctums when they were killed. Sung may have been careful to cover his tracks from conventional investigation methods, but his identity was captured on the scry network."

"He found their sanctums?" I asked. "And got in?"

"Yes."

That didn't make much sense. A wizard's sanctum was one of those things that they were damned secretive about. How the hell did Sung find them?

"Wow. This guy must be scary powerful," I said. "What are we talking about here? A vampire? Some kind of fairy? Some of them can sniff out magic, I think."

"No. Richard Sung is a junior advertising executive. He's been working at a local agency for the last three years."

I stared at my phone. "Wait, Richard Sung is... human? Just a normal human man?"

"Yes, as far as we know. The College already checked on Sung's home and he's not there. So they contacted his employer. They say that Sung is out on bereavement."

"There's some irony," I grumbled. "Anything else?"

"You will need to move quickly," said Stefano. "You don't know how to use the scry network, but the rest of the College does."

I nodded, though only Max could see it. "I don't have much time before one of the other hunters closes in on Sung."

"I'm more worried that Richard Sung isn't done," Stefano said.

That idea hadn't occurred to me, but now my blood ran cold. "You mean he's going to kill more wizards."

"That's what I'm afraid of, yes."

"I'm on it, Stefano," I said. "I'll get this guy. And quickly."

"Thank you, Lilith."

Stefano hung up and I pocketed my cell phone. Max pulled open a nearby ice chest and fished out a pair of water bottles. He tossed one to me and then pressed the other to his sweat-drenched forehead for a moment before twisting the cap off.

"Is everything okay?" Max asked.

"Stefano tipped me off on a new bounty. A man named Richard Sung killed a couple of College wizards in their sanctums," I answered. "Somehow."

"Sanctum?"

"It's a sort of secret magical laboratory where wizards do their spells and keep all their weird shit. Everyone at the College has a sanctum, though no one's ever let me visit theirs."

Max nodded. "If two people have been murdered, why aren't the police handling it?"

"The College is probably covering it all up for right now," I said, then took a long drink of water. "Even if Richard Sung is human, the people he shot were wizards. Their sanctums aren't exactly the kinds of places the College want the police poking around."

"That makes sense," Max agreed. "But how could a normal human kill two wizards? I know they're not like you, but Stefano can take care of himself. Can't they throw lightning bolts and stuff?"

"Yeah, they can. But for one, Stefano is a bounty hunter. He's got a lot more physical and combat training than your average wizard.

They do more heavy reading than heavy lifting. I doubt most mages even know how to throw a punch."

Max looked a little disappointed.

"But... but magic?" he protested.

"Sure, wizards can summon storms and create earthquakes. Or roast you with a fireball if they don't mind melting the sidewalk. But their magic isn't easy and it isn't fast. The divination ritual we used to track down Dominic took Stefano hours to cast. And the spell that cured Dominic of the werewolf curse? Three moons. They finished it last week."

"Moons?" Max asked.

"Yeah. As in three PMS cycles. That's how wizards measure out time." I handed the rest of my water to Max, who had finished his. "And that's assuming they get it all right. One extra pinch of sulfur or two wolfsbane leaves instead of three and it all fizzles or blows up in your face."

Max downed the rest of my water in a couple thirsty gulps.

"So even with all their magic, wizards are basically just normal people," he panted.

"Yeah," I said. "Sneak up behind them, put a bullet into their head, and they die just like anyone else."

"And so do you, Lil." Max reached out and touched my shoulder. "Without sex, you're as human as those wizards. Be careful on this, okay?"

"Don't you worry about me, Max," I told him with a grin. "I get more action than a rabbit on Tinder."

He laughed. "Wow, Lil."

I ran a finger over the hard, sweat-slicked ripples of his abs. "You just keep being all shirtless and sweaty. I'm sure it won't be long before we're fucking away that pesky human vulnerability of mine."

Max smiled and tossed the second empty water bottle back into his cooler. He picked up his sledgehammer once again and returned to work knocking out the south wall.

Stefano was right. I didn't have a lot of time to spare. I needed to get to Richard Sung before the other bounty hunters, and more importantly, before he could kill another wizard. How had he managed that at all? An ordinary human had no protections against magic.

My new target wasn't at home, though. Stefano told me that already. Was Richard Sung on the run for the murder of two wizards? But he had left notice with his employer, even if it was a lie. Why? Were the deaths of Bianca Taren and Orson Clark premeditated? And what if they were just the beginning of something bigger?

I had a name and something that even the great western society of wizards and all-round weird magic people didn't: an intimate knowledge of the internet. If the scry network wouldn't find Richard Sung for me, maybe social media could.

So I dug my phone back out of my pocket to do some research... with frequent breaks to watch Max work.

Chapter
TWO

I took a taxi down to Southport. It wasn't a part of town where I wanted to leave my Alfa Romeo unattended and the i10 was still in shreds, courtesy of Dominic and his werewolf curse. Vincent Myrdon had removed the curse, but there was nothing he could do to magic my favorite car back into one piece. Well, not that Vincent mentioned to me, at least.

But I didn't need any favors from the head of the College. I could wait for Max to work his own brand of magic on the i10. I guess I could have bought a new one, but damn it, I *liked* that car. And after all the time and effort Max had poured into it over the years, I didn't want to just throw it away.

I paid the cab driver from my cell phone, left a sizable tip – what's the point of being rich if you can't tip well? – and climbed out of the car.

At the sidewalk, I studied the photograph on my phone screen one last time: Tony Davidson. According to his profile and a bunch of tagged pictures, Tony was a good friend of Richard Sung's. And according to Tony's digital check-ins, he spent his Thursday lunch hour at The Poling Place. Not voting, though if ballots had neon outlines of naked women all over them, voter turnout might go way up.

Tony either really needed to check his privacy settings or else he *never* planned on getting married.

The strip club was a big, blocky gray concrete building completely devoid of windows. If it weren't for all the neon, I might even have called it plain. The Poling Place's parking lot was about half full with the lunchtime crowd and a blackboard in the shape of a woman's silhouette advertised *The best breasts and thighs in South port.*

Ha ha.

But the barbecue sauce and grilled chicken actually didn't smell half bad. Maybe I'd start coming here for lunch.

I paid my cover charge to a stern middle-aged woman and went inside. After a few blinks, my eyes adjusted to the dimness and I looked around. The Poling Place used to be a warehouse, back in the days when Southport was an actual thriving port. But now that airplanes had taken a serious bite out of the ocean shipping business, the warehouse was just located too far away from the waterfront to be worth using for its original purpose.

It made a pretty good strip club, though. The main room was large enough for three full stages – though at lunchtime, only the center one was occupied – with plenty of tables in between. Mirrors lining the rear wall made the place seem even bigger and doubled the slowly swelling crowd.

The club's distant ceiling was hung with strings of lights. Each tiny bulb was dim, but hundreds of them filled the club with diffuse illumination and created the illusion of a star-studded sky overhead. Not a very convincing illusion, but I had to give The Poling Place points for the attempt. I appreciate any strip club that tries to look like something other than a scuzzy back alley.

The club was full of throbbing music and throbbing cock. A few women, too, even if you didn't include the dancers. Lunch here was sounding better and better, but not today. I was on the clock and that clock was counting down.

I did my best to ignore the show on the main stage – which wasn't easy. The girl dancing around one shiny brass pole up there had skin oiled and burnished until it looked like she was sculpted from bronze. Her tits were luscious and her nipples pierced with je-weled barbells that glittered like far more enticing stars than the lights overhead. The dancer winked at me. I felt the hot golden needle of her lust and answered with a sharp little stab of my own.

It was only with a monumental effort of will that I tore my eyes off the stripper. My hesitation had given the patrons time enough to start noticing me, so I hurried on. I didn't want them staring at me. Not yet, at least.

I checked and mentally mapped out the doors in case I had to make a hasty exit. I noted the location of the VIP lounge and then headed for the restroom. For this intelligence-gathering mission, I had worn a little black dress, the kind that clings like a second skin and you can ball up into a purse if you have to. Which, when I reac-hed the bathroom and slipped into a stall, was exactly what I did.

The ceiling in the bathroom was low and not the warehouse original, so I stood on the toilet and got up on my toes to push aside one of the black-painted acoustic tiles, revealing empty space be-yond. I tucked my purse into the ceiling and then replaced the tile.

When I emerged from the stall, I was wearing the highest heels I owned, a tiny red satin g-string and shiny matching bra. I posed in front of the mirror, brandishing my breasts like weapons. Perfect. Minus a coating of glitter, I looked just like the other dancers. Satis-fied, I strutted out of the restroom to prowl the floor like the mas-terful sex beast that I am.

Luckily, The Poling Place was large enough that I could avoid the other performers, as well as the staff. Lust warmed me like sunlight on my skin, but there was a lot of competition working the growing lunch crowd that helped me keep a relatively low profile.

Still, I had an impressive wad of bills folded into my bra by the time Tony arrived.

Tony Davidson was a big guy, with broad shoulders under his t-shirt. I knew from digging around some old posts online that Tony had met Richard Sung on the college soccer team and the two had remained friends afterward. Tony had the slightly soft-focus muscles of an athlete who hadn't been on the field since graduation, but not yet lost all of that hard-won definition.

Tony headed for a seat a few tables back from the main stage. I tucked my earnings into the corner of an empty stage – I didn't need the money weighing me down and some stripper was going to get a nice surprise later – and made a beeline for Tony to make sure I got to him first.

I reached his table just seconds after Tony had sat down and dropped into his lap. He blinked in surprise, but swiftly hooked an arm around my waist.

"Hi. I'm Violet," I introduced myself. "I'm new."

"Hello there, Violet," Tony said with a huge smile.

"I'm doing half-price lap dances in the VIP lounge. You know, for practice. Interested?"

"Oh yeah," he agreed quickly. "That sounds great."

So far, so good. I took Tony's hand and led him across the club, then through the door labeled in purple neon. The lounge was a much smaller room, lined with booths even more dimly lit than the main floor. It was still early and the room was empty, but as I propelled Tony into one of the little padded booths, I pulled the curtain closed behind me.

Tony seated himself with the comfort of long familiarity and patted his lap, smiling. I stood with my feet planted on either side of his and my ass pointed right at his face. I bounced it in front of Tony, then inched the soft cheeks down his chest. Finally, I was sitting in Tony's lap and ground my satin-covered pussy against his cock. He was already rock-hard.

"You said you're new?" Tony asked.

I glanced back over my shoulder and nodded. "My first day. There was supposed to be some training and stuff, but I got here late. So I guess they'll do it tomorrow."

"Well, you're doing great."

Tony put his hands on my hips and guided my body as I rubbed against him. Touching a stripper without her *express* invitation is a definite no-no, but I let him take advantage of me. I intended to do the same, after all.

"Thanks," I said.

I turned toward Tony, this time brandishing my breasts for his ravenous attention. His breath quickened as I unfastened my bra and dropped it to the floor.

"Wow," said Tony.

When I leaned in to bounce my tits in his face, Tony stuck out his tongue and snuck a lick at one nipple. He really shouldn't have done that, either, but I'd be lying if I said it didn't feel good. I smiled and trailed my breasts down Tony's chest.

"So where's your friend?" I asked.

Richard Sung had been tagged in a few pictures at The Poling Place with Tony, though my murderer didn't frequent the club as devoutly as his friend. And the last of those pictures had been some time ago.

Tony's brow furrowed. "Huh?"

"Don't you usually come here with your friend?" I asked.

"I thought you were new."

Oh, right. Fuck.

I hadn't actually expected Tony to be able to think that much with all his blood down in his cock. Damn it. I rubbed my bare breasts over the impressive tent in his pants to buy myself a few seconds to think.

"Well, some of the other girls were telling me about their favorites," I said.

I rose to settle into Tony's lap and picked up his hands from the edge of his seat, pressing them to my chest. He didn't question me, just started squeezing my breasts with a contented groan.

"You guys usually come in together, right?" I asked. "I thought maybe I could make a deal with both of you. Like two for one or something."

"Rick's not coming," Tony told my chest.

Rick, huh? It was nice to know the name Richard Sung actually used, but it didn't get me any closer to finding him. I swiveled my hips in slow, sensual circles over Tony's lap. With a little moan, I reached between my legs and stroked the hard length of his cock.

"Why isn't Rick coming out today?" I asked. "The girls liked him almost as much as they like you."

"The girls like me?" Tony's eyes finally rose to meet mine. They were wide and I felt a little sorry for the guy.

"Every dancer has their favorite," I said. "And I was going to try you both out."

I continued petting Tony's dick with one hand and found his zipper with the other. Slowly, I pulled it down.

"Uh, you're not supposed to do that," Tony finally told me in a choked voice. Not that he stopped me or even paused in playing with my breasts.

"Well," I said in a throaty purr. "If I'm nice to you, then maybe you can be nice to me."

I reached into Tony's straining jeans and then his boxers until I felt the blazing hardness of his cock against my fingertips. He held his breath as I pulled it free. Tony's dick was thick and heavy in my hand. I gave him a bright grin.

"Wow," I said. It never hurts to flatter a guy.

Tony returned my smile a little more falteringly. He stifled a loud gasp as I rocked my hips back and forth over him, brushing the satin of my g-string against the head of his cock.

"So when is Rick coming back?" I asked.

Tony unclenched his jaw with a visible effort. Answering my strange questions had scored him a lap dance with benefits and he wasn't about to stop now.

"Not sure. I haven't seen Rick in like six months," Tony grunted.

That matched up with what I had seen on their respective social media profiles. I looked through lowered lashes at Tony. Good boy. Warm wetness made my tiny red panties cling to me, so I reached down and pulled them to one side.

"That's a long time," I said.

Long came out in a moan as I sank down onto Tony's cock. His eyes flew so wide that I could see white all around the irises. Tony was used to watching women, not feeling them, and his neglected dick throbbed. I whipped my coppery hair back and twisted my hips in slow circles again, moving him inside me.

"Is Rick okay?" I asked.

"Uh... oh, god," Tony groaned. He clutched at my tits almost desperately, like he was trying to hold on to something he thought might fade away. "Rick... his brother vanished about a year ago."

Interesting. I rose to the tip of Tony's cock and reached down to give his slick shaft a light squeeze with one hand. I put my fingers to Tony's lips and let him lick the taste of my pussy from them.

"What happened with Rick's brother?" I asked as Tony sucked at my fingertip like a man dying of thirst.

"No one knows," he gasped between licks. "The police stopped looking for Ben six months ago."

When Tony had sucked up every trace of wetness from my fingers, he pinched my nipples in each hand and watched, mesmerized by my breasts bouncing before him. He didn't even need another question to keep him talking now.

"Rick and Ben were really close. Oh, fuck... That feels so good... Rick won't get rid of his brother's stuff or sell his house. I mean, it's on the market and everything – his family insisted – but he turns down every single offer."

An empty house and a new name: Ben Sung, the missing brother. This job was getting stranger by the minute. I was glad Stefano had called me.

Tony slid his hands down from my chest to cup my ass and bounced me on his cock. I rewarded him with a few genuine moans and bit his earlobe gently.

"Poor Rick," I whispered into Tony's ear.

"I think he's actually living in Ben's house. Oh, fuck yes... It's kind of creepy, but Rick said he needed to do it."

"You're a good friend," I said. I squeezed Tony's dick inside me, making us both moan. "And a good fuck."

Tony was writhing under me. He gave a rough grunt that might have been a warning – Tony had been helpful, so I was willing to give him the benefit of the doubt – but I didn't need it. I know my way around a cock and can feel when a guy is about to blow. So I slipped myself off Tony with a wet sound and pumped him swiftly with one hand.

"Oh, shit...!" he panted.

Tony's dick spurted pale, sticky ropes that splashed against my belly. I stroked him through his orgasm until my stomach was painted in white and cum began to pool in my navel.

"Wow," Tony said in a breathless voice. "Holy shit. So... what do I owe you?"

I asked him what was fair and we agreed on a hundred dollars. Tony zipped up his pants, paid me with a twenty-dollar tip and wandered off with an absolutely shit-eating grin on his face. Well, we had both gotten what we wanted.

When Tony was gone, I threw his money onto the small VIP lounge stage for one of the other dancers to collect – I was sure they needed the cash more than I did – and looked down at the creamy mess oozing slowly down my belly. It had clearly been a while for Tony and the load he left on me was pretty massive. I trailed my finger through his sticky cum and licked it off as I sorted out my new information, searching for the important bits.

Rick's brother, Benjamin Sung, had gone missing a year ago. A few months after that, Rick began acting strange, withdrawing from his friends and moving alone into his brother's house. And then, just two days ago, Rick... started shooting wizards in their sanctums?

Why? And how? I wasn't sure, but I had the sneaking suspicion that Ben's disappearance had something to do with it.

I couldn't investigate any more of my strange new job until I managed to sneak back out of The Poling Place, though. I needed to get away before any of the large bouncers discovered I had been posing as one of their dancers and tossed me out on my ass. Not that I thought they could hurt me, but if someone called the cops, I was going to spend all day ducking the law. I had better things to do than play hide-and-seek with the police. Like catch Rick Sung before he could murder another wizard.

So I rubbed Tony's cum along my stomach and bare breasts until they gleamed. It wasn't going to pass for stripper glitter under any kind of close inspection, but I hoped it would be enough to get me back to the bathroom and into my clothes.

Chapter THREE

*W*hen I got home, I took a quick shower. I had gotten out of the strip club without getting caught, but only barely. A girl like me tends to attract attention. If I wanted to return to The Poling Place as a patron, I would have to wait a while.

I stepped out of the shower and wrapped myself in a towel without drying off first. I needed to get back to work, so I dripped my way across the pale bamboo flooring of my condo to the kitchen.

After the morning at Max's proto-garage and an afternoon of pumping Tony for information – and a load of spunk – I was more than ready for lunch, so I threw a couple of frozen burritos into the microwave. The smell as they cooked wasn't nearly as good as anything Max made in his kitchen, but I was hungry enough not to care... much.

Ignoring my burning fingers, I plopped my boiling burritos onto a plate. I was all juiced up on sex and healing any minor burns faster than they could form. Hurray for magical half-succubus lust-powers.

I carried my lunch into the living room. Once I wolfed down the first tortilla-wrapped mess of beans and chicken, I settled back on the couch. The leather was warm and pliant in the late afternoon sunlight. I grabbed my laptop off the coffee table and took the second burrito a little slower.

It didn't take much poking around Rick's online profiles to find his brother. Ben Sung's pages were all inactive, but no one had shut down his accounts yet. When I went back about sixteen months, I found all sorts of information.

Ben was older than Rick by a couple of years and worked as an antiques appraiser. He specialized in typewriters and clocks. Ben had been seeing a woman for a while, the owner of a successful local antique store, but a few weeks after Ben's disappearance, her relationship status went back to *single*. Now she was dating one of her employees, according to her profile.

Yawn. I still wasn't seeing how any of this connected to the murder of two Merlinic wizards.

I looked into the rest of Rick Sung's family. The brothers were third-generation Korean immigrants, if I was counting correctly. The Sung family was extensive, if a bit far-flung up and down the west coast. There weren't many posts about Ben's disappearance, but that might have been reserved for private letters and I didn't have access to Rick's email.

The most recent picture of the Sung brothers was from March last year – right before Ben went missing. They stood together at the end of one of the Quay wharves, each holding a fishing pole. Ben and Rick were in their twenties, with short, dark hair and deep brown eyes. They each had the same bright, sunny smile.

Ben and Rick Sung were pretty damned sexy. Too bad one brother was missing and the other was wanted for murder.

Tony said that Rick was staying at Ben's house. That explained why he hadn't been at his own home. So all I had to do was find Ben's house. Before his disappearance, the older Sung brother was smart enough not to list his home address online, so I checked through some of his year-old restaurant reviews. Most of them were up in a ten-block section of Northbay. Okay, I had a neighborhood.

From there, I hit the real estate websites. Tony also said that the family had put Ben's house up for sale, but Rick wasn't accepting any offers, so I narrowed my search to the ones that had been listed for at least four months. Seven results. The listing agent was posted on each one, but not the name of the seller.

Well, Tony said that Rick wasn't getting rid of any of his brother's stuff, so I scrolled through photographs until I found the house that had to be Ben's. The pictures showed a living room with a glass display case full of antique typewriters and an old-fashioned grandfather clock in the bedroom.

Bingo.

I copied the address into my phone and then went to my bedroom, tossing my towel onto the floor to clean up later. From the back of my closet, I pulled out some plain black pants and a matching shirt. Along with a pair of sturdy, well-worn boots, that made up my tactical gear. I don't like weighing myself down with a lot of unnecessary buckles and belts.

Seriously, what would I carry in a utility belt anyway? Anal beads and lube?

And while I look great in leather and vinyl, it tends to squeak when I'm sneaking around. I pocketed a set of handcuffs, but couldn't think of much else. My little session with Tony had given me not only information, but powered me up with enough lust to tear Rick's head off if he gave me trouble. If the fucker shot me, I'd just spit his bullet back at him. All I had to do was put Richard Sung in handcuffs and drag him up to the College to face justice.

Still... I frowned at my reflection in the mirror as I braided my hair back out of my face. After a day of researching him, Rick Sung seemed so normal. Just a normal human going about a normal human life, missing his lost brother like any normal man would.

I felt like I knew Rick better than the two College wizards he had killed. Except for this. What reason could Rick *possibly* have to shoot a pair of mages?

The Merlinic sorcerers aren't exactly a warm and fuzzy bunch. They can be cold and aloof, when they deign to look up from their books and alchemical potions at all. I don't know if it's the years of study or controlling magical forces, but I've yet to meet a wizard who would be any fun at a party. Maybe Stefano's friend, Bianca Taren, but now she was dead and I would never know.

The College works hard in secret to protect the world from the kind of weird, supernatural shit that most humans don't even realize exists. I didn't know how Rick had discovered the wizards, but whatever reason he had for killing them wasn't enough. The sorcerers were pretty much all that stood between order and supernatural chaos in this part of the world. Rick might not have been a werewolf or vampire, but shooting up wizards sure as hell made him a monster in my book.

His motive still made absolutely no sense, but I could ask Rick about it once I caught him. All I had to do now was go arrest his ass. I tied off the end of my braid and grabbed my car keys.

Chapter
FOUR

he sky was turning purple and frosted on the eastern horizon with stars when I parked the Alfa Romeo across the steeply sloped street from Ben's house. Or was it Rick's house now, since he was the one living there? Well, before long it would be an empty house, just as soon as I slapped some handcuffs on Rick Sung.

It was one of those tall, narrow townhouses that were so popular around the turn of the twentieth century. There was a lot of ornate gingerbread and patterned siding painted in dark green and a gold that had probably shone brilliantly twenty years ago, but which had now darkened to the color of brass. Light glowed through one of the diamond-paneled downstairs windows and I still had enough power to make out the fractured images of Ben's bookshelves and clocks inside. The source of the light was obscured, but came from the direction of the dining room.

I saw no sign of the other bounty hunters. I inspected the shadowed sidewalks, but didn't recognize anyone. There were plenty of people hurrying past with coat collars turned up against the early March chill, but none of them had the squat, clunky look of Sabra's homunculi. No one else had made the connection between Rick Sung and his missing brother. Not yet.

A dented little blue mini stopped and double-parked in front of the Sung house. The driver jumped out and trotted up the steps, carrying a plastic bag of takeout. I couldn't read the language of the restaurant name on the bag, but I didn't have to. Someone had ordered Chinese food.

The delivery driver knocked and the door opened, revealing Rick Sung inside. He was shorter and far more slender than Tony, with tawny skin and lovely oblique eyes. Rick wore a pair of jeans and a college t-shirt that had seen better days.

I breathed a sigh of relief. Rick was still at the house, not out hunting down some other wizard. The mental image of old Dorian Vandi slumped over a desk, eyes blank and blood pooling around him, made my chest clench.

Rick nodded to the delivery girl and dutifully signed the receipt, then accepted the bag of Chinese food. I was annoyed to find myself smiling. Not much taste for the cuisine of his family homeland, or maybe Rick just didn't feel like jjambbong tonight. If you expect Korean red noodle soup to be mild, you're in for one fire-spitting surprise. Bring a carton of milk or three.

Rick waved to the driver until she descended the steps, climbed back into her beat-up mini and drove away again. I drummed my fingers on the Alfa's steering wheel. Paying for takeout with a credit card and accepting it in plain sight of the street didn't seem very wise for a serial murderer. At least, not one smart enough to clean up his crime scenes. Or was Rick that confident no one would catch him?

This job just kept getting weirder. And I'm an expert on weird.

Rick went back inside and closed the door behind him. With my sharpened senses, I clearly heard the metallic click of the lock. So I wasn't getting in that way, not unless I felt like kicking a door down in full view of the evening pedestrian crowd. Pass.

I gave Rick five minutes to settle down and dig into his dinner, then climbed out of my car and walked down a few doors until I found a skinny alleyway between two more brightly painted gingerbread townhouses. I had to clamber up over some trash cans, but then I was on the narrow path that ran behind the row of tiny back yards. Each one was fenced in and gated, but that was hardly a barrier. It was already full dark in the shadows between the houses and I slipped silently through them.

Once I was behind the green and gold townhouse, I made sure no one was watching and then vaulted up over the fence. I landed lightly down on the other side. The back gate wasn't even locked, but fog and rust are the bane of all things metal in this city and I didn't want to risk any squealing hinges that might alert Rick to my arrival.

The back yard wasn't much larger than my kitchen, but then, you don't exactly find a lot of rambling farmsteads inside city limits. The Sung yard was a bit of a mess, not nearly as well-kept as in the months-old photographs posted online. Moss grew up between the patterned stones and the only plants were a few stringy weeds. I guessed that Ben hadn't been much of a gardener and Rick wasn't spending a whole lot of time outside.

He had better things to do. Like killing wizards.

Well, that stopped tonight.

The back door was locked up and the knob hung with one of those little blue lockboxes that realtors use. I could have snapped it in half with my bare hands to get at the key inside – my powers are awesome – but the realtor might notice later. I wanted Rick Sung's disappearance to be just as quiet and mysterious as his brother's.

The windows at the rear of the house were plain sheets of glass. I guess the pretty stuff was only for street-facing windows. It would have been even easier to break one of them, and probably raised fewer questions later than a crushed lockbox, but would make more noise than I liked.

Luckily, I didn't have to resort to smashing glass. The ground floor windows were closed tight, but one on the second story was pushed a few inches open to let in some fresh air.

I crouched, tensed and then leapt. A two-story straight-jump isn't easy, even when fully powered, but I managed to hook my fingers over the sill. I pulled myself up and shouldered the window open just enough to slither through. I landed with a soft thump inside the house. There were no lights on up here, but I didn't need them to see. Owls have nothing on my night vision when I'm all sexed up.

I was in the master bedroom. I recognized the grandfather clock in the corner from the photos. The brass pendulum swung back and forth in leisurely arcs and filled the room with a quiet ticking sound. Rick was still winding his big brother's clocks, it seemed.

The bed was made half-heartedly, though, white sheets and blankets tangled up around the pillows. There wasn't much else in the bedroom except an antique dresser. The drawers were closed, but a plastic laundry basket sat on top, full of clean socks and t-shirts. I doubted that folding clothes was exactly one of Rick's top priorities right now.

If I remembered the floor plan from the real estate website correctly, the stairs would take me down into the kitchen. I sniffed the air and smelled cashew chicken. The dining room was on the other side of the kitchen and that was where I would find Rick.

I crept out of the bedroom and along a dark, narrow hallway to the stairs. Cocking my head, I heard voices from below. Not like Rick was talking to someone, but the flattened tones of something playing through laptop speakers.

My foot came down on a step and it creaked beneath me, as loud as squealing tires to my supernaturally sharpened hearing. I winced. I'm not really much of a cat burglar. My job usually requires a bit more beating the shit out of big-ass monsters and little less sneaking around, but I'll do what I need to get the job done.

I eased my weight off the treacherous stair, stepped over it and continued down to the first story. The kitchen was dark, too, and there was a mountain of empty take-out cartons in the trash can. I caught myself smiling again. Rick ate a lot like I did. I wiped the smirk off my face and kept moving.

The townhouse was older than the concept of *open floor plan* and a free-swinging door separated the kitchen from the dining room. Yellow light glowed in a line along the bottom. I crouched beside the door and cracked it gently open.

Rick sat at the dining room table with his back turned to me. He ate his dinner right from the carton with a pair of chopsticks while he watched some mid-list crime drama play on his laptop. Was my murderer taking hipster irony to a whole new level?

I slid through the door and stepped right down on another creaky floorboard. Rick looked up from his dinner.

"Ben?" he asked.

My stealthy entrance was blown, but I was close enough now that it no longer mattered. By the time Rick was turning in his chair toward me, I had already grabbed him by the front of his t-shirt and slammed him down onto the dining room table. His laptop jumped and tumbled to the floor. The machine squawked once and then went silent. Rick stared up at me with wide eyes.

"Holy shit! Who are you?" he gasped. "What the hell are you doing in here?"

I leaned into Rick as he squirmed pointlessly beneath me. He wasn't going anywhere. The table groaned beneath our combined weight.

"I'm more interested in why you're killing College wizards," I said, then frowned down at Rick. "Wait, why did you think I was your brother? He's been missing for a year."

Rick shook his head.

"Ben's not missing," he said. "My brother... he's dead."

My frown deepened. Oh, okay. Thanks. That made things *way* less confusing.

"Then how the fuck did you think I was him?" I asked through gritted teeth.

"Because Ben is a ghost."

Chapter
FIVE

"There's no such thing as ghosts," I said. "Believe me, Rick – I know a lot about the shit that goes bump in the night."

"Like you?" Rick protested. "Let go of me!"

I didn't release him, but I did heave my prisoner to his feet and propelled him into the nearby living room. I held Rick by the arm and gave him a quick pat-down. Nice ass, but no gun. I could survive a few bullets, but they hurt and the charge I get off sex is finite, like a battery. Every time I call on it, there's less for later.

"Sit," I instructed as I gave Rick a firm push down onto the couch. "This whole job has gotten way too weird. You're going to explain *exactly* what the hell is going on here."

I seated myself at the other end of the couch. Even if Rick tried to make a run for the door, I was going to be on him in no time flat.

"Um, who the hell are you?" Rick rubbed his arm where I had grabbed him. He winced. "I'd love to know how much time you spend at the gym, but right now, I'm more curious what you're even doing here."

"You're the one who killed two wizards. So you're going to be answering questions first."

Rick's eyes flew wide and he held up his hands. "Wait, what? No! I didn't–"

"Look, I hunt monsters for a living," I interrupted. "So I know my supernatural shit. I've dealt with vampires, werewolves, fairies and elemental spirits. Just to name a few. But there are no ghosts. When humans die, their souls move on. Heaven, hell, whatever. But they can't stick around in this world."

Now Rick leaned forward, some of his suspicion fading away as he shook his head. "I swear it's true. Ben died, but he came back."

What the *fuck* was going on? I rubbed the bridge of my nose. Rick seemed honestly shocked when I mentioned the murders, and just as earnest about the ghost stuff. Was he crazy? At this point, anything seemed possible.

I dropped my hand once more to regard Rick. He didn't *seem* crazy. A little agitated, but I suppose that I couldn't blame him for that. I did kind of jump out and tackle the guy in the middle of dinner. To tell the truth, I'd have been a hell of a lot more pissed about it than Rick was. And he appeared to believe that I was a monster hunter, which certainly suggested that he had some sort of brush with the supernatural.

I sat back against the arm of the couch. As long as I had Rick here with me, he wasn't shooting anyone. I could afford some time for answers.

"Alright, Rick," I said. "You've got my attention. Talk."

Rick hesitated, though. "You said that you're some kind of hunter. Are you going to hurt Ben?"

"Honestly, I have no fucking clue," I admitted. "Right now, I just want some answers. Today's been one of the weirdest days in my life. Believe me when I tell you that's saying something."

"I... I'll tell you what I can," Rick said falteringly. "I don't seem to have much choice. But there's a lot of it that I don't understand yet. You would have to ask Ben about the details."

"And how might I do that?" I asked.

"He's coming back here tonight. I was waiting for him when you... sort of attacked me."

"Why is Ben coming here?"

"To possess me," said Rick.

Presuming that Richard Sung wasn't completely nuts, I needed more information. Was big dead brother Ben the one somehow hunting down and killing wizards?

"Okay," I said. "Start at the beginning."

Rick lowered his head, thinking. Dark hair fell over his eyes – it looked like he hadn't gotten it cut in a while. It was pretty sexy and I berated myself for smiling at Rick again. I managed to school my expression before he looked back up at me.

"What's your name?" Rick asked. "I feel weird talking about this when I don't even know that much about you."

"I'm Lily."

Now it was Rick's turn to give me a smile. It was even cuter in person than in the pictures. Damn it.

"Okay. Thanks, Lily." Rick put his hands on his knees and took a deep breath. "Well, you seem to know about some of it. A year ago, Ben just... vanished. I was supposed to meet him for lunch, but he didn't show. I called, but never got an answer. I reported the whole thing to the cops, of course. They poked around a few times, but never found anything they considered interesting. Everyone just figured that Ben left."

"But that's not what you thought," I said.

"It didn't make any sense. Ben was fine. Why would he leave without telling anyone?" Rick asked. He gestured toward the front door. "He gave me a key a few years back, so I came by to... I don't know. Take care of the place? Or maybe I wanted to find something the police had overlooked."

"And did you?"

"Maybe," said Rick. "There was this strange smell in the air, like incense. That was a year ago, though, so I don't remember much except that it was sort of weird and metallic. Ben always hated incense. It makes... *made* him sneeze, so I thought that was strange."

My heart skipped a beat. "Anything else?"

Rick nodded and began to stand, but then froze and looked at me with frightened eyes.

"Can I get up and turn on the light in here without you trying to snap me in half again?" he asked.

"Just don't try to get away," I said. "However fast you can run, trust that I can run faster."

"Um, okay."

Rick stood and went to flip the light switch. A pair of lamps flickered on and filled the living room with a pleasant amber glow. Incandescent bulbs, I noted absently. Ben really had a thing for the old-fashioned shit, didn't he?

Rick sat again and pointed to the center of the living room floor. Something black was ground between several of the floorboards. There were other darkened spots, too, arranged in a ring in the middle of the floor... Like someone had drawn a charcoal circle there and then tried to clean it up. But the black dust had gathered in the slight gaps between the creaky old wood boards. The last time I saw a charcoal circle on the floor was in Dominic's apartment, when Stefano used his magic to teleport the raging werewolf away.

What was Ben involved in? Was he a sorcerer? If Rick Sung's brother were a Merlinic wizard, surely Stefano would have mentioned it.

Rick was studying my face. "All of this means something to you, doesn't it?"

"Maybe," I said. "Keep going."

"Um, okay. I just sort of... stayed here. Stalling, I guess, and waiting for Ben to come home. It takes seven years to declare someone dead, but I... After six months, the police weren't looking anymore and my parents started talking about a funeral..."

Rick's voice cracked and he trailed off, wiping his eyes. He didn't seem to notice that he was doing it. I guessed Rick was pretty used to crying over Ben. He truly did love his brother.

I was really beginning to hate the idea of dragging Rick Sung to the College for judgment. But I don't leave jobs half done. If you doubt it, ask a nix named Adähr. Someone had to face justice for the deaths of Orson Clark and Bianca Taren.

Rick drew a shuddering breath and continued. "One night, maybe a week after New Year, the whole house went cold. I remember getting up and checking the thermostat. The heat was on, but I just couldn't stop shivering. I wondered if I was in some kind of shock... I hadn't been eating or sleeping very well for a while."

"Yeah, I saw your temple of takeout."

Rick flushed a little. "Sorry about that. Sort of. I mean, you're the one who was sneaking around."

"You should see my fridge. What happened after it got cold?"

"Then I heard Ben's voice," Rick said. "At first, I was sure I was having a total nervous breakdown, but Ben was... here. I couldn't see him, but I felt him here with me and I started to calm down."

"What did he say?"

"That someone had murdered him and he needed my help to fix it."

I narrowed my eyes. The kind of help that involved a gun and two dead wizards?

"And what did he want you to do?" I asked Rick in a flat voice.

"Ben said that he had to possess my body. He didn't seem very happy about it, but I told him that I was all his. Whatever he needed. After that, things get kind of... fuzzy. When I woke up, it was morning. I wondered if it had all been a dream or something, but I was sitting at the table and my laptop was open."

"What was on the screen?" I asked. If Ben had been looking up information or buying guns, I wanted to know.

Rick scratched his head as he tried to remember. "Um, some website about demons, I think."

Demons. Things weren't looking good for Ben Sung. It wouldn't have surprised me if this "murder" was a College hunter taking Ben Sung down for infernalism.

Except... I didn't remember any bounties like that being posted in the last year. If the College had caught someone summoning demons, I would know. Infernalism is pretty much the worst crime under College rules and bounties for demon-summoners are some of the most lucrative awarded.

"How did your brother die?" I asked. "What happened?"

Rick shook his head again. "That's one of the things I don't know. Ben won't tell me. He says that he wants to keep me out of it so I don't get hurt."

"Typical big brother," I said.

Not that I knew from personal experience. I was a child of the foster system – Max was the closest thing I had to a brother. Which, given the naked shenanigans we got up to, wasn't very close at all.

"How long has all this been going on, Rick?" I asked.

"Um, about two months. I don't know what Ben's working on, exactly. Mostly, it seems to be research. Sometimes about people, sometimes more mythological stuff. I've offered to help during the days, but Ben won't tell me what he's up to."

"Have you ever woken up somewhere strange?" I asked. "Like a basement or... a tower?"

My question sounded a little lame, but I had no idea what Orson or Bianca's sanctums were like. I'd never been in one. For all I knew, Stefano's dead lady friend had practiced her magic in a bowling alley. Rick seemed to find my question strange, too, because his eyebrows rose.

"Uh, no," he said. "Sometimes I wake up in different clothes, but that's it. If he goes anywhere, Ben always brings me... my body... back here."

Rick hadn't mentioned a gun yet, but Ben might have hidden it. Were the new clothes to conceal bloodstains?

"Look, I don't know what any of this is about," Rick said. He sounded young, earnest and frightened. "But if my brother needs my body to finish his earthly business, then I want to help him."

"That's creepy," I told him. "But sweet. Why didn't you call the police about any of this?"

Rick gave an unhappy little laugh. "And tell them what, exactly? That my brother's ghost said he was murdered? The cops would have thought I was crazy. And I could hardly blame them. For a while, I was pretty sure I was crazy, too."

I wasn't entirely convinced of Rick's sanity, either. There weren't supposed to be ghosts. His story answered some of my questions, but not nearly enough of them. Tony said that the two Sung brothers were close. Had Ben's disappearance or death caused some kind of psychotic break? And even if everything Rick said was true, it still had an unsettling flavor of the demonic.

"What time is Ben coming to possess you?" I asked.

"Usually about nine o'clock."

I checked one of the rhythmically ticking clocks hanging along the wall. That was about twenty minutes away.

"Alright," I said. "I need to get Ben's half of the story."

Rick eyed me up and down, nervous again. "You're not going to hurt him, are you?"

"I'm not even sure how I would hurt a ghost. But I need to know what he's been up to."

Rick didn't look terribly reassured, but he nodded.

"Can I finish my dinner?" he asked.

"Sure."

Rick stood and I watched closely as he retrieved the Chinese food from the dining room, then brought it back to the sofa. He sat once more, still eyeing me.

"So uh... do you think I'm crazy, Lily?" Rick asked as he began poking at his cashew chicken again.

"I really don't know yet. If it makes you feel any better, I hope not. You seem like a good guy, Rick."

He smiled at me and held out a carton of fried rice.

"Want some?"

"I'm not that hungry. I'll take your fortune cookie, though."

"Sure."

I fished around in the plastic bag until I found the cookie, then cracked it open and picked out the strip of paper.

"*You will not find love,*" I read out loud. "*You have always had it.* In bed."

"That doesn't work very well," said Rick.

"Yeah," I agreed.

We ate in silence for a few minutes, watching each other and the clock. Rick only took a couple of bites, chewing them slowly. He smirked wryly at me and dropped his chopsticks back into the carton.

"Not all of those boxes in the kitchen are mine," Rick said. "I think Ben misses eating. When he's using my body, he hits the ice cream pretty hard. I've put on a couple pounds in the last few weeks."

I laughed a little at that and Rick's smile grew wider. Then he blushed and pushed the box of cashew chicken a few inches away, dropping his gaze.

"Sorry," Rick said. "I... I've been in this house for most of the last year, ever since Ben died. I haven't gone to work in months. I'm not even sure how long it's been since I've seen a beautiful woman. One that wasn't on my computer screen, at least."

"It's been lonely, huh?" I asked.

"Yeah. Don't get me wrong, though... I'm in this as long as Ben needs me. I don't know if I even have a job to go back to anymore, but I don't care."

Rick was embarrassed and I had no idea what to say. I covered the moment as best I could by checking the time on my phone. It was far more precise than the antique clocks. Eight fifty-seven.

The temperature in the living room plunged. The air went ice-cold and the phone nearly fell from my suddenly numb fingers. Something felt... wrong. I shivered, but my breath didn't steam. The otherworldly chill wasn't in the house – it was in my soul.

On the other end of the couch, Rick sagged as though he had fallen asleep. Gingerly, I reached toward his shoulder to shake it, but Rick jolted upright. He ran quick, searching hands over his chest, stomach and legs. Then he raised his eyes to mine. They were still the same rich chocolate brown, but no longer shy or confused. These eyes burned with dark fury.

"I don't know who you are, but if you hurt Rick," he snarled, "I'll kill you, too."

Chapter
SIX

"Y̶ou're Ben Sung?" I asked.

"Yes," answered the man that until five seconds ago had been his younger brother. "What the hell are you doing in my house?"

So Rick wasn't crazy. Hell, he wasn't even here anymore.

"That depends," I said. "Did you shoot Bianca Taren and Orson Clark?"

"Yes."

"Your murder spree is over," I told Ben. "Don't try to run. That body isn't yours and I kind of like Rick. I'd really hate to hurt him chasing you down."

Ben sat back, but his jaw was tight and his eyes narrowed.

"Don't hurt my brother."

"He said the same thing about you. Now, my name is Lily Quinn and I work for the order of wizards that your victims belonged to."

Ben grabbed the edge of the couch and to judge by the bloodless white spots that appeared across his knuckles, barely resisted leaping to his feet.

"You work for them?" he hissed. "What? Are you here to kill me again?"

"Tell me why you're killing wizards, Ben!" I said. I stabbed one finger in the direction of the charcoal ground into his floorboards. "Did they stop you from summoning a demon? Is that what you were doing here?"

"What? No!" Ben's voice was raw with pain and anger. "I don't know anything about magic. *They* were the ones who summoned her!"

"What? Summoned who?"

"The succubus!"

I felt like he had just kicked me in the stomach. A succubus? On our side of the Seal of Avalon?

"Who summoned a succubus?" I asked. "What the fuck happened here, Ben?"

The ghost in Rick's body answered slowly. "I was here, home alone one night when this woman burst through my door. At least, I thought she was a woman at first."

"But she wasn't."

"No," Ben agreed. "God, she was so beautiful. And naked. Tall, with golden skin and the blackest hair I've ever seen. But she had horns, too. Little black ones that I nearly couldn't see against her hair. Her eyes were gold, too, and they burned like fire."

Yeah, that was a succubus. I had never seen one, but Evaine told me about them. A full-blooded lust demon has all my strength, speed and supernatural senses. They're tough like me, too. Maybe tougher.

But real demons aren't sweet like me. There's only one thing a succubus wants in all the worlds: sex. And she won't stop at anything to get it. Back before Merlin sealed all of the demons away in the Nether, succubae and incubi were said to enthrall humans so utterly that they died of exhaustion trying to please their demonic lovers.

"Before I could say a word, the succubus threw herself at me," Ben said. There was a mixture of helpless desire and horrified revulsion in his voice. "The next thing I knew, we were fucking on the floor. I was scared out of my mind, but that just seemed so unimportant. I couldn't stop myself and I didn't want to. All I wanted was her."

"Yeah." I sat down beside Ben on the couch. "That's succubus magic for you. They live on lust and they're the perfect monsters for getting it. Is that... how you died?"

Ben turned to look at me and shook his head. "No. I'm not really sure how long the succubus had been fucking me – it felt like forever and just a few seconds, all at the same time – when more people came charging through the front door. Not demons like her, though. Humans. There were four of them, all of them shouting at each other."

"Do you remember what they looked like?" I asked. "Or what they said?"

"Some," Ben closed his eyes and then scrubbed at them with clenched fists. "I've had a long time to think back on it, but right then, I didn't care. I just couldn't stop fucking the succubus."

Ben shifted a little on the couch, adjusting his weight. There was still pain in his expression, but I felt the desire rising inside him, too. Even a year later, that succubus had the power to arouse a dead man. I put my hand on Ben's shoulder and gave it a small squeeze, urging him to continue.

"But the humans... the wizards... There were three men and a woman. Two of them you obviously know, since you asked about them. One of the men was big and had a beard. The last guy had pale hair. I'm not sure if it was blond or white. I really didn't see much more than that."

Bianca Taren, Orson Clark and two other wizards. Stefano said Bianca liked a good time... I guessed that even he didn't realize just *how* good a time. If Bianca had a taste for demon sex, no wonder she wasn't interested in pursuing something more serious with Stefano.

"Bianca was screaming that they had to banish it before some-one found out what they had done. Orson tried to grab the suc-cubus off of me. But she swatted him away without even breaking her rhythm. So the other two men threw this... net over us."

"Net?"

"It was heavy and made of leather, with weird symbols all along the straps. God, even with that draped over us, all I did was... you know, keep fucking."

Ben's eyes were open now and fixed on me. That I could feel his desire meant it wasn't just for the succubus, I realized. I can sense it only when someone is lusting after *me*. My eyebrows rose a bit. Maybe ice cream wasn't the only thing Ben Sung had been missing.

"The wizards drew a big circle on the floor around us. There was other stuff going on, too, and I smelled something burning. By then, even the succubus was starting to notice. She started pulling on the net and I didn't get the impression it was going to hold her for very long."

"Demons are strong," I said. "It takes powerful magic to hold them for even a short time. That's part of why it's forbidden to sum-mon one."

Ben gave me a pained look. Clearly, it hadn't been enough to keep Bianca and her friends from doing exactly what they weren't supposed to.

"One of the men asked the others about me," Ben said. "I think it was the big one. Bianca told him that the banishment should only affect the demon."

Ben's voice turned hard, every word like cracking ice and I guessed that Stefano's dead friend had been dead wrong.

"They chanted in some language I didn't know," Ben went on. "And then there was firelight, but it was wrong. Cold somehow. The succubus started screaming... and so did I. Nothing's ever hurt like that. She vanished off of me, but something was ripping me out of the world, too. For just a moment, I saw my body on the ground, but I wasn't in it anymore. I was dead."

"Fuck," I said.

"And then it was like I was caught in a riptide or something. Their spell was trying to pull me to the same place as the succubus, but I smashed into some kind of barrier. Wherever they sent her, I couldn't follow."

The Nether. The realm of demons, the place from which they were summoned and then banished back to. I didn't understand magic very well, but it made sense that a human soul wouldn't be able to pass through the sealed wall between worlds. The wizards' banishment spell had torn Ben's soul out of his body and left it stranded.

"Shit," I breathed. My hand tightened a little on Ben's shoulder. "Shit, Ben."

"For so long, I was stuck there in the darkness," he told me. "I was just... lost. There was nothing but anger and pain. They were like white-hot wires cutting into me, pulling at me... I couldn't even scream. But eventually, I followed the threads back to this world."

Ben had been gone for a year. A year of pain and rage and darkness... I shuddered again and it had nothing to do with the ghost's unnatural chill this time.

"By the time I returned, my body was gone," Ben said. "I guess the wizards disposed of it. But I found Rick here."

Ben's voice finally softened. He looked down at my hand on his shoulder – or maybe it was his brother's shoulder right then – and smiled for the first time since possessing Rick's body. He touched one hand briefly to mine.

"For a few weeks, I couldn't do much," Ben said. "Whenever I tried to... gather myself, Rick would start shivering like he was cold. I hated it. But without a body, I was just as helpless as I had been in that net."

"None of the movie ghost powers?" I asked. "You can't throw dishes with your mind or anything?"

"Without a body, I'm nothing," Ben said in a harsh voice. "So I finally had to ask Rick to borrow... to possess his. At first, it was only research, trying to understand what had happened to me. But I still felt those threads tying me to my murderers, and they *burned*."

"Is that how you tracked down Orson and Bianca?" I asked. That would explain how Ben had discovered places kept as secret as their sanctums.

The dead man nodded. "Yes. I used to deal in antiques and it's not hard to get your hands on an old gun. They're considered show-pieces and aren't subject to the same laws as modern firearms. When I found two of the wizards, something... tried to keep me away. I felt it, but it couldn't stop me."

Wards, I guessed. College wizards used them to protect rooms and buildings. But ghosts like Ben weren't supposed to exist, so maybe the wards weren't enough to keep him out. It's hard to defend yourself from something you know nothing about.

"The first one, Orson, didn't even see me coming. The woman tried to fight, I think. She chanted and grabbed things from bottles on her desk. Just like when they killed me and turned me into... into this!" Ben's voice rose and his hands squeezed into fists again. But tears shone in his dark eyes. "I... I shot them. I thought that maybe, if I cut all the threads, I could finally move on. That maybe the pain would be over."

"Is it working?" I asked.

Ben swiped a swift, angry hand across his eyes. "I don't know. Two of them are dead, but everything still so cold. Except for those threads tying me to the other two wizards. God, they *burn* and I just... I just want it to stop."

I had no idea what to say to that.

"I can only feel anything else when I'm possessing Rick's body," Ben said. "And this isn't fair to him. I tried to clean up after... after what I did so we wouldn't get caught. But you're here, so it seems pretty fucking obvious that I didn't do a good enough job. I could get Rick in trouble."

"Rick would do anything to help you," I said. I put my other hand on Ben's shoulders and turned him to face me. "Look, what happened to you... that wasn't right. Summoning a succubus like that is forbidden by the College and when the High Magus finds out, he's going to be beyond pissed. But you *have* to stop hunting down the wizards."

"No!" Ben's voice rose to a shout. "They killed me! They tore me out of my body and turned me into... into *this*!"

"I want to help you," I said. "The College might be able to fix what's happened, but not like this. You're–"

I almost told Ben that he would get himself killed. But that wasn't what he was afraid of.

"Look, you surprised Orson," I said. "You managed to get Bianca because she didn't have wards against ghosts and shot her before she could fire off a spell. But now the College knows what you're doing. There's a bounty out on you. The next wizard will be prepared."

Ben glared at me, eyes full of dark fire.

I drew a deep breath. "You're going to get Rick killed."

That did it. The dam burst inside Ben. His fingers curled into fists so tight that his knuckles turned white, but hot tears poured from his eyes. Ben's pain was so raw and sharp that it hurt to witness.

"You're right," he whispered. "Rick, I'm so sorry..."

I wrapped my arms around Ben and held him against me. His fingers twisted into the black cloth of my shirt. The room still felt as cold as ice, but his tears were hot where they soaked through to my skin. Ben's need was sharply visceral, vulnerable but desperately commanding. It seemed to reach into the very oldest, most primal centers of my being and *pulled*.

The last year had been pain, confusion and horror for Ben that even I could only guess at. I admired his strength and even sympathized with his drive to somehow sever the ties that bound him here. But Ben needed justice, not vengeance. I wasn't sure yet how to give him that, but maybe there was something else I could give. That I *wanted* to give.

All of Ben's emotions were pouring out into the open now, and he didn't get to choose which ones. The lust had been driven under by anger as Ben told me his story, but now it came surging to the fore. I actually gasped at its intensity.

Ben Sung had known little but formless cold since his death and now hot desire surged through his borrowed body. The warmth of it burned even through the unnatural chill that clung to me in the ghost's presence and I felt an answering heat rising in me. Softly, I kissed his tousled hair, and then again as I listened to his heart pound. Ben looked up slowly and I gently kissed his forehead, the bridge of his nose, then his lips. He tasted like tears.

Ben's grip on me tightened, pulling me close. He kissed me hard, tasting my breath, my heat. My life. He drew away for a moment, staring at me with naked wonder in his eyes, and kissed me again, long and lingering.

I trailed my fingers up Ben's stomach to his chest, then pushed him down against the arm of the couch. His hands raced down my back and then lower. I moaned and lifted my hips, pressing myself into his touch. My underwear were soaked clear through and the damp cloth of my pants clung to my thighs.

Taking my moan as the invitation that it very much was, Ben grabbed the hem of my shirt and yanked it up over my head. He did the same with the purely functional black sports bra I wore beneath – I hadn't dressed for anything like this. But with an effort that made me groan aloud, I drew back and crossed my arms over my bared breasts.

"Wait," I panted. "Ben, stop."

He froze, his hands shaking on my hips. "What? I thought you wanted—"

"I do," I said. "Trust me, I really do. But you need to know something. I'm a cambion."

"A... what? What's a cambion?"

"I'm half demon," I told him. "My mother was a succubus."

Ben started as though I had hit him and his eyes narrowed again. All of that rage and pain was still so close to the surface. What would Ben decide I was? A woman? Or a succubus, just like the one who had assaulted him, raped him – demons aren't big on consent – and then got him killed.

"Look, I'm not like the demon that attacked you," I said. "I have... certain powers, but I use them to fight things like her."

The ghost stared at me. I was still going to help him – Ben had fucked up by killing Orson and Bianca, but not as badly as they had in summoning a succubus and then letting it escape to attack a helpless human. Someone at the College had to know how to fix that, right?

Ben grabbed my arm and pulled me close once more. When he spoke, his voice was rough. "I don't want to stop. Help me, Lily. I want to feel something beside rage and ice and pain."

And I wanted to give that to him. Lust poured through me, his and mine, mingling and burning together in a golden blaze. Ben kissed me with the soul-deep desperation of a man who wanted, who *needed* to feel alive.

Unwilling to break our kiss, I grabbed the collar of Ben's shirt. It tore easily down the front and I yanked the shredded fabric off his shoulders, dropping it to the floor. His tawny skin was feverish against mine, his borrowed body taut and lean. We tore each other's pants off in a hasty tangle of legs and shoelaces, fingernails raking over one another's skin in our urgency.

Naked at last, I fell back across the couch and pulled Ben down on top of me. His cock was like a length of red-hot steel, hard and searing between our bodies. It pulsed against the soft skin of my stomach like a second heartbeat.

Ben finally pulled his lips away, gasping for air, but he wasn't done kissing me. His mouth trailed over my cold skin and my body strained upward to meet the heat of his breath. My pulse pounded sensation through me as Ben took one of my hard pink nipples in his mouth. I moaned in pleasure when his tongue circled the other and then worked down my belly.

Gently, he nudged my legs apart to expose the slickness of my waiting pussy and I felt his lips move against my inner thigh, then questing down between them. Ben's hands slid under me, along the curve of my ass and held my hips steady as he ran his tongue over my labia. I gasped and twined my fingers in his black hair. It was thick and soft.

"Oh fuck, Ben," I breathed. "Yes!"

Ben needed this in a way that ran almost as deep as my own succubus-blooded instincts. The ghost's lust poured through me like a river of molten gold, the heat of his passion drowning out even the chill of his deathly presence. He clutched at my hips and resumed the kissing assault he had begun at my lips, sucking and licking at my pussy, then plunging his tongue into me. I arched my spine and my hips rose as he devoured me. My hands tightened in his hair when Ben's mouth found my clitoris and his teeth grazed that most sensitive part of me.

I moaned and Ben replaced teeth with the hungry heat of his tongue over my clit, but he didn't leave me empty. He slid two fingers into my velvety wetness and my voice rose as Ben worked them in and out of my body in long, swift strokes while his mouth caressed me more slowly. With a twist of his fingers in my pussy, Ben sent me over the edge. I screamed in pleasure and streamed juices down his wrist.

He looked up, fixing me with his dark-eyed gaze as he guided me over the peak. When I finally sagged back into the couch cushions, Ben sat up, licking his lips and giving me that bright, beautiful Sung-boy smile.

"Thank you," he said.

"Me? Thank *you*," I gasped.

Ben's smile widened and there was even a slightly wicked edge to it that made me grin right back.

"It's nice to know I can still do that," he said. "And to a... what did you call yourself?"

"A cambion."

Ben nodded and licked his lips. "I asked for something hot to forget the cold for a while. And you're definitely that. So... it was my pleasure."

"No," I purred. "*This* is your pleasure."

Seizing Ben's shoulders, I pulled him down to me. I kissed him and tasted myself on his lips. Ben let out a deep groan as I reached between our bodies to grab his cock. I stroked the silky skin and steely hardness beneath.

"Oh god," Ben said. "That feels so good... but strange, too."

I circled my fingers just below the crown and ran my thumb along the underside of his cockhead. Ben gasped and his fingernails scraped over the upholstery.

"Because this body isn't yours?" I asked.

Ben nodded. "This... won't hurt Rick, will it?"

"No." I reached up with my free hand to brush his cheek. "I'll take care of your brother, Ben. None of this is Rick's fault and I'm not going to let anything bad happen to him. I promise."

Wordlessly, Ben kissed me again. His desire was a brilliant golden beacon, calling to me. I wound my legs around his waist and Ben surged forward against me. His cock pierced and then filled me, eliciting sharp cries from both of us that were mingled and muffled by our kiss.

For a sweet, lingering moment, Ben simply remained buried inside me. His heart hammered against my breast and then the rest of his body followed suit. Ben drove his dick urgently into me and my head fell back against the armrest. My braid was swiftly unraveling and red hair fanned out around me like a truly demonic halo of flames.

When Ben drew back, sliding his cock from the wet tightness of my pussy, I wound my legs about his waist and pulled him into me once more. He filled me one thrust at a time. My body was no longer mine alone – I opened myself and shared it with Ben, just as Rick had done.

When it came, my orgasm was the first in a long line of strong, deep pulses of pleasure like the bass notes of some ethereal song. I moaned with each one and my nails raked down Ben's back. Gently, though... I said that I wouldn't hurt his brother's body and I intended to keep that promise.

Ben rose with me, plunging himself harder and faster into my streaming slit. His pace became frenzied, wild. Each thrust was short and sharp, matching his panting breath. My pussy squeezed and tightened in ecstasy until I could feel every subtle feature of his cock. And it was swelling inside me.

"Lily, I... I'm close," Ben groaned. "What do you–?"

I pulled Ben down to me and whispered into his ear. "Cum. I want you to fill me. Let yourself go and I'll take it all."

"Yes... oh, yes..."

Ben's words came out in a breathless rasp, an uninhibited gasp of release that sent me spiraling up into climax right alongside him. White-hot semen gushed into my pussy, filling me just as I had asked. He buried his face against the side of my neck as he poured himself into me.

I stroked Ben's sweaty hair, holding him close until our shudders of pleasure smoothed out and we could both breathe again. Thick, creamy heat oozed from between our joined bodies. As we lay boneless and panting on the couch, Ben kissed me one last time.

"Thank you, Lily," he said.

Chapter SEVEN

"Where's the gun?" I asked.

Ben was sitting now and raking trembling fingers through his disheveled black hair. Beads of sweat dotted his skin and ran down his bare chest.

I held out my hand, palm up, toward him. "I said you can't keep murdering the wizards and I meant it. Give me the gun, Ben, so I know you aren't going to hurt anyone else. There are better ways to get justice for what they did to you."

"How?" Ben asked.

"We're going to catch the bastards who did this to you."

I stood. I probably didn't cut the most imposing figure, naked and sweaty, with my hair a tangled cloud around my shoulders and cum rolling down my thighs in white drops. Sexy, yes, but maybe not so scary. Unless you knew me... which I guess Ben was starting to because he didn't laugh.

"I thought you wanted the gun so I couldn't do exactly that," he said.

"We're not going to kill them, Ben," I answered. "But that doesn't mean we can't drag these guys in front of the High Magus and kick their asses until they confess. Do you know their names?"

"No. I only learned Orson Clark and Bianca Taren because it was on their mail when I went to their houses."

"Sanctums," I corrected absently, then shook my head. "But you can feel those threads connecting you to them, right?"

"Yeah. I always feel them. And they always hurt."

I put a hand on his shoulder. "Give me the gun and then we're going to finish this."

Ben tensed under my touch and for a moment, I thought he might try to run, but then he looked down at his borrowed body.

"This is so strange," Ben said softly. He trailed curious fingertips over his chest and stomach. I don't think he was talking to me. "I wonder if it would weird Rick out to know I've seen him naked. Sorry, buddy. But... but I'm going to put a stop to this before it gets any worse for you, okay?"

Ben raised his eyes to mine. They were still red-rimmed from crying, but I saw the hardened resolve there, too. Slowly, the ghost nodded.

"The gun is up in my bedroom."

Both of us still naked, I followed Ben upstairs. I worried about how the hell all of this was going to play out, but that didn't stop me from admiring Ben's ass bunching and releasing with each step. Or Rick's ass, I supposed.

"Lily?" Ben asked.

I blinked. "Uh, yeah?"

Ben paused at the top of the stairs and looked down at me. His cock stirred at the sight, but his expression remained serious.

"That succubus they summoned," Ben said. "You don't think that was your mother, do you?"

I gave him a small, sad smile. "No. My mother's dead. She died right after I was born."

"What happened?"

"Succubae can't normally get pregnant," I said. "When they do, things get complicated."

I didn't really want to explain it any more than that. Ben seemed to understand, though. When I reached the top of the stairs, he touched my shoulder.

"I'm sorry," was all he said.

I guess a ghost understands death pretty damned well.

Ben led me into his bedroom and pulled a brass key down from the top of the grandfather clock. Twisting it in the lock, Ben opened the front of the clock and then reached inside. I suppose I could have told him to stand back, to let me do it. But I trusted Ben not to shoot at me.

He withdrew an antique revolver and held it out by the barrel, offering me the yellowed ivory grip. I took it carefully in two fingers.

"Thanks, Ben," I said.

He swallowed hard and nodded. I grabbed a fresh pillowcase and wrapped it around the gun. I didn't know if the College would need it later for forensic evidence or anything, but I figured that I should avoid getting my fingerprints all over it, just in case. Ben watched me curiously.

"What happens now?" he asked.

"I need you to lead me to the other two wizards. Can you possess a body other than Rick's?"

"I've never tried," Ben admitted. "But I think so."

I considered asking him to possess me, then release control of my body to let me tackle the wizards. And I thought I'd had a man inside me every way possible... I smirked, but then shook my head.

"I like the idea of leaving Rick out of this, but I think we're going to need him," I said with a sigh. "I don't want to be unconscious when the other hunters are out there. I might need my body."

"What do you mean, *other hunters*?" Ben asked.

"I'm not the only one. The rest are wizards and it's not going to take them long to find Rick. When you killed Bianca, they caught him on the scry network."

Ben's sweaty brow furrowed. "Scry network?"

"Think magical surveillance. The College doesn't know about you, Ben. They believe Rick shot Orson and Bianca. The wizards can use that same network to find him here."

Ben's face went pale. "Shit."

"Yeah," I agreed. "But there's no way I can find a pair of sanctums on my own. So I need you in Rick's body, giving me directions and following the threads. You get me there and then I want both of you to wait for me in the car."

"But–"

"You can't help me without a body," I interrupted. "But I need mine and we're not putting Rick's in danger, remember?"

Ben drew a deep breath and nodded. "Alright."

I set the wrapped-up gun down on top of the dresser. The bedroom window was still open a few inches and an evening breeze blowing through felt almost tropical beside the frigid chill of Ben's presence. But I took his hand and squeezed it gently.

"Let me talk to Rick for a minute," I said. "He deserves a chance to shoot all this shit down. I'm pretty sure what his answer will be, but I still need to ask."

Ben smiled wryly. "I'd like Rick to tell you to take a hike and not risk any of it, but you're right. He won't."

"Give us a little while to talk," I said. "But then be ready to go."

Ben nodded. "I'll see you again soon."

I released his hand and stepped back. Ben lowered his head and his eyes drifted shut. He stood there for a moment, and then the graveyard chill was gone from my senses. Rick's bare chest rose in a long, deep breath and his head snapped up. He blinked, then stared around the room.

"What happened?" he asked. "Is Ben–?"

Rick's lips and tongue crashed together like a three-car pileup when he saw me. He blinked a few more times as his shocked gaze roamed over my naked, slick body. His cock sprang up, instantly hard and Rick suddenly realized his own nudity. He yelped and grabbed a pillow from the bed, yanking it awkwardly down over his crotch.

"Um... what happened?" Rick repeated more urgently.

"It's okay," I assured him and took a little step closer. "Ben and I talked. He told me how he died and I'm going to help him bring the men responsible to justice."

"Really?" Rick's smile was nervous, but still adorable. "Great. What do you need me to do? Once I get dressed, I mean."

"Ben is going to show me where to find the people who killed him and then I'm going to arrest them... more or less. We need Ben in possession of your body for that and there's some risk to you–"

"That's fine," Rick answered at once. His posture remained awkward and stiff, though – in more ways than one. "But seriously... why am I naked?"

"Ben and I used your body," I said, taking another step closer until we stood only a few inches apart. "I hope you don't mind."

Rick's smile didn't fade. If anything, it brightened like a crescent moonrise. "No. That's... weird, I'll admit, but I'm glad. Ben deserves something good. It uh... was good, right?"

Even after death, the bond Rick shared with his brother was strong. It almost made me wish for siblings of my own, but mostly just made me grin at Rick. We could spare a *few* minutes before hunting down two more wizards. I had promised Ben that I would take care of his little brother, after all.

"Yes," I told Rick. "It was very good. Want to see for yourself?"

"Huh? What do you–?"

I put my hand against Rick's chest and gave a small push that sent him staggering back toward the bed. Another gentle shove and he tumbled down into the sheets, somehow still clutching that pillow over himself. I crawled up into the bed and prowled along Rick's lean body. He eyed me like a mouse watching a cat. His smile was shaky as hell, but it didn't fade one bit. Fuck, it was adorable.

"Oh," he whispered. "Yes... I... want to see."

I grabbed the corner of the pillow and pulled. Rick's bashfulness was no match for my sex-powered strength. I tossed the pillow aside, leaving him hard and exposed.

"Oh god..." Rick groaned.

His hips rose as I closed my fingers around his cock. It was strange how different Rick felt in my hand. This was the same dick that had been inside me twenty minutes ago. Hell, I still smelled the sharp scent of my pussy on Rick's skin. But without Ben possessing his brother's body, everything felt entirely new.

I knelt between Rick's legs and made sure he was watching when I closed my lips around his dick. The taste of sex was strong on my tongue. I licked up and down every inch of his cock, lapping up the wetness I had left before.

Rick's dark eyes remained wide and his expression charmingly confused. Would you think less of me if I admitted that I loved it? After what happened to Ben, I supposed I could have felt guilty about what I was, about the demonic power that runs in my blood, but the truth is that I don't. I never have.

Holding Rick's hips against the bed, I slowly took his cock inch by inch down my throat. He was trembling and his rapid breathing was just this side of a whimper by the time my lips were wrapped around the base of his shaft. Rick's lust was hot as flame and his slick, salty precum trickled across my tongue. I drank them both into me and let out a muffled moan.

"Lily," Rick sighed. "Yes..."

I worked my mouth back up along Rick's length just as slowly as I had gone down. I stroked my tongue over the crown and more precum streamed from the tip until his cock was slippery with it. Rick clutched at the sheets, trying and failing to keep his composure. His eyes were slit almost closed, but he couldn't stop watching my head bob up and down over his dick.

Rick's smile was drawing tighter, up into something close to a grimace of pain. It wasn't pain, I knew, but overwhelming sensation.

The most overwhelming sense is usually pain and at the moment of orgasm, it can be hard to tell the heights of pain and pleasure apart.

Rick was rising swiftly toward that peak now and I wanted to drive him over the edge. I shoved my mouth down onto his cock, back up and then down again. Faster and faster, until he couldn't take it anymore.

"Lily, I'm going to cum!" Rick groaned.

I popped his dick out of my mouth with a loud, wet sound and smiled at Rick. My hand closed around his slippery length and pumped him just three times before he let out a choked cry of pure pleasure. Hot cum boiled up from his tightened balls and splattered my lips until they were painted in white. I licked them and tasted the thick musk of Rick's orgasm.

He lay panting in a tangle of sheets, staring up at me in wonder as his spunk oozed messily from my mouth and between my legs. I wondered if Ben was watching us, too. I really hoped the ghost hadn't gone far, and not just because I enjoy an audience some-times.

Reluctantly, I stopped licking Rick's load from my lips. It would only make me want more. So I slid off the bed and went to the laundry basket for a towel. I would have liked to stay and get fucked again, maybe even see if I could somehow get both of the Sung brothers into bed.

But not right now. It was time to go.

When I had cleaned up, I tossed the towel to Rick. He caught it and scrubbed briskly at his sweat- and sex-slicked skin.

"Put on some clothes," I told him. "We need to get moving. We've got a couple of wizards to catch."

"Wizards?" Rick dropped the towel and grabbed a pair of boxers from the laundry. "I really missed a lot, didn't I?"

"Yeah. But it'll be over soon."

I took the cloth-wrapped revolver off the dresser and Rick followed me downstairs, clutching a shirt in his teeth while he zipped up his jeans. I collected my clothes from the floor and re-dressed quickly. I've had a lot of practice.

"Ben?" I called out. "Tell me you're still around."

An icy shiver worked its way up my spine and Rick cocked his head as though listening. I looked at him.

"That means he's here, right?" I asked.

"Yeah. Can't you hear him?"

"No, not unless he's using your mouth," I said with a smirk. "I guess you have special ghost-brother privileges."

"Does he need to possess me again?" Rick asked.

"In just a minute. Do you drive?"

"Uh, I have a license, but I mostly take the trolleys," Rick said. "I carshare for work."

"Come on, then. I'll drive. I'm parked at the bottom of the hill. Hold on to this for me."

I handed Rick the balled-up pillowcase. He took it with a con-fused expression, then his dark eyes widened as he felt the shape and weight of the gun inside. Rick looked up at the empty living room and I broke out in another fit of shivering.

"Ben, what's going on?" he asked.

"You boys can talk on the way," I said.

I went to the front door of the townhouse, unlocked and opened it. Outside, the steep, narrow hillside street was quiet. The freeway was a low, steady roar in the hidden distance, but there was no one on the road.

"Okay, let's go," I said over my shoulder to the living and dead Sung boys.

Rick was still wide-eyed and stunned, but he stepped out of the front door and followed me down the stairs. He was looking at the empty air beside him and the icy fingers tugging at my nerves told me he was listening to Ben.

It really wasn't that late... I pulled my phone from my pocket and checked the time. Just past ten o'clock. Where the hell was everyone? There should have been cars on the road or at least someone out walking their dog.

Frowning, I unlocked my phone and scrolled quickly through the contacts. Maybe Stefano or Dorian Vandi could give me the High Magus' number. I was starting to think it would be a good idea to let him know what was going on...

Then I smelled it: iron and salt, magnesium and fennel. Magic.

"Stop!" I said. I threw my arm across Rick's chest and halted his progress down the sidewalk.

"What's wrong?" he asked.

"There's a wizard out there."

I had known it was only a matter of time before one of the mages tracked Rick down through the scry network. Was that time up? There was wizard blood on Rick's unwitting hands. Would they try to take him alive? Or kill him?

Beside me, Rick's eyes went wide. "Lily..."

"Sssh!" I hissed. I raised my voice and raked my gaze along the street. "Clio? Doyle? Is that you? Are you out there? I've got this–"

"Lily, Ben can feel them," said Rick. "The wizards who killed him. They're here!"

"What?" I asked.

Strands of tousled red hair rose up off my shoulders, floating around me as though I were underwater. I blinked in surprise. What the hell? There wasn't even a hint of wind. Next to me, Rick gulped nervously. And then I smelled something burning and red light bloomed in the darkness.

I spun and shoved Rick back, sending him tumbling along the sidewalk just before the ball of fire slammed into the spot where he had been standing. It blasted a crater into the sidewalk and flung me against the side of the nearest car, shattering ribs and glass. My clothes were in flames and my skin was burning. The air in my lungs seared with smoke.

"Lily?" Rick cried. "Lily!"

"Ben!" I shouted. "Get him out of here!"

For a moment, Ben's cold presence swirled around me, soothing the flaming agony of my body, but then Rick's head snapped back as his brother's ghost seized control. His eyes blazed with dark fury and Ben reached for the gun on the ground at his feet.

"Don't you dare," I shouted. "Get Rick the fuck out of here! I can handle this!"

Ben's jaw clenched hard, but he nodded. He spun on his heels and bolted up the hill.

"He's getting away," called out a male voice I didn't recognize. "Muir!"

Another voice chanted strange words in a thick Scottish accent and another miniature sun kindled in the street, momentarily illuminating a pair of figures: one tall and blond, the other broad and bearded. I don't think I had ever seen them before, but I already knew exactly who they were – Ben Sung's murderers.

"You saved me a trip," I said. My voice was roughened by smoke, but it carried down the road. "Now how about saving me some time and just giving yourselves up?"

At the big Scottish wizard's command, another fireball hurtled down the street toward Ben's retreating silhouette. My half-demon blood roared in my ears as power surged through my body, healing and strengthening me. I leapt to my feet, wrenching the dented door off the car. I held it up like a shield and threw myself into the fire's path. A magical inferno billowed over the metal, blistering paint and then blasting it to ash. The fireball drove me back to the ground and I dropped the ruined car door, beating at the flames quickly consuming my shirt.

Footsteps pounded on the pavement and I squinted through swimming spots of color at the smaller wizard dashing across the street. He wore a long, dark coat that reminded me more than a little of robes and was reaching into one of the deep pockets. His hand came out with a polished length of wood – a wand.

Ben was at the top of the hill and his arms pumped at his sides, pushing Rick's body as fast as he could make it go. The blond wizard pointed his wand toward Ben and drew a breath to chant some kind of spell.

"Hey asshat!" I shouted.

I kicked the red-hot car door at him as hard as I could. My aim wasn't great, but the wizard threw himself down to the ground with a surprised exclamation. The warped and smoking hunk of metal slammed into the bus stop behind him, shattering the glass walls into sparkling cubes that spilled out across the empty road.

The other wizard, Muir, was running at me. Unlike his pale-haired friend, he was stripped to the waist and built like a fucking bear. The man was muscled and massive enough to give Max a run for his money. I didn't recognize him, but a lot of younger wizards pay the magical bill by working as bounty hunters until they can graduate to higher magic. It's a bit like being a college athlete. I would have bet his weight in gold bars that Muir used to hunt. And I guess he was doing it again now…

Blue paint swirled over Muir's exposed skin, designs across his face and broad chest that made him look like an extra from a Scottish romance. I struggled to stand, but smoke rose from my hair and my clothes hung in smoldering rags from my healing body. Muir towered over me.

"Finn! She's down," he called out in his rumbling brogue.

"She's a cambion," said the blond one. Finn, I supposed. "Hit her again!"

"I know what I'm doing," grumbled Muir.

"You couldn't even contain that succubus you summoned," I snarled. "What the fuck makes you think you can beat me?"

Muir stepped back, pulling a pouch from his wide leather belt. The bag was sealed with some kind of red wax that began to smoke as the big wizard brandished it over his head and chanted. My hair and charred bits of cloth levitated up around me once more.

Shit. I'm tough, but I wasn't sure about my chances against a fireball at this range. Healing from two indirect hits was already draining my power badly and if Muir nailed me right in the face with that spell, I was pretty well fucked.

He threw the smoldering bag at me and I hurled myself out into the road as hard as I could. If a car came by right then, I would be picking bits of fender out of my teeth for a week, but that was better than being wizard barbecue. The fireball blasted a parked minivan a dozen yards up the hill and the alarm inside blared. Lights were flickering in house windows, though no one opened their doors. Who the fuck could blame them? Normal people don't run *toward* strange explosions.

But I've never been a normal person. I was healed enough to roll up to my feet in the street and whirl on Muir. I lunged at him. The big painted fucker was going to regret ever hurting Ben Sung. And for what? So he could get his rocks off with a succubus? I couldn't wait to toss these two assholes at the High Magus' feet.

Something flew out at me, up over my head this time. Not another one of Muir's fireball pouches, but a net of braided and branded leather. Just like the net they had used to immobilize the succubus. I swore and veered off course, but the net came down, tangling around one of my arms. It yanked me to the ground as if made of something a hundred times heavier than lead.

"Quickly, Muir!" Finn shouted.

I tried to wrench my arm out of the net, but it seemed to be tightening around me, snaring me in enchanted tangles. Muir knelt over me, holding a strangely ordinary folded washcloth in one huge hand. It stank sweetly of chloroform. Trust wizards to know how to get their hands on all sorts of useful chemicals.

"Fuck you," I hissed.

I swung my free arm and punched Muir right in his big bearded face as hard as I could. I should have knocked the wizard into low orbit, but the blue paint across his skin flared with azure light and then faded.

Muir didn't even flinch as he pressed the cloth over my mouth and nose. I thrashed and struggled to pull free of the net. Finn grabbed the twisted leather, threw it over the rest of my body and suddenly I couldn't move at all. My eyes rolled wildly, but I couldn't see Ben anymore. Had he gotten away?

My sex-fueled body burned valiantly through the chloroform for almost a minute, but I had already exhausted too much power fighting the wizards. Eventually, the darkness swallowed me.

Chapter
EIGHT

I woke up alone in a basement. No, not just a basement, I realized a moment later. A sanctum. After eight years of working for the College, I finally got to see one. I really would have liked to be more excited about it.

The basement sanctum had gray stone walls and a low ceiling supported by thick wooden beams all hung with bundles of drying herbs. I guessed that this place belonged to Finn. The oversized Muir would have a hard time moving around in here.

Thick carpets were strewn across much of the floor, but not all of it. I counted at least thirteen open patches of flat, bare stone, all covered in circles and diagrams. Some were cut directly into the rock, while others were drawn out in charcoal, wax or what appeared to be blood.

Great.

Desks, worktables and bookcases lined all of the sanctum walls. Every surface was covered in neat rows of books and scrolls, clay pots and glass jars of chemicals or herbs, stones and crystals. There were knives with silver and iron blades, rods tipped in iridescent stone shards, and even bones arranged in orderly stacks. Merlinic magic isn't a good profession for the disorganized.

Slowly, I sat up. Something that felt like a cargo strap cinched my wrists behind my back. A quick inspection revealed that my ankles were bound with strips of leather branded with marks that looked a lot like the ones on the net Muir had thrown over me. Not that I had been examining them all that closely.

I was naked, too. My injuries had healed, but all that remained of my clothes were a few smears of ash across my pale skin. I could guess what Muir's fireballs had done to my handcuffs. They were probably little more than unrecognizable lumps of melted steel on the sidewalk outside Ben's house.

Swearing under my breath, I pulled at my bonds, but they didn't budge. Trying – and failing – to fight off two fully-trained and pre-pared wizards had consumed every glimmer of the sexual energy Ben and Rick gave me. I was no more than an ordinary human woman now. Just like Max had warned me.

It was times like this that I really wished I could power up off of masturbation. It would serve Finn right if he came down here to find me fingering myself. And while he was busy getting the biggest boner of his life, I could kick his stupid head right off.

I was trying to get my feet under me – maybe I could hop over to one of the desks and get a knife to cut myself free – when I heard footsteps creaking overhead and then voices.

"We should just go back ta the observatory," Muir said. That Scottish accent was pretty helpful in identifying the big bastard. "We can use the scrying mirrors ta find him again."

Him must have been Ben in Rick's body. So that was how the wizards found him tonight. I was so worried about the College hunters using the network to beat me to Rick that it never even occurred to me that the other sorcerers had access to it, too.

But then I smirked. I might not have succeeded in capturing Finn and Muir, but at least I had managed to buy Rick and Ben enough time to escape. I had thoroughly fucked up the wizards' little cleanup attempt.

I can be damned heroic when I put my mind to it.

As long as Finn and Muir hadn't caught Ben, there was still time for me to finish the job. Maybe not the job Stefano had called me for, but the one that needed to be done now.

Things had gone utterly tits-up... But where I'm concerned, that's not always bad news.

"We've been spending too much time at the scry stones," said another voice. Finn. "And we already had to suppress too many memories. The High Magus will notice that something's going on. We can't risk that."

"What, then?" Muir asked.

"We ask Lilith where they went."

"And after that?"

"We'll have to kill her. You heard what the spirit told her," Finn said. "She knows what happened last year."

"Kill her?" Muir sounded surprised.

"She's a cambion, Finn said. "Half the council's wanted her dead since the beginning. You should have hunted her years ago."

I rocked back onto my heels, but the leather knotted around my ankles was unnaturally heavy and I fell to the ground with a thump. Holding my breath, I lay against the stone floor, but Finn and Muir didn't seem to have heard me. They were too busy arguing.

Muir's deep voice again. "Zane says that she's got friends. Like that hunter Bianca fucked sometimes."

"I know Stefano Rossi," Finn said dismissively. "Bianca and I studied summoning with him. He won't be a problem. The man cares more about his dog-catching crusade than *true* magic."

Stefano was my friend? At least, someone at the College thought so. Well, that was kind of neat – I didn't have many friends – and I even spared a moment to be annoyed at Finn for shit-talking Stefano behind his back. But unless his friendship came with the power to summon Stefano to dick-punch some sense into his fellow wizards, he was just going to be another seat-warmer at my funeral.

I wiggled my toes experimentally, but the enchanted leather bonds only tightened around my ankles in response. Standing was out of the question, so I started squirming across the sanctum floor toward the nearest desk.

"What about Evaine?" Muir asked, his voice dropping so low that I nearly couldn't hear it.

"So long as the Lady doesn't have any reasons to suspect us," Finn answered firmly, "we will be fine. So let's be more careful this time."

One of my elbows came down on my hair and tugged. I swallowed a few choice oaths. Hair this long looked great, but sometimes it could be a real pain in the ass. And scalp.

"What is that supposed ta mean?" asked Muir. An ember of anger flared in his voice.

"A messy cleanup is worse than none at all," Finn answered. "Carelessness is what got us into this in the first place."

"No, *you* wanting ta gangbang a succubus is what got us all inta this!"

"That was Bianca's idea," Finn said, unruffled by the other man's temper. "The best fuck imaginable, she promised."

"Well, she was right about that," Muir rumbled. "We're even more fucked than I ever imagined."

I heard footsteps again, thumping down the steps toward the basement. I was nowhere near close enough to something sharp for cutting myself free to be an option anymore. Biting my lower lip, I racked my brain for some other idea.

"Orson was too eager to get his cock sucked," Finn said with a low sigh of frustration. "His circle wasn't strong enough to contain the succubus. If it had been one of mine..."

I rolled awkwardly back across the floor, as close to my original position as I could. My cheek pressed against the cold stone and I forced myself to go limp, like I was still unconscious. I slit my eyes nearly shut and watched the sanctum entrance.

Muir stepped out of the shadowed stairwell and into the basement. The protective blue paint was gone from his skin, though he still hadn't put on a shirt. His hair and beard were dark and neat, but so thick that I seriously wondered if there were were-bears over in Scotland.

Finn strode past Muir to stand over me. He had removed his coat and wore a pair of neat fog-gray slacks and a button-down shirt. Now that he wasn't trying to kill Rick or throw an enchanted net over me, I got a better look at Finn.

My captor was older than Muir, clearly the voice of experience in all this. Finn was long-limbed and slender, with graceful hands well-suited to his magical trade. The shoulder-length hair that I had first taken for blond was actually closer to white and gave Finn an ethereal look that would have been pretty damned sexy if I didn't so badly want to kick his ass.

Okay, maybe it was still a *little* sexy.

Muir stared around Finn's sanctum with frank curiosity, but then his eyes fixed on me.

"Gods, can you imagine what it would have been like?" The anger was gone from Muir's voice as his gaze raked over my bound, naked body. "We never even got ta touch that succubus before she escaped the circle. And then she jumped some fucking... civilian."

Finn thrust his hands into his pockets. "She ran because she knew we could banish her. But I must admit that some part of me has long been jealous of Benjamin Sung. He tasted the sweetest of forbidden fruit. It cost him his life, but still..."

I felt their desire swirling, warming me but too unfocused to give me anything like the power I needed. Finn sighed and knelt beside me. He grabbed my chin between his fingers and turned my face toward him. I opened my eyes.

"How long have you been awake, Lilith?" he asked.

"A while now," I admitted.

"Where are Benjamin and Richard Sung?"

"I don't know," I answered honestly.

Muir grabbed a massive handful of my hair and hauled me up to my knees. I bit back a moan of pain and the big wizard's desire swelled as I squirmed in his grip.

"Are you sure you don't want to change your answer, Lilith?" Finn asked.

"The Sung brothers could be on an airplane and halfway across the country by now," I said. "I don't know."

Finn stood and smoothed the creases of his gray slacks. "Then you no longer serve a purpose. Muir–"

"Really?" I interrupted in a low voice, looking up at him through my eyelashes. "You can't think of *anything* else to do with me?"

Finn blinked and cocked his head to one side. "What?"

"Guys, I'm writing you a blank check here," I said, then gasped as Muir's grip on my hair tightened. "I... I'll do anything. You have no idea how much I want to live. I'll work hard for it."

The two wizard's lust flared up like gasoline thrown onto a fire and Muir's voice was an ursine growl.

"Gods, is she serious?" he asked

"You guys wanted to fuck a succubus," I panted. "This is your chance."

Muir dropped me to the floor and his hands flew to the buckle of his belt. His pants were thick wool, but still prominently displayed a bulge befitting the rest of his huge frame. But Finn glowered at me with pale green eyes.

"Wait," he said. "I'm not taking any chances this time. Put her in the circle of binding. This one isn't getting away from us."

Finn pointed to the largest circle cut into the stone floor of his sanctum. The interlocking sigils running all around it made my eyes water just to look at. Muir scooped me up again and carried me across the basement. I felt something as he took me into the circle, like an air pressure change, but my ears didn't pop. The carvings bloomed with cold silver light. My whole body felt... strange.

"I'm far more careful than Orson was," Finn said. He stepped into the ring of runes. "*This* spell is strong enough to hold most any demon. Don't even think of trying to escape it, cambion."

He unfurled a small, rich red carpet in the stone circle's center that I suspected was for their comfort, not mine. Muir shoved me down onto it.

"Untie her," said Finn.

The Scottish wizard produced an iron knife from his belt. He sliced through the straps holding my wrists and ankles, then tossed the sheared bits of leather out of the runic ring.

Finn had already made short work of his clothes and they lay outside the circle of binding in a neatly folded stack. On my other side, Muir probably broke some kind of land-speed record for ditching his pants and boots. His dick was just as huge as it had looked when still dressed, already hard and flushed with desire.

I didn't waste any time rubbing my wrists or stretching. I was sore from lying all trussed up for who knew how long, but there were two cocks waiting for my attention – and two asses for my kicking, if I could only get enough power from them to defeat two seasoned wizards.

"You've both been waiting for this," I purred.

"Aye," Muir said.

I pulled myself up onto my knees and grabbed his thick cock in one hand. I ran the fingers of the other down Finn's length. He was shorter than his friend by a few inches in all respects. But considering that Muir was a humanoid mountain, that was hardly paying Finn any kind of disrespect. His dick rose more slowly, though. The white-haired wizard was hard to impress... I was starting to see why he'd been willing to violate the College's strictest rules to summon a succubus.

Well, I was a fucking cambion. I was my demoness mother's daughter and these two mages were going to get exactly what they wanted. And then some.

I fed the darkening head of Finn's cock into my mouth and circled it with my tongue. My hand stroked along Muir's monster shaft on the other side, making the tip brush my cheek and leave sticky wet streaks across the skin. Finn's fingers wound through my hair and then tightened, insistently pulling my head down over his growing length.

"More," he told me.

Another moment of sucking, then I popped my lips off of Finn's dick and squeezed my fingers around the slippery head. I raced my hand down, spreading my drooled wetness all along him. Jacking his quickly slicked shaft, I turned my face to lick at Muir's flushed cockhead. The big wizard groaned deep in his broad chest.

"Ah, shit," he grunted. "Don't stop."

"I won't. I'll do whatever you want," I said. "You can do everything you've ever dreamed of to me."

He did. Muir rammed his long cock down my throat. I had a lot of practice and knew what I was doing, but I choked a little on the sudden invasion. Saliva ran from one corner of my mouth and splattered my tits. Wetness streamed from between my legs, too, as Muir mercilessly fucked my face.

Finn's dick prodded at my cheek in a none-too-subtle demand for attention and I pulled off of Muir. I gasped once for breath and then Finn forced my mouth open, filling it with rigid heat. My lips slid easily over his wet shaft and Finn's breath grew rapidly hard and heavy.

Muir was so slick that my hand almost slipped right off of him, but I held on and stroked him swiftly. I couldn't even close my fingers around his girth, so I twisted my hand along him in a wet spiral that soon had Muir panting, too.

I pulled my mouth from Finn with a moan and whipped my head back, making my hair fly. I arched my spine, thrusting my tits out to show off the peaked strawberry nubs of my nipples. My curled fingers moved up and down along both stone-hard cocks.

"Fuck yes, boys," I gasped. "I can feel how close you are. Come on, cover your little demon whore in spunk."

I looked up at both of my captors and opened my mouth to receive their cum. I licked my lips in an invitation that was too much for Muir. Thick heat gushed hard against my cheek and oozed down my face. Another pulse sent semen running across my tongue and dripping down my chin.

The sight of my messy face pushed Finn right over the edge. He still held my hair in his clenched fingers and pulled my head back.

"Yes," Finn said.

His load shot out and laced through my red hair in white like a wet witch's streak. Another gooey ribbon of cum splashed down across my cheek and then Finn emptied himself between my lips, helping Muir to fill my mouth until their jizz was streaming from the corners.

I kept my hands working until I was sure I had milked every drop. Swirling my tongue through my mouthful of cream, I showed off the huge mess they had made. Then I closed my mouth and swallowed it all.

"Shite," Muir groaned.

When I was done, I opened my mouth again to show Finn and Muir that their double load was gone.

"I hope you two aren't finished yet," I said. "For me, that was just an appetizer."

I wiped my white-streaked cheek clean with the back of my hand and smirked at the two as I licked their cum up from my skin. Muir stared at the sight with his mouth hanging open. His cock hadn't flagged one bit. The big bearded wizard went down on one knee, but he sure as hell wasn't proposing.

Muir grabbed my breasts in his huge hands. He wasn't gentle and I felt his lust more like a hot golden blade than the sweet stream of energy Ben and Rick had given me. But it was still doing the job: the aches and abrasions of my imprisonment faded swiftly. I might have been down, but I sure as hell wasn't out.

Finn stood back at the edge of the glowing circle, watching. He wrapped one long, elegant hand around the prominent length of his dick as Muir squeezed my breasts together and gave the nipples a pair of hard pinches. Finn's pale eyes roamed all over my exposed body.

"Fuck her," he commanded.

Muir didn't need to be told twice. He moved behind me and seized my shoulders, shoving me roughly down onto my hands and knees. I lifted my hips and thrust my ass up at Muir.

"Yes," I said. "Fuck me–"

I broke off with a gasp as Muir's hand cracked against my backside. He spanked the other cheek of my ass, too, hard enough to leave a bright red print on the white skin. It faded quickly, though. I could take a lot more than Muir was dishing out.

The Scottish wizard seemed to know that, too. He gave me no warning at all before he grabbed my hips and slammed his dick deep into my pussy. My gasps became a sharp moan as he suddenly filled me.

"Fuck, she's so wet," Muir grunted.

"Of course I'm wet," I said. "I'm half succubus. I can't help it. I need to be fucked. Give me your cock!"

I pushed back into Muir and bounced my ass against his tensed thighs. His hands tightened on my hips and he pounded himself ruthlessly into my pussy. Muir was intent on putting as many 'O's as he could on that blank check I wrote.

He fucked me hard, slamming his long, thick dick into me over and over. I threw back my head and let loose a stream of loud, slutty moans that would have made any succubus proud and which drove Muir wild. He hammered himself into me like an engine piston, making his hips slap against my ass with every blow. The sound was like clapping, faster and louder, building to thunderous applause.

Then I supposed that Finn was giving me the standing ovation. He loomed over me, jerking his dick in swift, smooth strokes while he watched Muir fuck me.

I raised my face up to the pale-haired wizard and lifted one hand to hook a finger at him. Muir's cock pistoning in and out of me just about drove me down to my belly on the ground, but I was strong enough now to remain on my knees.

"Finn, come here," I gasped. "Give me your dick!"

Even the restrained and distrusting Finn couldn't resist *that* invitation. He stepped closer and knelt, circling his fingers around the base of his cock. He held the hard length out to me. Muir pounded into my pussy from behind and I moaned as he shoved me forward again. But this time, I just let him push me and my moan became muffled as he forced my mouth down over Finn's dick. Another hot, heavy blow of Muir into my pussy rocked me on my hands and knees, making me deep-throat his only slightly smaller partner, whether I liked it or not.

Don't worry – I liked it. Maybe I was playing it up a little for Finn and Muir, but I wasn't lying when I said that I wanted and needed their cocks.

I reached up, balancing on my knees and grabbed Finn's ass to pull him closer. The slender mage started and then seized a handful of my hair, but I was just helping him to fuck my face. I rocked back until only the crown rested between my lips, then Muir slammed me forward and I swallowed Finn's entire length down my throat. Again and again, more and more until my whole body trembled and I fought for the breath to whimper out my pleasure.

"She's so tight, Finn," Muir said in a low growl. "Fucking unbelievable. You've got ta try her."

He yanked his cock out of my pussy, eliciting a disappointed moan from me. Finn's dick popped from my mouth as big, rough hands rolled me over onto my back. I had only a second to reorient myself before Finn was kneeling between my legs and spearing himself into me.

Hard heat filled me again and I gasped at the sensation. I lifted my hips, taking all of Finn's cock. Wetness slicked my parted thighs and ran down the cleft of my ass. I squeezed Finn deep inside me, making us both pant and moan. Was he finally impressed?

Finn grabbed my ankles and began to work himself in and out of me. My back arched and my toes curled as his cock stroked me inside and the thick, warm weight of orgasm built low in my belly.

Something hard and hot touched my cheek and I opened my eyes to see Muir, his dripping dick thrust insistently out toward me.

"Don't forget me, Lilith," he said.

"Oh, I haven't," I gasped. "More...!"

I opened my lips and sucked Muir's big, slippery cock into my mouth. He tasted of my pussy and heavy, masculine musk. I ran my tongue along as much of his length as I could and felt the desire pulsing through him.

Muir cupped one of my breasts and squeezed hard. I moaned around his dick so loud that it vibrated through the huge wizard and made him grunt in wordless reply. His thumb and forefinger found my nipple, giving it a brutal twist that made me moan all over again.

Finn slid one hand down my leg, then up along my belly to seize my other breast. His fingers were just as deft as they looked and the smaller wizard teased my flushed, sensitive skin. Finn brushed my nipple so lightly that I whimpered in disappointment and pushed myself into his touch.

"Gods, you really can't get enough, can you?" he said.

I moaned hungrily around Muir's thick cock in answer.

Finn's voice was strained and the wizard was panting. His build was long and slender, but I was reminded that neither of these men were hunters. At least, not anymore. Most wizards did their magic in sanctums like this, not out in the field. Banging me was likely the most athletic thing either of them had done this year. The spells Finn and Muir used against me at Ben's house had probably been prepared right here. How long did it take to put together one of those fireball bags? I couldn't even imagine the hours of cold calculation that had gone into trying to murder Ben Sung all over again.

Muir's cock suddenly withdrew from my mouth and my whimpering moans were shockingly loud without it gagging me. Finn was slowing his smooth thrusting inside me, too, and pointed to a patch of red-carpeted floor in his circle of binding. Muir laid back, his large dick towering up from his body.

"Go," Finn ordered.

He withdrew himself from my pussy and I rolled up to shaking hands and knees. Finn sat back on his heels and slapped my ass smartly. I crawled across the circle and threw myself on top of Muir. Not even using my arms to steady myself, I sank down onto his long cock in a single desperate thrust.

"Oh, fuck!" I moaned.

I didn't need any request or command to start riding Muir like a prize stallion. He grunted in surprise and grabbed my breasts with almost crushing force. A human girl would have been bruised for weeks, but I just moaned and bounced atop Muir even faster.

Finn watched with a smug smile. "She's insatiable."

"Isn't this what you wanted all along?" I asked. "The hottest demon bitch to fuck however you want?"

I leaned down across Muir's expansive chest as I took his impressive length deep inside me and ground myself hard against him. Then I reached back and grabbed my ass, spreading the soft, smooth cheeks.

"That succubus ran before you could have your fun," I gasped. "But not me. I'm not running away. You can do *whatever* you want to me."

Finn rose swiftly to cross the distance between us. Then he knelt behind me and shoved my hands out of his way. I pressed my cheek to Muir's chest as Finn's fingers replaced mine and then I felt his cock against my backside.

"Aye, Finn," Muir rasped in breathless, mindless pleasure. "Fuck her hot little ass!"

Finn pushed the head of his dick against my anus. Muir's already huge presence in my pussy swelled as his friend forced my ass open slowly and then popped inside. I squealed and squirmed between them. Finn rubbed his thumb over the sensitive, stretched ring of my ass and I gasped.

"Yes!" I cried.

"Gods, she took it all," Finn said. "Every inch. From both of us. And the little demon whore loves it."

With Finn filling me from behind, I could only manage tiny movements between the two mages. But even that was enough to make their cocks press against one another deep inside my body. Lust and pleasure flooded me as Muir grabbed my waist, holding me up so he could drive himself into me with savage intensity. Behind me, Finn gripped my ass and worked his dick more slowly in and out.

"Fuck me deeper," I moaned. "Harder! I'm going to cum!"

They pounded me front and back. Hardness slammed into me again and again, stretching my pussy and ass, cocks pressing against one another to overfill my trembling body. I streamed hot wetness that slicked Finn and Muir's skin both as they surged wildly in and out of me.

"Yes! I'm cumming!" I screamed.

The orgasm began in my pussy, high and sharp and ripping through me. Then it was in my ass, too. There was a storm raging between my legs, through my whole body. Lightning crackled along my nerves and shot up my spine. Thunder boomed in my chest with every slamming heartbeat. Finn and Muir's heavy breathing rushed like wind in my ears. I lost control of my voice and screamed wordlessly as they used me hard.

The dripping, convulsing climax was too much for my captors. Muir went rigid beneath me and buried his huge dick to the hilt inside me. Finn was pressed against my back, gasping as he hammered his cock into my clenching asshole.

Their twin volleys went off so close together that I couldn't have told you which man fired their load first. All I knew was that I was suddenly full with hot golden light. Cum gushed into my pussy and ass in paired fountains that sent pleasure coursing, churning all through my body. They flooded and filled me until I could take no more.

Muir sagged, his chest heaving like bellows, and Finn collapsed on top of me. Cum trickled from my body in creamy streams that I knew would turn into rivers as soon as either of them summoned the strength to pull their cocks from my well-fucked holes.

I wasn't going to give them that much time. Muir and Finn had given me just what I needed and now it was time to finish this.

I heaved myself to my feet, hurling Finn off of me. He fell back with a startled shout. Beneath me, Muir blinked in surprise and grabbed for my throat. Wrong move. I swatted his hand away with a force that cracked bones and made the Scottish wizard howl in pain. I seized Muir by his thick, dark beard and lifted his face to mine. His eyes were huge and frightened.

"Ben Sung is done paying the price for your mistakes," I said.

Before Muir could stammer some kind of bullshit answer, I smashed his head down against the floor. His eyes went blank and blood flew bright red from his mouth. I left Muir breathing – I needed him alive when this was over, but I definitely wanted the big fireball-throwing bastard damned sleepy.

I stood. Cum streamed down my legs and left moonstone droplets on the stone floor as I whirled toward Finn. The tall wizard was smirking at me.

Not for long. I was going to wipe the floor with that smug face. I bunched my legs beneath me and leapt at Finn, but I slammed midair into something and slid to the ground still two feet away from my target.

Finn stood outside the circle of binding and the runes at his feet glowed with cold silver light. His grin grew wider.

"I'm far more careful than Orson was," Finn said. "And you're only half succubus. There's no way you're strong enough to break through my spell. You know, I don't think I'll kill you after all. You are mine, cambion."

"Fuck you, Finn!" I snarled.

He laughed. "Whenever I want. Which will be often, I suspect."

I tried to punch Finn, but my fist impacted against the circle's warded perimeter again. White-hot sparks flew glittering through the air and I pulled back with a gasp of pain.

But I frowned. I raised my hand and put it against the invisible barrier. There it was, cold and curved under my fingertips. Hair rose along the back of my neck as I pushed against Finn's magical circle. It was like trying to swim through solid ice. I pushed harder and chilly sweat poured down my spine. Light blazed around the place where I touched the binding spell and Finn laughed again.

I pushed until I screamed with the effort. Fuck, it burned. It froze. I poured every ounce of strength and power against the circle of binding. Finn's spell grabbed onto everything that was demonic inside and held on with unbreakable might.

But then something... slipped. The empty air in front of me spiderwebbed in cracks. Another shove and it shattered. So did I. For a second, there were two halves of me: the human and the succubus. And they *hated* each other.

Then my hand was through the circle. Everything inside me came crashing back together and my head spun. But there was still a job to do, so I seized Finn by the throat and yanked him close. The wizard wasn't smiling anymore.

"What...?" Finn choked. "Why didn't the circle hold you?"

"You said it yourself, asshole. I'm only *half* succubus."

Chapter
NINE

*I*t took the College a few days to get everything in order. This had gone far beyond a simple bounty.

One of the first things I did was drive out to the firehouse and jump Max's bones to make sure I could still power up. That feeling of separation, of being torn into two hateful halves as I pushed my way through Finn's spell had been... awful. But I could still smash the brick walls of the firehouse without breaking a sweat and no permanent damage seemed to have been done to my half-demonic nature.

The wizards put their scry network to good use and discovered Rick Sung hiding out with some of his aunts about fifty miles up the coast. They wanted to send Sabra out to get him, but I insisted on being the one to bring Rick and his brother to the College.

Now I waited on a bench deep in Dresden Hall, in a vast room I had never seen before. A hundred wizards or more sat in galleries along the sides, all dressed in formal-looking black robes. I had no idea there were so many. Dorian mentioned some of them had come from other campuses across the country. There was a trio who wore intricate crosses on silver chains around their necks that I was pretty sure had traveled all the way from the Castle.

At the end of the huge hall, the council sat behind a tall, inscribed stone bench like King Arthur's own supreme court. High Magus Vincent Myrdon was seated in the center, holding a long, polished wooden staff that he banged against the floor to call the room to order. Vincent looked older than the last time I had seen him. There were new streaks of gray in his auburn goatee and his already dagger-like widow's peak seemed even more pronounced.

"To order," the High Magus intoned. His voice boomed like thunder through the courtroom. "Merlin himself forged the Seal of Avalon to safeguard Earth from demons. He banished even his own father to protect this world. And so there is no greater violation of Merlinic law than to summon those evils which he sealed away."

Wizards are a disciplined lot, but a murmur rippled through the crowd. Vincent slammed his staff against the floor again and silence fell.

"Four of our own stand accused of infernalism," he said in a deep, dangerous voice. "Of summoning a succubus from the Nether for their earthly pleasure, of failing to properly bind her and then allowing her to attack an innocent mortal man."

I shivered. The College didn't take this shit lightly.

Good.

"If these accusations prove true, Bianca Taren and Orson Clark have already paid the ultimate price for their treason. And if they are false, then Benjamin Sung will answer for their murders."

The High Magus looked down at me. There was something in his tired, angry eyes that I couldn't quite read. But when he gestured, I rose to my feet.

"Lilith Quinn, you are called to testify," Vincent said.

Which wasn't as easy as it sounded. I was given a carved black scarab and told to put it in my mouth. The High Magus waited until I had tucked the little beetle into place to inform me that it would animate and sever my tongue if I spoke anything but the truth.

Holy shit. I almost spat the fucking thing out, but managed with an effort to simply nod my understanding.

And then I told the College everything, from learning about the bounty on Richard Sung to the night I deposited Finn and Muir naked and unconscious in the foyer of Dresden Hall. No one laughed.

I wasn't the only one to speak. Next came Ben Sung, wearing his younger brother's body. He came into the courtroom escorted by Stefano Rossi – who had been summoned back from Canada – and a dark-haired young wizard I only vaguely remembered seeing around the College a couple of times before.

Ben caused quite a stir, first by being a ghost and then again by initially refusing to accept the truth scarab, lest it harm Rick. But after some stern persuasion, Ben put the stone beetle in his mouth and recounted the same story he had told me, about how he had become a bodiless spirit and how he killed two of his murderers an a vain attempt to end his torment.

After that, Muir and Finn had little choice but to confess everything. Even if they were willing to get their tongues snipped off for lying, my testimony and Ben's were pretty damning.

There were a lot of technical questions about what Finn and his friends had done, first in summoning and then banishing the succubus. How exactly had snaring a human in the banishment wrenched him from his body and turned him into a ghost? Had the spell malfunctioned or was Ben's spiritual state a result of the Seal of Avalon...?

And so on. I hate to admit it, but I eventually got a little sleepy and bored. When wizards get into the minutiae of magic, it's like talking tax code with an accountant. But even I came awake when the hall's huge doors swung open and Evaine strode through. My mentor wore a white cashmere sweater and plain gray slacks, but she glided into the courtroom like a runway model or princess.

"My Lady," said Vincent.

Evaine nodded once to the High Magus. You could have heard a pin drop in that room. Hell, a feather hitting the floor would have been a thunderclap. But Evaine just stepped back and the questioning resumed.

Evaine went to the side of the hall where I waited. I gave her a quick hug, but refrained from any more enthusiastic forms of greeting. Evaine kissed my cheek with cool lips and then seated herself beside me.

"Are you alright, Lily?" she asked in a quiet voice.

"Yeah," I answered. "I think."

Ben sat in Rick's body with his dark eyes fixed on Finn, who still stood before the council of wizards. There was rage there, and pain. Those burning threads still bound Ben's soul to his killers. Was there any way to cut them? *Besides* murdering people?

I sat silently for a minute, trying to listen to Finn explain... something.

"What's going to happen to them?" I asked Evaine. "Finn and Muir. Vincent's not going to let Ben kill them, right?"

Evaine shook her head. "No. I suspect that they will be imprisoned for the remainder of their natural lives. They may find some way to repay the wrongs they have done. But I doubt it."

"...I've been thinking about my parents," I admitted, surprising myself.

I hadn't meant to say that. I poked my tongue around my mouth to make sure the creepy black scarab thing wasn't still in there.

Nope.

"This is not the first time that a young sorcerer – flush with power and lonely in their responsibilities – has dabbled in dangerous areas," Evaine said. She looked up at the council as they grilled Finn. "The unmatched carnal magic of the succubae and incubi are powerful temptations, even to those who should know better. And the demons are always eager for a chance to escape the Nether."

"The succubus they summoned... could she have gotten pregnant?" I asked.

"A succubus can only conceive a child in love," Evaine said. "You know that."

"Hey, I'm not saying that she would have fallen for any of those assholes who summoned her," I said quickly. "But Ben is nice."

"Perhaps, but I don't think it likely that the demoness had the chance to know Ben Sung very well. He was her victim, not her lover. And love doesn't come easily to the demons, when it does at all."

At the head of the room, Vincent hammered his staff down and we looked up to find everyone in the courtroom staring at us. I flushed a little and wondered how long they had all been listening. Evaine squeezed my shoulder once and then rose gracefully to her feet.

"High Magus." Her voice was soft, but it carried all through the hall.

"A demoness was summoned," Vincent said. "It was a year ago, but we must know if her actions here poses any danger to the human realm."

"The Seal of Avalon remains intact. All that moves on the isle are shadows and dreams."

There was an almost ritual note to Evaine's words and Vincent Myrdon nodded slowly. He looked thoughtful.

"Thank you, Lady," said the High Magus. He stood and banged his staff again. "This hearing is at an end. I will consider the appropriate punishments for the guilty and what may be done for those they have harmed."

Finn and Muir were led from the courtroom at wand-point. Ben watched them go with a storm of emotions warring on his borrowed face. Then he stood and spoke briefly with the wizards guarding him. Stefano and the mage I didn't know followed Ben across the room to me. Evaine melted back a few steps.

"Hey, Stefano," I said as the three men approached. "How're you doing?"

The other bounty hunter shook his head. His usually close-cut beard was unkempt and I doubted it was just from his time in the Canadian wilderness.

"I'm not sure yet," Stefano admitted. "I guess that I'm not entirely surprised to learn what Bianca did. She always had a deep fascination with the demons of lust."

"The fantasy is a lot more fun, isn't it?" I asked quietly.

Stefano blushed a little behind his beard. "Yes."

"I'm sorry," I said. "I doubt this is exactly what you had in mind when you asked me to go after that bounty."

Stefano offered up a tired smile. "I asked you to do the job right, Lilith. And you did."

"Thanks."

The other hunter inclined his head and then stepped away to give Ben some semblance of privacy. In a room full of curious wizards, it was a pretty thin façade. But it was nice of Stefano to try.

Ben cleared his throat. "I... didn't get the chance to thank you. For what you did before, fighting Muir and Finn. I don't know if they could have hurt me again, but they would have killed Rick."

I winced. "You really shouldn't thank me for that."

"Why not?"

"If I hadn't taken the time to get you two into bed, we might have gotten out of there before Finn and Muir attacked. It's my own fault that Rick was in danger."

Ben caught my eye and his voice dropped to a whisper. "Please don't regret that. You were good to me. And to my brother."

"How do you know that?" I asked and then laughed. "You *were* watching, weren't you?"

"I had to be sure Rick would be okay." Ben blushed a little and pulled me into a brief, fierce hug. "Thanks for... everything, Lily. We'll never forget you."

I hoped that was true, though it was more the College's decision than that of the two Sung brothers. If they decided to take Rick's memories, there wasn't much either of us could do about it. But I held Ben close for a moment before releasing him.

"You two boys take good care of each other," I said.

Ben nodded as Stefano took his arm and escorted him from the courtroom. Evaine reappeared at my side and put her hand on my shoulder. I looked up at her.

"Can the College help them?" I asked, looking in the direction Ben had gone.

Evaine followed my gaze. "Perhaps. True ghosts are almost as rare as cambions. But Vincent and his magi will study the spell that created this one and may be able to undo the damage that was done to his soul."

The rest of the wizards rose, too, and filed out of the hall with heads together, whispering animatedly about everything that had happened. Many of them paused as they passed Evaine and a few even dropped briefly to one knee. Evaine inclined her head and smiled to each of them. But then Vincent Myrdon stepped down from the raised dais and the crowd parted as he approached us.

"Lady, will you speak with me in my study?" he asked. "Many strange things have happened in the last year and I was hoping you could help me make sense of them."

"Can we talk some more later?" I asked.

"We will speak again, Lily. There's still time," Evaine said. She touched her fingertips to my cheek and then turned back to the High Magus. "I'll offer what answers I have, Vincent. But you may not like them."

"That's certainly never stopped you before," the High Magus answered sourly.

Evaine smiled and cocked her head. The tiny beads of water in her waist-length blonde ringlets caught the light and gleamed like diamonds.

Vincent turned to me. "Lilith."

I stood under the High Magus' sharp-eyed gazed and waited. Evaine, too, watched with a curious expression on her lovely face. Finally, I raised my eyebrows.

"Yeah?" I asked. "Time to kick me out again?"

Vincent rubbed one hand over his graying beard and sighed. "You've done well, Lilith. Richard Sung has been brought to us. The deaths of Bianca Taren and Orson Clark have been explained. You have met the conditions of the bounty request and more. Dorian will see to your payment."

"Oh," I said. I'd actually forgotten about the bounty. "Thanks."

With that, Vincent turned to Evaine. "If you'll accompany me?"

Evaine looked over her shoulder and smiled at me once before Vincent led her away. I headed out the courtroom door to go find Dorian and collect my gold.

LILY QUINN BOOK #7

ONE NIGHT
Sand

Chapter ONE

I knew where the auto shop was, of course, but that didn't stop me from smiling at the big red sign set up out front: *Max's Garage.*

I turned into the parking lot. Since the garage wasn't open for business yet, the sign was dark and there weren't many cars outside: just me in my Alfa Romeo, Max's old truck... and a little domestic sedan that I didn't recognize. Did Max already have a customer?

It was still early in the morning and a family of pigeons squabbled with the seagull roosting on a corner of the old firehouse roof. A night's worth of sea-scented dew dripped along the brown brick edifice and trickled through the gutters. It would evaporate to join the dawn fog when the sun rose a bit higher, but for now, the water wound in wandering pewter lines across the face of Max's Garage like curious quicksilver snakes.

I made my way across the parking lot toward the front door, but it swung open before I got there and someone came out. It was a woman, maybe a year or two older than me, with smooth olive skin and long, straight black hair. She pushed a pair of glasses up her nose and when she could see through them, she blinked at me in surprise.

My smile became a huge grin. I know the walk of shame when I see it. The other woman's clothes were rumpled, her hair still wild, and the remains of makeup was smudged around her wide eyes. Her high cheeks colored darkly as I approached.

"Hi," I said, waving. "Is Max in yet? I just wanted to check on my car."

"Oh um... hi," the other woman answered, ducking her head to hide her flaming face. "Yeah. I'm sure he'll be down soon."

"Thanks."

She turned away and hurried to her car. Despite being absolutely afire with curiosity, I let her go. I didn't want to interrogate the poor girl. I was saving that for Max.

I went into the old firehouse. The renovations were going well. Max had finished ripping out the outdated wiring and fixtures. The garage that long ago used to house fire engines was now full of Max's tools and even a second-hand hydraulic lift. My little i10 was parked on it, but the lift wasn't raised into position and all of the lights in the garage were still dark.

I poked my head into the office. One of the few things Max hadn't thrown out was the old fire chief's big wooden desk. It was pretty beat up, but after Max thoroughly cleaned the walnut and applied several new layers of varnish, the desk just looked well-used and well-loved.

There was a neat stack of invoices on top of the desk that momentarily arrested my attention. I flipped through the pages and my lips turned down into a contemplative frown. Invoices. Max would never forgive me if I stole the bills and paid them off behind his back, but I was seriously tempted to do it anyway. Opening this garage was expensive and I wondered how long it would take Max to pay it all off.

But with a monumental effort of will, I returned the invoices to Max's desk and went upstairs. What used to be a row of firefighters' bunkrooms, Max was now converting into a spacious apartment.

Construction was nearly complete and I had helped Max move in a couple weeks ago so he could stop paying rent on the old place. After a quick blowjob, I had been strong enough to make short work of even Max's heaviest furniture. I have no idea why more moving companies don't employ half-succubae like me.

Oh, right. Because I'm the first cambion since Merlin and my existence is a secret from most of the world. Pesky details.

I heard running water and went to the bathroom. It had been designed for several firefighters to use at once and Max had kept it more or less the same. The bathroom was a long, open concrete room with a line of shower heads lining the rear wall. My best friend stood naked beneath one of them, head bowed and his body bathed in steam. Max faced away from the door and hot water cascaded down his muscular back. His blond hair was slicked and darkened a few shades by the shower. Max didn't hear me yet, so I paused in the doorway to admire his firm, wet backside.

But I was curious, so I crept across the bathroom and found the wastebasket under one white porcelain sink. I peeked inside. Three used condoms lay tangled at the bottom. Magnums, of course. That was my boy.

"Good morning, Max," I chirruped brightly as I replaced the trash can.

"Holy shit!"

Max jumped and spun to face me, nearly slipping on the wet floor. I laughed and he pressed the heel of one hand to his chest, struggling to catch his breath.

"Oh, god. It's you," Max said after a moment. He turned back into the spray of water to finish rinsing away the soap. "Sorry, Lil. I didn't hear you come in. Do you want breakfast? Coffee?"

"Well, I brought some donuts," I said. "But I kind of forgot them in my car when I saw that surprise."

"Surprise?" Max's voice echoed a little in the bathroom.

"The woman I saw leaving. Who is she?"

"Her name's Taya," Max said. "She's the lumber department manager over at the hardware store and I've been going there a lot."

"I thought you told me that you didn't have time to date. She must be something pretty special."

"Taya uh… gave me a few ideas to save some money on the remodel and we started talking. I invited her over when she said she wanted to see where all the wood was going in."

"Yeah, I bet you showed her," I said, smirking.

Max turned off the shower and then rewarded my joke with a dimpled smile. I tossed him a towel from the wire rack beside the sinks and he began scrubbing water off his big, muscular body. I was willing to bet all the donuts in the city that Taya was impressed. And if she wasn't, then the girl obviously needed glasses.

Oh wait, she already had glasses.

Well, I'm sure she was impressed.

"So is it serious?" I asked. "You haven't dated much since high school. The only woman besides me you've slept with in the last year was Evaine when she was in the city for Finn and Muir's trial."

"Hey! You were there, too," Max protested. He blushed.

"Exactly my point," I said triumphantly. "So what about Taya?"

"Uh, we've only been going out for a week. I really don't know our relationship status right now," Max said. The towel muffled his voice as he dried his face. "So what are you doing over here, Lil? I've been working on the i10 when I've got time, but it's not ready yet. Sorry, I hope you don't need it for a job."

I waved dismissively. "I'm not working. Actually, I came to see if I could help out with the garage. I mentioned the donuts, right?"

Max finished drying his hair, turning it into a wild thatch of pale gold, and draped the towel around his broad shoulders. "I can make some coffee to go with them…"

"That sounds great." I poked him in the ribs. "But you're not escaping me that easily, Max. I want to know *every* detail about you and Taya. Who asked who out? Which one of you made the first move? Did she let you cum on her glasses?"

"I don't know if she's ready to get kinky, Lil."

"Oh, come on! That's what glasses are for!"

"No," Max objected mildly. "They're so she can see."

"Yeah? And did Taya see your cum splashing all over her cute little face? Details, Max!" I demanded.

Just to spite me, my phone rang. I gave Max a mock-stern glare and shook one finger at him.

"You're not off the hook," I told him. "Not by a long shot."

Max held up his hands in surrender and eased past me through the door to his bedroom. I pulled my phone out of my jacket pocket and followed. My finger hovered over the red *decline* button, but the caller ID displayed Vincent Myrdon's name. After everything that happened last month with Ben and Rick Sung, I had finally managed to get the High Magus' number and programmed it into my new phone in case of another emergency.

Why would Vincent be calling me, though? I *really* wanted to grill Max about his new girlfriend, but I accepted the call.

"Hello?" I said.

Vincent skipped right past any kind of greeting. "Lilith, I need to see you at the College today."

Even on the phone, the High Magus' voice rang with deep gravitas. I watched Max bend over next to the bed to retrieve a pair of jeans and barely resisted the urge to smack his tight ass. Taya was a lucky girl.

"When?" I asked. "What's going on?"

"Immediately," Vincent answered. "A situation has arisen. The Castle and the College need it resolved as soon as possible."

I didn't know if this *situation* was serious or if it was just because the High Magus always sounded like that, but pretty much all I heard was *doom, doom, doom, doom.*

Max pulled on his jeans and frowned as he buttoned them. I gave a slightly uncertain thumbs-up to reassure him.

"Uh... alright," I said into the phone. "I can be there in about an hour."

"Very well. Goodbye, Lilith."

Vincent hung up and I pocketed my phone. Max led me out to the kitchen and arched his pale eyebrows.

"Is everything okay?" he asked.

"I'm not sure. That was High Magus Myrdon. What the hell? He never talks to me unless he absolutely has to."

"I doubt there's a man on Earth that doesn't like seeing you, Lil." Max stepped behind the kitchen counter and looked at me. "No time for breakfast, then?"

"I'll go grab those donuts from my car, but then I need to drive out to the College."

Max nodded and got to work filling his coffee pot from the kitchen faucet. "I can at least make you a cup for the road."

"Thanks," I said. "I'll be back to hear all about Taya as soon as I can. She better know how lucky she is."

Max smiled at me and blushed again. "We'll see, Lil."

Chapter TWO

The College is a secret order of wizards, which is exactly as scary and cool as it sounds, and their headquarters are right across town from my condo. They do teach magic at the College, but it's not exactly the kind of school you can just enroll in and then ditch class because you got drunk at a frat party. The College is one of the largest organizations of Merlinic mages in the world, second only to the Castle in Europe.

I think the Castle is based out of England somewhere. Probably in an actual castle.

I turned my car down a driveway long enough to be its own road and the massive wrought iron gate at the end swung open at my approach. It was possible that the wizards had cameras and operated the gate remotely when they saw me coming.

Possible, but not likely. I suspected that it had more to do with the huge stone gargoyles perched on top of the gateposts. Every single time I visit the College, I swear those things are in a different position.

After parking beneath the old oak tree out front, I headed for the largest mansion, Dresden Hall. The main foyer was full of suits of armor and the cork bounty board that was my usual destination.

Deeper inside were the vaults where the wizards kept transmuted gold to pay me and the other hunters when we brought in monsters.

But this morning, I didn't even make it as far as the bounty board. Dorian Vandi was waiting for me at the big double doors of Dresden Hall. He was one of the senior wizards of the College, both in age and position. The old man was shorter than me by a head and wrapped all in long black robes that were perfectly clean and pressed, but still managed somehow to look dusty.

"Good morning, Lilith." Despite the early hour, Dorian didn't yawn. He did, however, run his hand over his balding brown pate and then point off down one of the white-paved paths leading further into the College. "I'm supposed to take you to the observatory."

"Um, what?" I asked.

In eight years of working for the wizards, I had only ever been allowed inside Dresden Hall. And I didn't even get free run of that. Dorian nodded, though, and escorted me across an overgrown green lawn. We passed the pond and walked through a strange garden full of herbs being tended by another robed old man. He inclined his head respectfully to Dorian and stared after me in frank curiosity.

The observatory was a much smaller building than Dresden Hall, topped with a verdigrised bronze dome split down the middle and open to the pale morning. Dorian gestured to a tall front door made of the same green-tinged metal as the dome and depicting a handsome, bearded man gazing contemplatively skyward. Merlin, maybe?

I opened the door and followed Dorian into the observatory. It was dim inside and since I hadn't jumped Max at the garage, it took a few seconds for my eyes to adjust. Most of the observatory was taken up by a single room. The curved walls were lined with complicated star charts showing constellations I'd never heard of. There was nothing as simple as the Big Dipper here. At the top of a winding bronze staircase, another wizard peered through the eyepiece of the telescope with way too many lenses. I had no idea what she could possibly be looking at during the day, but whatever it was, she seemed *really* focused on it.

In the center of the ground floor room stood a huge table covered in more charts and stacks of scrolls. A few younger wizards gathered around one of the antique celestial maps and appeared to be arguing about something written on it. Most of them were about my age, which probably meant that they were still just acolytes. It takes decades of study to master magic.

Or so I've been told. I certainly haven't learned any magic and would have gotten some scowls if I tried. Merlin was a half-demon like me, but sometimes I think his successors fear their founder's legacy as much as they revere it.

The little apprentice wizards looked up as we came in. Each of them inclined their heads solemnly toward Dorian, then started when they caught sight of me. I guess my tiny denim shorts and favorite leather jacket didn't exactly fit in with their prep-school-meets-Hogwarts dress code. But that didn't stop me from picking up golden flares of lust from most of them.

Especially the dark-haired one. He seemed familiar – about six feet tall, with short, wavy brown hair and sharp, intelligent eyes the same chestnut color. When Dorian led me around the table, the young wizard actually stepped away from the debate and held out his hand to me. I shook it.

"Good morning," he greeted me with a smile. "My name is Zane Colton."

"I'm Lily Quinn," I answered.

Zane nodded. He hadn't released my hand. "Oh, yes. I know. I attended Finn and Muir's inquiry."

That was where I knew him from. We hadn't been introduced at the time, but Zane had worked with Stefano Rossi during Finn and

Muir's trial. The ghost was the primary witness in the not-so-minor matter of several wizards summoning a succubus last year. Which had promptly escaped their control, of course.

"Yeah," I answered. "I thought I recognized you. Is that what you're working on right now?"

Zane's smile faltered. His eyes flicked back to a thick book that lay open on the table where he had been standing.

"No," he said. "There's a celestial alignment coming up this autumn that interests us."

I peered over his shoulder at the book and blinked. I recognized that, too. "Is that *The Gates of Avalon*?"

"Yes, it is," Zane said. He sounded surprised. "You know it?"

"Lilith is the one who retrieved the book when it was stolen last year," Dorian told the younger wizard, who seemed duly impressed. "But I'm afraid she has an urgent meeting with the High Magus."

Zane released my hand and stepped away, nodding. "Of course. I should get back to work."

He returned his attention to *The Gates of Avalon* and Dorian led me away across the observatory. I glanced back at Zane again. You know, it might have been worth the effort to spend some more time with the College wizards. Mostly I just interacted with the other bounty hunters...

But I kept following Dorian. The study of alchemy took years. Zane would still be here when I was finished with whatever the High Magus wanted.

"Hey, Dorian...?" I asked. "Speaking of *The Gates of Avalon*, do you know anything about the shadow that came to get it? Has Kalen spilled the beans yet about his employer?"

Dorian shook his bald head. "No, not yet, I'm afraid. And perhaps not ever. But the High Magus has spoken to Finn and Muir on the issue."

Those were the College wizards that I had busted for breaking the number one rule of the Merlinic order: don't summon demons.

"And what the hell would those two bastards know about it?" I asked, frowning. "Wait, do you think demons were involved in the theft? Was Kalen working for a demon?"

"It's an unsettling possibility."

Dorian stopped me at a narrow door. A tarnished bronze plaque on the front was etched with a name in neat copperplate letters: Vincent Myrdon.

"Is this the High Magus' office?" I asked.

Dorian nodded. "You're surprised?"

"I was expecting something... grander, I guess."

"This has been his study for longer than he's served as High Magus," Dorian said. "When Vincent ascended to his current position, he kept it."

I had no idea what to make of this information, so I returned to staring at the door. There was no sign of animated knockers or little brass gargoyles, so I knocked.

"Enter," came Vincent's voice from inside.

Dorian twisted the knob and pushed the door open, then stood back. Reluctantly, I stepped through.

"Lilith Quinn to see you, High Magus," he announced.

Then Dorian shut the door with a thud that made me jump, leaving me alone with Vincent Myrdon. I shot the place where he had been standing a scathing look. Traitor.

The High Magus' office – or study, as Dorian had called it – was bigger than it appeared from the outside, though not by much. The walls were lined in bookshelves, of course, but most of the room was dominated by a desk so vast that I swear it was made for a werewolf. The top was stacked high with books, each one so big and old that you would have to call them *tomes*.

I wondered how many apprentices it took to carry those things. You know, after actually seeing the books the wizards had to tote around, maybe I shouldn't have been so dismissive of the College exercise regimen.

Vincent sat behind his monstrous desk, frowning down at an equally monstrous tome. One of the yellowed pages was inked with tiny script that I couldn't read, but which looked like Arabic. The other page was a hand-drawn map that seemed to be of the Middle East, to judge by the coastline, but I didn't recognize any of the borders drawn on it.

The High Magus was an imposing man, angular and tall even when seated. His shoulder-length hair was the color of steel and combed neatly back into a gray tail. There were still a few streaks of auburn left in his closely trimmed goatee, but they had faded considerably in the years I've been working for the College. Sometimes I wondered how many of Vincent Myrdon's gray hairs were because of me.

"You know, that old book smell you all like so much is kind of toxic," I said as casually as I could. "Mold and stuff. You should really digitize all of this. A whole library could fit on a flash drive or phone. Or maybe you could do audiobooks. Then you could take them jogging."

Vincent looked up from the map and fixed me with a sharp gaze. His eyes were a dark green like dried leaves. I didn't think I had ever noticed before, but it seemed like I was talking to the High Magus more and more these days.

"That would be unwise," he said gravely. "There are things in many of these books which should never be spoken aloud."

I swallowed. The High Magus didn't crack jokes, apparently. Ever.

To business, then.

"You wanted to see me?" I prompted.

"There is a job," Vincent said.

I frowned. "You mean a bounty? Why didn't you just post it to the board?"

"It's not a bounty. And there would be no point in posting the request. Our hunters cannot undertake this task. One or two might be willing to make the attempt, but no wizard can do what I must ask of you."

"Sounds interesting," I said. "So what can I do that the other hunters can't?"

"There's a mummy who has managed to corner the market on quicksilver."

I blinked, trying to wrap my head around the apparent change in conversation. "Uh, do you mean mercury?"

"No, though the ancients often mistook one for the other. They confused the two in name and use with disastrous results. To this day, alchemy remains a discredited science because early scholars lacked the knowledge to make distinctions between substances that superficially looked and acted alike."

I nodded and wondered how many of those old alchemists had blown themselves to bits while trying to figure out which runny silver stuff was what, but mostly I just let the lecture wash over me. The High Magus probably didn't ask me here for an alchemical history lesson, but it was his show and I didn't exactly think I could tell him to hurry it up.

He didn't.

"Quicksilver is liquid and silver in appearance, much like mercury, but brighter in color and considerably heavier. It is not toxic, nor can it be found in fish. In fact, there are only a few places in the world where quicksilver can be collected. The most abundant font lies in the Ultimate South, but since ice claimed that land, it has been lost to us."

"South? Ice?" I asked. "You mean Antarctica?"

Vincent shrugged. "If you prefer that name, yes. It has been known by many. But the largest remaining font of quicksilver is located in Egypt."

"Font? So it... what? Bubbles up out of the ground?"

Not that I was terribly interested, but somewhere in all of this alchemy talk was a job for me. I was really curious what the High

Magus thought I could do that was beyond the skill of his own wizards. And there was apparently a mummy involved, which I had never dealt with before.

"It would be simplest to say that quicksilver is the blood of the Earth," Vincent told me. "It communes with everything that it touches, carrying vital nutrients like our own blood carries oxygen. Quicksilver is a precious and irreplaceable alchemical commodity. It must be harvested with care, since like blood, draining too much can harm the lands from which it is drawn…"

There was more. A *lot* more. I tried to follow the High Magus' lecture. Not very hard, but I did try for a while. My eyes glazed over, though, and Vincent's voice became a nonsensical, droning buzz in my ears.

"That's why we need you," he said at last.

Oh, shit. I'd missed the important bit.

"Uh, what?" I asked.

Vincent Myrdon was far too cultured to roll his eyes at me, but he heaved a soul-deep sigh that was somehow even worse.

"The mummy is called Ptah," he explained slowly. "An Egyptian alchemist of a powerful and ancient tradition. During the recent unrest in his country, Ptah was able to seize all of the remaining quicksilver. He controls the entire trade and is now making… unreasonable demands."

"You guys can make gold out of candy bars. Why don't you just step up production to meet his price?"

"Ptah is an accomplished alchemist himself, as I said. He has no need of our gold. His requirements are more serious and problematic than that."

"So what does this mummy want?"

"Unique artifacts," Vincent said. "One-of-a-kind magical tomes. Political favors. Women."

I scowled and shook my head. "Women? What the fuck does that mean?"

"Relations to the wizards that would serve both as hostages to strengthen Ptah's control over us, and to expand his own growing harem. Insult upon injury."

"This guy sounds like a giant dick," I said.

Vincent's eyebrows rose a bit at that, but he didn't argue. "Ptah's made these same demands of the geomancers of China and Korea, as well, preying upon their great need for quicksilver to maintain their ties to the local ley lines."

"You didn't send this Ptah guy any of your relatives, did you?" I asked, probably with more heat than was really wise with the most powerful and influential wizard in all of North America. "Some wife or daughter I've never heard of?"

Which was entirely possible. I didn't really know much about the High Magus' personal life. But Vincent's eyes went wide for a moment and then narrowed into dangerous green slits.

"No," Vincent said flatly. "We have refused his demands. Lilith, the College is willing to pay a fair price for quicksilver, but we must come to an understanding with Ptah about the trade. That is why we need you to speak with him."

"Why me? I'm not a diplomat or negotiator. Plus, I don't know shit about quicksilver. You just spent ten minutes lecturing me on the stuff and I still can't tell you anything about it. Why don't you go talk to Ptah and hammer this out yourself?"

Vincent sighed and ran his fingers through his gray-streaked beard. I wasn't sure if that was commentary on my response or a general indicator of the High Magus' stress level.

In the past six months, the College had lost one wizard at the claws of a werewolf, two more to Ben Sung's murderous attempts to sever the ties that bound his spirit to Earth, and then had to imprison Finn and Muir for turning Ben into a ghost in the first place. A strange gold-eyed shadow had forced perhaps the most accomplished fairy thief in the world to steal the original *Gates of Avalon*, and despite being held in the College's most secure magical prison,

Kalen Silverwind still wouldn't give up the name of his employer. It had been a rough year for Vincent Myrdon.

I wondered briefly if *The Gates of Avalon* was one of those unique old tomes that the College didn't want to give up, but the High Magus was speaking again before I could ask about it.

"The magi of the College and the Castle are no longer welcome in Egypt and much of the old Persian Empire. In ages past, Castle wizards tried to wrest control of the region from the djinni. They did not succeed, but the djinni have long memories."

I didn't scoff, but I badly wanted to. What? Meddling in Middle Eastern politics backfired into a mess of complications and trouble? Color me shocked.

"Now all Merlinic wizards are forbidden to set foot in Egypt and many of the surrounding nations," Vincent finished.

"But I'm not a wizard," I said. "That's why you need me to go."

The High Magus nodded. "Before you can deal with Ptah, you must present yourself to the djinni and secure their permission to do so. The djinni do not overly concern themselves in the affairs of mortal sorcerers in their territory, but they would not take kindly to the unannounced presence of a foreign representative."

"So you want me to negotiate the flow of quicksilver with Ptah," I said. "But first, I need to get permission from a genie to even talk to the guy."

"Djinn," Vincent corrected. "Djinni is plural. And show them the utmost respect. Those who anger the djinni usually end up inside lamps, prisoners suspended bodiless in eternal limbo."

No thanks. I had a lot of fun with my body and wasn't in a big hurry to lose it. I cocked my head at Vincent.

"And you're *sure* I'm your best option?" I asked. "I'm a bounty hunter. You might have noticed that I'm not exactly the delicate diplomatic type."

"If there were anyone else I could send to deal with Ptah, I would do so. You are our last and only choice."

"Thanks," I said sourly.

"There's no one else that we can trust with this, Lilith."

I blinked. "You... trust me?"

"There are still those in the College who believe that you are dangerous. But others have noted your service."

I doubted it was anything I'd ever actually done that worried the wizards. They were afraid of what I *was*. My mother was a succubus and my father was a mage. One of their own.

And as I had been reminded so emphatically last month, summoning a succubus was a *very* serious crime under College rules. Merlin and generations of his students have spent over a thousand years keeping the demons locked away in the Nether, so my half-demon blood was an understandable strike against me. But now it occurred to me that *both* of my parents were probably points of anxiety among the College – not only was my mother a succubus, but my father was a wizard willing to summon her.

"So which side are you on?" I asked Vincent. "I seem to remember you not being too thrilled when Evaine first brought me to the College..."

If the High Magus heard my question, he didn't answer it. Instead, he gestured to one of the outlines on his ancient map.

"Ptah's home is in Cairo," he said. "The most prominent djinn in that area is Madu Tau. He is a djinn of the air, which makes Madu Tau somewhat more affable than the djinni of fire or water, and less territorial than the earth djinni. But none of them are to be trifled with. The djinni are elemental forces and since the erection of the Seal of Avalon, they are among the most powerful beings left in this world."

Erection. I fought the adolescent urge to snicker.

"What about Ptah?" I asked instead. "Assuming I can somehow get Madu Tau's blessing to go knock down this mummy's door, what should I know about him? You said he's an alchemist. So he's like you?"

"Ptah was human once, long ago. But he mummified himself in order to gain immortality." Vincent said it with a subtle note of distaste in his voice. "Ptah is one of the canopic undead."

"Okay," I said. Whatever *that* meant. "Well, I've dealt with vampires. I'm pretty sure I've got a handle on how a thousand-year-old man thinks."

"We estimate that Ptah is closer to three thousand years of age."

I whistled. "So I need to charm an air djinn who hates wizards and negotiate trade terms with a millennia-old mummy who is abusing his monopoly on quicksilver to build a harem of hostages. That's the job?"

"Yes," said Vincent.

"Great. When do I leave?"

Chapter THREE

The city spread out below me was bigger than my home and older by thousands of years. From the air, I stared out across Cairo and marveled at the mix of ancient stone buildings side by side with modern glass skyscrapers. Churches and geometrically decorated mosques from traditional to starkly contemporary stood glaring across city squares at each other. The colorful sprawls of plazas and strip malls twisted between crowded housing developments, all connected by a vast web of roads and freeways, though I was still too high up to see the people and vehicles traveling along them. And winding through it all was the dark silver of the Nile River. Quicksilver in its own right, I supposed: the lifeblood of an entire nation.

Navigating this job and this city was going to be one hell of a challenge.

I settled back into my cushy first-class seat and watched the ground rush up toward us as the airplane began its descent into Cairo International Airport. About half of my flight was full of locals returning home after business or travel abroad. The other half were foreigners like me, just beginning our journeys as we climbed off the plane and made our way out across the airport.

I handed my passport to a tall customs agent who spent more time examining me than my papers. I wondered if my short navy-blue skirt suit was too much. Or too little. I had tied my hair up in a tight red bun to at least try to look professional, but my succubus blood felt the stirrings of lust from a number of men and a few of the women.

When I had collected my passport again and started searching around for the baggage claim, I spotted a man in an impeccable black suit holding a sign with my name printed on it. I crossed the gleaming airport floor to him and wasn't sure if I should offer him my hand.

"Hello," I said. "I'm Lily Quinn."

"Master Tau is expecting you," the neatly-dressed man answered in flawless English. "He asked me to meet you."

My escort bowed slightly and took my carry-on bag, then led me to the baggage carousel. When I pointed out my suitcase, he picked it up and refused to let me lift a finger to help. I figured I should give the guy a tip or a handjob – or maybe both – but I wasn't sure of the etiquette and was supposed to be on my best behavior while in djinni territory.

Feeling a little useless, I followed him away from the thick flow of passengers and their families. He guided me through a smaller side door that was labeled *Authorized personnel only* in English, French and Arabic. We stepped out onto a concrete sidewalk that shimmered with heat despite the deep shade of an overhanging red awning. The crimson cloth flapped in a swift, hot wind.

There was no car at the curb, though. I turned to ask my escort where we were going, but he had vanished. I had just enough time to gasp and wonder what the fuck was going on before smoke billowed up all around me. I smelled sweet sandalwood and wind rushed in my ears.

When I waved the smoke away, the airport was gone and I gasped all over again. I was standing in a penthouse that made my four-million-dollar condominium back home look like a cardboard box by comparison. A moldy one.

The floor beneath me was pale marble, so smoothly polished that I could look down and see right up my own skirt. All of the furnishings were expensive, tasteful and either silver, white, gray or glass. The walls were covered in huge floor-to-ceiling windows that displayed soaring views across Cairo. We had to be at least fifty stories above the city.

I turned in a slow circle, staring. It was like being in a cloud. But I seemed to be alone in the aerial penthouse. There was no sign at all of the man who had picked me up at the airport, though my luggage sat in a neat stack beside the doors. My host didn't expect me to stay long, apparently.

I was wondering if I should have a seat on one of several ivory couches gathered under a magnificently glittering crystal chandelier, but when I turned to do so, there was a man standing in front of the window that I *swear* wasn't there before.

He was easily seven feet tall and so impressively muscled that I wouldn't have bet on even Max to last ten seconds against the guy in an arm-wrestling match.

Sorry, Max.

The unexpected man's skin was the color of polished wood and both his short, thick hair and beard were ink black. His clothes were a simple pair of khakis and a crisp white linen shirt unbuttoned halfway down his expansive chest. He wore no jewelry, but there was a platinum Lange & Söhne watch around his wrist that probably cost as much as my car.

"Welcome to my home," said the man in a voice so deep that it made my bones vibrate. "I am Madu Tau."

His English was deeply accented, if thunder was an accent. Madu Tau extended one large hand and when I did the same, he closed his fingers over mine. The djinn shook my hand carefully, like he was somehow weighing it.

"Lily Quinn," I said. "Thank you for the uh... ride, I guess... from the airport. I'm not sure why we bothered with the plane at all, actually."

Madu Tau turned to gesture toward one of the deeply cushioned white couches. I smoothed my skirt and sat.

"We have a mutual agreement with the Castle, and by extension, the College," rumbled Madu Tau. "So long as Merlinic magic does not cross their borders, neither does ours."

That sounded a little ominous. Vincent wasn't kidding about bad blood between the djinni and the College. Madu Tau gave me a smile that was dazzlingly bright, though his gaze remained watchful and cautious. The djinn of air seated himself on a couch opposite me, leaning back and spreading thick arms across the pillows.

"Besides, it would have been extremely rude to merely pluck you from your home," he said.

"Uh, thanks." Oh yeah, I was a *natural* at this diplomacy shit. I cleared my throat. "Look, I'm here on behalf of the College to negotiate with a mummy in Cairo."

"You are speaking of Ptah," said Madu Tau. "Few humans have succeeded in unlocking the secrets of immortality, and there is only one canopic mage in my city right now."

The djinn's tone was neutral, but I thought I detected a brief flicker of distaste in his expression. Was it for me or the College? Or was it the same thing I had heard in Vincent Myrdon's voice when he talked about Ptah? Well, no matter the answer, I still needed Madu Tau's consent to deal with the mummy.

"That's the guy," I said. "I'd like your permission to talk to him."

Madu Tau regarded me with dark, mysterious eyes. "You are no sorceress. So who are you, Lily Quinn, that the College trusts this delicate matter to you? Or perhaps it is more accurate to ask *what* you are."

I drew a deep breath and briefly weighed the benefits of lying, but it just didn't seem like a smart move.

"I'm a cambion," I admitted. "Half succubus on my mother's side."

Madu Tau considered that for a moment. When he exhaled, a warm breeze blew through the penthouse and tugged lightly at my clothes.

"I sensed something of the Eternal Dark about you," said the huge djinn. "Interesting. The Castle sought out and locked the demons away centuries ago. But Merlin himself was half-damned, as well. Such contradictions."

Madu Tau gave me a long, contemplative look. I worried that he was still thinking of Merlin, of the cambion who was also a wizard, and getting ready to poof me out into the middle of the ocean or something.

"Before the Seal of Avalon," said Madu Tau, "I thought often of bedding a succubus."

That got my attention, and not just because Merlin had sealed the demons up in the Nether over a thousand years ago. I felt the warm stirring of lust from Madu Tau. Even the mighty djinni were not above temptation, it seemed.

"How was it?" I asked.

"I never found out. Taking a demoness was dangerous, especially in those days. I could not risk it. But I have always had some... regrets."

Madu Tau's growing lust was like the heat of the blazing Egyptian sun streaming in through the windows. His desire was powerful, elemental. When a djinn wants something, I guess he *really* wanted it. Good. I expected no less.

I rose and crossed the scant feet between us to stand before Madu Tau. Even seated, he didn't have to look up to meet my eye. I smiled at him.

"Eternity is too short for regrets," I said. "Don't you think?"

Madu Tau stood, towering over me. He eclipsed the sun, but his answering smile was radiant.

"Yes," he agreed in that stormy baritone rumble.

He put one strong arm around my waist and there was another scented swirl of smoke. When it cleared, we were in a bedroom.

Madu Tau gave me a moment to take in the heavenly view. Like the rest of his penthouse – assuming that's where we still were – it was all finished in silver and ivory and shone like a celestial jewel. That included the bed, which was far bigger than even a California king, so I'll just call it an emperor bed. It was covered in soft sheets of pale silk that made me want to throw myself into the middle of them.

The bedroom was lovely, but that wasn't what made the blood rush in my ears and the heat kindle between my legs. I turned back to Madu Tau and trailed one hand down his dark, hard chest. It rose and fell with the air djinn's swift, deep breaths and his heart-beat was strong, a powerful throb through his body that I couldn't wait to feel inside of me.

Madu Tau's shirt was in the way of my exploration, so I set to work unbuttoning the fine white linen, then slipping it off of his wide shoulders. I walked my fingers over the rippled knots of im-pressive abdominal muscles to the buckle of his belt and pulled it slowly open. I tried not to be too eager as I unfastened Madu Tau's khakis and pushed them down. This was a diplomatic mission, after all.

I wondered for a moment if this was *exactly* what the High Magus sent me to do. I couldn't decide if the idea was insulting or if I should get Vincent Myrdon a thank-you card. But I didn't waste much time pondering those particular mysteries. I had far better things to do.

Madu Tau stepped out of his pants and then onto the bed. White silk rustled softly around the djinn as he leaned back, re-clining against the headboard. His cock was a massive length along one thigh. Even untouched, he was longer and thicker than most men were fully hard.

The djinn watched me and I felt his powerful desire brewing like a thunderstorm. He had been contemplating this since before Merlin created the Seal of Avalon and I intended to make it worth the wait.

I unbuttoned my tailored jacket and draped it over the back of a stylish gray-upholstered chair, then undid each tiny pearl button of my blouse. I turned to let Madu Tau watch me unzip my skirt and slide it down my long legs – slowly, but not quite with the rhythm of a striptease.

It was working. Maybe I would be good at this diplomacy stuff, after all. I felt the storm building, rising and swelling inside Madu Tau. I couldn't wait to get a taste of the sexual energy an elemental force like a djinn put out.

As well as a taste of his cock. It was rising, too, more and more with each slow movement that I made. And *still* rising. As I slid my hand along my spine to unhook my bra, I wondered just when Madu Tau's dick would stop growing. It was a pillar, and I wasn't being poetic. That thing could have held up the roof of the Parthenon. Not even magnum condoms would have fit Madu Tau.

But I'm no fragile little flower and I didn't balk. I slipped my fingers under the wet lace of my panties, easing them down and off. I wore a pair of thigh-high stockings, but I left myself clad from the soles of my feet to mid-thigh in sheer black silk.

Finally I reached up, unwound my long red hair and shook it out. Freed, it cascaded down my back and teased a chill out along my spine. I was still facing away from Madu Tau, but I felt the djinn's lust blazing and I turned toward him again. His intake of breath at the sight of my naked body made me grin. It's nice to be appreciated.

I climbed up onto the vast bed, sliding through yards of white silk. It caressed me, soft as a breeze, and then I was climbing up Madu Tau, too. The huge djinn was a mountain of taut muscle and warm skin that felt even better than his silk sheets.

My breasts brushed against the searing heat of his cock, my nipples peaking swiftly with pleasure. Madu Tau sighed and I did the same as his desire kindled into hot gold sexual energy – my own special style of alchemy.

"You are beautiful," Madu Tau breathed.

I grabbed it in both hands and would have needed a third and fourth to cover the whole thing. My fingers couldn't close around his girth, but I slid them up and down his dick, exploring midnight skin that was just as smooth as his silk sheets. I licked my way along Madu Tau's massive length, tasting him. I don't know who groaned louder, him or me.

My mouth watered as I traced my tongue around the huge, dark head until it was shining wet. I wanted more, though the djinn's cock was so big that I struggled to fit the crown past my lips and then into my eager mouth. But I managed it and moaned as the thick weight pressed against my tongue.

Hard and fast, I pumped Madu Tau's dick with my hand to make up for how slow I had to take it with my lips, but that didn't mean I was done. Not by a long shot. I pushed my hair out of the way and forced Madu Tau's huge cock deeper. Even with only half of it in my mouth, the djinn was shoved to the back of my throat. I swallowed against him, squeezing and massaging, but the other half of his dick was still mournfully not stuffed into my slutty little mouth.

Madu Tau reached out to settle one big hand on my head, perhaps granting me wordless permission to stop, but I didn't need it. I grabbed his wrist. I wasn't giving up that easily. This was my first diplomatic mission for the College, and I was in the middle of sensitive negotiations. I worked my lips lower, devouring Madu Tau's great dick inch by inch. He was so hard and hot on my tongue that I wasn't just dizzy from holding my breath. I was nearing my limit. Saliva ran along Madu Tau's smooth ebony shaft and the bedroom was full of the muffled sounds of my hungry moans. But I absolutely refused to be beaten by this huge cock.

In a desperate gulp, I took the last inches. I swallowed them down and held my lips there, wrapped around the base of Madu Tau's dick. My head was lowered and my ass thrust into the air to angle myself for the feat. A hot shiver of well-earned pleasure slid through my body and I felt wetness streaming from my pussy.

I raised my eyes, looking up through the coppery lattice of my lashes at Madu Tau. I wanted him to see me with my mouth around him and his whole fucking cock down my throat. The djinn's eyebrows rose and his grin was wide. If there's a world record for deep-throating giant dicks, then I'm coming to claim my prize.

The rush of victory and the brilliant golden surge of desire from Madu Tau gave me a few more seconds of rubbing my tongue against his cock and swallowing at the massive length stuffed down my throat before I had to pull away. I sat up, throwing back my hair and gasping for air. Madu Tau's dick was dripping wet and even his heavy balls gleamed.

"Incredible," he said. "I would not have believed it possible."

"I'm a very determined girl."

I wiped the back of one hand across my chin, and crawled up along him like a hunting cat. The djinn was so tall and broad that it was hard to straddle his body. But if I could manage to suck every bit of that mighty cock, then I sure as hell wasn't going to stop now.

"Oh, yes," I said, still gasping for breath. "I'm definitely going to fuck you."

It might have been stating the obvious, but in bed, no one really seems to care. A running commentary of dirty talk is fun and sexy, no matter how obvious. I grabbed Madu Tau's slippery wet tower of a dick and held it between my stocking-clad legs. The huge cockhead nuzzled against me and I dripped with anticipation.

I swiveled my hips in small circles, rubbing the soft pink of my pussy over the djinn's dick. Madu Tau let out a rumbling groan as I dropped my ass a few inches and he forced me open. I writhed on the end of his cock and gasped for air.

"You're so big," I moaned. "I don't know if I can take all of you."

"I hope you are not discouraged."

"Fuck no. I want it," I told Madu Tau. "I want to take it all!"

I lifted my hips and worked them down again. The sounds of my efforts were wet and loud, interspersed with my breathy moans. I moved astride Madu Tau, just fucking myself on the tip of his beautiful, monstrous prick until I couldn't stand it anymore.

I dropped my full weight, impaling myself on the djinn's entire length. I stiffened and threw my head back with a sharp cry. I'd be lying if I said it didn't hurt, but the pleasure of being so utterly filled drowned out all other sensation.

"Oh, shit. It's so big," I said. "Is it inside me? Did I take it all?"

Madu Tau propped himself up on one elbow, making his huge shoulders bunch and tense beautifully, and looked down. I leaned back a little, as best I could with his massive dick buried inside me, to give him the best view of his cock overstuffing my pink slit.

"Yes. You have taken it all," the djinn said proudly.

"Fuck!"

Men aren't the only ones who enjoy hearing the delightfully obvious. At Madu Tau's pronouncement, I ground my hips urgently against his and came hard. Every nerve was pulled taut as violin strings through my body, vibrating with ecstasy. My pussy squeezed and milked Madu Tau desperately, though I was so full of cock that the contractions were just soft flutters along his length.

My orgasm lasted for several long, shuddering breaths before I could open my eyes and smile down at Madu Tau. His answering grin was brilliantly white in the midnight of his beard. I leaned forward with a groan and planted my hands in the center of Madu Tau's vast chest to give myself the leverage to begin rolling my hips against him. I kept his cock buried in my pussy, reluctant to release him after all the gloriously painstaking effort of taking the djinn's whole dick. So I worked him inside me, swirling and twisting and making him stir the pleasure deep within me.

"Fuck," I said again. "Fuck, fuck, fuck…"

My entire body trembled in a tightly coiled string of orgasms. I dug my nails into Madu Tau's mahogany skin. It might not have been very diplomatic to leave scratches on your host's chest, but I felt too good and he didn't seem to mind one bit.

"Fuck me," I said.

Madu Tau reached for me. His hands were so large that his fingers actually touched around my waist. The djinn made me feel like a doll as he effortlessly lifted me. He raised me almost up off his cock, but I whimpered and squeezed, strong enough now with my half-succubus lust-power to make Madu Tau grunt and keep his dick from popping free of my pussy. I writhed in his grasp until he lowered me again, filling and stretching me once more. Again and again, Madu Tau pumped his cock into me and forced out long gasping moans of pleasure.

But I wanted it faster, harder. I flexed my thighs and moved with Madu Tau, encouraging him to pick up the pace, but for some reason, men rarely fuck me as hard as I can take it. They always underestimate me. So I grabbed Madu Tau's wrists again and shoved them up toward the headboard.

There was a heavy moment of hesitation and the djinn's tree-trunk arms went taut. Seven feet of muscle or not, a human man could never have stopped me, but when Madu Tau tensed, I felt as though I were trying to move a mountain. It was like I had no power at all. I had no trouble believing that the djinni were the mightiest creatures beyond the Nether.

But Madu Tau relented and let me pin his big hands against the bed. I held him there and rode the great djinn, driving myself faster and harder than he had dared. I lifted my hips until only the huge crown of his cock spread me, then slammed my body down to take Madu Tau in quick, wet thrusts. At those speeds, I was lucky that his dick didn't slip out of my pussy and hammer right up my ass. But that wouldn't have stopped me for a second.

Madu Tau grinned up at me, impressed all over again. Sweat glistened like dew on his dark chest and must have stung along the scratches I had left there, but he didn't seem to notice. I quivered and streamed wetness that made Madu Tau's cock shine as though polished. If possible, his dick swelled even bigger inside me. The sexual energy between us was building swiftly to a crescendo and I rode him wildly, reaching for that dizzying peak.

And then we were there, sensation and desire crashing over the edge. I screamed out my pleasure as Madu Tau's cum gushed hot and thick into me, so deep that he seemed to be shooting it straight up into my stomach. In a couple hard spurts, I was full and the djinn's load streamed down my thighs.

"More," I said, gasping as I pulled myself off.

And there was more – a hot ribbon of bright, pale cum that splashed up against my hammering heart. I seized Madu Tau's slick cock and pumped out the rest of his huge load in great geysers all across my breasts until I was dripping from collarbone to navel in creamy white.

The djinn lay back in his vast bed, his chest heaving like bellows and sending warm wind swirling through the room. I shivered, but I wasn't cold. Far from it. Sticky cum ran down my chest, beading on my nipples, and hung there like pearl jewelry.

I grabbed my slippery tits, squeezed them together and made sure Madu Tau was watching as I bowed my head to lick up thick drops of his semen. His breath caught and then came out in one of those delicious thunder-growls. Madu Tau flexed his freed hands and reached for me again.

Negotiations were going long today.

Chapter FOUR

I finished toweling off my wet hair and considered the robe hanging from a hook beside the shower. It was far too small to fit Madu Tau, so I assumed it was for me. How considerate. I wrapped myself in white silk and emerged from the bathroom to find Madu Tau standing on the bedroom balcony, dressed in a flowing pair of cream-colored pants. His broad, muscular back was to me and his hands spread across the railing.

"I remember the demons." Madu Tau's voice was quiet, but the wind obediently carried his words to my ears. "They respected no borders, no agreements. They ruled this world and all others. None of us could stop them."

I stepped through the open door to stand beside the djinn. An insubstantial-looking barrier of waist-high glass enclosed the penthouse balcony, but I supposed even that was a mere technicality for a djinn of the air.

The view from Madu Tau's penthouse was dizzying, but lovely. We had been in bed for hours and now the sun was setting over Cairo, turning the city into a living mosaic of gold and amber spread out below us. A hot evening wind tugged insistently at my robe and hair.

"One by one, the demons plunged the empires of the world into darkness," said Madu Tau. "I remember the carnage of the great rage demons, hundreds of khets of fertile river land turned into barren sand by a single demon of greed. I remember Asmodai, the Lord of Lust, and the terrible beauty of his succubae. I rejoiced when the demons were banished once more to the Eternal Dark."

"And how about those regrets? How are they doing?" I asked.

Madu Tau turned to me with a scimitar grin. "I have bedded a succubus at long last, have I not?"

A half-succubus, but Madu Tau certainly didn't seem to think he had been cheated. I mirrored his smile, feeling pretty damned proud of myself.

"I have not been so well-pleasured in centuries," said the djinn. "For that, it is only right that I grant you a gift in return."

"Like three wishes?" I joked, then wondered if that was culturally insensitive.

Madu Tau laughed. It was a deep, rich sound. "You were good, my beauty, but not *that* good."

"Oh."

The djinn hooked a finger under my chin and looked down at me. "One wish seems fair, however."

"Oh," I repeated, then finally registered his words. "Wait, really? I... get a wish?"

Madu Tau nodded.

"Do I have to use my wish for permission to meet with Ptah?" I asked suspiciously.

The djinn laughed again and stood back, twisting a finger through his thick black beard mockingly. "Ha! You have watched too many movies, my lovely one. No. This wish is a gift, not a trick."

"Wow. Thank you, Madu Tau," I said, inclining my head. "What about Ptah? Can I talk to him?"

"You may, if he will agree to the meeting. We do not rule over him. That is not the way of the djinni. Ours are the earth and sea and skies. So long as you bring no violence on Ptah, you may do as you wish."

"So no beating a better deal out of the mummy?" I asked, frowning. I didn't like restrictions.

"Our lands have war enough already," said Madu Tau with a shake of his huge head. "Do not start another between Ptah and the students of Merlin."

"Alright," I agreed. "I'll figure out a peaceful way to do this."

"Resolve this matter with Ptah swiftly. The canopic mage pays us all due respects and is careful enough in extracting the quicksilver that he does not anger the earth djinni. But Ptah is overreaching, extending his power through unwise means."

"I thought he wasn't screwing with you guys. I mean, Ptah's not asking for *your* daughters."

"He would not dare. But we do not want Ptah's enemies and we will not play host to a war of the alchemist's making," Madu Tau rumbled ominously. "It is in Ptah's own best interest to reach some kind of compromise with his customers before he gives me cause to become involved in the matter."

"I'll manage somehow. I can be very persuasive."

The smile returned to Madu Tau's face and he gave me another short, booming laugh. "Indeed you are! I would never have believed that I could welcome a half-demon into my city, much less into my bed."

"You're not the only one who enjoyed that," I said, winking. "But I should get going."

Madu Tau looked down at me with deep, ageless black eyes. "It is late to go calling on Ptah tonight. Will you not remain until morning, here with me?"

It was a tempting invitation, but I don't do sleepovers. Hoping it wasn't a bad political move, I shook my head.

"Thanks," I said. "But I've booked a hotel room."

"Very well."

Madu Tau followed me inside as I went to collect some fresh clothes from my suitcase. When I finished dressing, the djinn held out a slick black business card that read *Khamsin Limousine*.

"For now, Ptah pays his tribute to us and respects the elements, so we do not interfere with him," said Madu Tau. "Which includes sending you to him by my own magic. But I can offer this small help. When you are ready, one of my people will take you to Ptah's home."

I buttoned up my new jacket, then zipped my suitcase shut and smiled at the djinn. "You've done a lot more for me than you had to. Thank you."

"The pleasure was mine."

Madu Tau walked me to the front door of his penthouse. With an afternoon of wild djinn sex under my belt, carrying all of my luggage was easy. I could have juggled an entire baggage carousel.

Madu Tau held the door open for me and a light breeze caressed my cheek.

"Remember your wish," he told me. "Simply speak my name and I shall answer. If your desire is within my power – which is considerable – then it will be yours. Do not forget."

"I won't," I promised.

Chapter
FIVE

I checked into my hotel just after dinnertime. The place was nice but felt a bit like a truck stop after the effortless opulence of Madu Tau's penthouse. I didn't bother unpacking my suitcase – I hoped not to be in Cairo that long. After ordering up some room service, I went to bed and got a few hours of sleep.

In the morning, I had eggs and basbousa – a cake soaked in rose and lemon syrup – for breakfast. Okay, I had two orders of the basbousa. And a half.

When I finished, I found the business card Madu Tau had given me and called Khamsin Limousine. They were expecting me, of course, and within ten minutes, I was climbing down into a sleek black town car.

I sat and the driver shut the door behind me. As we pulled out into the bustling Cairo streets, I watched through the tinted windows and brushed my fingers over my new suit. It was a lot like the one I had worn to talk with Madu Tau, but this time in a deep burgundy. I wanted to look professional for my meeting with Ptah. And sexy. And professionally sexy.

I had considered calling the hotel concierge earlier that morning to find me some more suitable clothes, but I wasn't quite sure what those would be. And even if Ptah wasn't familiar with the term *cultural appropriation*, he might still be offended when a caucasian girl showed up at his door in his homeland's traditional clothing. Madu Tau said to handle this without a fight and I didn't want to find out what happened if I failed to do so.

Besides, I doubted that I could really buy whatever it was that all the ladies were rocking three thousand years ago, when Ptah was born. Too bad, because I found some belly-dancing outfits online that would have looked great and completely historically inaccurate.

I ran my fingers along the leather upholstery of the town car and watched Cairo streak past, bright signs and pale minarets and dark glass towers that gleamed like obsidian in the morning sun. My clothes were probably going to end up being a moot point, and not for whatever naughty reason you're thinking. Ptah had plans – like lording his quicksilver monopoly over the College – and mine were to walk my dainty size sevens all over those plans. I suspected that *offended* was going to be just the beginning of what awaited me with Ptah.

How could I get the Egyptian alchemist to agree to anything? My usual persuasion tactics included sex and violence, and not always in that order. Violence was off the table and Ptah was a mummy, so I wasn't sure about sex. Vincent told me that Ptah had a harem of women coerced from his clients. But *harem* only sometimes meant a stable of sexual partners. It could also refer collectively to the female members of a nobleman's family.

Can you tell I spent breakfast hitting up Google? But even the internet couldn't give me any information on what a *real* mummy would be like. Sometimes the movies got it right, but more often, they got the supernatural shit dead wrong. And there's no easy way to know which one it's going to be.

The car pulled to a stop in front of what looked like some kind of government facility... or maybe an arboretum? It was a small compound surrounded by a tall wall, but I could see the green leaves of trees over the top and a few lush vines draping along the stone. They must have cost a fortune to maintain in this climate.

The Khamsin driver came around and opened the door for me.

"Thank you," I said as I climbed out.

He bowed in my direction and slid back behind the wheel, then drove away. I was alone on the narrow sidewalk, but I still had the Khamsin Limousine business card and supposed I could call them again when I needed another ride.

After waiting for a bicycle to pass me on the sidewalk, I made my way along the stone wall of the compound. It was broken every few yards by the blocky pillar of a support, each carved with a stylized eye that glittered in a way that had nothing to do with the bright sunlight. I guessed that they were the equivalent of the College's watchful gargoyles. Ptah was probably aware that a stranger had arrived.

I walked until I finally found a break in the imposing expanse of the encircling wall. Not just a gate, but a pair of solid bronze doors three times my height that reminded me of the ones leading into the College observatory. These were decorated in bas-relief with a woman crouching, her winged arms outstretched.

There was a slightly old-fashioned call box attached to the wall beside the door. I pressed the button at the bottom.

"Hello?" I said. "My name is Lily Quinn and I would like to speak to... to the master of this house."

I wasn't sure if Ptah was the mummy's original name or how discreet the supernatural forces were here in Egypt, but it didn't hurt to be careful. Especially when I could be flattering, too.

For a moment, there was no answer. I tried the call box again and was wondering if I could climb over the wall quickly enough to avoid being spotted when the doors finally swung open. I stepped back and gulped at the pair of stern-faced Egyptian men inside. They were dressed in neat black security uniforms that had to be absolute hell in this heat, and each one cradled a machine gun. The weapons weren't leveled at me, but they weren't exactly pointed away, either.

"Uh..." I said. "Hi."

I sketched a tiny bow. I wasn't sure if it was the local courtesy, but Madu Tau's men had done it and I figured that it couldn't hurt my chances. But either the two guards didn't speak English or were just assholes, because both remained silent as they gestured me through the open doors. I wondered if they were some kind of animated statues like those Sabra used back home.

One of the stoic men led me inside, the other following close behind. Their hands never strayed far from their guns. The big bronze doors clanged shut after us with a sound like a huge gong.

We were in a large room with no windows and more stone walls. There was a door at the far end, but a massive steel security desk devoid of any insignia or branding stood between me and the exit. Mutely, the guards waved me into a boxy metal detector, but I hadn't brought a gun or even handcuffs. There was no bounty on Ptah, and Madu Tau had made it pretty clear that things wouldn't go well for me if I shot the mummy in the face.

I walked through the metal detector and let one of the security guards run a wand over me. Next, I smirked through a pat-down that put tents in both men's black pants and reassured me that they were, in fact, flesh and blood. When they were satisfied that I carried nothing dangerous, the two silent guards escorted me to the room's far door. One of them unlocked it with a security badge and the other heaved it open. They gestured me through.

Expecting another sterile hallway, I was a little surprised to find myself walking out into the vibrant green garden that I had just glimpsed over the walls. There were trees and bushes and flowers everywhere. The foliage was so thick and lush that within three steps, I could no longer see the compound walls, much less the city beyond. Brightly colored birds trilled musically from branches and

I heard water trickling somewhere nearby. The warm air was heavy with the sweet scent of jasmine.

I looked behind me, expecting Ptah's men to prod me along at gunpoint, but the door was already swinging shut behind me with another resounding clang. Before I could wonder what the hell I was supposed to do, a pair of women emerged from the dense green of the garden.

The one standing on my right had smooth, dark brown skin and a perfectly round ass that just begged to be spanked. The other girl was shorter and paler, with angled eyes and black hair pulled back into a braid that reached all the way to her slender waist.

Both women were a few years younger than me, dressed in completely period-inappropriate transparent loincloths and nothing else. Every inch of their bodies was on display and I practically had to pick my jaw up off the ground. I don't think harem girls *ever* dressed like that, but I was starting to get the feeling that this place was someone's fantasy.

No need to guess who. But when you've lived for three thousand years and control the entire quicksilver trade, I supposed you feel entitled to write your own version of history.

"Hello, ladies," I said. "Where do I get an outfit like that?"

"You are here to see Master Ptah," said the shorter woman. Her accent sounded Chinese. "We are commanded to prepare you."

"Oh, hey. You speak English," I said with a sigh of relief.

But I didn't relax just yet. I wasn't sure if I liked the sound of being *prepared*.

I followed the two women through the lavish oasis of palms, jasmine and dozens of other plants I couldn't name. The floral perfume of the thick, humid air was sensually sweet, especially with the two shapely asses swaying in front of me with every step.

They led me into a long rectangular building, also built out of stone but much more finely polished and finished than the hidden compound walls. A huge rectangular pool of gently steaming water dominated the interior and was occupied by several more naked young women. They sat or stood waist-deep in the massive bath, scrubbing at their skin and speaking to one another in low voices.

At my entrance, the other women fell silent and looked up at me, but then they quickly returned to their own work. While I was busy staring around the bathhouse and wondering what the hell was going on, my two beautiful new escorts began tugging at my clothes. It didn't take long for me to connect the big bathtub and getting naked, but this was still a first for me. I had expected something more like sitting in a waiting room and flipping through outdated magazines.

"Okay, this is weird," I said as the two girls slipped me out of my jacket and went to work on my skirt. "Can you two at least tell me your names?"

"I am Jun Zhi," said the smaller girl. She gestured to her companion. "This is Akua Makena. Master Ptah wishes you cleansed and readied before he will see you."

I was pretty sure Jun was related to the Chinese geomancers. Akua seemed to be from further down south in Africa, but I sincerely doubted that she was any more willing an employee in Ptah's miniature Eden than Jun. Frowning, I looked around the bathhouse again. The other women were of every ethnicity, from all over the world, but none of them any older than I was and all gorgeous enough to make me tingle between the legs.

Ptah's harem of hostages.

Warm, wet air washed over me and I realized that Jun and Akua had finished stripping me while I was still assessing the bathhouse. They had shed their sheer loincloths, too, I noted. Jun pulled me gently down into the water while Akua lathered up a soft sponge with soap that smelled like vanilla and honey. I sighed. *So* much better than out-of-date magazines.

Jun and Akua gently scrubbed me all over, soapy sponges gliding smoothly along my back and breasts. As pissed as I was getting at Ptah, I had to admit that the bath felt amazing. Akua tugged on my shoulders until I leaned back so she could clean and comb out my long red hair. Jun worked down my legs with the soap and I let my toes trail lightly along her arm. Her eyes widened a little and I smiled at the hesitant thrum of lust from her.

When my body was clean – no amount of washing was *ever* going to cleanse my dirty, dirty mind – Akua and Jun helped me up out of the bath. They toweled me off gently but thoroughly, which was almost as much fun as the washing part had been. Then they led me to a richly cushioned table beside the pool. Akua gestured and I lay down.

"I get a massage, too?" I asked. "Nice."

"Our master is generous," said Jun.

I craned my neck to look up at the young Chinese woman. She schooled her expression well, but there was no way she meant a word of that. This wasn't generosity. This was a show of power. A really hot one.

Jun and Akua poured oil into their cupped palms from a small gold ewer. I smelled olives, fir needles and lanolin as four delicate, dexterous hands began rubbing the oil over my feet and calves. Crossing my arms under my chin, I watched the other women in the bath. There was a pretty apt adage about a gilded cage still being a cage, but I was having a hard time remembering exactly how it went as Akua and Jun worked their fingers up my legs, massaging and stroking.

The tingle inside me bloomed at their touch and I parted my legs so the two women could massage my thighs. There was only room for one pair of hands there, though, so Akua kneaded her strong fingers into the pale flesh of my ass while Jun rubbed tight circles closer and closer to my pussy.

"Mmm, yes," I sighed.

Jun's hand brushed against my wet slit and my sigh became a soft moan. Akua moved her finger down until they tangled with

Jun's, sliding together over me. I lifted my hips and spread my legs further open.

I sensed Jun's desire, though there was a tremor to it that made me wonder if she had ever been with another woman before. From Akua, though, I felt nothing. Her fingers were skilled as they swiftly found and caressed my clit, but I didn't get even a glimmer of lust from the midnight-skinned beauty.

Damn.

I reached back and grabbed Akua's wrist. I shook my head.

"Don't," I said.

She tugged her hand from my grasp and replaced it on my ass. I closed my fingers around her wrist once more and held on a little harder.

"Hey, I know you're not into this," I said. "I don't care what Ptah told you, but he can go fuck himself. Don't do anything you don't want to, okay?"

Akua didn't seem to speak a single word of English, but at the sound of the mummy's name, she stiffened and her eyes narrowed. I looked back and gave her my best reassuring smile, shaking my head again.

"I'm not going to complain to Ptah," I told her. "Promise."

Akua held my gaze for a moment, then nodded slowly. When I released her hand this time, she stepped away and crossed the bathhouse to retrieve her discarded loincloth. I sighed at the sight of Akua bending over. Too bad she wasn't interested, but I only take what's offered freely.

"Do you wish me to stop, as well?" Jun asked.

"Only if you want to," I told her. "I'm not going to rat either of you out to Ptah. But if there's anything *you* would like to do, I'm all yours."

I laid my head down again. Jun's lust warmed a few degrees and I basked in the feel of it, but I didn't want to push her. I closed my eyes. The anticipation made me run wet.

Tentatively, Jun's hand traced a faltering line up my thigh to the softness of my pussy. I groaned. There was another hesitation and then two slim fingers slipped into me. With Jun's decision and the penetration of my body came the smooth liquid flow of her sexual energy.

She probably had no idea she was giving it to me, but it felt just as good as her fingers when they began to move inside me. Jun worked in and out of my pussy in slow, shy strokes. Her touch was curious, exploring the tight, wet heat of me. I urged Jun on with moans and whimpers of pleasure, angling my hips to help guide her touch to where I wanted so badly to feel it. She pressed curiously against the back of my vagina and rubbed there, making me feel almost as though there were something in my ass, too. I gasped in pleasure and Jun twisted her fingers inside me to stroke against the front of my pussy.

"Yes," I panted. "Right... right there. More!"

Jun did as I asked, moving her fingers faster. Her other hand traced inquisitive circles down my spine, slicking my skin in massage oil. I drank in the sharp scents of olive, fir and dripping feminine juices. Not only mine, but Jun's as well.

My body jerked and I cried out. For a fraction of a second, Jun's hands froze. But when she realized that I was cumming, she redoubled her efforts, thrusting and rubbing and caressing me with exquisite fascination. I rolled my hips back against Jun and gushed wetness all down her wrist.

When I finally descended from my orgasm, Jun withdrew her fingers from me with a slick wet sound. She reached for a towel and I grabbed her wrist. Jun looked surprised, but I winked at her as I sucked each of her fingers clean.

I rolled onto my back, still holding Jun's hand, and then pulled it gently down once more. I fed the other girl's fingers into my hungry pussy again. Jun gave me a shy smile and resumed stroking me. But now I could properly watch her bending over me. Jun's small, perfect breasts bounced with every thrust of her fingers inside me and her ass was just within my reach.

I trailed a single finger over Jun's leg and the delicate crest of her hip. Slowly, though, in case she wanted me to stop. But Jun didn't say anything and her desire leapt up several degrees. I feathered my fingertips over her ass. It was smooth and firm. For a moment, I simply reveled in the feeling of it under my hand, but then I traced the silky curve down between Jun's legs.

Her pussy was blazing hot and dripping wet. I pushed one finger into Jun and felt her tighten at the intrusion. I smiled up at the other girl and swirled my finger inside her. Jun gasped sharply and her own touch faltered against me as I started working in and out of her. She was so tight that I only needed a single finger to return the sweet pleasure she was giving me.

"Oh, oh, oh," she moaned.

Jun bit her lip and tried to stifle the soft whimpers of pleasure. She leaned into me, brushing my belly with the hard little peaks of her nipples and began to quiver. Jun's body tightened on my finger as I pumped it inside her. Reaching down between my legs, I grabbed her wrist in my free hand and rocked my hips. I fucked myself there on her trembling digits as Jun lapsed into Mandarin and gasped something that I didn't understand. Her convulsing pussy milked my fingertip. The knot of my own ecstasy exploded in answer and I came, too, letting out a loud moan that echoed through the bathhouse.

Panting, I slid my finger from Jun and held up my hand to show her how shiny wet it was. While she stared with wide brown eyes, I opened my mouth and wrapped my lips around my finger, tasting her sweet pussy on my skin. Jun blushed brilliantly, but didn't look away. Slowly, she stuck her own fingers in her mouth and licked my juices from them.

I grinned at Jun. Good girl.

I sat up and drew a deep breath. "Alright, I think I'm ready to go meet Ptah."

Jun nodded and wobbled over to retrieve her flowing loincloth from where she had draped it across a chair. She tied it around her waist and smoothed out the fabric. I looked around for my clothes, but while I was busy with Jun, someone had collected my suit and taken it off who knew where. In fact, the bathhouse was nearly empty.

"Uh," I said.

Akua was still there. She slipped in beside me, as silent as a shadow, and held out a length of sheer cloth folded over her arm. Wordlessly, she helped me fasten the loincloth around my hips. I caught my reflection in a polished silver mirror and smirked at the sight. If Ptah had one ounce of red blood left in his body, then he was going to give me *everything* I wanted.

Chapter
SIX

*J*un and Akua escorted me from the bathhouse to a large sandstone building rising up from the middle of the lush green garden. Carved men with proud faces and unnaturally perfect posture loomed three times life-size all around the exterior. A pair of doors with scarab-shaped handles stood open at the front. Following Jun and Akua, I stepped through into a... well, I'm going to go with *throne room*.

It was vast and lined in stone pillars with tops cut into the shapes of blooming flowers. The long walls were inscribed with a dense network of hieroglyphics that reminded me at once of the books on Vincent Myrdon's desk. I couldn't read them, but somehow doubted that the writing was ornamental.

The throne room was as immense and splendid as Madu Tau's penthouse, but in an entirely different way. Here was a slice of ancient Egypt as I had imagined it since I was a child, grand and older than anything I had ever seen before, even at the College.

There were dozens of cases spaced along the walls, full of tattered papyrus scrolls and priceless Egyptian relics of bronze and bright blue stone. The largest display case was reserved for a row of beautiful canopic jars, each sitting in their own pool of light and adorned with the heads of animals in lapis and gold: falcon, lion, jackal and a serenely lovely woman.

But it wasn't just the size or priceless antiquities that made me call the place a throne room. On a raised dais sat an intricately carved wooden chair, accented in burnished copper and gold so that the whole thing shone richly.

And seated on his throne was the mummy. I jerked to a halt before the dais and stared. What sat on the throne was a tall human shape, every inch of his body wrapped in bandages that reflected a faintly mirrored sheen.

A real fucking mummy.

My scantily-clad escorts and I weren't the only women in the throne room. Five of them – all in the same filmy loincloths that I wore and little else – gathered around the mummy. Their hands moved over his body in long, delicate strokes that made my heart and stomach flutter inside me. It took me a second to realize what they were doing: unwinding the mummy.

"The immortal master, Ptah," Jun announced.

She and Akua bowed low. I followed their example, feeling far less professional than I had in my suit. But I didn't try to cover myself, either. If you've got it, flaunt it. And I've got it.

"We have brought you Lily Quinn, my master," Jun said. Her accented voice was even and careful. "She has been readied according to your command."

The mummy's hand rose from the arm of his carved throne and one of the girls began unwinding it. I held my breath and tried not to flinch in anticipation of the gnarled gray corpse claw beneath.

But the hand being uncovered as his bandages were peeled away wasn't withered at all. Ptah's skin was golden-brown and his fingers looked almost cast out of bronze. Literally... As the attendant women removed strips of cloth from the mummy's chest and stomach, the revealed skin had a burnished shine to it that I've seen on no other man, no matter how sweaty I got them.

"Welcome to my house," Ptah said in accented but perfect English. "Come and sit."

The mummy gestured to the bottom of his dais. A silk cushion had been set there for me. I knelt at Ptah's feet as the other women continued unwinding him. It was pretty clear that he didn't regard me as anything even close to an equal in these negotiations. For the moment, Ptah held all the cards, but I was confident that wouldn't last for long. We were playing strip poker, apparently, and that's my game.

Bandage by shimmering bandage – all soaked in quicksilver, I guessed – the women unwrapped their master like a present. It was a slow and laborious process, but now the anticipation was sweet. Beneath, Ptah was no wasted skeleton. In fact, despite millennia of existence, the man looked to be in the prime of his life, oddly ageless and exotically handsome.

Ptah was smaller than Madu Tau – so were some mountains – but still tall, with a toned and svelte build. His head was shaved utterly smooth and his eyes were edged in dark liner. Or I guess you would more properly call it *kohl*. Ptah's eyes weren't brown or even the deep bronze of his bare chest, but a brilliant, almost mirrored silver. I found myself staring into them.

"Did Jun and Akua attend to your needs?" Ptah asked, looking down his sharp, hawkish nose at me.

"Oh yes," I answered. I wasn't sure if the girls had been under orders to pleasure me, but I gave Ptah a sensual smile. "They took excellent care of me."

My two beautiful escorts were ascending the dais to help the others in their elaborate unwrapping ceremony and Jun blushed brilliantly. Ptah saw it and a slow, lazy smirk crossed his face. He stood so his harem could unwind the cloth from his waist.

Ptah wore nothing beneath the strips of silvery bandages and I barely kept myself from whistling. Kneeling on the soft cushion at his feet, the immortal alchemist's cock was right at eye level. It was long and his balls were shorn just as silky-smooth as the rest of his body, the skin oiled to the same bronze shine. Ptah's dick stirred, rising slowly. I have that effect on most men, though the mummy didn't seem the slightest bit embarrassed by his swelling erection.

"On behalf of the College, I thank you for your hospitality," I said.

This diplomacy stuff wasn't so hard. I only had to ask *What would Princess Leia do?* Now uncovered and quite naked, Ptah seated himself gracefully.

"You serve the College, then?" he asked.

"I work for them," I corrected tactfully. "The wizards hire me to do... a variety of things. Including speak with you."

"I didn't expect the western sorcerers to find any ambassador willing to enter Egypt and meet with me."

"And you're not exactly what I expected from a mummy, either," I said, looking Ptah up and down.

His black-lined silver eyes met mine. "My magic is not really so different from that of the Merlinic sect, but we both have our secrets."

"Like these?" I pointed to the piles of bandages.

Two of Ptah's scantily-clad harem gathered the silvery cloth up into reed baskets and carried them away. The others clustered around the mummy's throne and began rubbing sweet-smelling oils into his already gleaming skin. The scents weren't strong or cloying, but with my sex-powered senses, every breath was full of exotic fragrance.

"Immortality requires great dedication," Ptah said. He leaned back in his throne. "Every day and every night, the mummification ritual is performed. But it has brought me eternal life, which in turn has brought wisdom, power and wealth."

Akua rubbed her oil-slicked palms along Ptah's toned stomach to grab his upthrust cock. Her hands worked slowly up and down his length, massaging the oil into his skin. Ptah continued watching me with his eerily beautiful silver eyes, utterly unfazed by Akua's attentions. I guessed this was all part of the ritual, too, or at least part of the daily routine. I was beginning to understand why Ptah demanded a harem of lovely women. He was still an arrogant bastard, but I could see the point.

Another young woman – a stunning, round cherub of a girl with curly black hair down to her waist – slid her hands down over Ptah's ribs and then lower along the line of a scar just visible on his left side. It was a neat incision and looked very old, only barely a shade paler than Ptah's skin. Somehow, I doubted that was a battle scar – Ptah was more likely the type to hire or maybe build someone to fight for him. Was that mark from something else?

Ptah didn't show any other signs of injury across his flawless bronze skin. His body was so perfectly formed that I wondered just how much of it was magically crafted. Those bright silver eyes certainly weren't human anymore.

It was a little difficult to talk to Ptah with all of those other women crawling all over him. Jun stood at the mummy's right side, watching me as she rubbed one of Ptah's shoulders. Her small, lovely breasts trailed along his smooth skin. At Ptah's feet, Akua stroked his cock and I had a hard time not staring at her hands wrapped around that long, shining shaft.

Another girl poured more scented oil from a gem-studded golden bottle across Ptah's chest. It was a fairly ridiculous display of excess, which I supposed was part of the purpose. Just how rich was Ptah? How powerful? As long as he didn't piss off the djinni, the elementals had no reason to stomp him into dust. But Ptah and his quicksilver monopoly held the rest of the world by the balls. He understood the balance of power and played it well.

"The College wants to talk about the price of quicksilver," I said, then thought to add: "The Castle, too."

"The Castle and their American offspring's repeated refusal to adhere to my terms has offended me."

Ptah looked down at me, kneeling on the floor in nothing more than a nearly transparent loincloth. I felt his desire for me flowing through him, uncoiling like a gleaming, dangerous golden snake.

"The Merlinic magi were wise to send someone as beautiful as you," Ptah said. "Perhaps I could be persuaded to discuss the matter further."

Oh yeah. These were definitely my kind of negotiations. I stood slowly and swept long hair back from my shoulders to display my naked breasts in their full soft and bouncy glory. My nipples were rising swiftly to pink points. As far as I knew, Ptah couldn't sense my lust like I could his, so I would just have to show him.

I stepped up onto the dais and knelt at Ptah's feet. What would Princess Leia do? Well, probably not this.

I put my hand lightly on Akua's wrist, just like in the bathhouse. She glanced up at me and then to Ptah. The mummy nodded and Akua removed her hand. I took her place between Ptah's knees and a hot shiver ran down my spine as I reached out to wrap my fingers around his slick cock.

The other women exchanged brief looks, but did not flag in their attentions. Hands ran over Ptah, over his chest and shoulders, caressing every inch of his toned bronze body. The mummy remained reclined in his throne, reminding me of a leopard lounging in a tree.

I ran my fingers up and down Ptah's dick, feeling the utter smoothness of him. His cock stood out like a mast, hard and long and proud. The skin under my curious touch was silky and slippery, the flesh beneath hot and unyielding. A glistening drop of pale pre-cum shined on the flared tip. I bowed my head to swirl my tongue over it and my hair fell around me in a scarlet curtain. I pushed it back again. I wanted Ptah to watch me.

Which he was. Raptly. Those kohl-lined quicksilver eyes were fixed on me, but Ptah's heartbeat and breath didn't quicken at all. In fact, I didn't hear either one, not even with my sex-enhanced senses.

Ptah's smooth, lean chest didn't rise or fall and I felt no pulse throbbing through his cock. He should have been panting – I certainly was.

My gaze rose to the scar on his left side, the only mark marring the man's flawless cinnamon-colored skin. Vincent had called Ptah a mummy and I was beginning to think that was about more than just the nightly bandages. What else had the High Magus and Madu Tau called him...? Canopic undead. As in the canopic jars where ancient Egyptian priests put organs they had removed from the dead. Ptah didn't *have* lungs or a heart anymore.

But he sure as hell wasn't missing my favorite organ. My tongue slipped over his cock. I tasted sweet honey, nutty marula oil and Ptah's own hot musk. His dick blazed with searing desire. Good. I wanted Ptah to want me. That was kind of my whole bargaining position. You know, like reverse cowgirl. That's a bargaining position, right?

I reached up with my other hand to cup Ptah's balls. He looked down his long body at me, but didn't tense or shy away at all as I closed my fingers around the most sensitive part of him. They grew tighter and heavier at my touch and Ptah nodded.

"Hmm, yes," he said. "Continue."

Jun leaned in low, her shoulder brushing mine, and poured slippery oil over my hands so they made loud wet sounds as I stroked Ptah's cock. The mummy still wasn't huffing and puffing, but I could tell that he was just about to blow the fucking house down. Sweat gleamed across his already shining skin and his sharp jaw tightened. He let out a breath that hissed like a snake and his hips rose a fraction of an inch from his throne – the first involuntary reaction I'd seen from the mummy.

"Prepare yourself," said Ptah.

That was perhaps the most imperious warning I'd ever received from a man and it made my pussy ache to be filled. Ptah's cock swelled in my hand and his balls pulsed with heat. A huge fountain of brilliant ivory cum arced up from his dick and splashed all across Jun's flushed breasts. Her eyes went wide, but Jun remained utterly motionless as I jerked one rope of slick white after another out onto her tits.

Making sure that Ptah's ethereal eyes were still on me – and they were – I pulled Jun close. She was short enough that even on my knees, the other woman's dripping breasts were right in my face. Jun gasped in shock and pleasure when I sucked one of her nipples into my mouth and licked it clean of her master's load. I kissed the hard little peak and then made my way across Jun's chest, drinking every drop of Ptah's cum. By the time I was done lapping up the mess, Jun was panting and her legs trembled. I smacked my lips in satisfaction and looked back at Ptah.

"I'm listening," he said. "Let us negotiate."

"Yeah," I agreed. "Let's do that."

I rose and tugged at the ties of my loincloth. The flimsy garment fell into a puddle of gauzy cloth at my feet. I turned to point my pale ass right at Ptah. Most of the other girls had stepped back to stand with Akua, watching the "negotiations" in silence. Except for Jun, who sank down onto her knees nearby, waiting.

Moving sinuously, I slipped back until I felt Ptah's cock between my buttocks. It was still hard and slippery with fragrant oil. His dick nestled hot and heavy in the cleft of my ass.

"You control the largest source of quicksilver in the world," I said.

"The only source," Ptah corrected.

"Perhaps."

Vincent had mentioned one in Antarctica and maybe I could convince Ptah that the College had some other access to quicksilver. I raised my hips and rubbed my ass up along the underside of Ptah's cock until the slick head brushed against my pussy. Then I dropped again, stroking his length between my buttocks.

I wanted the mummy thinking about my ass, not me lying out of it. I moaned a little as Ptah's dick slid against me, teasing us both.

"No," the mummy told me firmly. "I control the entire quicksilver market and therefore the price. I believe you call it the law of supply and demand."

Ptah remained reclining in his throne, letting me service his dick with the soft cheeks of my ass. His silver eyes were sharp, not lulled at all into complacency by the pleasure I was giving him.

"The supply of quicksilver is low and demand is high across the world," Ptah said. "I can set whatever price I wish."

I didn't come halfway across the planet for an economics lecture. I also didn't fly out to Egypt to fuck Ptah, but I was damned well going to do exactly that. I would do whatever I needed to. And wanted to.

Watching Ptah's face over my shoulder, I brushed my ass one last time up along his length, then spread my legs to straddle him. Jun reached between my thighs to hold her master steady. I smiled at her and sat slowly down into Ptah's lap. His dick parted and then filled me.

"Oh," I sighed. "Yes...!"

I sank myself onto Ptah's cock, taking him deep in a single long stroke until I felt Jun's hand against my labia. She traced my spread slit with her fingertips, staring at where her master pierced me.

Ptah reached out and opened my legs even further across him until I hooked my knees over the gilded arms of his throne. Good thing I'm flexible. I put my hands on his and slid them along my body to my breasts. Ptah seized my soft tits and pulled me back against his hard chest. He held me there and began working his cock up into my pussy while his harem looked on.

Ptah wasn't gentle or careful with me, which kind of pissed me off. I know that I've complained about being treated gently, but it wasn't me that I was concerned about. I could take pretty much anything the mummy had to dish out, but if this was any indication of how he treated Jun and the other women, then he was nearly as cruel as he was arrogant.

But I had to admit that it inflamed me, too. Madu Tau had tried to take it easy on me, but Ptah had no such compunctions. He hammered his cock up into my spread pussy, spearing deeper and faster, stoking the furious fire inside me rather than quelling it.

"If your terms are so steep that no one will buy from you," I said in between sharp moans, "then demand drops to nothing. You're undermining your own position."

Ptah held me against him and shoved his cock deep into me. I felt his lips brush my ear as he spoke softly into it.

"The Castle and the College will exhaust their quicksilver stores within a year. Do you truly believe that *my* patience will break before theirs?"

My head fell back onto Ptah's shoulder and my hair spilled across our sweat-slicked bodies. Jun reached between my legs and closed a small hand around Ptah's balls, massaging them with practiced grace. With her other hand, Jun flicked one fingertip over my clitoris and made me gasp sharply. She stroked me again, more gently in counterpoint to Ptah's deep, possessive fucking.

"You're making enemies for yourself," I told him in a breathless moan. "A lot more of them than you're going to want in the end. Wouldn't you rather make them allies by being a reasonable trade partner?"

Ptah pinched my nipples until my back arched. Sparkling droplets of my juices flew through the air.

"No force left in this world would dare fight me over the quicksilver or its price," he said in a steady voice, utterly unperturbed by the motions of his dick driving up into me. "Not here in the domain of the djinni."

I squeezed the immortal alchemist's cock inside me, coaxing low grunts from him with each thrust into my tight, wet hole. I still couldn't hear Ptah gasping or feel his heart pounding in his chest, but I felt his dick filling me and Jun's nimble fingers between my legs. I wasn't sure which of them made me cum first, but once it began, neither one would let me stop.

Ptah and Jun traded my pleasure back and forth until his long cock and her fingers were dripping in my wetness. The mummy's fingers pinched my hard pink nipples while Jun did the same to my clit below. I writhed in Ptah's lap, filling the throne room with all of the cries and gasps that he refused to voice.

There was no way he could hold out much longer, though. I rolled my hips atop Ptah, milking his engorged length with my tightness. With my back pressed against him, I couldn't see the mummy's face, but I felt the sweat running down his skin. His desire swelled huge and golden as a rising sun inside me.

"Even the djinni won't protect you forever, Ptah," I panted. "They'll destroy you themselves if you make enough trouble."

"I know Egypt and its powers far better than any American."

"I think that in the end, you'll give us the quicksilver at a fair price," I said. "So come on! Give it to me!"

Ptah slammed his cock home into my pussy and I felt it throb. I slipped my legs off the arms of the throne and pulled myself from his dick. But when I tried to stand and turn toward Ptah, I was surprised to feel him shoving me down to my knees on the dais. Jun knelt there in front of me with an expression on her pretty face that I didn't quite have the chance to read.

I could have been on my feet in an instant, regardless of what Ptah wanted, but then I felt him sweeping my hair away over one shoulder. He uttered a short command in Mandarin to Jun. Her jaw clenched unhappily, but Jun grabbed his wet cock and stroked it swiftly. Ribbons of cum arced out from Ptah's cock and splashed hot across my back. Jun squeezed his balls with the certainty of experience and more thick white semen splattered onto my skin. It oozed in creamy lines down my spine and then ass, making me shudder with pleasure.

Now I stood and turned to face Ptah. That hadn't been the finish I was expecting. Hands ran up my legs, raising goosebumps and then I felt Jun's mouth running warm and wet over the curve of my ass. Her lips traced the dripping lines of Ptah's cum and her tongue swirled through it, lapping at her master's spill.

I moaned and looked down at the mummy, who still remained seated in his throne. A pair of the girls who had waited so patiently while I fucked Ptah came forward now with soft cotton towels and began wiping him clean.

"So what do you say?" I asked.

Ptah's silver-eyed gaze didn't waver. "Tell your masters that my price remains unchanged. And that I have a new demand – you."

"...What?"

"You will stay with me, Lily, for my pleasure and as assurance against the Castle and College's disrespect."

Well, I had succeeded in making myself desirable, but this was *not* the result I was going for. I scowled at Ptah and my eyes narrowed. At my sides, my hands balled into furious fists, but then I felt Jun's fingers light on my wrist. I looked down at her. Jun didn't shake her head, but there was a warning in her eyes. I doubted she knew I was strong enough to rip Ptah's shiny head off his body, but she was right. Even if this was a fight I could win, it wasn't one I could afford to start.

"You may consult with your masters in America, of course." Ptah lounged back in his throne, smiling with supreme confidence. "And you are welcome to remain here while I reach an agreement with the College."

"I'm not big on cuddling afterward," I said coldly. "I'm going back to my hotel room."

Ptah shrugged sinuously. "If you wish. I am in no hurry. Soon, you will belong to me."

Chapter
SEVEN

*J*un Zhi led me back through the colorful and fragrant garden to the bathhouse. I slid down into the water with a splash while one of the other women laid out the maroon suit I had arrived in. Apparently, it had been steam-cleaned while I was busy with Ptah.

Jun remained there with me, even joining me in the bath and spiking the hot water with the sweeter heat of her desire for me. Normally, I would have been all over Jun, but I was too pissed off to have fun. Ptah wanted me as a part of his price for the quicksilver he controlled. Just like Akua and Jun and all the other women here, demanded and imprisoned like slaves. There was never a time when that was acceptable – I didn't care *how* old Ptah was.

Jun advanced on me with a soapy sponge. I tried to wave her off, but I couldn't really scrub my own back. So I leaned over the edge of the bathing pool and had to admit that the warm lather felt good. I crossed my arms and rested my cheek against them.

Damn it, why did men keep trying to somehow own me? Finn had done it just a month ago, attempting to contain me in his circle of binding. Until I broke out, beat and then hauled his demon-summoning ass to the College to face the music.

I desperately wanted to do the same to Ptah. He was strong, but certainly not stronger than me. I had enough lust from Madu Tau, Jun and even the mummy himself to tear down the bathhouse. I wouldn't even break a sweat beating the alchemical shit out of Ptah.

But that wouldn't solve anything. Madu Tau had made it pretty damned clear that the price for starting a fight with Ptah was too high for me or the College to pay. This diplomacy stuff was right back to being a pain in the ass.

And I wasn't certain I could actually kill Ptah. Break all of his bones, sure, but he was undead and I didn't think a wooden stake would do the trick like it did on vampires.

"The bastard doesn't even have a heart anymore," I muttered. I huffed out a long breath that swirled the steamy air of the bathhouse.

The strokes of Jun's sponge across my back slowed.

"You're speaking of Ptah?" she asked.

"Yeah. Sorry. I didn't mean to grump out loud."

She scooped up water and rinsed the soap from my skin. "Not in his chest. But Ptah is still a man. Even he requires a heart."

I looked over my shoulder. "Are you saying that smug, sexy bastard didn't just chuck his heart in the nearest trash bin?"

Jun nodded.

"That's... pretty weird," I said. "How do you know?"

"We have studied immortality for many centuries."

For a moment, I wasn't sure who "we" were, but then I realized that Jun meant the Chinese geomancers. I had assumed that she was... I don't know, just one of their relatives. But most magic is a closely guarded secret and often passed down through family lines. Jun was a geomancer. I started to turn toward her, but succeeded only in slipping and dunking myself into the bath.

I came up a moment later, gasping for air and feeling like a jackass. Jun wasn't smiling at my clumsiness, though. The young geomancer gave me that same look she had back in Ptah's throne room.

I finally recognized it: sympathy. Had Jun come here just like me, perhaps as a member of the Chinese delegation to negotiate for their people's needs, only for Ptah to demand her as part of his ridiculous price?

By the time I could breathe once more, Jun had climbed out of the bath and was redressing in a fresh loincloth. She gestured to me and then to my suit.

"Ptah *is* patient," said Jun. "But you should act quickly. He is offended easily and then his price will rise."

I stepped out of the bath. "Spoken from experience?"

Jun nodded again.

"I'd better get moving then," I said.

I pulled on my underwear just as another pair of Ptah's harem arrived. The two newcomers helped me with my suit and hair without saying a word. I don't know if they didn't speak English or had simply been instructed not to talk to me. When they were done and waved me toward the bathhouse door, I paused to give Jun a short kiss. She blushed and smiled a little. I wanted to say something reassuring, but I had no idea what to do next.

The other women escorted me swiftly and silently back to the security vestibule, where the two black-uniformed guards searched me again. Were they really afraid I had stolen something from their master? But when their pat-down turned up nothing interesting, Ptah's security goons pulled open the big bronze front doors.

I made my way out onto the Cairo streets once more. It was like stepping from one century into another and I suddenly remembered that I had a cell phone. I could call the College right now to tell them about Ptah's new demand. Or summon one of Madu Tau's drivers to take me back to my hotel. But I left my phone in my pocket. I needed time to think, so I started walking.

Ptah said that the College quicksilver stores would only hold out for a year and I had the unsettling feeling that was accurate. Eventually, Vincent would have to pay up and give the mummy what he wanted. Minus me, probably. Even if I could convince myself to surrender to Ptah for the sake of the College and Castle, there was no way that was going to last. Being a sex slave might be fun for a day or two, but then I was going to be kicking down the doors. The only reason Jun, Akua and the others were still behind those walls was because they weren't half demon like me.

No. That wasn't why, I realized. Jun was a geomancer and I guessed that most of Ptah's harem were members of one magical community or another. They were all smart, capable women who could have figured out some kind of escape plan months ago. But their homelands needed the quicksilver that Ptah sold. Escaping his house would shatter those agreements, so they remained.

I didn't think that I could be so selfless and I was furious that they had to be. Negotiations with Ptah were far from over... I just needed a new angle.

From beside me on the sidewalk, a woman in a pretty blue hijab snapped at me in Arabic. Her husband – or maybe brother, I wasn't sure – didn't share her opinion of my short skirt. A few other people muttered around me, but not many. I guess they were used to foreigners in Cairo.

I had made it a couple of blocks from Ptah's house and found myself in a lovingly preserved section of the immortal city. The busy street was cobbled but well-maintained in a centuries-old style, the buildings all finished in carved brown and yellow stone. Everything was marked out and labeled in English and French as well as Arabic. The sidewalks were full of tourists pointing and taking photos on their cell phones.

The whole world is fascinated by Egypt. There's something about the country and its ancient civilization that captivates the imagination. And I was surrounded by shops and galleries all catering to that sense of the exotic. Bookstores and libraries held thousands of texts and photos of Egyptian beauty. Huge museums showcased thousands of years of history and cultural pride.

I couldn't blame Madu Tau for wanting to protect all of this.

The air djinn still owed me a wish. Madu Tau told me to just speak his name and he would grant a single request. I actually considered it for a moment before shaking my head. Screw that. I wasn't wasting my wish on Ptah.

I wasn't even sure what to wish for, anyway. For Ptah to die or something? Given how emphatically Madu Tau had cautioned me against beating the shit out of the mummy, I doubted that he would do my dirty work for me.

And besides, as angry as I was with Ptah, I didn't really want him dead. Just... more reasonable. The man was clearly intelligent and resourceful, but I needed to teach Ptah some of the humility that he subjected his customers to.

When the flow of pedestrians stopped, waiting for the light to turn in our favor, I pulled out my phone. Not to call anyone, but just to check my GPS. The hotel I had booked myself was one of the nicest in Cairo – on the College's tab, thank you very much – and was only about ten blocks away.

The light over the crosswalk switched and I followed a throng of locals and tourists across the street. Here, there was no sign of the revolution and war that Madu Tau spoke of. Only well-maintained culture and history. I guessed that this part of the city was well protected. It all certainly looked very important.

About half of the mid-morning crowd was splitting off at the opposite street corner and streaming up the steps of a huge building finished in red and white: the National Gallery of Egyptian History. I'd never been a particularly good student, but even I recognized that museum. The National Gallery housed the world's largest collection of famous treasures dug out of the Egyptian sand. The government had to fight hard to get some of those prizes back from old explorers and grave robbers. Every time they succeeded in returning a priceless piece of heritage back to Egypt, it made international news.

Nothing like that recently, though. Today, the sun-bleached banners hanging over the entrance advertised one of the longest-running exhibits of the National Gallery, a collection of beautifully preserved Old Kingdom relics. But one of the rippling banners made me lurch to a stop in front of the museum. It displayed the enlarged photograph of a set of canopic jars – four of them, polished and intact. They were adorned with the blue and gold heads of a jackal, a lion, a falcon, and a stern-faced woman.

Canopic jars, the containers that held the organs removed from a mummy before burial. They looked exactly like the ones in Ptah's throne room. Jun said that he still had a heart – it just wasn't in his chest. But I guessed that Ptah would want to keep his vital organs close and safe...

Several security guards arrayed across the front of the National Gallery watched me. I wasn't doing anything threatening, but they seemed to think that I was acting strangely enough for one of them to say something into a radio clipped to his shoulder. I smiled at the guard and waved. Before anyone could get too concerned, I turned away from the museum and walked briskly in the direction of my hotel.

I grinned to myself. Jun said that Ptah still required his heart, as well as the rest of the organs in the canopic jars on display in his throne room. Well, it wasn't exactly what people usually meant by giving me their heart... But if I could get my hands on Ptah's canopic jars, then maybe I would finally have the leverage I needed to negotiate with the mummy.

Chapter
EIGHT

I had the hotel concierge pick up some black cargo pants and a long-sleeved shirt, along with a pair of boots in my size and a dark scarf to cover my hair. I had plenty of those kinds of clothes back home, but hadn't thought to pack any of them for a diplomatic mission. As it turned out, though, diplomacy required more of my usual skill set than I expected.

Waiting until the sun went down left me time to call Vincent Myrdon and double-check my information. The time zone difference made the High Magus a little cranky, or maybe it was just talking to me that did it.

"A mummy still requires their organs, even after removal," he verified. "It's a slightly different collection than those excised by historical preparation of the dead, though there is some overlap. If you can procure the canopic jars – *without* harming them or provoking a confrontation with Ptah – then it would strengthen our bargaining position."

"Great. I'll call you again tomorrow," I said and then hung up.

By that evening, my sexual energy had begun to fade, but Ptah and Jun had given me enough that I still felt more than ready to break open a safe. Unless there was a werewolf between me and Ptah's canopic jars, I would be fine.

I also asked the concierge to rent me a car. Something small and unobtrusive that would blend in better than anything Khamsin Limousine would send for me. An hour after sunset, the little gray sedan was parked beside the curb a few blocks away from Ptah's house. I sat behind the wheel, playing Candy Crush on my cell phone and waiting.

Just before eight o'clock, a Cairo police car raced past, lights flashing and siren blaring, followed quickly by a yellow-striped red fire truck. It had only been five minutes since setting that trash fire down the street and the local response times were everything a homeowner – or a half-demon thief – could ask for.

With the nearest cops distracted, I slipped out of my rental car and made my way along the sidewalk. I walked swiftly, but not so fast that the thinning evening crowd would notice. When I reached the walls of Ptah's compound, I kept my head lowered. I circled until I found a place where lush green vines had grown up from the garden inside and draped over the stone, covering the carved Eyes of Horus. I still wasn't certain those were surveillance spells, but I didn't want to risk it.

When there was a break in the pedestrian traffic, I used my sex-fueled strength to leap up, hook my fingers over the edge and then scramble onto the wall. Perched on the top, I squinted down into Ptah's expansive garden. It was dark beneath the interlaced tree branches, but my senses were honed to razor sharpness. Confident that I wouldn't land on a patrolling security guard, I jumped down onto the other side of the wall.

I landed in a patch of sweet-smelling white flowers and green leaves. I was back in the mummy's territory, but this time on my own terms. There was the bathhouse off to my right, just barely visible through the thick jungle of Ptah's garden. I began picking my way between the plants in that direction.

The warm breeze carried the smells of flowers, stone and the vital fragrance of plants cooling after a day in the hot sun. I detected gunpowder and dog fur, too, almost buried by the more pleasant garden scents. The smells were neither close nor recent, but they meant that Ptah's Uzi-toting guards *did* patrol the grounds. If I wanted to avoid a fight with them, I had better keep moving.

I crept to the bathhouse and followed the wall until I found the path Jun had used to take me to the throne room. Main thoroughfares are usually a central part of any patrol pattern, though, so I jogged in a low crouch between the trees and neatly trimmed hedges. I didn't see any guards patrolling the path, but neither was it empty.

A lithe young woman carried a basket full of rolled bandages in her arms. Ptah had one hell of a beauty routine. The cloth gleamed like moonlight, though the stars and moon were hidden overhead. I recognized the girl as one of those from the throne room and she remained dressed much the same, nearly naked but for the flowing white and gold loincloth around her hips. She muttered unhappily to herself in Tamil, but then fell silent as she neared the great silhouette of Ptah's house.

I followed her at a distance, just another shadow flickering through the garden. The young woman carried her basket not to the arched front doors – the ones that led into Ptah's throne room – but around the side to another entrance. These doors were only slightly less grand and flanked by another pair of Ptah's black-uniformed guards. The two men looked the approaching girl up and down as she came closer. She offered a stiff bow and they pulled the doors open for her, then shut them once more after she stepped through.

The two men's attention returned to the green-tinged darkness of the garden and I crouched down behind a sycamore tree. Now what? I had more than enough strength and power left to beat the shit out of the guards, but I was pretty sure that fell under the same heading as starting a fight with Ptah himself. I could do it, but then the djinni were going to stick me in a lamp. And if we were lucky, the College would only have to spend the next fifty years apologizing for my fuck-up.

I had to get in there without hurting anyone. Peeking out from behind my tree, I didn't see any windows along the carved sandstone edifice and couldn't remember any from my audience with Ptah. I could probably break down the front doors, but not without making a lot of noise that would attract the guards' attention. That would lead to a fight, then me in a lamp and Ptah laughing while he continued to fuck over the world and hide behind the might of the djinni.

There was no way I was going to let that happen. So I grabbed the hem of my shirt and pulled it off over my head, then did the same with my pants, boots and underwear. I rolled all of my clothes into a ball and stuffed them up between the spreading branches of the sycamore tree I was hiding behind. Warm wind tugged at my hair and I shook it out, combing my fingers through it until it fell loose down my bare back.

Naked and with my head held high, I strode out onto the path, toward the door. The two guards caught sight of me and tightened grips on their guns. I walked right up to them and bowed, just like the girl with the bandages had done. The men looked at me and then at each other.

"I've been summoned by the master," I said in as demure a voice as I could manage. "He commands my... service before his windings are applied tonight."

Ptah's guards regarded me silently, though I would've had to be comatose not to feel the hot sparks of their desire for me. But I supposed that Ptah's harem was for his enjoyment alone – his men opened the doors for me without so much as a whistle.

I stepped through and the doors thumped shut behind me. A wide hallway spread out to either side, lined in burning oil lamps that glittered with golden light and expensive gemstones. I guessed that Ptah knew about electricity, but if the College wizards were archaic, then the mummy was downright antiquated.

The hall led off in two directions. The smooth tile floor was cool beneath my bare feet, but it was the sounds and smells that raised goosebumps along my skin. From the left-hand hallway, I heard the soft, seductive moans of female voices, the rustle of cloth and the musical sounds of flesh against flesh. I smelled sweet perfumes and sex. Ptah and his harem. There was a part of me – and not a small one – that desperately wanted to go join the party.

But I had a job to do, so I made my way quietly down the right fork of the hall in the direction of Ptah's throne room. I moved cautiously, watchful for more guards or maybe magical defenses like the wards that the College employed, but I saw nothing. Did Ptah's arrogance and confidence know any limits?

Well, it was about to.

I crept through the hall, past several carved doorways until I reached an open arch. The throne room. The lights inside had been extinguished for the night, but I didn't need them. The trickle of amber lamplight from the hallway was more than enough for my awesome sex-o-vision.

With a final check around for magical or other precautions, I stepped into Ptah's throne room. It was just as I had left it that morning, a slice of the mummy's strange and beautiful fantasy version of ancient Egypt. Treasures and statues of the old world surrounded me, like standing in a museum. And in their glass case sat Ptah's canopic jars. Four of them, inscribed in hieroglyphics and topped with gold and polished lapis lazuli faces that shone in the dim lamplight.

I inspected the case carefully. The door was on the back and closed up with a small steel lock. I actually broke a bit of a sweat crushing the metal in my hand. Maybe I should have topped off with the concierge when he delivered my clothes. But the shank of the lock snapped free. It almost fell to the floor, but I caught the bit of steel before it could clang on the tiles. I doubted anyone would hear it, but I didn't feel like taking chances.

I didn't see any other security, so I eased open the case's door and studied the canopic jars inside. Each one was about ten inches tall and as big around as a coffee cup. Getting all four out without pockets or a box was going to be problematic. Maybe all I needed was Ptah's heart. If I had that, surely the mummy would become more reasonable...

I picked up the jar on the right end, the one with the carved woman's head and a prominent feather hieroglyphic. I guessed that the pretty lady was Ma'at, who weighed the souls of the dead against her feather and seemed like a logical protector for Ptah's heart. Thanks again, Google.

The jar was heavier than I expected, though, and when I tipped it a little, I heard a dry hissing sound from inside. Frowning, I grabbed the top. Was my research wrong? Ptah's collection of jars was certainly unique. I hadn't found any others quite like them anywhere online. Or maybe Ptah's ancient viscera were little more than dust by now...

I had to know. I pulled open the inlaid golden lid and looked inside.

"Shit," I hissed.

Sand. The canopic jar was full of sand. Not dust – this was gritty, red-brown sand right out of the desert. I stuck my hand into the sand and felt around, but there was nothing else inside the jar. I pulled the other three jars down from the case, pried them open and stared.

Nothing but sand.

I replaced the canopic jars in their case and closed it. Fakes. They were all fakes. So where were the real ones?

I stood in the darkness, thinking. I was missing something important. But what? I stared at the jars for a long time.

Finally, I made my way quietly out of Ptah's throne room again and out across the garden. As soon as I retrieved my clothes and made it back over the compound walls, I pulled my phone out of my pocket and called Vincent Myrdon. It was time to cut a deal.

Chapter
NINE

I returned to Ptah's little palace the next afternoon. A new set of security guards patted me down and searched me again, but I knew it was just for show. The mummy wasn't worried about anything I could do to him. Security handed me off to Ptah's harem once more, who bathed and clothed me in another wispy loincloth.

No fingerbanging this time, though. There was business to take care of. A couple of the women took my suitcase, too, which I had brought from the hotel. I didn't argue. It wasn't like I planned on going back there.

Ptah awaited me in his throne room, already unwrapped from a night swaddled in magical quicksilver and dressed like the pharaoh he was setting himself up to become. He remained bare-chested, gleaming bronze skin and sleek muscle on display, but wore a skirt of fine white linen belted with beaten gold. Ptah even held a crook and flail to complete the image. And as his brilliant silver eyes fixed on me, I had to admit that it *was* striking.

I approached Ptah's throne and bowed, then turned to the nearly-naked girls kneeling before him. Jun was prostrated at the end of the line. She looked up at me with an inquisitive expression.

"I'm pleased that you've come back to me so quickly," Ptah said. He twisted the flail between his fingers and there was already an impressive bulge growing under his linen kilt. "The College understands what must be done."

"Yes," I agreed. "And they're doing it now."

I stepped onto the dais and stood before Ptah. The mummy ran the curve of his crook down along my shoulder and over my bare breasts. The cold, heavy metal made me shiver. It moved along my belly to the waist of my silky loincloth.

"You may be the finest prize in my entire collection," Ptah said.

His eyes followed the path of the gold-banded crook down my body. I slid my hand up his thigh and firm muscles bunched under my touch. Ptah's cock was hard, waiting for me. I gripped it tightly beneath the skirt of linen and gave a single long stroke.

"Mmm, yes," Ptah said. "You're eager to resume what we began yesterday."

I nodded and waved my free hand back in the direction of the other women.

"You can go get dressed," I told them. "Master Ptah is all done with you."

The mummy raised one slick black brow at me. "You're bold if you think that you can satisfy me alone."

I grinned at him.

"I am going to enjoy you a great deal," Ptah said with a languid smile.

Jun and the other two women looked at me and then at Ptah, but when he didn't countermand my request, they rose and filed out of the throne room. Jun glanced over her shoulder at me, but I winked at her and the young geomancer left.

I turned to Ptah again and climbed into his lap. Tossing my hair back, I trailed my fingers up along his arm and then cupped his cheek, leaning in for a long, deep kiss. The alchemist tasted like cinnamon and coriander. He didn't need to breathe and pressed his lips possessively to mine until I had to break away with a loud gasp for air.

"You will find me a pleasant master," Ptah said. He ran the flail down along my spine to my ass. "*If* you can learn obedience."

"Obedience?" I asked. "Me? You might have noticed that I'm a bit of a handful."

"Indeed."

I reached down to tug aside the white linen until I could touch Ptah's cock again. I stroked his already hard length slowly and felt it twitch eagerly in my hand. The mummy didn't hurry me, though. He was eternally patient and confident. I rocked my hips to rub my silk-covered pussy over his dick until my loincloth grew damp.

"You should have joined me last night," Ptah said. "Instead of wasting your time trying to rob me."

I swept the soft fabric of my loincloth back out of the way. "You knew I was here?"

"I suspected the College would become desperate, but knew that they dared not risk open battle against me. So it was apparent what you would try to do."

"Well, you do drive a hard bargain."

With the word *hard*, I sank myself down onto Ptah's long cock. There's an art to this, you know. He chuckled, making his dick throb inside me. A soft sound of pleasure escaped my lips.

"I allowed you to leave last night," Ptah said. "But now you belong to me and I will expect better behavior."

Did he now? I leaned forward and shoved my tits into Ptah's face. He smiled indulgently and sucked one ripe pink nipple into his mouth, running his tongue in tight circles over it. I squirmed there in his lap, grinding myself desperately on his cock. The man had three thousand years of experience at sex and it showed. Ptah bit sharply at the soft flesh of my breast. Ecstasy lit up between my legs and across my breasts, meeting in the middle and rushing through my body. I let out a long, loud moan.

"Was I a bad girl, then?" I gasped through the haze of climax.

"Yes," said Ptah.

"Then either drop those old relics or show me what they're good for!"

The mummy's eyes narrowed. He was still smiling, but he raised the flail. It was a lovely piece of work, with a short handle banded in gold and obsidian, topped by strips of leather beaded with polished wood. Ptah cracked it down across my flank and left stinging red lines that wrapped around my hip and buttock. I gasped at the sudden hot flare of pain and pleasure.

"Come on," I moaned. "Is that all you've got?"

Ptah smacked the flail over my skin with just the right amount of force to tease my nerves into ecstasy. I lifted my smarting ass and rammed it down again, bouncing on Ptah's hot, hard cock. My toes curled and I only managed not to fall out of his lap because I knew what I was doing, too. I might not have been as old as the mummy, but I was pretty damned sure that I had at least a thousand years *worth* of sexual experience...

I leaned against Ptah and pressed my lips to his ear. "I tried to steal your heart and hold it hostage. Show me how bad I was."

He cracked the flail across my ass again. The sensation was exquisite and I threw my head back to cry out another orgasm. I rode Ptah hard as he spanked me, sending pleasure and pain searing through my whole body.

"Ah, fuck!" I screamed. "Yes!"

Ptah's desire burned hot and bright, his cock turning to blazing steel inside me. But I wrenched myself up and off of him.

"Not yet," I gasped. "I'm not done with you."

I fell to my hands and knees before the throne and raised my ass into the air. Ptah rose, setting both the crook and flail aside. He unbelted his linen skirt and let it drop to the floor. Even now, hours after his morning preparations, Ptah's skin remained gleaming and smooth. His long dick dripped with my wetness.

Ptah reached down and grabbed my loincloth. He didn't bother untying it; the mummy just ripped it off my body and stood over me like a conqueror.

"Yes," I moaned. "Fuck my naughty little ass...!"

The man who considered himself my master knelt behind me and rammed his cock all the way up my ass in a single brutal thrust. But I'm a professional and my anus yielded easily before the hard intrusion with a soft, wet pop.

Ptah seized my waist and held me in place as he forced his cock into my ass with sharp, swift strokes. I panted and cried out with every blow, but his hips rolled fluidly, his long dick churning in and out of me. Ptah stretched and filled my ass relentlessly, making me tense reflexively against him, but my tightening heat only drove him harder.

"Oh, fuck!" I cried.

He pounded the words out of me. Wetness streamed from my pussy and down my legs. The surging, overstuffed sensation in my ass burst and flooded through my body in orgasm. You don't even realize there's a place that deep inside you until a hard dick is slamming into it. Pleasure surged up from my core like a primordial eruption, something powerful and ancient – the kind of orgasm that killed the dinosaurs.

"Yes!" I screamed. "Cum in my ass!"

Ptah's fingers tightened on my hips in a possessive grip. His cum gushed boiling into me, so deep that I swore I could taste it. I felt the hard pulse of Ptah's orgasm in the pit of my stomach and the torrent of searing hot spunk sent me moaning up into climax right alongside him.

I sagged to the throne room floor as Ptah released me. His cock slid free and the massive load he had poured into my ass began dripping out, slicking my thighs in white. The warm lassitude in my limbs was no match for the strength of the sexual energy Ptah had given me. I stood.

The mummy was on his feet, too, giving me a smug smile. He reached out and rested one perfectly preserved hand on my head. Ptah's instruction was clear, for me to get on my knees and suck his cock clean. But I didn't move. Not on general principle – it looked damned tasty – but I had kept Ptah waiting long enough. It was time to finish our negotiations.

I brushed the ancient alchemist's hand aside with force enough to make him take a surprised, staggering step back. Ptah narrowed his beautiful silver eyes at me.

"I told you that I require obedience," he said, "if the College is to get what they need."

"Actually, I think I'll be going now."

Ptah frowned, perhaps trying to figure out some American joke in my words, but I shook my head.

"Your decoy canopic jars were good," I admitted. "You almost got me with those. But then I realized where to find the originals."

Ptah's gaze flicked over to the display case I had raided the night before and his frown deepened.

"If your organs are still that important to you, it wouldn't do you much good to keep them in your own home. One bomb or fireball from a dissatisfied customer and they go up in flames right along with you. The djinni would be pissed, of course, but you would be too dead to enjoy it."

Ptah cocked his head, listening as I spoke. Assessing the threat and readying his defense.

"But they would have to be safe, right?" I went on. "Somewhere close enough that you could get to them if you needed to. A place where they would be watched and constantly protected. Tell me, Ptah, do you get off on the tourists lining up to stare at your guts?"

The mummy's expression went from angry curiosity to smirking victory in the blink of an eye. He raised one dark finger.

"You are clever, but lying," Ptah told me. "You could not have broken into the National Gallery."

I put my hands on my hips. "I didn't have to. I recognized the photographs on the banners outside. The museum's prize collection of canopic jars aren't just similar to the ones you have here. They're *identical.*"

"Then you may go admire them," Ptah gloated. "When I permit you out of my house at all. Even if you managed to breach the National Gallery, the djinni would never allow foreigners to plunder the home of Egypt's greatest treasures."

"You've got me there," I said, nodding. "I wouldn't dare break into the National Gallery. But here's the thing: *you* might not care about all the gold that the College has been offering you for quicksilver, but museums... They just love wealthy donors."

"What?" Ptah asked.

"I called up the College and they made a little donation to the National Gallery. And by *little,* I mean fifty million dollars. I'm pretty sure the museum director creamed his pants when I told him. He fell all over himself agreeing to send one of their exhibits to America on tour."

"My... heart. My lungs..." Ptah gasped. I wondered if his heart was racing, sealed away in its beautifully crafted canopic jar.

"Right about now, they should be getting loaded onto a plane, ready to begin their museum tour. Probably for a couple of years in the States, but then your jars are going all over the world. Europe, Asia... Everywhere. There are so many people who are going to want a look at them."

Ptah seethed. "How *dare* you?"

"Don't worry, your organs will be perfectly safe," I told him. "Protected, even. And they'll be returned to Egypt. We've already promised the djinni to treat your remains with a hell of a lot more respect than you've shown anyone else's body."

Ptah's rage was beyond words.

"We aren't trying to rob anyone," I told him. "But your heart will be in the hands of your customers long enough to work out a fair price for quicksilver. And for you to release every single woman from this palace."

I retrieved my loincloth from the floor and used it to scrub myself clean. Ptah regarded me with fury in his silver eyes. I leaned against his throne and grinned.

"Oh, cheer up," I told him. "Sure, we've got you by the balls... Well, by the heart, stomach, liver and lungs. But you're still going to be insanely rich, Ptah. And you know, you're not half bad in bed. How about a pity fuck?"

The mummy stared at me, his jaw clenched too tight to even speak. I guessed that was a *no*.

I shrugged and turned away, heading for the door of Ptah's throne room. I'd taken up enough of his time. By now, Jun and the other women should be dressed and a dozen Khamsin limousines were parked outside, ready to take us away to the airport.

It was time for us all to go home.

LILY QUINN BOOK #8

Tangled
LIMBS

Chapter ONE

I chased the vampire through Gates Park, my bare feet churning up sandy clods of grass as I raced southwest toward Mission Beach. Lights flickered past along the darkened jogging paths, but the fog was so thick tonight that they were little more than hazy yellow dots zipping by through the swirling shadows like speeding fireflies.

Any of the other bounty hunters would have lost track of the vampire long ago. He darted between the spindly silhouettes of coastal willows and redwoods, a black blur only barely discernible against the deeper darkness. But I could smell the blood that soaked his clothes, and tracked the vampire's scent through the misty night.

This wasn't exactly how I had planned to spend the evening. *My* plan was a lot more fun: identify the vampire, sweet-talk him, and then – let's be honest – fuck him until I was strong enough to impale the demonic blood-sucker on his own bedpost. Bam! Dead vampire, happy Lily.

But then I hit a tiny snag: the fucker was gay. My stellar pick-up lines and cleavage had accomplished exactly dick... or not, as the case may be.

I suppose I should have guessed there might be a problem from the moment I read the bounty posting. This vampire had a bad habit of ripping his exclusively male victims apart and using their limbs as bloody paintbrushes to scrawl nasty messages across their walls.

Who says all gay guys have good taste? Screw stereotypes.

There were still a few people out in Gates Park, jogging or walking their dogs even in the middle of the foggy night, but I wasn't worried that they could see much. Both the vampire and I were burning through our demonic powers at a voracious rate as we shot through the darkened park like a pair of greased cheetahs on crack. Thick gray clouds hung heavy in the sky and the impending storm had driven most humans indoors. Those few who remained out would see little more than a couple of blurs through the fog.

I clutched my gun and vaulted over one of the streams that wound through Gates Park, landing on the other side hard enough to pound my footprints an inch into the ground. Damp dirt squelched between my toes and then I was off again, kicking my way through fallen branches that the landscapers hadn't cleaned up yet. Wood snapped and cracked under my feet.

It was a race. Who would run out of power first? The vampire's speed and strength was fueled by the blood he drank, mine by fucking the cute bartender back in the stockroom... which was what had given my quarry his head start.

The vampire sprinted into a copse of willows and I ducked beneath a low-hanging branch to avoid a mouthful of leaves. I spotted a flash of bone-white skin and tattered black clothes – like I said, no taste – before he vanished between the trees. The low black sky rumbled as though hungry and rain began pouring down through the fog. My dress was quickly soaked and my bare feet slid across wet willow leaves. Ditching my high heels was one of the first things I had done when the chase began. If I couldn't find my shoes later, then I was adding them to this vampire's tally. Good thing monster hunting pays well.

I burst into the clearing at the center of the willow grove and immediately had to throw myself back as my vampire lunged out of the shadows. Even the driving rain wasn't enough to wash away all the blood and I smelled him coming. His pale fist whistled audibly through where my head had just been and splattered raindrops out of the air.

"Finally done running?" I asked. "Great. Then let's dance, you smelly demonic fucker."

The vampire's next punch blasted a splintered hole into the tree trunk behind me, but I was already sliding under the blow. Not that I was any faster than the vampire, but the difference between him and me was that I knew how to fight. Creatures like this tended to rely on pure brute power. Hitting a vampire was like hitting a brick wall, so why should he bother learning how to duck? Our strength was evenly matched, but Evaine knew that I would spend my life up against assholes like this, so she taught me to fight well. And she wanted it to be a long life, so she also taught me to fight dirty.

I shoved my wet red hair out of the way and slid in close to knee the vampire in the balls. He bared dagger-sharp fangs at me and hissed like the most pissed-off cat you've ever seen. I blocked another punch that came hard enough to shatter one of the bones in my arm and jammed my gun into his stomach. I pulled the trigger again and again, pumping four shots into the vampire's guts before he managed to bring up his foot and kick me away. I flew back and smashed into one of the trees. Ribs and wood cracked with the impact.

I rolled up to my feet, wheezing a few choice oaths and grabbed one of the broken willow branches. It was still attached to the tree by a strip of tough green wood that bent impressively before finally ripping free. I was really starting to lament the lack of a sturdy bedpost.

The vampire flung himself at me, vaulting unnaturally high up into the dark night and then falling through the rain down on me like a bolt of lightning. I slid away barely fast enough and kicked up wet willow leaves that stuck to my legs. The vampire landed in a silvery spray of rainwater and whirled on me.

I whipped him across the face with my springy willow branch. It wasn't enough to hurt the vampire, but it kept him on the defensive for just a second while he recovered his balance. Before he could, I kicked out and swept his feet out from under him. With another alley cat hiss, the vampire fell into the mud and I jumped on top of him.

"This would have been so much more fun in a bedroom," I said.

The vampire bucked and squirmed savagely beneath me, but I straddled his waist with my thighs and held on like I was riding a rodeo bull.

"Fuck you, bitch!" the vampire snarled.

"That *was* the idea."

I slammed the broken branch through his ribs. The pale green willow wood bent and bowed, but my sex-powered super-strength forced the point. No pun intended.

My improvised stake punched through the vampire's ribs and down into his heart. He howled in fury, but the sound fell away as though into an abyss as his skin went from white to gray, and then crumbled to dust. Falling rain hissed through the pile of ashes and within moments, the vampire's remains had washed away into the leaves and grass. Too bad. The wizards at the College paid extra for the ashes and it never hurt to earn some more gold.

Oh, well. The vampire was dead and wouldn't be killing any more men.

I stood up and shook rainwater from my hair. Now to find my damned shoes.

Chapter TWO

*A*fter a week of research, I dug up a few leads on my dead vampire's creator, the one who drank blood straight from a demon and became undead in the first place. Her last known location was somewhere out in eastern Germany, so the task of hunting her down was handed off to the Castle bounty hunters. I contemplated calling Remy Saville to see if the sexy French wizard wanted to partner up on the job, but quickly decided against it. With only a few rare exceptions, monster hunters work alone and that includes yours truly.

I was a little cranky about the whole thing, but even without catching the progenitor vampire, my bank account was stuffed. I had more than enough money to sit on my incredibly fine ass on some tropical beach for the rest of my life, but that's boring. I'm a cambion, the daughter of a succubus and some unknown wizard, with an extensive suite of sex-fueled super powers. I love my job and I'm damned good at it. What the hell else would I do with my life?

I couldn't stay grumpy for too long, though. It was Friday night and I had plans. Important plans. Tonight, I finally got to meet Max's new girlfriend, Taya.

Well, I'd seen her once before, when she was leaving his place a few weeks ago, but that doesn't count. This time I wanted a real chance to talk to Taya and feel her out. And maybe up.

I chose a short black dress and some tasteful silver spiral earrings, then tied up my hair into a sleek red ponytail. I applied a dusting of bronze eyeshadow, examined the effect in the mirror and began fiddling. After another fifteen minutes of work, I was finally satisfied. I picked a pair of shiny black pumps from the closet and then went to the kitchen to collect the bottle of wine I had bought earlier that day just for this special occasion.

Evening traffic along the freeway moved smoothly enough, but some kind of accident bogged me down in midtown. It looked like a driver had hit one of the trees planted along the side of the road. At least, there was broken glass and green leaves everywhere, though I didn't see much damage to the trees themselves. When I stopped at the next red light, I tapped out a quick text to let Max know that I was running late.

The sun was setting and turned the sky into a cloud-streaked ceiling of celestial fire when I pulled into the little lot in front of the old converted firehouse. I parked beside Max's old truck and caught sight of my i10 parked on the other side. I climbed out of the Alfa Romeo and pumped my fist victoriously. My favorite car looked smooth and silver and perfect, as though a werewolf had never tried to have angry sex with it.

Thanks, Max.

I wanted to take a moment to inspect the repairs, but I was already late and I trusted my best friend's work utterly. So I cradled the bottle of wine in the crook of one arm and hurried across the parking lot to the antique brownstone firehouse. I ignored the doorbell and unlocked the front door with my keys. There was a light on down in the office, but no one inside, so I went upstairs.

Max's garage didn't officially open until next week, but the renovations were more or less done, including his apartment upstairs.

Max had preserved as much of the firehouse's original wood and brickwork as he could, accenting it with polished but functional stainless steel. The furniture filling his new living room was still battered and outdated, but I was determined to fix that on Max's next birthday.

Most of the walls upstairs had been removed – I remembered sweaty Max and his sledgehammer fondly – leaving behind only a few of the old supports. The rest of the apartment was open, with brick walls striped in tall, narrow windows full of red and orange sunset.

Max leaned against the patterned steel kitchen counter that ran along one side of the apartment. Taya stood around the other side, talking to him. They hadn't heard me arrive, so I paused at the top of the stairs to enjoy the view. Max was wearing a pair of jeans and a button-down blue shirt with the sleeves rolled up to his elbows. Honestly, I'm not even sure why Max owns anything with full sleeves. He always needs the cuffs out of the way to work on cars or food. His blond hair was combed back so neatly that I barely suppressed the impish urge to go run my hands through it.

Taya was in the middle of what sounded like a story from work. She was the lumber manager down at the hardware store Max had been spending a lot of time and money at while renovating the firehouse. He tends to miss anything more subtle than *Hey, I think you're pretty sexy, but I'd like to tear off all your clothes just to be sure*, but Taya had managed to flirt with Max flagrantly enough that he eventually got the hint.

I was glad Taya was stubborn. Max doesn't date much. Maybe five or six girls in the last eight years. I go through that many partners in a month. More, if I'm busy.

Taya looked like quite a catch, though: islander dark skin, with tan legs that went on forever and which she showed off in a deliciously short red dress. Her hair was long and as shiny as obsidian, falling in a slick black cascade around her lovely round face.

Max listened to Taya's story, then smiled and put his hand over hers on the counter when she finished. She smiled back at Max and leaned over to give him a quick kiss.

Damn, that was a *lot* of sexy. I would have given the entire stack of gold I had just earned from that vampire's bounty to see Max pick Taya up onto the counter and eat her pussy right there. I went swiftly hot and wet between the legs.

Down, girl!

"Hey, Max," I said. I dropped my purse next to the stairs and waved across the living room.

Max's smile widened and the dimples appeared in his cheeks. "Hey, Lil."

He came out of the kitchen and swept me into a tight hug. I returned it and gave him a kiss on the cheek that took some serious restraint. Saying hello to Max usually involved tongue and a blow-job. But he was seeing someone now, so I had to behave.

Max let go of me and gestured to Taya, who was approaching us with an uncertain smile.

"Lil, this is Taya," he said. "Taya, Lilith Quinn."

I grinned and hoped it didn't look too evil. This was it: the Friend Test.

I was Max's best friend and meeting me was a rite of passage. Taya had to win my approval or their relationship wasn't going *anywhere*. Max had only brought a few girls to face the Friend Test – and fewer had passed.

Taya regarded me with large, dark eyes and I was a little disappointed that she wasn't wearing the glasses I'd seen last time. They were adorable. But her lips were gorgeous and painted the same red as her dress. Taya's hair was swept back and tiny, delicate diamonds sparkled at her ears. She was really trying to impress me.

Good. Tonight, I had *all* the power. Mwah ha ha!

I held out my hand. "Nice to meet you for real this time, Taya."

"Hi, Lily," Taya said. "Max says you prefer that."

Taya took my hand firmly and kept eye contact. Her handshake said *I'm ready for this. I'm confident. I'm good enough for your friend. Also, you're hotter than I'd like his best friend to be, so don't get any ideas.*

She was off to a strong start.

When Taya released my hand, I offered up the wine. She took the bottle and whistled softly.

"Next of Kyn? This stuff is expensive," she said. "Are you sure you want to drink it tonight?"

I nodded and followed Taya back to the kitchen. Max took the wine and got to work opening it up. Three glasses already sat out on the counter.

"Lil, your i10 is ready to go," Max said as he twisted a corkscrew into the top of the bottle.

Mmm. Screw.

Calm down, Lily.

"I saw it parked outside. Thanks, Max. I've really missed that car," I said, then looked at Taya. "I just about turned it into a paperweight a few months ago. Max has got her back in perfect working order, though."

"I'm sorry. What happened?" Taya asked, her eyes widening. "Were you hurt?"

"I'm fine. I was trying not to hit a dog."

Which was sort of close to the truth... I had actually been aiming *for* the dog and the dog was a six-hundred-pound werewolf.

But I couldn't exactly explain that to Taya. Not even Max was supposed to know about the monsters I hunt, even though he was right there when I punched a wyvern in the face on Valentine's Day. If the College wizards ever discovered that I said too much, they would wipe Taya's memory like a chalkboard and probably put me on a magical time-out or something. There's a reason that normal people don't know about demons and Unseelie fae and all of the other monsters that try to fuck with our world. Because I hunt them down and the College keeps it quiet.

"Thanks for coming out tonight, Lil," Max said quickly. "I hope we aren't interrupting work?"

I shook my head. "Nope. Dinner with you two is the only thing going on tonight."

Max beamed at me. He poured three glasses of my nice red wine and held his up. "I don't have a toast ready, but here's to a great night."

Taya smiled and we all clinked our glasses together, then took long sips of wine. When she had swallowed, Taya leaned across the counter to give Max another kiss.

"Tastes great," she said, then raised one fine black brow at me. Was the best friend going to object to public displays of affection?

I smirked. Taya had *no* idea.

Max set down his wineglass. "Wow, Lil. This wine is amazing. It'll go great with the lasagna. Are you hungry?"

"For your cooking?" I said. "Always."

Max smiled at that and waved us over to the dining room table, where lasagna and salad were already laid out. I sat across from Taya and smoothed a napkin over my lap while Max filled our plates with pasta, cheese and homemade red sauce.

"It's nice to finally meet you, Lily," Taya said. "Max talks about you all the time. I've been excited about tonight. And nervous, of course."

Honesty. That scored Taya a few points on the Friend Test. I gestured at her with my fork and grinned. "Hey, you've faced Max's cock. That's not for the faint of heart."

"Lil!" Max choked.

"Just pointing out that she's got nothing to fear from me."

Taya's cheeks darkened in an adorable blush. I laughed and accepted my plate from Max. It had more lasagna heaped on it than his and Taya's combined. Max knew how much I had to eat to keep up with the caloric demands of my sex powers. Taya's eyes widened, but she was too polite to say anything about it. I wasn't sure if that was worth points or not.

I dug into my food and it was delicious, of course. Max isn't a gourmet chef or anything, but he took home economics twice in high school and is a master of comfort food.

"So... Lily," said Taya. The words came out a little awkwardly, but she was really trying. "What do you do for a living?"

I get that question a lot. I gave Taya a brilliant smile. "Oh, I'm a porn star. You've probably seen me online."

This time, it was Taya who choked on a mouthful of salad. Max shot me a panicked look and kicked me under the table. I laughed again and shook my head.

"Only kidding," I assured Taya. "I'm an investment banker for Alcott and Martin."

It was my standard response. It explained away my money and was boring enough that no one *ever* asked for more details. Taya just nodded and Max gulped down a long drink of wine.

"Max tells me that you're in college and going for a business degree," I said.

Taya nodded. "I am. I've still got a few semesters left to go. It can be hard to schedule the classes I need around work."

"Any plans for what to do with that degree when you're finished?"

Taya took a bite of lasagna and appeared to be weighing her answer carefully.

"Well, nothing concrete," she said at last. "I'm thinking of trying to get into business management, running a store... or maybe a garage."

Taya met my eye and held my gaze. Gutsy move. Yeah, she was talking about Max's new shop. Not by name – that would have been too much this early in the relationship. But Taya was letting me know that she considered Max long-term boyfriend material, perhaps even the kind of man she could marry.

Twenty points to Taya for recognizing what she had in Max. Five more for telling me so without making him uncomfortable.

"Speaking of garages," I said. "Are you ready for your grand opening next week, Max?"

"More or less," he answered. "I'm waiting on a few more cases of parts and that sort of thing. But everything else is ready to go."

"I don't suppose you'll let me hire a caterer?"

"No way, Lil. I'll just bake some cookies."

"Have you tasted Max's cookies?" I asked. "They're amazing. He puts toffee in them or something."

"I haven't tried them yet, but I guess I will next week," Taya said.

So she planned to attend Max's grand opening, too. Ten points. Unless she was just doing it for the cookies – in which case, five points for good taste.

Over dinner, Max and Taya took turns telling me stories about working at the lumberyard and Golden Touch Auto. I admitted to Taya that I was the reason Max had gotten fired from GTA, though neither of us got into the details of exactly how that had happened.

"I tried to give Max some money to start this place up," I said. "Seemed like the least I could do."

"It was a shitty job anyway," Max assured me with a dimpled smile. "And some of my customers from GTA have already called me to open accounts here."

Taya smiled. "That's going to give you a good start on business. Getting those first customers is always the hardest."

The conversations were all strangely... normal. Max has known about my half-demon heritage and the supernatural world since we were teenagers. I've never had to pretend to be human around Max. But for tonight, I was just an ordinary woman – an ordinary woman scrutinizing her best friend's new girl. I'd never trade my powers, but it was rather fun to be normal for a night.

Max stood, collected our plates and carried them away. I picked up the empty wineglasses and followed him into the kitchen.

"Nice catch, big guy," I said as I set the glasses down beside the sink. "Need any help breaking her in?"

"Be good, Lil," Max said, then raised his voice. "Anyone want another drink or some coffee?"

"Coffee," Taya called from the dining room. "Black, please."

"I'll take a cup, too," I said.

Max nodded. "Sure. Go sit down, Lil. I've got things in here."

I sauntered out of the kitchen. Taya had already relocated to Max's well-worn couch. She leaned back, folding her long, olive-skinned legs beneath her. I sat down at the other end of the couch and kicked off my high heels. Taya considered for a moment and then did the same.

"Lily?" she asked hesitantly.

"Yeah?"

"You and Max seem very close. I think he really wants us to get to know each other."

Broaching an awkward subject that was important to Max. Ten points. I grinned at Taya.

"I think so, too," I said. "And I've got an idea. How about a game of Truth or Dare?"

Max came into the living room, carrying two mugs of coffee. He set one of them in front of Taya and handed the second to me. Tons of cream and sugar, just how I liked it.

"Truth or Dare?" he asked, arching an eyebrow. "Lil, are you still in high school?"

"Hey, it's a good way to get to know someone," I protested. And it was still fun, age be damned. "We've been proper grown-ups all night. It's time to relax. I'll even let Taya go first."

Max retrieved a third gently steaming cup from the kitchen and then grabbed a chair out of the dining room. He sat down on the other side of the coffee table from us.

"No asking about work, though," I said, waving one finger. "We did that over dinner. Truth or Dare has to be fun."

Plus, this was so Taya and I could get to know each other. If she asked about my job, I'd *have* to lie to her and that would ruin the whole game.

"Fine by me, then. If it's okay with Taya," Max said.

Taya took a sip of coffee and nodded. "Sure. I'm game."

Playful, at least when prompted. More points for Taya.

She tapped one finger against her lower lip as she thought. The nail was painted red, a few shades darker than her dress and lipstick. It must have been hell to maintain fingernails like that in a lumberyard.

"Okay, I've got one," said Taya. "Lily, truth or dare?"

I waited to answer long enough for Max to start giving me adorably nervous looks. Just because we had sworn off discussing work didn't mean he still didn't have *plenty* to worry about. I winked at Max.

"Truth," I said.

"How did you and Max meet?" Taya asked.

"I was the girl next door."

Taya frowned a little at this, but I gave her a reassuring smile.

"We were five years old," I told her. "My foster family lived right next to his and we played together pretty much every day. Max always went along with my wild-ass games and never made fun of me for being a girl, whether I wanted to climb trees or play house. And I made Max have fun."

"Made him?" Taya asked.

"Well, both of Max's parents worked a lot of long hours. That left him on his own to take care of his two little brothers most of the time."

"Jake and Peter," Max told Taya. "They moved away from the city a few years ago."

"So someone had to drag Max out to play," I said, then pointed to myself. "That was me. But I was a foster kid and eventually that family had to get rid of me."

Taya's expression was shocked and then turned swiftly sad. I waved her off.

"Don't blame them. Really. I was a crazy kid," I told Taya. "I wouldn't have kept me, either. Max begged his parents to adopt me so I wouldn't have to leave. But they couldn't afford it, so Max and I only saw each other at school after that."

"You stayed friends all those years?" Taya asked.

"That's another question," I said. "I think it's my turn now."

Taya nodded and sat back. She laced her fingers around her coffee cup while I looked between her and Max.

"Okay," I said. "Max. Truth or dare?"

"Truth," he answered quickly.

"Who asked who out first?"

Max smiled, flashing his dimples at Taya. "She asked me."

I twirled my fingers. "Details, Max!"

"After four trips to the hardware store in one week, Taya wanted to take a look at what I was doing. I showed her around and then Taya um... sort of kissed me. Later, she asked me if I wanted to get some dinner."

"Later?" I grinned at Max and put down my empty coffee mug. "You mean after you guys had wild sex three times in one night?"

"Uh, that's two questions, Lil," Max said, flushing. "But... yeah."

Taya was blushing furiously, too, but she smiled. Good. She *should* be proud of fucking Max. If the woman didn't appreciate his cock, then that would cost her major points in the Friend Test.

"Alright, my turn," said Max. "Taya, truth or dare?"

Taya sipped her coffee and hesitated for a moment, then chose truth.

"Nothing boring, Max," I told him. "I'm supposed to be getting to know your girlfriend here, remember? How about *What's your favorite sexual position?*"

"Lil!" Max laughed. "Sorry, Taya. You might have noticed that Lily's a bit... blunt."

"It's okay. I can handle her," said Taya.

Hell yes, she could handle me. Any time she wanted. But I managed not to say so out loud. Barely.

"What's the first thing you look for in a potential partner?" Max asked.

Taya cocked her head slightly. "You mean sexual partner?"

"Yeah."

"Physically or personality?"

"Uh, physically," Max said as a concession to me.

"Hands," Taya answered. "Strong hands, long fingers. And you have great nails, Max. A lot of girls would kill for fingernails like yours and you keep them really clean. Most guys who come into the store have enough grease caked under them to oil an engine."

Taya stuck out her tongue and made an exaggerated face of disgust. I laughed. Max curled his fingers and examined his nails with a curious expression, which made Taya laugh, too. She wasn't wrong, though. When Max worked at GTA, he was the only one there without permanently black nails and I knew he spent ten minutes scrubbing on every break to keep them that way.

"And in women... I like lips," Taya said.

I blinked. So did Max. I wasn't expecting an answer for women, too. Taya blushed again and her smile faltered. I guessed that she didn't have much experience with other girls, but I felt a pale, warm glow of lust from her, like sitting in front of a fireplace. Maybe Taya was bisexual, maybe just fooled around once in college, or maybe never at all and I was giving her new ideas.

"Wow," said Max.

Taya ducked her head and brushed her fingers over her darkened cheeks. "Lily, truth or dare?"

"I'll spare Max a heart attack for a little longer. Truth."

"Have you and Max ever... hooked up?" Taya asked.

"Oh hell yes," I answered at once. "Sooo many times."

"Lil!" Max choked.

"What? I'm supposed to tell the truth."

"Yeah, but you could tell it more... gently."

I looked back to Taya. She was still blushing, but the corners of her lovely lips turned down. Taya watched closely, appraising me.

"Max and I have been best friends ever since we were kids," I told her. "And we've been best friends with benefits since high school. Max was the first guy I ever slept with and we've had a ton of sex since then."

"Ah," said Taya.

I held up my hands. "But *never* when he's seeing someone."

"Never?" she asked.

"Never. That's the rule and we've always held to it."

I glanced at Max, who nodded. Taya seemed to weigh my answer for a moment, but then her mouth quirked back up into a smile. She gave me a nod of respect and I felt the soft heat of her desire again. Taya earned a few more points.

"My turn," I said. "Truth or dare, Taya?"

"I think it's time for a dare," she answered.

Well, I *had* been planning to ask Taya if she liked my lips, but now the gauntlet was thrown. I slipped a few inches closer to Taya on the couch.

"I dare you to make out with me," I said.

"Um... for how long?"

"Until you can't stand it anymore, and then it's your turn."

"Are you okay with that, Max?" Taya asked.

Good girl. Ten points to Taya, though I had lost track of how many Friend Test points she'd won by now. Max blushed and spluttered and made a bunch of noises without managing any actual words.

"That's a *yes*," I told Taya.

Max nodded dumbly and leaned forward in his chair, half to watch and half to poorly hide the growing tent in his pants. Taya turned to face me and hooked her hands behind my neck, pulling me swiftly into a kiss. Was she eager or just trying not to lose her nerve? Either way, I was determined to reward Taya's unhesitating execution of my dare.

Her lips were soft and still tasted faintly of coffee and the wine we had shared over dinner. I flicked my tongue lightly along them and Taya's mouth opened to allow me entry. Her tongue met mine hesitantly and I drank down her nervous, shuddering breath. I gave her a little moan and gently put one hand on her knee. When Taya didn't shy away, I slid it up to her thigh, just below the hem of her dress. Her desire flared, turning from timid lust to the hot golden flow of sexual energy that made my half-succubus blood boil.

I felt Max's lust, too, without even looking up at him. I wasn't exaggerating how much Max and I had fucked. I knew my best friend's desire like I knew his face.

With their lust coursing through me, I felt like I could jump over buildings and my senses honed to a razor edge. I smelled the hot scent of Max's testosterone surging through his body as he watched me make out with Taya. I heard her heart jackhammering and I could practically *feel* the smooth tawny color of her skin under my fingertips. I wanted to lick every inch of her.

The power that Max and his girlfriend's blazing desire gave me meant that I had to be careful of my inhuman strength as I crushed my lips against Taya's. But Evaine had spent a long time teaching me restraint. I used my tongue and lips gently, tasting and teasing Taya. The lace of my panties was beyond soaked by the time she broke the kiss.

"I dare you to do a shot out of my belly button," she gasped.

"Max, go get some booze," I said.

He was already on his feet and sprinting for the kitchen so fast that I almost wondered if he were a cambion, too. Technically, Taya was supposed to ask me if I wanted truth or dare, but let's be honest: we weren't really playing anymore.

Not Truth or Dare, at least.

Max returned a second later, holding a bottle of tequila and breathing hard. He spun the cap off and held the open bottle up. I smirked at Taya.

"You're going to have to show me your belly button for me to drink anything out of it," I informed her.

Taya looked down at her dress. She lifted her butt a few inches so she could pull it up and over her head. With an answering grin, Taya threw her dress over the back of the couch. It landed on the floor in a puddle of red fabric. Beneath, she wore matching crimson lace panties and bra. They concealed the dark shapes of her pussy and nipples, but only barely. She definitely planned on fucking Max tonight.

I slipped off the couch and down onto the floor while Taya leaned back to make her stomach relatively level. Carefully, Max poured a small shot into the shallow dip of his girlfriend's navel. I knelt down at Taya's feet and put my hands on her knees. She hesitated slightly, then spread her legs to allow me between them. Her delicate red underwear were soaking wet. I trembled with the effort of restraining myself from diving right in to drink up a shot of *that*.

Tequila first. More later... if I was lucky, and if Max and Taya were game.

I leaned in slowly and ran my lips along the sensitive skin of Taya's inner thigh. The closer I got to her wet panties, the slower I moved until my mouth was almost stopped right over her fever-hot pussy. Taya whimpered when I skipped up to the top of the lace. I traced my lips across her smooth belly until I reached her navel. Her breath came so fast that the tequila threatened to spill out over her stomach.

Feeling her lust and Max's like open flames, I drank up the shot from Taya's belly button and tasted the burn of alcohol. I licked around the soft edge of her navel and then dipped the tip of my tongue inside for the last drops. Taya sighed in pleasure.

Now it was my turn. I sat up.

"Don't you wear glasses?" I asked.

Taya lay back in the cushions, panting. It took her a moment to process my question, but then she nodded.

"Yeah," she said breathlessly. "They're uh... in my purse."

Max handed Taya a leather handbag and she pulled a pair of black-framed glasses from a case inside. She held them out toward me with a curious expression on her face.

I took the glasses from Taya's hand, unfolded the stems and slid them into place over her ears. They rested just perfectly against her high, blushing cheeks and made Taya look like a schoolteacher. Well, with her hair a little tousled and wearing nothing more than a few bits of red lace, she was a really slutty teacher. But those were my favorite kind. I instantly wanted to tie my hair up in pigtails and report to her office for detention and spankings.

"I dare you to take a load of Max's cum on your glasses," I said.

Taya adjusted her glasses and looked up at Max. He stood at the arm of the couch, eyes wide and his muscular chest heaving like bellows. Max's jeans appeared about ready to rip open from the strain of containing his massive erection. Taya straightened and slid her hands up his legs.

"Well, Max?" she asked. "Is that something you want to try?"

I bit my lip. I had three pairs of costume glasses just for this particular fetish – sometimes I liked to be the schoolgirl and sometimes I was the teacher – so this wouldn't exactly be Max's first time. But it sounded like it was Taya's and my heart raced to think that I might be the one to introduce her to the glories of a massive load of spunk all over her glasses.

"Come on, Max," I said. "Cum all over your incredibly hot girlfriend's face."

"Oh fuck," he panted.

I took that as another *yes* and stood to unbutton Max's shirt. I pulled it off his shoulders to display my friend's broad chest, muscles hardened by years of working on cars and keeping up with me.

A faint sheen of sweat already gleamed across his skin. Taya drew the zipper of his jeans down and we grabbed Max's pants and boxers together, yanking them off. She gasped as her boyfriend's cock sprang free and bobbed in front of us, long and hard and darkly flushed with desire. I guess Taya still wasn't quite used to the view and I smiled indulgently. It can take a while.

Taya slid down onto the floor and seized a double handful of Max's taut ass. She pulled him close to wrap her red lips around the blunt head of his dick. She slurped and licked noisily at my best friend's big cock. Max held on to the back of the couch tight enough that his knuckles went white.

I wondered if I should go. I hoped not... Things were getting damned sexy between Max and Taya. I was impatient to get them somewhere with a bed. If I was lucky, I'd get front-row seats to some serious fucking. If I was *very* lucky, I might get invited onto the court. Not if it would cause trouble, though. If either of them asked me to leave, I would, without complaint. Not out loud, at least – privately, I'd hate to miss out on watching Max and Taya together.

But I still felt her desire and his, and I can only sense lust that's directed at me. I could certainly see how much Taya wanted Max, but I didn't feel it the same way. That heat was for *me*. Max met my gaze with dark blue eyes that were wide, dilated with excitement. I answered him with my own giddy grin.

Taya was already stripped down to her delicates, so I figured that I should do the same. I pushed my dress off my shoulders and then wriggled out, tossing it aside to join Taya's in a growing puddle of cloth. I unfastened my black satin bra for good measure, and then I was wearing less. So it was only fair if I removed Taya's, too. She knelt in front of Max, holding his cock and licking at the crown like it was a lollipop. I ran one finger down her spine to the catch of her bra. Taya shivered and let out a muffled little moan at my touch. I unhooked her bra, peeling it off her shoulders, and she removed her hands one at a time so I could pull the lace away.

I crouched and leaned against Taya's bare back so I could reach around her to cup her breasts in my hands. They were silky soft and firm. I ran my thumbs over the small, stiff peaks of her nipples. With a moan, Taya pressed herself forward, into my touch and gulping down another inch of Max's cock.

She didn't seem to have much experience with dicks the size of his – she was only managing to suck the top half – but Taya more than made up for it by being wet, enthusiastic and loud. There's a lot more to a good blowjob than just stuffing a guy all the way down your throat. Nothing is sexier to a man than a lover who is really excited about his cock, who takes pleasure in his pleasure.

"Oh fuck, Taya," Max said. Sweat beaded along his hairline and his expression was rapt.

Told you.

Taya popped her mouth off her boyfriend's dick to gasp for breath. Then, to my surprise, she pointed it toward me, blushing as she offered me a taste. How the hell could I decline that invitation?

I leaned over Taya's shoulder and slid the hot head of Max's cock into my mouth. He let out a long, hissing breath and his dick twitched between my lips. Now, I *can* deep-throat Max, but this wasn't a competition. So I licked and sucked at the crown with every ounce of the desire that soaked my panties, piling my cock-lust on top of Taya's.

"Lil!" Max groaned.

His girlfriend kissed her way along his rigid length until her mouth brushed mine. Together, we ran lips and tongues up and down every inch until Max's cock was all shining wet. When we reached the crown, I tasted the slick saltiness of his precum and lapped it up. I twined my tongue with Taya's to share and turned Max's dick into the innocent bystander caught in the middle of our kiss.

Max's jaw was clenched tight and he was as hard as steel against our lips. I felt heat pounding through him, on the verge of eruption.

Reaching up, I closed eager fingers around the slippery shaft of Max's cock.

"Ready?" I asked Taya.

"Yes," she whimpered. "God, yes."

Taya stared up at Max with beautiful dark eyes. I put an arm around her, cradling one of her soft breasts and pinching the nipple gently. I stroked Max swiftly with the other hand. My fingers made wet sounds racing up and down his hard length.

"Go ahead," I told him. "Show Taya just how fucking sexy she is in those glasses. Give her a big load of cum all over them!"

He did. Oh fuck, how he did.

I aimed Max's pulsing cock right at Taya's glasses and a huge streamer of spunk lanced out, splashing all over one lens. Creamy white shot across her cheek and even up into her black hair. Another pair of hard spurts painted the other lens in thick cum.

Taya's eyes widened behind her glasses and her mouth hung open as she panted. Max's jizz oozed down and onto her lips. She pulled away a bit, blinking, but then opened her mouth and swirled it around with her tongue, tasting. With a soft sound of pleasure, she swallowed.

I leaned in to lick delicately at the semen dripping from Taya's glasses. She watched me through the sticky lenses and gave a shy smile. I lapped up the rest of Max's thick white load from her skin like the excited little cum-slut that I am, then pulled Taya into a deep kiss. She let out a surprised moan when she tasted the slick mess still on my tongue. Taya drank it all up and swallowed with hardly a pause.

When she sat back and licked her lips, I grinned at her. Fifty points. No, a hundred. Whatever. Taya had totally aced the Friend Test.

Chapter
THREE

$\mathcal{M}$ax gave me the shirt off his back. Well, off of his floor, at least. I buttoned it up while Taya went to take a quick shower. Max's cum had kind of splashed everywhere. Personally, I thought it was an excellent look, but sticky is only fun for so long. Especially in long hair.

Max pulled his jeans back on and I followed him downstairs to collect the paperwork for my i10's repairs while Taya cleaned up. He tried to convince me that I didn't owe him a penny as we stepped into the garage.

"Not a chance," I told him. "Unless you want to let me forgive the loan I gave you for this place."

Max smiled, showing off his dimples, and shook his head.

"Nope."

I enjoyed a swell of pride at the sight of his finished garage. The workbenches were all bolted into place and there was even another car on the lift – a red sedan with the hood propped open to reveal an engine that looked like someone had taken a pickaxe to it.

While Max collected a couple last invoices for my i10's file, I hopped up to sit on one of the workbenches. The metal surface was cold against my ass and drenched panties. I kicked my bare legs and smirked at Max.

"Taya seems pretty great," I said.

A fresh blush crept up into Max's cheeks. "Yeah."

"How are things going with her?"

"Well, I think. She's busy with school and work, but always makes time for us to go out."

"Taya's sweet," I said. "And hot as hell. You can tell her that she passed the Friend Test with flying colors. Or flying cum."

Max laughed and leaned beside a rack of wrenches to look at me. "Not that I'm complaining, Lil, but did your test have to involve all of that?"

He pointed up at the ceiling, indicating upstairs where his girlfriend and I had gone to town on his dick. My pussy tightened on nothing and I felt my wetness running across Max's workbench. I hadn't gotten off at all yet.

"Hey, I had to get to know Taya," I said.

"She told me once that she always wondered about being with another girl. And I think she liked the uh... stuff with the glasses."

"You don't think she'll freak out, do you?" I asked Max. "Sometimes I get a little carried away."

"Yeah, but I doubt it. Taya's never talked about a three-way before, but she seemed to love it... Of course, you sort of have that effect on anyone with a pulse," Max said, then looked back at the door to make sure we were still alone and smiled at me. "And even on people *without* a pulse."

He wasn't wrong about that. I glanced past Max to the red sedan again and pointed.

"So what the hell is the story there?" I asked. "Vengeful girlfriend?"

Max went to the car. He ran one hand lightly along one of the deep rents in the engine block, streaking his fingers with grease. When he put them to his chin, thinking, they left black smudges across his skin. Shirtless Max, dirty and sweaty, sex-tousled blond hair... I can't tell you how badly I wanted to pounce him, but I held back. When Taya was playing along, it was an incredibly hot threesome. While she was away, though, it was just cheating and I don't do that shit.

"I'm not sure," Max said. "Actually, I was hoping you could take a look at it."

I frowned. "Why me? You're the mechanic."

"One of my old customers from GTA had it towed over a couple of days ago. He was pretty vague about what happened."

I slid down off the tool bench and came to stand beside Max, inspecting the ruined car. It was bad. Max's customer would need every bit of his magical touch. Something had shattered three windows and punched right through the entire engine. I felt Max's eyes on me and looked up at him. He was still rubbing his jaw, smearing the black grease there.

"It reminded me of what that werewolf did to your 110," Max said slowly. "At first."

"At first?"

Max leaned over the front of the car, showing off his well-sculpted ass, and pointed to the largest hole in the engine.

"This is just as bad as what Dominic did," said Max. "But that was mostly claws, tearing damage. This is different."

I barely resisted the urge to smack Max's butt and busied myself examining the ruined car instead. He was right. There were several holes all the way through the sedan's engine. The metal edges were rough and buckled upward.

"Something hit the car from beneath," I said.

Max nodded. "I can't think of much that could do this. Maybe some kind of underground explosion kicking up rebar, but even then, it takes a lot of force to punch through an engine block."

I grabbed the sedan's front bumper and lifted up the car with one hand – the blowjob upstairs had been *really* fun. With my sex-heightened senses, I inspected the undercarriage. Lots of scuffing, dented frame and dirt packed into every crevice, but I still wasn't quite sure what I was looking at.

"What could do this, Lil?" Max asked.

"I don't know," I admitted. "Where did this happen? Up in the mountains?"

Max went to another workbench to retrieve the tow slip from a clipboard there. He glanced over it. "Nope. Vijay had it brought in from Mission Beach."

That was down at the southern end of Gates Park, not too far from Max's garage. Mission Beach was one of the larger beaches, popular with the tourists and locals alike for jogging, surfing and making out. What the hell could be smashing up cars like this out there? And why wouldn't his customer, Vijay, tell Max what had happened?

There was something pale wedged in the sedan's undercarriage. I lifted the car a little higher and bent to examine it more closely. It was a long splinter about the length and thickness of a finger. I ran a curious hand over the slender piece of wood. It was springy and green – this was from a living tree.

"Hmm..." I said.

"What are you thinking, Lil?" Max asked. I felt his lust at the sight of me bent over, but there was curiosity in his voice, too.

I opened my mouth to answer, but then heard footsteps on the stairs. Max didn't hear them yet, so he started when I straightened and hastily dropped the car back to the lift. Metal creaked ominously and then settled just as Taya stepped into the garage. Max and I whirled to face her.

"Uh... hi," said Taya.

She stood in the doorway, wrapped in a short pink robe that definitely didn't belong to Max. Her hair was wet and her dusky skin had a freshly-scrubbed glow. I had to give Max credit for his taste in women – Taya looked delicious.

Had she overheard anything she wasn't supposed to? It was bad enough that Max knew about my world – if the wizards ever discovered how much I told him, they would wipe his memory back to high school. Max understood the danger and had accepted it since he was eighteen years old, but Taya was different. I didn't want to get her into trouble with the College just because I couldn't keep my mouth shut.

Max strode across the garage to Taya. His jeans were already straining again to contain his swelling cock. He planted an incredibly delectable-looking kiss on Taya's lips and she followed him into the garage. I leaned over the front of the ruined sedan again.

"Hey there," said Max.

"Hey," Taya answered with a smile. "What are you guys looking at down here?"

"Max has his first customer," I said, pointing to the red sedan. "Besides me, I mean."

Taya came to stand beside me, shifting her bare feet on the cold concrete while Max scrubbed his hands carefully clean and dried them with a towel.

"That's great," she said with a smile. "Wow, looks like it's going to be a lot of work."

"Yeah," Max agreed. "It's going to be expensive. I'll see if I can cut Vijay some kind of deal."

Taya leaned over the engine next to me, but luckily, didn't seem to be paying too much attention to the strange damage in front of us. She spoke quietly.

"That... what we did upstairs was... unexpected. I've never done anything like that before."

"You had fun, though," I said. "Right?"

Taya nodded and blushed brilliantly.

"Good, because I think there's about to be more," I said.

I felt a bright flash of lust from Taya and she licked her beautiful full lips. "What?"

"Well, we're both bent over this car here and neither of us are wearing much. We're showing off a lot of incredibly fine ass and I'm not sure if Max will be able to resist much longer."

Taya gasped as Max stepped up behind her and reached under the hem of her robe.

"Nope," he agreed in a low growl.

I felt one of his strong hands between my legs, too, cupping the wet satin of my panties. I pushed back against his fingers and moaned. Taya was right about Max's hands – they were amazing.

Peeking back over my shoulder, I noted that Max had taken advantage of my quiet conversation with his girlfriend to strip out of his jeans. He stood naked behind us, his cock so hard that it was nearly pointed right at the garage's ceiling. Max pushed Taya's robe up until it was bunched around her waist. She stared back at him, panting, and pressed her ass into his hand. She wore nothing beneath and my mouth watered at the sight of her slick pussy.

Max's thumb brushed over me through the sopping cloth of my thong. His other hand held the dark curve of Taya's hip as he slid his cock into her. Max moved slowly, starting with small, shallow thrusts to let Taya adjust to the massive intrusion. She sighed in pleasure every time his dick shoved deeper into her and then a surprisingly loud moan when she took it all.

"Wow," I said.

Max wasn't done. He hooked his thumb through my soaking wet panties and pulled them to one side so he could feed two fingers into my eager little slit. Taya and I moaned together as Max fingered me in time with the long, slow thrusts of his cock.

"Yes, yes, yes!" Taya chanted.

I was impressed that she could take him all the way. Max is a big guy and handling his cock isn't easy. Rewarding as fuck, but difficult. I figured I should show Taya how well she was doing, so I angled myself across the front of the car to brush the wet black hair back from her face.

Taya's dark eyes were wide and dilated. I took her chin between my fingers and turned her face toward mine. I gave Taya a short kiss and then another, tasting her moans and panted cries, but not stifling them. I wanted to hear them all. And more importantly, I didn't want Max to miss a single one.

His fingers were moving swiftly inside me, twisting and curling to touch all of my most sensitive places. Taya bounced against the front of the car, grabbing at the engine for a handhold as Max began working himself faster in and out of her pussy.

"Are you going to cum?" I asked.

Taya moaned and nodded. I bit her lower lip gently and then released it as Max pounded himself into her, making the other woman rock against the car. His fingers slid in and out of me with loud wet sounds, and then his thumb found the tight pink of my asshole.

"Fuck!" I cried.

"Oh god...!" Taya screamed out.

Taya and I kissed savagely as we came, wet and messy. I shoved desperate hands under her robe and she did the same with my borrowed shirt. Her skin was so warm and silky... There was dark engine grease on our hands and we smeared it across each other like war paint. Every hammer-blow of Max's cock into Taya made her gasp and squeak in pleasure. His fingers were like live wires between my legs, jolting with ecstasy so intense that I writhed helplessly against Taya.

"I... I want to lick your pussy," she whimpered.

"Oh fuck," I gasped. "Really?"

"Yeah..."

We looked up at Max, each trying to suck down enough breath to ask if he was okay with that, but he was already stepping back and withdrawing his dripping cock from Taya's pussy. I sighed when his fingers slid out of me, but pushed myself upright. Taya grabbed the sash of her robe and untied it with hasty, shaking hands. I shoved it down off her delicate shoulders to display the stark black lines of grease across her perfect tan skin.

My fingers flew to the buttons of the shirt Max had given me. There was grease ground into the cloth and I doubted that he would ever get it entirely clean again. I stripped the shirt hastily off, dropped it to the floor and promised myself to buy Max a new one.

Step by step, I backed up until my ass hit the edge of the nearest workbench. The textured metal surface was chilly against my skin, but I pulled myself up onto the top and hooked one finger at Taya. She crept closer, her lips parted and dark eyes wide. Max watched over his girlfriend's shoulder, breathing hard but holding himself back.

I raised both of my legs together, toes pointed at the ceiling, and then grabbed the waist of my panties. The cloth was soaked clean through. I pulled them up and off. Taya stared at me with hunger in her dark eyes. Her lust was red-hot as I slowly let my legs fall open to reveal my naked sex.

"You still want to try it?" I asked.

"Yes," Taya panted.

She glanced up at Max, who gave her a kiss and then nodded. Taya practically ran the final steps to me, bending to press her face between my parted thighs. For a moment, she just traced her fingers over my slick labia and inhaled the warm scent of my arousal. I didn't have to ask if she liked it – I could feel the blaze of her pleasure, flaming in contrast to the cold of the metal tool bench under my ass.

I didn't want to push Taya. It was difficult not to and I gripped the edge of the workbench hard enough to leave dimples in the steel. Max shot me a wide-eyed look. I gulped and loosened my hold. Instead, I slid my fingers into Taya's long black hair. I didn't pull, but guided her face in closer until her lips brushed my pussy. We both sighed at the hot, wet sensation. Max's untended cock twitched in sympathetic pleasure.

And then Taya was off. She kissed my slit deep and thrust her tongue into me, tasting my streaming juices. My fingers tightened in her hair and my hips rose up from the workbench. Taya devoured me with little technique – this was her first time with another woman, after all – but so much enthusiasm. Remember what I said about enthusiasm being a huge turn-on for guys? Well, the same goes for girls. Watching Taya down between my legs, eyes bright with excitement as she licked and nibbled and explored my body pushed me right to the edge of climax.

"Taya," I moaned. "Shit, you're going to make me cum!"

My wetness smeared Taya's flushed cheeks as she pulled back just enough to speak. "Max, fuck me."

He was there behind her in an instant, those hands that first attracted her to Max running over the smooth bronze curve of her ass. Taya arched her body so Max could plow his cock straight up into her core. The motion rocked her forward into my pussy and her tongue plumbed my depths again. Taya's mouth was wet and hot on me, never still as Max filled her with his hardness. I rolled my hips against her face and threw back my head with a cry when the pleasure peaked. Taya moaned and I felt her panting breaths intimately as she joined me in orgasm.

"God, you two are so hot together," I said. "Fuck her, Max!"

His fingers tightened on his girlfriend's hips, holding Taya as he shoved his slicked cock into her. His blue eyes were riveted to the sight of Taya licking me out. And damn, that was hot, too. If smoke had started pouring from any one of us, I wouldn't have been the least bit surprised.

"Lick her clit," Max told her in a strained voice. "Firmly, up and down."

At his instruction, Taya's tongue made its warm, wet way to my hard little nub and stroked a long line over the most sensitive center of my body.

"Yes!" I cried. "Fuck, yes!"

Taya's arms hooked around my legs and pulled me closer to lick and suck at my clitoris like a piece of candy she was determined to finish. My back arched and I nearly put more dents in Max's workbench. My pussy gushed, leaving shining streaks across Taya's cheeks and my quivering thighs. Max's hips slammed into her ass as I came and his jaw tightened.

"Damn it," Max grunted. "Taya, I'm close."

Her dark eyes went wide and I remembered the condoms from their first night together. I may not have needed to worry about stuff like pregnancy and disease, but most women do.

With an almost pained-sounding moan, Taya straightened and pulled herself off Max's steel-hard dick. My wetness ran down her chin and throat in gleaming lines. Taya grabbed Max and stroked his huge length so fast that tiny drops of her own juices spattered my stomach. And then Max's body went taut and something hotter and thicker splashed against my skin. Cum arced out from his cock so hard that it flew across the space between us and painted my belly in white, running down to pool in my navel.

My head fell back and I just sat there on top of the workbench, panting as Max's spunk rolled down my skin. It felt amazing and I shivered on the verge of another orgasm, but then I was distracted by the incredible wet sounds coming from below me. I sat up to find Taya on her knees in front of Max, naked except for the swirling smudges of black grease all across her lithe body. Her head bobbed over Max's dick, drinking up the slick mixture of his cum and hers.

Taya gave Max one last hard suck, swallowed and looked up at me. I trailed a finger through the pale mess of semen oozing across my stomach and held it out.

"Do you want this?" I asked. "I mean, it's all rightfully yours."

Max offered his hand to Taya and helped her to her feet. She slid in close to me again and caught my finger in her teeth, then sucked it into her mouth. Taya bit the tip gently and I moaned.

When she had lapped up Max's cum from my finger, I sat back once more and Taya leaned in to trace her tongue lightly over my slippery skin. She licked a tightening spiral that raised goosebumps across my body. In and in, until Taya reached my navel. She looked at me with bright, beautiful eyes.

"I dare you to do a shot out of my belly button," I whispered.

Taya swept her hair back and dove in again, drinking up Max's gooey cream from my stomach. When she had tongued the final drops from my navel, Taya straightened and I gave her one last kiss. Her lips tasted like pussy and jizz – probably my favorite flavor combination in the world.

"You're going to need another shower," I said.

Taya looked down at her oil- and pussy-slicked body. She blushed and laughed. "Yeah, I guess you're right."

She scooped her robe up off the floor and inspected it. The pink fabric was miraculously clean, considering what it had just been through. Taya draped it over her arm, threw a coquettish wink over one shoulder and then headed for the stairs. Max and I admired Taya's firm backside with each step until she was gone.

"I think we've unleashed her kinky side," I said with a grin. "You're welcome."

"I don't suppose you can stay here with us?" Max asked. "We might not get any sleep, but..."

I shook my head. "No, I'd better head home."

"Are you sure, Lil?"

"Yeah. You know me. Besides, this was really fun, but I doubt that Taya plans to make it a regular thing. She's going to want you all to herself."

"Maybe," said Max.

He smiled a little and dimples appeared on his flushed cheeks. I kissed one of them lightly.

"She should," I told Max, then smacked his ass. "So get up there and make Taya's shower interesting."

Max's blush was scarlet, but his cock was swiftly rising again. He kissed my tangled red hair. "The keys to your 110 are on my desk in the office."

"Thanks, Max."

He followed Taya out of the garage and back upstairs. I gave him a minute or two while I found the lights in the downstairs office, retrieved my keys, and then crept up to the apartment. To judge by the mingled sounds of cascading water and deep moans, Max had already joined Taya in the shower. I grabbed my clothes and purse, then quietly let myself out.

Chapter
FOUR

*A*fter a shower of my own and then a few hours sleep back home in my downtown condo, I was in the i10 once more and weaving my way through the thin veil of silver fog and cranky early-morning commuters. It felt great to be driving my i10 once more. The car handled perfectly. I patted the steering wheel and mentally thanked Max again for fixing her up.

But I wasn't on my way back to my friend's garage. I got off the freeway and wound my way out along the narrowing roads outside the city until the i10's tires crunched over the gravel of the College driveway. I stopped in front of the big iron gates and waved to one of the stone gargoyles perched on the posts. A moment later, the gates swung smoothly open and I drove through.

I parked beneath the spreading branches of the huge oak out front. The tree's tightly furled buds were bursting into miniature green fireworks of leaves and the sprawling gardens of the College were bright even in the pale morning light. A few robed figures were already picking their way through the extensive herb gardens, pruning and collecting.

A pair of wizards stood beside the pond, deep in discussion. I still had enough delicious sex power after last night to recognize

Dorian Vandi and one of the apprentice wizards, Zane Colton, even through the fog. Not enough to hear what they said, though. I waved, but I don't think either of them saw me. Dorian shook his head and Zane turned away, frowning. One after the other, the two wizards walked off in the direction of the bronze-domed observatory.

I pushed my way through the heavy oak door of Dresden Hall, the largest and most prominent of the ivy-cloaked mansions on the College campus. I made my way across the marble-floored foyer and down the right-hand hallway, lined along one side by a row of shining suits of medieval armor. On the opposite wall hung the old-fashioned corkboard covered in a hundred pieces of paper, many of them yellowed at the edges and written in languages or codes that I couldn't even guess at. But the bounties were always posted in English.

A knee-high little figurine squatted under the bounty board. It was reddish brown and had rough, blunt features. A homunculus – Sabra's specialty. A pair of black stones were pressed into the clay of its face to make eyes and they flicked across the board.

I pulled off my leather jacket and dropped it over the homunculus' head. Sabra used much larger versions of the same constructs to corner and capture her bounties. She didn't even have to come check the board herself. Sabra's homunculus struggled under my jacket – they're not terribly bright – and I stepped past to examine the board.

I paced the length of the hall, chewing my lower lip and scanning over the pages. I wasn't sure exactly what I was looking for, but *something* had messed up Vijay's car. Something supernatural.

There was a new bounty at the end of the board. I stopped and frowned. A sizable reward in gold for... a dryad? No, that couldn't be right. Dryads were graceful, peaceful creatures. You see, when a hippie loves a tree very much, they share a special hug and you get a dryad. Or something like that.

In nearly a decade of hunting monsters, I'd never before seen a reward offered for a dryad. They're sweet, pretty and harmless, but the bounty listing said that this one was roaming the city and... holy shit. She was raping people. At least seven of them in the last week – one each night.

Okay, dryads were kind of famous for seducing men, but not like this. And according to the hand-written bounty poster, this dryad had attacked several women, too. What the hell?

Suddenly the fucked up car in Max's shop made sense. Dryads could control trees and plants. The splinter of wood must have been from roots, which would have attacked it from below. I remembered Max saying that his customer, Vijay, wouldn't tell him anything about what happened. Too many rapes go unreported, including by men.

And even if Vijay told the police who did it, there was no way the cops would believe that some kind of magical tree lady attacked him.

Or it was entirely possible that the College already knew about Vijay's encounter and he was one of the seven victims – in which case, High Magus Myrdon must have ordered some of his subordinate wizards to swoop in and scrub out Vijay's memory. Was that what Dorian and Zane had been talking about? If the mortal mainstream news got ahold of verifiable information that some dryad was sexually assaulting citizens, it would raise all sorts of dangerous questions about magic and supernatural shit.

Poor Vijay. I'd never met the guy, but I couldn't help feeling bad for him. One more to put on this renegade dryad's tab.

The bounty was marked *urgent* in ornate red handwriting. The longer this dryad ran around raping humans, the harder it would be to keep it quiet and the harder it would be to protect people.

I snapped a quick photo of the poster on my phone to reference later. The College didn't send out email alerts for bounties, so I had to make my own copies.

"Get this thing off me!" the homunculus shrilled from the floor. Its voice sounded like Sabra's, but came out small and squeaky, like she had taken a hit of helium. I grabbed my jacket up off the squirming little clay man and pulled it on again. It was time to go. I had work to do.

Outside Dresden Hall, the fog was beginning to burn off, but wasn't quite gone yet. It swirled around my feet as I half-jogged back in the direction of my car, wondering where to start my hunt. I didn't know very much about dryads... Generally, I dealt with the dangerous sorts of supernatural shit that lurks in the shadows, but that had never included a dryad before.

Something glided across the misty surface of the pond a hundred yards away – another human shape, but there was nothing crude about this one. She stood tall and slender as a willow tree, dressed in a flowing white gown. Blonde hair so pale that it was nearly silver fell to her waist in a cascade of ringlets.

I changed direction midstep and ran toward the pond, waving. "Evaine!"

She turned toward me and walked across the water to the shore. No sooner had Evaine's bare feet hit the grass than I threw my arms around her neck and pulled her down into a long kiss. My teacher's lips were soft and cool. Her gentle fingers brushed my cheek as she returned my kiss.

"Lily," she said when I finally released her. "It's a pleasure to see you again."

"I missed you, too," I answered breathlessly. "Are you here about the dryad?"

Evaine frowned. The warm spring breeze tugged at her long white dress and the rippling edges seemed lost in the fading mist, like she wasn't quite real.

"I know nothing about a dryad," Evaine said in her beautifully, arcanely accented voice. "I came to speak with Vincent. Shadows are stirring on Avalon once more."

"Shadows? Like... like the one that came after me and Kalen last year?"

Evaine nodded. "Yes. Avalon is the intersection of all worlds. Even those who cannot set foot in the human world may cast shadows on the island across all realms. One of those worlds is the fae realm, however... Tell me about this dryad."

"Fae realm?" I asked. As usual, Evaine's mind moved just a little faster than I could immediately follow. She always kept me on my toes. I thought for a moment. "Does that mean that dryads are fairies?"

"They are. They were wild creatures once, but that was long ago. Humans have tamed many of the world's forests and the dryads that make their home in such places have become more civilized, as well. They have lived peacefully under the law of the fairy king and queen for many centuries."

"Really?" I asked. "Well, we've got one somewhere in the city that's running around assaulting people."

Evaine's frown deepened and her perfect pink pout just begged to be kissed. If we were back at my place, I might have done exactly that and made dryads our pillow talk. But I settled for walking with Evaine through the damp green grass in the direction of the observatory.

"Each dryad is bound to her tree," Evaine said. "Her tree is not only her home, but her very soul. The dryad of an oak is bold and strong. Hazel dryads are wise. But the dryads are Seelie fairies. Not even the dryad of the coldest northern fir is brutal enough to attack a human. Something is wrong."

"Like this one's gone rogue, maybe?" I suggested. "She's raping human men and women. At least seven of them that the College knows about."

Evaine stopped walking and her fine silver-blonde brows drew down. Oh good, I wasn't the only one who thought that was especially fucked up.

"That makes no sense," Evaine said in a soft voice. "Dryads require human seed to bear new daughters. But they do not rape men and have no use at all for mortal women."

"I'm going to stop her, but the bounty posting doesn't give a description or a location. How am I supposed to find this dryad? I can't exactly run around the city just hoping she'll decide to jump my bones."

"No," Evaine agreed. "But the center of any dryad's world is her tree. Find her tree and you will find the dryad."

"But there are thousands of trees in the city," I protested. "Millions if you go east into the mountains. How am I supposed to find one dryad's tree in all of that?"

I remembered what Max had told me, that his client's car was towed up from Mission Beach in Gates Park. Maybe I could start there, but the park was massive. By the time I knocked on every tree to see which one had a crazy dryad living in it, she could hurt a lot more people. Damn it...

Evaine squeezed my shoulder gently and I looked up at her.

"There may be a way to speed your search," she said.

"Yeah?"

"The dryads were once a wilder sisterhood than they are now."

I nodded. Yeah, Evaine had said something about that, how humans taming the forests had changed the dryads, too. Made them more civilized and Seelie.

"In those days – which were before even my time – the fairy queen required a token from the dryads to symbolize her dominion over them. So they gave to the queen a ring of living green wood that granted its wearer the ability to find the tree of any dryad."

I whistled. "Wow, that's a hell of a gift. I bet the fairy queen liked that little trinket."

"Indeed she did," Evaine said. She nudged me lightly and we resumed walking across the College toward the observatory. "But the ring was stolen many years ago."

"Oh," I sighed. "Well... fuck."

"Do not despair just yet, Lily. There may yet be hope in acquiring the ring and using it to discover this dryad before she can harm more innocents."

I wasn't so sure. Finding a stolen ring sounded even more problematic than finding the dryad. At least I knew the dryad was somewhere in the city. But Evaine gave me a sidelong glance and a sly smile.

"The ring's location remains a mystery, true... The thief who stole it from his own queen, however, was anything but humble about the deed."

I blinked. "A fairy thief? An arrogant one? You can't mean–"

"Kalen Silverwind," Evaine finished. "The very man who stole *The Gates of Avalon* from the College."

I'll admit that I jumped up in the air and clapped. "Yes! And Kalen's spent nearly six months stuck in some kind of magical prison for that, right? He's got to be getting lonely."

"I believe there was talk of a visit when you saw Kalen last," Evaine said in her cultured voice. "Perhaps it is time to make good on that promise."

Chapter FIVE

"I want access to Kalen Silverwind," I said.

I stood in the High Magus' personal office, which was tucked away into the back of the College observatory. Vincent Myrdon sat on the other side of a desk so vast that you could have used it as an emergency helipad. If it weren't already covered in stacks of books, at least.

The most powerful wizard in North America steepled his fingers and regarded me evenly. One of his eyebrows rose up toward his sharply angled gray hairline. I gulped and barely managed to hold his stare. Vincent shifted his gaze to Evaine and scowled.

"You've been speaking to Lilith," he said. "Again."

Evaine nodded. "I have. Strange things are happening in this world. Lily will discover many truths."

Vincent did something I've rarely seen before – he looked away. The High Magus closed his eyes and rubbed at them like he was tired. For a moment, he looked almost like any other aging human man. But when Vincent raised his eyes to mine again, they were as hard as jade.

"Very well, Lilith. You may speak to Kalen and attempt to secure his assistance. This dryad must be found and stopped," he said, then held up one long finger. "However, we still need him. You have no authority to bargain with Kalen. You cannot pardon the fairy or commute his sentence."

I shrugged. "Fine. I just want to talk to him."

Vincent opened one of the drawers in his massive desk and withdrew a heavy ring of keys that looked like something out of a fantasy movie. He stood and circled the desk to the office door, then stuck one of the old-fashioned keys into the lock. Vincent gave it a twist and I wondered what he was doing. The door was already unlocked – Evaine and I had walked right in.

The High Magus pulled the key out again, metal scraping on metal, and pocketed the ring. I gave Evaine a bewildered look. She just smiled at me and cocked her head in the direction of the door. Vincent turned the handle and opened it.

The observatory was gone. It was still early morning, but the sky outside Vincent's office was now a smoky, swirling gray shot through with ribbons of midnight blue, blood red and deep indigo. The colors swirled and eddied like a dark aurora over a great chasm. *Chasm* was definitely the right word. This was no little ravine that you could jump a dirt bike over. This thing fell away into shadows so deep and distant that even my enhanced senses couldn't see to the bottom. It made the Grand Canyon look like a drainage ditch.

A single bridge stretched out from the door and across the vast depths. It seemed about as substantial as a strand of spaghetti against that drop. Vincent gestured toward the open door and the bridge beyond. I looked back at Evaine again.

"Are you coming?" I asked.

"No, Lily. This is not my task," she told me, shaking her head.

"Follow me, Lilith," said Vincent. "I will return shortly, Lady. And then we will talk."

The High Magus bowed a little perfunctorily to Evaine and then stepped through his office door. I gave Evaine a tight hug in case she was gone when I got back – she's a mistress of that whole mysteriously disappearing thing – and then followed Vincent out onto the bridge.

He set a brisk pace. The bridge was wider than I first thought, wide enough that I could have driven my i10 down the center. It felt sturdy under my feet, but I still followed close behind Vincent. My sex powers are pretty awesome, but they didn't let me fly and I wasn't at all sure that the chasm stretching out below us even had a bottom.

"Where are we?" I asked, trotting to keep up with Vincent.

"Our prison," he answered shortly. "It's called the Tower."

"But where is this place? Are we in Siberia or something?"

It should have taken us all day to cross the miles-long bridge, but when I glanced back, we were already halfway across. There had to be all kinds of magic at work here. The High Magus slowed a little until I was walking beside him.

"We are no longer on Earth," he said.

"What... like another planet?"

"No. This realm was crafted by the Castle many centuries ago. The Tower can only be reached by means of certain keys. We keep here those who are too dangerous to hold anywhere on Earth."

"Another realm? Like the Nether, where the demons are?"

"This is much smaller, but yes," Vincent answered. "The Nether is an entire world unto itself, like our own."

"Madu Tau called it the Eternal Dark."

"The Nether has many names, few of them pleasant. It is the realm of demons."

The High Magus didn't break stride, but looked out of the corner of his eye at me. What did he see there? An employee? Maybe an ally? Or just a half-demon girl that he could never really trust?

I turned my attention forward again. Something was looming up through the murky twilight in front of us. A mountain rose from the depthless shadows, a single steep crag topped in a vast tower built out of dark volcanic-looking stone. Thousands of arched windows ringed the tower and glowed with flickering yellow light. The bridge on which we walked led right to the prison tower.

"Wow," I said.

The Tower appeared no less substantial than the mountain it was built on top of. If this was the College's jailhouse, then I shuddered to contemplate the supermax prison of the sealed Nether and the horrors it contained.

"So the College and the Castle and... the Tower?" I asked. "Creativity isn't exactly the wizards' strong suit, is it?"

Vincent stopped and narrowed his eyes at me, trying to gauge if I was mocking him. It wasn't easy, but I managed not to crack. The High Magus scowled at me for a moment before he resumed walking. As soon as he wasn't looking, I grinned and followed.

It wasn't cold in the Tower's strange little pocket realm – which felt weird, being this high up. But it wasn't warm, either, and the air was absolutely still. No wind tugged at my hair. I couldn't even smell the earthy scent of the stone. Were the bridge, mountain and tower really built out of stone at all... or just something that *looked* like stone?

We were already approaching the far end of the bridge. If the Tower had cast a shadow, Vincent and I would have been walking into it. Another door was set into the vast base, so wide that I could have dragged a fully transformed werewolf through. And flanking that door sat the Tower's guards.

Sphinxes. They weren't carved out of stone like on a postcard from Egypt, but huge and beautiful flesh-and-blood creatures that stood more than twice my height. Part human and part lion, with wings spreading out from their shoulders long enough to shade a soccer field between them.

The pair of sphinxes – one male, one female – were almost unbearably bright against the dark stone of the Tower. Their lustrous fur was golden and their wings brilliant blue-green like the feathers of a peacock. Their thick hair was the same color and the male sphinx sported a braided emerald beard. While their front limbs ended in something more like paws than hands, their chests were well-built and far more human – except for their shining bronze skin.

Vincent and I stopped before the door and two pairs of large, gleaming sapphire eyes turned down to stare. Since the sphinxes were only part lion, would it still be bestiality if I admitted that I kind of wanted to fuck them?

"What are they doing here?" I whispered to the High Magus. "Sphinxes are Egyptian, right? Doesn't that mean they belong to the djinni?"

"My sister and I were born in Kemet," the male sphinx rumbled like a rockslide. I figured that *Kemet* must mean Egypt. "But we belong to no one."

"The Merlinic order made us a better offer," added the female. Her voice was more melodic than her brother's, but still so deep that I felt it in my bones.

"Let me guess," I said. "Gold? Lots and lots of gold?"

"No." Her face may have been human, but her grin was feline. "Riddles."

"The Merlinic wizards are more interested in mysteries than the djinni," said the male.

Both sphinxes turned their eyes to the High Magus, who met their gaze and considered for a moment.

"The one who makes me does not need me. The one who buys me does not want me. The one who uses me never sees me," Vincent said. "What am I?"

"A coffin," the female sphinx answered promptly.

"Although," said her huge brother, "the answer could also be a sarcophagus."

"Semantics. The only difference is cultural," his sister sniffed delicately.

Vincent raised a finger. "Not so. Coffins are the final resting place of a body, while a sarcophagus is believed to be a home to the *ka*. And so, in a sense, the *ka* of a dead man would see its sarcophagus often."

The sphinxes looked at each other and rumbled. Only when I saw their long, gilded tails lashing lazily back and forth did I realize that the deep sound like an oncoming storm was the two huge creatures purring. I guess the mages' obsessive study of... well, everything... proved occasionally useful.

The sphinxes let us pass and the great stone door of the Tower swung open at our approach. Vincent guided me into a wide gray corridor lined at intervals with burning torches like something out of a Dungeons and Dragons game. Well, I supposed that we *were* technically in a dungeon. And knowing the College, I wouldn't have been at all surprised to learn that there was a dragon somewhere in this mountain.

Vincent and I walked up a steep spiral staircase in uncomfortable silence. He cleared his throat once as if to speak, but the quiet just stretched on. And on. By the time we had climbed a few levels, I almost missed the bridge and its daunting view down into nothingness.

I wondered why Vincent was bothering to do this himself. Surely the High Magus of the College had better things to do than show his least favorite bounty hunter around a magical prison. He could have ordered one of the other wizards to do it or left me to fend for myself. Was this dryad job really that important?

If Zane or even Dorian had been there, I might have passed the time flirting and teasing, but Vincent Myrdon was so... unapproachable. And that was putting it mildly. I doubted even my ability to pry the High Magus' lips open with innuendo and cleavage.

"Here," Vincent said at last.

I nearly ran right into the austere old wizard's back before I realized we were no longer climbing. Vincent had stopped at a door and held it for me. We stepped through into a curved hallway. The inner wall was lined in wooden doors and more glowing torches. The outer wall was mostly tall, narrow arched windows that looked out across the ethereal silver-gray sky and the bridge far, far below. Even the massive sphinxes seemed like winged kittens from this height. Vincent and I had been climbing for a while, but not *that* long. I guessed that the Tower's strange distance-shrinking magic was at work again, just like on the bridge.

I turned to the nearest door. It was thick and made of some kind of dark, reddish wood. A small window with a sliding metal shutter was closed at the top. So the mages could look in on their prisoners without opening up the door, I supposed.

"Is Kalen in here?" I asked.

I pulled back the shutter, expecting a dank stone cell, maybe with a cot and a bucket. But on the other side of the door was something much more like a well-sized hotel room. There was a bed, a desk with a potted plant sitting beside it. A few paintings even adorned the walls.

Something moved on the desk. A large glass pitcher stirred and then the water inside rose up, pouring itself into the shape of a man. As the transparent features solidified into black hair and shockingly blue eyes, Adähr smirked at me.

"Lily," said the nix. "I knew you would come for me."

"I couldn't stay away," I told him breathlessly. "I think about you all the time. I need you, Adähr... Oh, wait. No, I don't."

I snapped the little window closed and turned back to see Vincent frowning at me. I shrugged.

"We have a history," I said by way of explanation.

Vincent sighed and then gestured me further along the curving hallway until we stopped at another door that looked identical to Adähr's. The High Magus put his hand against it and murmured something I couldn't understand. A lock thunked inside, but he kept his hand on the wood, holding it closed.

"This door will open for you, but not for Kalen," said Vincent. "The fairy is bound in iron to prevent him from using his magic. Do not remove those bindings, Lilith, and be careful."

"I can handle Kalen," I assured the High Magus. "Trust me. You know, as much as you can."

Vincent held the door shut and eyed me a moment longer, then nodded and stepped back.

"You're not going to stick around, are you?" I asked, suddenly nervous. As Taya could now attest, I sometimes enjoyed an audience, but I didn't want Vincent Myrdon watching me at work.

"No," he said. "I should return to speak with the Lady."

We stared awkwardly at each other until Vincent finally turned away and strode off around the curve of the Tower hallway, leaving me alone outside Kalen's cell. I combed my fingers through my hair and momentarily lamented that I wasn't wearing something sexier than jeans and a tank top, which I had chosen to take advantage of the blooming spring warmth. It wasn't exactly lingerie, but I would manage – I don't depend on accessories to make men stop thinking with the big head.

The door swung soundlessly open at my approach, and then shut just as smoothly behind me when I stepped through. Inside, Kalen's prison was much like Adähr's: a bed and desk, a full bookshelf with a lamp hanging from a hook beside it and an armchair below. Kalen Silverwind, Unseelie fairy and master thief, lounged sideways in the chair with his long legs angled over one padded arm and his wings draped across the other. A book lay open in his lap.

"That's not *The Gates of Avalon*, is it?" I asked.

Kalen looked at me and smiled, then closed his book and held it up. The man on the cover had airbrushed abs and a face entirely cropped out of view.

"You must be really bored," I noted.

"You have no idea," Kalen said.

Manacles of black wrought iron encircled his wrists and their chain clattered as he replaced the romance novel on the bookshelf.

"How're the wizards treating you?" I asked.

"Not badly. I've certainly been in far worse places."

The fairy stretched in his chair. He seemed to be doing well in captivity. Kalen was still whip-thin and lithely muscled. His bright violet hair was longer than the last time I had seen him and now curled slightly against the golden skin of his neck. The shirt that the College had given Kalen was tailored so that his iridescent dragonfly wings could flutter freely.

"I am, however, growing rather tired of the wizards asking me about *The Gates of Avalon*." Kalen cocked his head at me. "Is that why you're here, Lily? Some new attempt at persuasion?"

"No," I said. "But if you're so tired of the questions, you could always answer them."

A haunted expression crossed Kalen's sharp, foxy face and his violet eyes narrowed.

"You're still afraid of him," I said. It wasn't a question. "The one who hired you and the shadow he cast after us. He wasn't from Earth, was he?"

"You say that like you're *not* afraid. You should be, Lily. He didn't so much hire me as... coerce me. And if you knew anything about him, you would stop asking for more."

"Hey, we would if you would just tell us who he was." I shook my head before Kalen could argue yet again. "Never mind. *The Gates of Avalon* job isn't what I'm here about, anyway. I want something else."

Kalen's amethyst eyes glittered. He turned in the armchair to face me, leaning forward to make room for his elegant wings and resting his elbows on his knees. The chain of his manacles dangled between them and couldn't help but make me think of something else that dangled between the Unseelie thief's legs. I licked my lips at the thought.

"Oh yes?" Kalen asked. "And what's that?"

"You stole something from the fairy queen," I said. "A ring. I need to know where it is now."

He arched a perfect purple-blue eyebrow. "The dryad's ring?"

"Yeah, that's the one."

Kalen considered for a moment, then spread his gossamer dragonfly wings carefully and leaned back in his chair. His smile had returned and was quickly becoming a sly grin. I swear his pointed ears twitched.

"Oh, I remember it," Kalen said. "Until *The Gates of Avalon*, that ring was the most dangerous job I've ever taken."

"So you were working for someone then, too? Who was it?"

"Why should I tell you?" Kalen asked.

"Protecting the identity of *another* client? Damn it, Kalen!"

The fairy thief laughed musically. "Oh no, I'll tell you who has the ring. He's not like the one who sent me after the book. I have a strong sense of survival, Lily, not honor. I'll give you exactly what you want. But first, you have to give me what *I* want."

"I can't release you," I told Kalen. "And I'm not allowed to reduce your sentence or anything like that."

"Oh, I know. This ordeal with *The Gates of Avalon* is far too important for the wizards to let me go just yet. But it's boring up here in the Tower, Lily. And I'm lonely."

Kalen stood in a quick, fluid motion and took my hands in his. I gasped a little and let the fairy pull me into a kiss. I breathed in his scent: honey and clover. Kalen's tongue moved a graceful dance over mine, taunting and promising all at once.

"I don't suppose you'll take off the iron," he murmured against my lips. "So we can do this right?"

"Not a chance," I whispered back.

"Can't blame me for trying."

No, I couldn't. But I also couldn't risk being the one who let Kalen Silverwind free. I grabbed the chain binding the fairy's wrists and pressed him slowly, inexorably back against the nearest wall. Kalen's eyes widened when I removed the lantern from its metal bracket and set it on a shelf.

"What are you doing, Lily?" he asked.

"Giving you what you want. But I'm not going to risk you slipping away from me."

I hoisted Kalen's arms up and hooked the chain of his manacles over the bracket. His wings splayed like shimmering murals across the stone wall behind him. The fairy gave me a quizzical look.

"What? You know I don't mind handcuffs," I told him.

Kalen grinned at me. I took a moment to admire the sight of him hanging from the wall, but quickly decided that it would be a lot more fun to admire the irreverent fairy thief without clothes. Kalen's shirt was tied along the sides so it could be pulled on over his wings and chains, so I unlaced it impatiently and tossed the useless garment away across the nearby armchair.

Better. I slid my hands up Kalen's lean chest and then raked my fingers down across all of that perfectly smooth butterscotch skin. The nails left faint red tracks in their wake and Kalen let out a soft hiss of pleasure.

I grabbed the waist of the fairy's plain linen pants and then pulled them down his long legs. The floor of Kalen's cell was strewn with thick carpets, so he wasn't wearing shoes, which made my job that much easier. Good, I was in a hurry.

When I had Kalen stripped completely naked, I stood back, biting one fingertip as I properly admired the view. Indigo and gold all over, skin like fine golden silk over svelte muscle, and his delicious cock rising swiftly before my eyes.

"Lily?" Kalen asked.

I raised my eyes to his bright violet ones. His lust was sharp and hot. We both wanted this badly and as much as I loved watching the long, graceful curve of Kalen's growing erection, I wasn't going to get it inside me just staring.

So I kicked off my shoes and slithered out of my jeans. I left the tank top for last. When I pulled it up and off, Kalen breathed a deep sigh at the sight. It was warm enough out in the real world that I wasn't wearing a bra underneath. I cupped the softness of my bare breasts and squeezed them together. Kalen's eyes were riveted to me. I bowed my head to lick lightly at my stiffening nipples and when I looked up again, Kalen was straining against the iron manacles. His lust was almost blinding in its brilliance.

I closed the distance I had created between us and ran one finger along his hardened length. Kalen groaned. His cock was searing steel under my touch.

"How long has it been since you got laid, Kalen?" I asked, quite frankly taken aback by the intensity of his reaction.

"Nearly six months. Since the College put me in here," gasped the thief. "Fuck me, Lily, and I'll tell you what you want to know."

His dick throbbed in my hand and I felt the rising pulse of wet heat inside me. This was going to be the best trade ever – I would have fucked Kalen for free. I remembered the sweet taste of the fairy's spunk all too well and badly wanted more. I stripped off my panties and held them up. They were soaked right through. I ran the sopping lace over Kalen's lips. He groaned again and bit my panties out of my hand. Damn, he *really* wanted this.

Kalen wasn't the only one. I'd enjoyed every minute of playing with Max and Taya the night before, but now I ached to feel a hard cock inside me.

I gave my breasts another firm squeeze, then slid my hands down my belly and between my legs. I lifted one foot and planted it on the arm of the reading chair. Spreading the soft pink of my slit open, I speared two fingers into my dripping hole.

"You hear that?" I asked. "How wet I am?"

"Mmm," Kalen said through a mouthful of my panties.

I worked my fingers in and out of my pussy, filling the room with the wet sounds of my desire. The scents of clover and honey grew stronger as the deep rosy-golden flush spread across Kalen's chest. He pulled and strained against the iron of his bonds. The crown of his cock pressed into my stomach and even that brief contact made pearlescent precum ooze from the tip. It traced a shimmering line across my pale skin.

Before I could get off, I withdrew my fingers. Not yet. Kalen had been waiting for the better part of six months. I could manage a *little* bit of waiting. But you may have figured that I don't exactly have the patience of a saint. Or anything else a saint might have. I ran one of my fingers around the dip of my navel, where Kalen's aching cock had left its slippery mark, then sucked his sweetness off my finger with a low moan. It was just as delicious as I remembered.

Wetness rolled warm and slick down my thighs at the taste. Okay, I was done waiting.

I pivoted up on the balls of my feet to put my back to Kalen's smooth, lean chest. Every inch of him was feverishly hot against my skin – especially the burning brand of his cock where it pressed insistently into my ass. I rubbed my body in slow strokes against Kalen's, then rose on my toes, bending slightly at the waist to angle my hips.

"Mmmm!" Kalen said through the panties clenched in his teeth.

I wasn't gagged, but I said the same thing when the head of his dick spread and pierced me. I straightened and reached behind me, hooking an arm around Kalen's neck as I sank down onto him. The Unseelie thief's cock was far longer than my fingers and came to rest deep inside my body. The pressure of penetration sent pleasure flaring through me.

Kalen finally spat my thong out and his groans were much louder without a mouthful of lace to muffle them. I rose and fell on my toes, lifting and dropping myself on the fairy thief's long prick. I swirled my hips in tiny circles with each thrust, brushing the soft curve of my ass over his taut stomach.

The iron chain rattled as Kalen pulled against his manacles again. He made a low, melodic sound of frustration. But not even iron could slow him down for long. Kalen trailed hot kisses along the side of my neck until he reached my ear.

"More, Lily," he said, running his tongue around the rim of my ear to punctuate his demand. "Make me cum and I'll tell you who has the ring."

I almost didn't care about the information as I plunged myself back onto Kalen's smooth caramel cock, though I knew better than to say so. He stirred and stroked deep inside me, making my breath come faster and faster. The fairy's wings fluttered against the wall as he stared down at my bouncing breasts and hard pink nipples. Kalen pushed his hips up to meet my thrusts and I writhed on his cock in a quickening dance of urgent desire.

"Fuck!" I screamed as my orgasm crashed over me.

My head fell back against Kalen's shoulder while I cried out my pleasure. Wetness gushed down my thighs. He bit my ear.

"More," Kalen gasped into it. "More, Lily!"

The thief had his price and I was more than happy to pay. So I reached down with my free hand between my trembling legs. My fingers brushed my peaked little clitoris and I let out a moan. The ecstasy burning through my nerves jumped a few degrees and I slid my hand back until I could feel the hardness of Kalen where he penetrated me. I ran my fingers over the slicked heat of his shaft.

"Yes," Kalen hissed. "By the Queen, yes...!"

How irreverent was the Unseelie thief that he swore in the name of the very monarch he had robbed? I grinned up at Kalen. The fairy panted and sweat shone in his indigo hair. I caressed his rigid cock again and felt him shiver against my back. With my thumb, I rubbed my clitoris in tight circles while my fingers traced lines of blazing sensation around the base of Kalen's dick.

I bounced on the balls of my feet and fucked myself on Kalen's long cock. Tightening my arm around his neck, I angled my hips and let Kalen and his chains support most of my weight so I could take another inch of his length. The fingers of my other hand were now stroking my dripping pussy as much as Kalen's dick. I slid and writhed against his sweat-slicked chest, gasping and moaning. It was too much.

"Kalen!" I cried.

I stiffened under the onslaught of pleasure and my pussy tightened on Kalen's cock, milking the sensitive head and making the fairy gasp. His hips hammered forward and drove his dick into me. I craned my neck up and Kalen kissed me, pouring months of pent-up lust into my overwhelmed body. His gossamer dragonfly wings beat a soft, rapid drumbeat against the wall that matched my racing heart as he pumped himself frantically deep into my streaming slit.

Kalen buried himself to the hilt inside me. His cock throbbed and then I felt the thick, liquid heat of his cum gushing into me. Shit, it seemed to go on forever, Kalen unleashing one hard spurt after another until my pussy was overflowing. Everything went hot and sticky between my legs and I swore that I could *taste* how sweet it was. My senses spiraled off into bliss, every part of my body giving itself over to the peak of ecstasy, and I clung to Kalen by reflex alone. I came on his pulsing dick until I had taken every drop.

Finally, Kalen sagged back against the stone wall of his cell. I pulled myself off of his cock and wobbled, feeling his massive load dripping from my well-fucked pussy. A thick drop of shimmering, iridescent white rolled down my leg like liquid opal and then spattered to the carpet.

There was no way I was letting a sweet treat like this go to waste. I glanced around the room and saw another water pitcher on the desk, smaller than the one in Adähr's cell, but probably not containing a nix. A few staggering steps brought me close enough to grab the glass sitting beside it.

I put one foot up on the desk and held the cup to my pussy. The glass was cool against my hot skin. I let Kalen's load ooze from my sensitive slit, shivering and gasping all over again as his gooey, slippery jizz dripped out of me. With a moan, I squeezed – I have some truly impressive muscles down there, especially when I've just been fucked – and spurted the final drops of Kalen's spunk into the cup.

When I was finished, there was about a finger of shining cum at the bottom of the cup. I lifted it up to show Kalen, swirled it once around the glass, and then knocked the whole thing back with a single long gulp. It was creamy and sweeter than honey, with the sharp tang of my own juices around the edge. Delicious.

I replaced the empty glass on the desk, licked my lips and then turned back to Kalen. His smooth body was shiny with sweat and the fairy's purple-blue hair was a tousled mess. He leaned against the wall, panting and grinning.

"Wow, Lily," he said. "You almost make being in prison worth the trouble."

I winked. "Damned right. So who has that ring you stole?"

"What makes you think I'll keep my promise?" Kalen asked, returning my wink. "I got what I wanted and you seem to forget that I'm not exactly trustworthy."

I put my hands on my hips. I don't like being stiffed. I mean, I *do*, but not like this. Though I wasn't really surprised. Kalen was right – he was a thief and an Unseelie fairy, and I knew that. Unfortunately for Kalen, I didn't have much more in the way of a sense of honor than he did. Once I take a bounty, I'll do just about anything to catch it.

"Yeah?" I asked. "Well, if you're not going to tell me what I want to know, then I might have to start making shit up."

Kalen cocked his head to one side. "Oh? Like what?"

"Perhaps that you almost slipped up, almost told me who sent you after *The Gates of Avalon*. You think the questions have been annoying so far? Just wait until I tell the High Magus you're about to crack. You won't have a moment to yourself."

I sashayed across the room to Kalen and ran a finger down his chest to his half-hard cock. It rose at my touch.

"Or," I purred, "I can tell Vincent that you helped me with this dryad bounty. Then the next time I say that I want to see you about a job, he says *yes* and we get another chance to... visit."

Kalen stared at me, then began to laugh. He inclined his head toward me in respect and his dick rose another inch.

"Ah, Lily," Kalen said. "You're truly an astonishing woman. The man who hired me to steal the ring is named Edward Ashton. Ash. He's half human, like you."

I bet both my eyebrows shot up at that. You don't meet many of those. Most of the weird shit out there can't breed with humans.

"He's not a cambion, is he?" I asked. Surely I would have heard of another half-demon like me.

"No. Half dryad," said Kalen, shaking his head. "Every spring, dryads take human lovers. The female children are true dryads, but the males are only part fairy. Ash is one of those."

"And he has the ring?"

"Yes. Ash traded me a dervish ring for the wooden one." Kalen laughed again, but there was a soft, faraway sound to it this time. "I would have done that job for free. I took the dryads' ring from Titania's chambers while she made love to the king just beyond a curtain of sunset clouds... I even snapped a few pictures."

"You're impossible," I told Kalen while I collected my clothes. "Where is Edward Ashton?"

The fairy shrugged as best he could with his arms chained up over his head. "I gave him the ring years ago. He could have gone anywhere... but his mother's tree is somewhere north of the city. I doubt he's ventured too far from it."

"What's this Ash guy like?" I asked.

"Seelie," Kalen said with lightly mocking disgust in his voice. "Like his mother. Responsible, honorable... Boring. His house is interesting, though. Ash is a collector. I would have robbed him blind years ago if it presented the slightest challenge."

That sounded promising. I nodded to Kalen. "Thanks."

I pulled my clothes on again and checked to make sure my wallet was still in my back pocket. I was pretty certain I had kept track of Kalen's hands the entire time I was in his cell, but you never know with him. When I was satisfied that nothing was missing, I headed for the door. Would the sphinxes demand a riddle on the way out? I hoped not – I hadn't studied any. Maybe they would take a dirty joke instead.

"Uh... Lily?"

I stopped at the door and turned back to Kalen. He waved his hands, making the iron chain rattle above him.

"Want to let me down from here?" he asked.

Chapter
SIX

The sphinxes let me leave the Tower with a pair of regal nods, but no riddle contest. After another weirdly swift trip across the long bridge, I found myself in front of a sheer cliff with a single door set in the sooty black stone. It was unlocked, though, and I stepped through into Vincent Myrdon's office again.

Evaine was already gone, having finished whatever business she had with the High Magus while I was busy fucking Kalen Silverwind's brains out. I guess the disappointment showed on my face because Vincent's brow furrowed so deeply that it looked like the steely gray dagger of his widow's peak was about to stab his nose.

"Did something go wrong?" he asked.

I shook my head. "No. Just hoping Evaine would stick around, I guess. I don't get to see her a lot. Not like I used to, at least."

I realized that I was whining to the High Magus and snapped my mouth shut. But he actually didn't say anything belittling. He just closed the book he had been reading and steepled his fingers. As promised, I reported that Kalen had been a good and forthcoming boy. Vincent nodded his curt approval at the information I had managed to gather.

Vincent recognized the name Kalen had given me. The College wizards kept an eye on all supernaturals, of course. Edward Ashton – or Ash, as he was generally known to the magical community – was a paper manufacturer. Ash owned several hundred acres of woodland in the northeast of the state from which the trees to make his paper were carefully culled. In fact, he had built a house in the woods he owned, up in the mountains about twenty miles outside a town called Pacific Grove.

"I don't suppose I can just call him up?" I asked.

Vincent shook his head. "Ashton is a creature of trees and earth. He has little to do with the human half of his ancestry and values his privacy."

I pulled out my phone and looked up Pacific Grove on a map. It was a bit of a drive, but I checked the time: about ten o'clock in the morning. If I got moving now, I could make it out to Pacific Grove before rush hour.

"Go quickly, Lilith," said Vincent. "We need to stop this dryad. She's attacked most of her victims at night, but she is acting unpredictably and may change her tactics at any time."

"Don't worry, I'll be back by evening," I promised. "And then I'll find that crazy tree-hugger before she hurts anyone else."

———

I stopped briefly by my condo to clean up and change my clothes, choosing a short brown skirt, leather boots and a soft white blouse that I left buttoned low. Maybe earth tones would go over well with a half-dryad man.

While I was in the closet, I also pulled down a duffle bag and then went to the safe in the back. I punched in my code and opened the reinforced steel door to reveal the rows of gleaming gold bars inside. It didn't represent my entire fortune, or even the majority.

But it was valuable and untraceable, so I loaded up a few hundred thousand dollars worth of gold bullion. One way or another, Ash would give me that ring.

I zipped the bag of gold shut, hefted it over my shoulder and made my way quickly back down to the garage. I entered Ash's address into the i10's GPS and set out.

By noon, I was winding my way up into the foothills. As the hills turned into mountains, spring's flowery scent became something sharper, more evergreen. I followed the mountains north through afternoon light that was as thick and golden as honey. I drove past Pacific Grove – a small, old-fashioned town that probably used to be a mining outpost – without stopping. My GPS led me up increasingly steep, narrow roads until the i10 bumped along a single-lane dirt track in the deep green-gray shadows of pine trees.

"You have arrived at your destination," my car said in a calm female voice.

I parked in a relatively clear patch of pine needles and climbed out of the i10. For the moment, I left the gold in my car. The forest was deep and quiet, serene in the slanting rays of afternoon sun. I almost missed the house entirely, but then spotted the glint of light reflecting off of glass and made my way toward it.

Edward Ashton's home was a tall wooden manor, so covered in dozens of floor-to-ceiling windows that I could see right through into the deep forest on the other side. The house sprawled and wound in long hallways between the trees, apparently built around each of them. No wonder I had nearly mistaken it for another part of the forest.

It took a bit of wandering, but I eventually found a carved cedar front door and knocked, then fidgeted as I waited for someone to answer. It was hard to fight the sense of dreamy lassitude up here in the thick amber sunlight. But back in the city, a crazed dryad was getting ready to find her next victim.

At last, the door swung open and a man stood holding the knob.

"Good afternoon," he said. "Are you lost?"

"Edward Ashton?" I asked.

He nodded. Despite being here in his own home, Ash wore functional-looking clothes and sturdy hiking boots, along with a pair of wire-rimmed glasses. His skin was a warm, dark brown that I guessed was the color of an ash tree's wood, and thick black hair curled close to his scalp. His features were broad and handsome, but it was his eyes that arrested my attention. Behind his glasses, they were the bright, vibrant green of new spring leaves.

"Hi, my name is Lily," I said. "I'm a bounty hunter for the College."

Ash's shockingly green eyes were curious. He put his hands in his pockets, but I saw the corded muscles of his arms tensing beneath his wood-hued skin. The half-dryad's tone, however, remained even and polite.

"And what brings one of their bounty hunters to me? There are no werewolves in my mother's forest, or else it would be Mister Rossi knocking on my door."

"You know Stefano?" I asked.

"He helps to keep my woods safe," Ash said with another nod and a small smile flitted across his face. "A handsome young man, if I do say so."

Young? Ash appeared to be somewhere in his thirties, about the same age as Stefano. But dryads lived as long as their trees, Vincent had told me, and even their male offspring were known to live several hundred years. So I supposed that, by comparison, Stefano *was* quite a young man.

And the half-dryad was looking me up and down, too. I felt Ash's interest, warm and inviting as the spring itself. Remember what I said about dryads being pretty notorious for seducing mortal men? They're not succubae or anything, but I guessed that dryads passed something of their appetites on to even their male children. Ash's smile widened and I really wished I had the time to compare half-dryad passion to half-succubus. But I didn't.

"Mister Ashton, I don't want to be rude," I said. "But it was a long drive and I'm in a hell of a hurry."

"Ash, please. You hunters are a rather... grim lot. A bit rough for sorcerers, but I suppose you have to be."

"I'm not a wizard," I said reflexively.

Ash smiled a little. "No. You are a cambion, the daughter of a demon and a mortal. My kind are rare, Miss Quinn, but yours are even more so. You're the first half-demon born since Merlin himself."

"You've heard of me?"

"Of course. I am a collector of rarities and take an interest in anything unique," Ash said, then laughed. "And Mister Rossi has mentioned you many times."

I wondered what Stefano had told the half-dryad about me, but I felt time pressing down on me like a tangible weight.

"Look, I need your help. Kalen Silverwind said he stole a ring from the fairy queen for you. A ring that lets its wearer find any dryad's tree."

Ash's expression went from curious to guarded in an instant. "Surely the College is not in the business of enforcing fae law."

"I'm not trying to get you or Kalen into trouble, but I need to borrow the ring. I'll buy it or rent it or whatever you want. I have to find a certain dryad somewhere near Southport and I need to do it tonight."

Ash had been lounging against the frame of his open front door, but now he straightened up and crossed his arms over his chest. His lust was gone in an instant, snuffed out like a candle. Ash looked over his glasses at me.

"No," he said.

"No?" I repeated, blinking. "What do you mean, *no*?"

"That ring was crafted as an act of submission by the dryads long ago. Things have changed since those days, but the ring's existence remains as a stain upon the honor of my aunts and sisters. I will not give it to you."

Chapter
SEVEN

I sat in Ash's dining room. It was long and wide, with walls covered in so many windows that it barely felt like I was indoors at all. Yellowing sunlight flickered through the overlapping leaves of madrone trees and turned their smooth reddish bark a brilliant copper color.

There were glass cases placed at artful intervals around the dining room, displaying their contents on beds of green velvet. I saw a crown of interwoven branches, still blooming with delicate pink blossoms, laid out beside an intricately inscribed bow. There was a carved idol that looked Greek – *ancient* Greek, not the white marble classical era stuff – next to an elegant wooden bowl.

Wood. Every single thing that Ash collected was made from wood. Of course it was. The half-dryad sat down across the table with a pair of glasses and set one down in front of me.

"Cider," he said. "Try it. I make it myself."

It was the color of the sunlight streaming through the trees and smelled like distilled spring. I turned the glass of cider in my hand and wondered how quickly I could ransack Ash's house for the ring. I didn't like the idea, but I *had* to find that rampaging dryad and stop her.

"I serve the trees," Ash said after taking a long drink from his own glass. "Forests need deadfall and blighted trees removed. I work with my aunts and sisters to make sure that only the right trees are sent to my paper mills, to promote the forest's health."

"Nice deal," I answered flatly. "Not sure why you're telling me, though. I really don't have time for this shit."

I was staring around the room, wondering where Ash kept the dryad's ring. The case behind him held only a graying, rough spar of aged wood that didn't look particularly special. I didn't see the ring, but the house was huge. It could be anywhere. For all I knew, Ash might have even destroyed the thing.

"For the same reason I invited you into my home," he said. "It is proper... and because I have questions. What does the College want with the ring? The Merlinic order and the Seelie court have been allies since the days of Camelot."

Ash set his cider down and looked over his glasses at me. I didn't think the half-dryad could take me in a fight, but had little doubt that Ash would try if he thought for a second that I was going to hurt his trees.

"If you're searching for a dryad, then perhaps I can come with you," Ash offered. "I could help you find her. *Without* the ring."

Kalen was right about the guy being Seelie. Even half-blooded, Ash had a truly impressive sense of honor and duty. But I shook my head.

"Absolutely not," I answered. "Even if you can help me figure out which tree is hers, she'll just rape you and I don't want that shit on my conscience."

"Rape me...?" Ash frowned and adjusted his glasses. "That's ridiculous! Dryads don't rape people."

"Yeah, yeah. I know. Dryads are all sweet and gentle and they fart pretty rainbows," I growled impatiently. I shoved the cider away and narrowed my eyes at Ash. "Look, I've been doing this job for almost nine years and I've never seen a bounty posted on a dryad before. But for some reason, this one is completely off her nut."

"This is just impossible. Pollution can make a dryad sick, but not drive her to rape."

But then Ash hesitated and an uneasy expression crossed his face.

"What?" I asked. "If you have an idea, spit it out. We're on the clock here."

"She may have been... poisoned," Ash said slowly. "Dying before her time. That could be why she's attacking humans – trying desperately to seed before she withers."

"Trees die all the time," I pointed out. "But their dryads don't usually go around raping humans to get knocked up."

"Dryads are as tough as ironwood," Ash agreed. "Nothing humans make is sufficiently toxic to kill them. But a poison terrible enough to be killing a dryad may well drive her to this insanity, too."

"So she's trying to make a little seedling dryad before she dies. But because she's sick, she's insane enough to rape humans to get it done, right? What could make a dryad that sick?"

"Nothing in this world, but perhaps something... demonic?"

"Demonic?" I repeated.

My mouth went dry and I forgot all about the ring. Demonic, like the werewolf curse or... vampire blood.

"But who would poison a dryad?" Ash was saying, shaking his head. "Not even the Unseelie would do such a thing."

"Ah, fuck!" I put my face in my hands and my words came out muffled. "It was me."

Ash understood me just fine, though, and his verdant eyes went wide. "What?"

"I chased down and killed a vampire about a week ago," I said. My stomach knotted up into a painful ball of guilt. "It was raining.

The blood and ashes... washed away. Right into the ground under the willow tree I used to stake him. Would that do it?"

"If that willow tree belonged to a dryad, then... yes."

I stood up. "I don't need that ring anymore. I know where to go. How do I fix this, Ash?"

"If her tree is sick enough to kill the dryad, then the corruption is in her heartwood," Ash answered. His voice was heavy. "Even iron will not do the deed. There is only one thing to do when the blight runs so deep – you must burn it out."

Chapter EIGHT

I raced back through the deep violet twilight as fast as I could. It nearly cost me more time when a cop pulled me over for speeding. I was in such a rush that I didn't even try to flirt my way out of the ticket. If I had taken the time to suck his cock, I'm pretty sure I could have gotten a police escort all the way back home, but I was in one fuck of a hurry.

The dryad's insanity was *my* fault. All of her attacks were my fault, too. This wasn't just a bounty anymore. I had a responsibility to deal with her.

It was dark and getting late by the time I threw the i10 into *park* on the bottom level of my building and practically flew upstairs to my condo. I stripped in record time – and for me, that's saying something – then redressed in a black shirt, pants and boots. As I cinched my hair up into a ponytail, I ducked into the back of my closet, using my elbows to push aside boxes and cases until I found the hatchet shoved in one corner. There wasn't much call for stuff like that in the city – a price tag was still attached to the handle by a plastic tie. I snapped it off.

I thrust the hatchet through my belt and pocketed a lighter from a drawer in the kitchen, then made my way to the elevator and down to the garage again. I ran a few parking spaces to the Alfa Romeo and grabbed the empty gas can from the trunk. The i10 was electric, but the Alfa had a gasoline engine.

There was a gas station around the corner and it was dead quiet at this hour. I swiped my card at an empty pump and held the nozzle in place with my bootheel while I checked the time on my phone. Nearly ten o'clock.

I wasn't sure if I should hope the dryad would be at home in her tree. After offering to come help me – again – Ash admitted that killing her tree would kill the dryad. Burning down her tree would be a hell of a lot simpler without the mad dryad there, but it would also mean she was out grabbing some human and having her way with them. If I were lucky, he or she would be into weird tree-fairy sex. But even in this city, I doubted it.

I tried to console myself that if my vampire-poisoned dryad had already cornered a new hopeful but unwilling father for her seed-ling, it would be the last one. But that thought didn't make me feel any better.

When the gas can was full, I capped it off and jumped back into the i10. I hauled ass with as much speed as I dared out to the coast and Gates Park, then followed The Parkway south to Mission Beach. There was a scenic turnout with a few other vehicles parked overlooking the sea and the slender crescent moon rising up from the dark waves.

I pulled in between two of the cars and climbed out of the i10. The teenage couples inside didn't even look up. I guessed the police didn't hit this spot very often. That served my purposes well – if a cop caught me lugging gasoline and an axe into the park, I would have to do a lot more than flirt to get out of *that* citation.

Through a long, dark break in the late evening traffic, I trotted across the road and up onto the grass of Gates Park. As the moon rose higher into the sky, I circled around south until I found the stream I had jumped over while chasing the vampire. From there, I retraced my steps to the willow grove. The largest tree loomed up out of the creeping silver fog, drooping branches hanging like strands of green hair. The leaves rustled in a soft night breeze.

"I'm so sorry," I said.

I pulled the hatchet from my belt and hefted the gasoline over my shoulder. Tomorrow, there would be a news story about some arsonist hitting Gates Park, but I could live with that.

I pushed my way through the curtain of willow branches and jerked to a stop. A slender woman crouched naked in the branches of her tree. Her skin was the same pale celadon color as moonlight on the willow leaves. Her long hair was silvery-white and there were tiny flowers woven into it. Or maybe they just bloomed there naturally.

"Oh, shit," I whispered.

The dryad stood gracefully, balancing effortlessly on a single bough. Her body was lithe and slim. Willowy. She had small, green-tipped breasts and another soft hint of verdant green between her legs. She stared down at me with eyes the same brilliant jade color as Ash's.

"Who are you?" the dryad asked. Her voice hissed like wind through leaves. "What are you doing here?"

"I'm Lily Quinn," I said. "You're sick and it's my fault. I hunted and killed the vampire that poisoned your tree. I wish I could do more to help you."

My fingers tightened on the hatchet and gasoline. I was nearly out of sexual energy. I really should have fucked Ash or that cop before I came out here, but I had been in a hurry and didn't expect to find the dryad at her tree.

That was my first mistake.

"I am Salix," the dryad said in her soft willow-whisper voice. She cocked her head at me. Her flower-filled white hair slithered around her shoulders and a few petals fell like flakes of snow. "I need you, human."

"Need... me?"

I stared at the branches fanning out around Salix. The curtain of her willow surrounded me, silver and green in the dim moonlight. But I could see the marks of Salix's sickness, curling and blackened leaves shuddering with more ferocity than the ocean breeze could lend.

I was frowning up at the dryad and her tree, not paying attention to the ground at my feet. That was my second mistake. I had seen Vijay's car in the garage and the damage to the undercarriage. I should have been ready.

Roots burst from the damp earth and whipped toward me. I jumped back, but half a day had passed since I fucked Kalen and I wasn't faster than a desperate, demonically poisoned dryad. Strong, flexible roots and vines wrapped around my wrists and ankles, squeezing until I dropped the gas can. Another twist and they wrenched the hatchet from my grasp, too. It bounced away across the grass.

Salix waved her hand and the roots pulled me off the ground, up into the air. I writhed in their grip, but they were too tough for me to break. What the hell? Was the dryad trying to kill me? But then I felt the heat of her lust. It was hot and burned out of control like wildfire.

Oh yeah.

Oh shit.

More green rose up from the earth and dropped from the branches of Salix's willow tree. A long, leafless vine slithered through the grass toward me. It was almost as big around as my wrist and terminated in a rounded tip that looked an awful lot like the head of a cock.

That *definitely* wasn't a normal part of a willow tree.

The dryad's eyes flashed with emerald fire and the thick tendril reared up out of the dew-dampened grass like a snake about to strike. I yanked against the roots binding my wrists and ankles.

There was a snapping sound from somewhere along its woody length, but Salix's tree held me firm.

The ropy green vine twined itself up my calf and then my thigh, winding along my body. I gave a startled gasp as the thing slipped under my shirt. The texture was cool and smooth against my bare skin, slightly rubbery and more like a dildo than a flesh-and-blood cock. I'd be lying if I denied the little shudder of pleasure that coursed through me.

Salix leapt lightly from her branch and caught herself in a net of roots and limbs. They wove themselves into a seat in front of me and the dryad leaned back in their embrace to display her slender, naked body. Despite the danger of my situation, another hot shiver slid up from between my legs. Ash was right – Salix didn't need to hold men down to get into their pants. But the demonic taint that poisoned her tree made her do it anyway. Even without a man.

The dryad spread her legs across her seat of twisting plants, revealing the soft green of her pussy. It was slick and wet, but Salix wasn't just showing off for me. A pair of blunt-tipped tentacles rose from the willow grove and wove through the air toward their mistress. One of them nuzzled at her dripping slit for a moment and then slid inside. The other pressed at the tight emerald pucker of her ass. Salix let out a whorish moan and arched her back as the vine pushed into her anus. My breath caught at the sight.

I didn't have long to feel perversely jealous of the dryad, though. The magical plant cock winding under my shirt flexed, making the fabric strain and then burst. Shreds of black cloth rained down around me. Salix's tentacle moved again, curled under my bra and ripped it off, exposing my bare skin to the warm spring evening.

The cock-headed tendril slithered across my chest, looping over my breasts and then finding the warm, soft cleft between them. The cool crown pushed into my cleavage and Salix moaned. I echoed her helplessly as the tentacle began to thrust up and down against the sensitive skin of my chest.

The green tendrils pumping in and out of Salix mimicked the rhythm and she writhed sinuously in her living seat. I wasn't sure if the dryad was purposefully fucking my tits or if she was just so crazed that she didn't know what she was doing. But Salix's eyes were riveted to the sight of her plants molesting me and with her next cry came the first hot, golden rush of her sexual energy.

Her serpentine plant cock moved faster and faster between my breasts, growing thicker against me. My head fell back and I let out a moan of pleasure. The rising moon had vanished behind the growing gray clouds, but the beginnings of Salix's sexual energy sharpened my vision enough that I could still see clearly.

I didn't need heightened senses to feel Salix's fiery lust building, though. Did she feel what her plants were doing? Was this the dryad fucking me or just her enjoying watching them do it? But the question fell right out of my thoughts as the tentacle thrusting urgently against my chest swelled and then began to gush something thick and pale green across my skin. I didn't think trees – even magical ones – could cum.

The substance felt slippery yet sticky as it dripped down my body, but the dryad's plant cock was still pulsing. Another coiled vine shoved my head from behind, pushing my face closer. I opened my mouth in a gasp and the sap-cum spurted between my lips. I was too veteran a cocksucker to choke, even when surprised, and I swallowed down the mouthful of spunk. It was a strange taste – both salty and sweet, but utterly devoid of the distinctive musk of male semen.

"Ooh," Salix moaned as I gulped down her tentacle's seed.

She arched her back, pushing her small breasts skyward. The dryad's nipples were a deep jade color and just as hard as the gemstone. Her vines tightened around my wrists and ankles.

"Salix, stop!" I said. "This isn't really what you want. Let me go. Let me help you!"

"No!" hissed the dryad.

Her plants jerked my limbs out taut, hanging me spread-eagle before their mistress. More of Salix's cock-headed green tendrils slithered down from the willow branches and reached for me. They curled around my belt and under my pants, tugging until they tore the clothes off my body. The vine that had just painted my tits in seed now ripped away my panties.

The spring evening was warm, but the tendrils winding across my skin raised goosebumps. I opened my mouth to plead with Salix again. Beneath that vampiric taint, she was a fairy of life and earth. Surely she could understand what had to be done. But before I could say a word, the dryad pointed and one of her pale willow tentacles plunged itself into my dripping pussy.

"Oh, fuck!" I screamed out.

The vine shoved deep between my legs and writhed there inside me, twisting and stroking me from within. I squirmed in the tree's grip, not yet strong enough to tear free. The plant cock withdrew a few inches, glistening and wet, until the flared head just barely spread me open. Then it rammed back into my body and my struggling became shaking as the slick length penetrated me over and over. I couldn't help cumming, crying out in helpless pleasure.

Salix sat forward, her lush green lips pursed while she watched. Sinuous vines writhed inside her pussy and ass, making the dryad's lithe body tighten and wetness drip from between her legs. It ran in shiny streams down the twisting plant cocks fucking her and Salix moaned her pleasure in a loud, heedless voice.

Another vine slithered closer, but the sight of Salix writhing in the throes of desperate passion distracted me. The tentacle inside my pussy wriggled until I cried out and before I could clench my jaw shut, the new vine slid into my mouth. I choked as it slipped deeper and deeper, fucking my throat with the same hard, savage thrusts as the one plundering my pussy. My saliva ran hot along the green length.

"Yes!" the dryad said. "More!"

Salix's cries rose as her plants took me from both ends. Her wild sexual energy poured into me and every part of my body felt too full of heat to be contained.

But I was wrong again – I was about to be even more full. Salix's vines lifted her face-to-face with me as I hung and squirmed in the suspended grip of her willow tree. The dryad's glistening thighs were spread wide to display the tentacles piercing her. The one plunging itself in and out of her pussy bulged and Salix threw her head back as the magical vine pulsed, filling her. Pale spunk gushed from her slit, making the dryad shudder and moan. She fixed her eyes on me and a manic grin spread across her delicate face.

"More," she demanded.

The tentacle whipped out of Salix, making more pale cream drip from between her legs, and then lashed toward me. It coiled behind me and then sprang forward, impaling my ass in a single fluid motion. The cock-headed tendril was so slippery with its own strange seed and Salix's gushed juices that it popped into me almost without resistance. I screamed out in pleasure as it surged deep up my ass, but the sound was muffled into a wet whimper by the long green cock stuffed down my throat.

My senses were utterly overwhelmed by Salix's maddened lust and my own wild ecstasy. The tentacles filled my every hole in hard, desperate thrusts. They pressed against one another from inside my pussy and my ass, the one in my mouth gagging my endless stream of whorish moans. The dryad's power held me aloft, spread open on display as my body was ravished from top and bottom, front and back.

"More," Salix cried. "More!"

I was dimly aware that the vines' thrusts and thrashing were becoming more erratic. The verdant tentacles swelled thicker and thicker, too... And then they shot their loads deep inside me. The tendril in my mouth spurted thick, floral seed down my throat, straight into my belly. The other two poured so much sticky spunk into my ass and pussy that it ran in bright lines from my overfilled holes and down my sweat-slicked body. Salix writhed and moaned out our unwillingly shared pleasure.

The tendrils pulled away slowly, sliding free of my stretched, well-used holes with milky showers of seed. Salix made a hungry sound as her plants slithered back to her, where the dryad began lapping the sticky mess dripping from each of them. I gasped down a deep breath and forced myself to focus even as the aftershocks of orgasm made me twitch and shiver.

A new set of writhing vines rose from the earth, but I didn't have time to go another round. Under other circumstances, I would have happily let Salix fuck me all night. But she was sick, dying, and not everyone was as excited about being ravaged by her plants as I was.

I *had* enjoyed it, though, and now the sexual energy blazed through me. Salix said she wouldn't help me end this, but she had done exactly that. I wished I could have thanked her for it. But at least I could give her peace.

I yanked and pulled against the tree's grasp. Wood creaked as I strained, then splintered and I wrenched myself free. I fell and landed hard on the leaf-strewn earth, grabbed the last tough plant tendrils from around my wrist and tore them off. The hatchet was sunk blade-first into the ground a few yards away, but thanks to Salix, I didn't need it anymore.

The dryad screamed in fury and willow branches swung toward me, lashing out with vines and roots. One of them wound around my arm, but I seized it, snapped the wood and hurled the twitching green length at Salix. She screeched in horror and I dove across the grass, grabbing the fallen gas can.

I ripped the cap off without unscrewing it and hurled the whole thing at Salix's willow tree. It spun through the air, spraying gasoline into the branches and then exploded when it impacted the tree trunk. I jumped over another pair of thick tendrils bursting up from the ground toward me and ran to the torn remains of my pants.

"Stop!" Salix snarled.

I snatched up a shred of fabric, shook it and swore. Grabbing desperately, I searched through my ruined clothes until I felt the weight of the lighter in one pocket.

"Yes!" I shouted as I yanked the little rectangle of metal free.

Roots curled around my ankles and pulled, sending me sprawling onto my stomach in the grass. The lighter tumbled out of my hand.

"Ah, shit!" I shouted. "No!"

I sank my fingers into the earth as Salix's roots pulled me back toward her tree, but the ground was still soft from the spring rains and all I accomplished was digging eight shallow furrows into the earth. Mud streaked my naked body and my hands were green with grass stains. I must have looked even wilder than the dryad. The air reeked of gasoline.

"You *will* give me what I need," Salix hissed.

Even now, the roots of her willow tree tried to pry my legs apart and I felt a pair of her vines nudging at my sticky pussy. I had to admire the dryad's tenacity and wished like fuck that I didn't have to kill her.

Salix's tree dragged me another few feet toward her, further away from the lighter... but closer to the hatchet. I writhed like the furious little hellspawn I am and managed to close my muddy fingers around the hatchet. I rolled over and flung it as best I could. With all of my sexed-up strength, the throw was hard and the blade whistled as it flew, but Salix's vines were fast and tough. They snatched my hatchet right out of the air before the blade could bite into the willow tree.

Snaring the flying hatchet was enough to momentarily break the dryad's focus, though. Only for a moment, but that was all I needed. I tore my way out of her vine's grip again and they were too slow to catch me as I sprinted toward the lighter. I dove, grabbing it just as Salix's attention snapped back to me.

Vines whipped themselves around me once more and pulled. This time, I let them, focusing instead on the lighter in my grass-stained hand. I flicked up the lid and thumbed the wheel. Sparks flew and then the flame caught as the plants yanked me up to face Salix. Her emerald eyes were wide and glowed with demonic desire.

"I'm sorry," I said. "I'm sorry..."

I dropped the lighter to the gasoline-soaked ground and furious red fire billowed up around us. Salix wailed and her tree contorted. I heaved myself out of her tentacles' grasp and leapt back, but still felt furious heat exploding from the burning tree. Willow leaves blackened and curled, scrubbed away into gray smoke that twisted up toward the cloudy sky. Branches cracked and splintered as fire consumed them. Salix clutched at her tree through the flames, screaming and weeping. I don't think it ever occurred to her to run. Even in death, the dryad would never abandon her tree.

I cried, too, but the tears evaporated swiftly in the heat. I didn't run away, either. I made myself stay and watch Salix die. I owed her that much.

The gray sky above opened up and a cool rain began to fall. The fire wouldn't spread, but it raged too hot through the branches of Salix's tree to be quenched. The dryad was gone, consumed by fire, and her scorched tree snapped with a loud, brittle sound. A crack started at the fork of branches where Salix had stood and raced down the blackened trunk. Sap popped and hissed in the heat.

There was something bright green nestled in the cracked and burning tree trunk. I squinted through the flames. It was about the size of a large walnut and I thought I saw a round-cheeked face inside. Like Salix's face, but younger, like an old baby picture.

I reached into the fire. My fingers burned, but I closed them around Salix's seed. It was smooth and pulsed as though with a tiny heartbeat. I pulled it out of the flaming tree and cradled it against my chest as the rain fell.

Chapter
NINE

Max didn't go to nightclubs often enough to have a favorite, so I reserved the biggest table at The Base to celebrate the grand opening of his new garage. The cookies and business cards we handed out all day were nice, but now that business hours were over, it was time for some *serious* celebration.

Several of Max's old Golden Touch Auto co-workers showed up to congratulate him, along with most of the garage's first customers. Max and Taya sat at the head of the table, of course, thanking everyone for coming out and trying to keep up with a dozen conversations at once. I took the fourth round of drink orders – they were getting pretty slurred by now, but I speak *drunk* quite well – and headed for The Base's bar. The club was all polished metal, glossy black surfaces and blue neon. It reminded me of a science fiction movie, like something out of *Blade Runner*.

Shut up. That movie is a classic.

Synthesized bass pulsed through the nightclub. I didn't know the song, but the beat was good enough to get me swaying my hips as I cut my way through the thick Friday night crowd. When I reached the bar, I had no trouble waving down the blue-haired woman behind it.

I had just finished reading off the order when I saw Max weaving across the packed dance floor. He had changed out of his mechanic's coveralls, now dressed in dark jeans and a black t-shirt that showed off his muscles impressively. Max leaned against the bar beside me and bumped his hip gently into mine.

"Put the drinks on my bill," he told the bartender.

"Put them on *my* tab," I countered. "I tip better."

The bartender nodded and winked at me. Max sighed as she got to work mixing the tray full of cocktails. I sat down on a barstool to wait and Max pulled another seat up close beside mine.

"So you're a real business owner now," I said. "You've been so busy I haven't really had time to congratulate you properly."

"This is all thanks to you, Lil," Max told me. "And thank you for coming out this morning to help hand out cookies and stuff. At least half of those guys only came in to talk to you."

"I picked up a few phone numbers. If they don't bring their cars in, you tell me and I'll have a word with them."

I laughed to let Max know that I was joking – mostly – but the sound came out flat and brittle. Max frowned and slid in a little closer.

"Lil... are you okay?" he asked, quietly enough that his voice wouldn't carry at all over the loud music. "I saw you talking to Vijay at the table."

I glanced back over my shoulder before I could help myself, but the table full of Max's friends and new customers was hidden on the other side of the dance floor. I turned back to Max with a sigh.

"Vijay doesn't remember anything that Salix did to him. I... I can't help wondering if he was the one who fathered that seedling. What Salix did was terrible, but he might be a father. It's a girl, you know."

Max put his arm around me and smiled gently. "A baby girl? Wow... That means she's going to be a dryad, right? So what happens to her now?"

"I took the seed to Ash. His aunts doubt that she inherited any of Salix's demonic taint, but they'll watch out and take good care of her."

"Do you think you'll ever go see her?"

I shook my head. "How could I, Max? I... I killed her mother. I'm why she got sick in the first place."

"That's not your fault, Lil. You could blame the vampire – if he hadn't carried the demonic blood, his ashes wouldn't have poisoned her. If it hadn't been raining, you could have cleaned them up. Or even that dryad..."

"Salix," I said so quietly that Max nearly head-butted me getting close enough to hear.

"Salix," he repeated. "It was an accident, Lil."

"Maybe. But it was *my* accident."

"And you fixed it. You saved her in the only way you could."

I laid my cheek against Max's shoulder. He was right, of course. He usually was. I smiled and looked up at Max so he could see it.

"Yeah," I said. "I did... I'm still the best damn hunter in this city, right?"

"In the whole world, Lil. Never doubt it."

The bartender returned with a tray of glasses, all full of ice, alcohol and swirling colors. I nodded my approval and told her which table to have them delivered to. Max nudged me with his hip again.

"None of those were for you," he noted.

"I haven't bought my own drinks since high school."

Before Max could comment on that, Taya was pushing her way through the club to her boyfriend's side. She wore the same red dress that she had at dinner last week and, if possible, looked even hotter in it than before. She had her glasses on, too.

"Hi there, Lily," said Taya. She put her arm through Max's and pulled. "Can I borrow him? He promised to dance with me."

Max's eyes flew wide. "Wait, what? When did I say that I would dance?"

"Just now," Taya said.

"Max is kind of slow to warm up," I warned. "And he will say he can't, but your boy can really dance."

Taya flashed me a quick thumbs-up and then resumed tugging at Max's arm. But he didn't move.

"What about you, Lil?" Max asked.

"Go on," I told him. "I'm fine."

"Are you sure? I can stay and talk, if you need me."

"I said I'm fine, Max. Want to see?" I turned to look down the bar and raised my voice. "Hey, who wants to buy me a drink?"

A dozen hands shot up into the air. I grinned at Max.

"See?" I said. "I'm all set."

Max smiled and he let Taya drag him off in the direction of the dance floor. I took a stack of his brand new business cards from my pocket, the ones that I had written my phone number on, and began handing them out.

LILY QUINN BOOK #9

Coming
INTO POWER

Chapter
ONE

My slinky, strapless red dress made me feel just like Jessica Rabbit. With my equally red hair and a little dark eyeshadow, the image was complete. Although I was barely wearing the dress now, if you wanted to get technical about it. The hem was shoved up to my hips, the top pulled down until the whole thing was only a sparkling crimson sash around my waist.

Derek's fingers pressed into my hips just below the glittering line of red, holding on for dear life as I rode him so hard that I wondered if we might break the bed frame. It wouldn't be the first time.

"Oh my god, Lily!" Derek gasped.

That's me, Lily Quinn. I'm a bounty hunter. Specifically, I hunt down supernatural monsters. And being half succubus myself, I get the superpowers that I need for my job from fucking guys. And girls. And everything else.

I twisted my hips, swirling Derek's thick cock inside me and making him groan. I swiveled in the other direction and Derek groaned louder. Our bodies slipped and slid against one another, skin slick with sweat and the wetness streaming from my pussy.

My headboard slammed into the wall as I impaled myself onto

Derek faster and faster. He was close again. I felt it in the hot, swift throb of his cock inside me, tasted it in Derek's urgent, panted breath as I kissed him. My body went taut in response and I gasped.

"Please, Lily," Derek begged.

I raked my nails down his chest. I keep them short for work – manicures don't last long when you're punching ogres in the face with sex-powered super strength. But I still left eight reddening welts across Derek's skin that echoed the curving lines of the tattooed snakes winding over the hard muscles of his heaving chest. I leaned back and traced my fingers more gently along the dark ink dipping down below Derek's navel to coil at the base of the biggest serpent of all – the one stuffed deep in my tight pussy.

"Lily!"

Derek's hips rose from the sweaty tangle of my sheets, straining toward me. His cock speared up between my legs and I threw my head back with a wild cry of pleasure.

I could have dismounted Derek right then and walked away if I wanted to. My power comes from drinking in the sexual energy of my lovers, their passion and desire, not their semen or anything creepy like that. I'm not a vampire. I could get enough bright golden sexual energy from a sensual kiss to crush concrete with my bare hands. I had what I needed from Derek, but I wouldn't leave him there in my bed, hard and begging for release. I'm not that kind of girl.

At least, not tonight.

Derek's hands slid up my sweat-slicked body to my breasts, curling his fingers into the soft flesh in a silent but eloquent plea for release. Derek was a big guy, at least twice my size, but I caught his wrists easily and pushed his arms down into the bed. With Derek pinned there, I lifted myself to the tip of his cock and balanced with the crown just nuzzling my entrance.

"You're so impatient," I said.

Like I was one to talk. I needed this power to run down my next target, so I had found Derek in ten minutes flat at some nightclub. He had deep, dark eyes that promised passion and a long, fit body that promised to keep up.

So when I asked about Derek's tattoos and he began showing them off, I had no trouble getting his shirt away from him and went right for his pants. I tried to fuck Derek in the club bathroom, but it looked like it hadn't been cleaned in... ever. I'm a nasty slut, but I'm not a filthy slut, so I had to wait until I got Derek back to my place.

Since I'd had to wait, I guess I was making Derek wait a little, too. I rocked my hips with a low moan, teasing the blunt head of his thick cock with the softness of my hungry pussy.

Okay, waiting over! My fingers tightened on Derek's straining wrists and I speared myself onto his long dick again. I took every inch in a single plunge and red-hot sensation shot through me.

"Yes," I moaned.

Derek's breath came in hissing, wordless sounds of primal need. His dick was a blazing pillar inside me. Every time I rose, Derek's slicked cock shone in the colorful city lights spilling through the window until I sank down onto him once more. Hardness churned the sweet ache within me, stoking it up and up into something brighter, hotter.

"Fuck!" I screamed.

Brilliant ecstasy shot through me, surging to fill my core and out along fingers and toes that curled in pleasure. I rode Derek's cock in swift, furious thrusts and then yanked myself up off of him.

Derek opened his mouth to groan, to beg, but I was already grabbing him in both hands. His dick was heavy and pulsed with heat against my touch. Derek's jaw went tight, biting down on a loud grunt as his cock turned to steel in my grasp. Bright cum arced into the air and spattered my cheeks in creamy droplets. More spunk poured in an oozing river of white across Derek's lean stomach and the dark ink of his tattoos.

After a moment, his muscles unknotted and Derek fell back into the sheets, panting.

"Shit, Lily. That... that was fucking amazing."

"That's the only way I know how to fuck," I told him with a smirk.

I held my hair back from my face and licked my way along the curves of Derek's snaking tattoos, over warm skin and hard muscles, lapping up his sticky load. It was hot and thick on my tongue and I swallowed it all down.

When I had drunk my fill, I slid off the bed and stood. Derek reclined in my twisted sheets, thick arms crossed behind his head. I stretched in front of the open window, feeling the blaze of sexual energy coursing through me, and Derek's expression became hungry again.

Nope. I scooped up Derek's pants from the floor and dumped them onto the bed. His shirt lay in a heap beside the door that led out into my living room. I kicked it up into my hand and tossed that at Derek, too.

"Go on," I said. "Get dressed. I've got things to do."

"I... uh, what?"

Derek's gaze moved only reluctantly from my naked body to the pile of his clothes on the bed. I made a little shooing gesture toward the door. Derek blinked and I rolled my eyes. I'd emptied the guy's balls, sure, but did I empty his head, too?

"Time... to... go," I said, enunciating each word carefully. "It's late. I have work."

Derek bit his lower lip. It looked like fun, but my target was already on the move and I had to catch up. I needed to get out of town tonight and didn't have time to waste, even on Derek's dark, soulful eyes and thick, mussed black hair. Finally, he reached for his clothes and began getting dressed.

"Thanks for the fun, Derek," I said.

"Darren," he corrected.

Oops.

Once I ushered Derek/Darren firmly from my condo, I slipped out of my shimmery red dress and tossed it aside to send to the dry-cleaner later. I took a quick shower and got dressed again. Nothing slinky this time – functional jeans and shirt, boots and belt. Still, I checked my reflection in the mirror. It's an old habit.

There were my long legs and tits that looked great even in plain clothes. I saw my red hair and pale skin that never seems to tan, no matter how many of these rural hunts I went on. But it's always my eyes I stare at. I guess I'm still not entirely used to them. They're hazel – a dark, green-flecked gold that attracts just as much attention as my figure. But they weren't always that color. When I was a kid, my eyes were just green. I was eighteen when they changed and even after all these years, sometimes they don't feel quite... mine.

I tied my hair back into a damp ponytail and picked up the duffel bag beside the door. There were spare clothes inside, some granola and a flashlight. That about did it for my camping supplies, though, so I really hoped this job wouldn't take too long or I would be one miserable bounty hunter.

Just in case, I threw a few candy bars into my bag, then zipped it shut and grabbed the key fob for my i10. The sleek little silver electric wasn't made for the bumpy dirt roads up where I would be hunting, but it didn't have to be. For now, the i10 only had to go as far as Max's garage.

I drove up the freeway to midtown, cruising through the river of red taillights at the thinning end of the nighttime traffic. When I turned off East 32nd Street onto Valley Road, I spotted the darkened sign of Max's new repair shop and pulled into the parking lot. The windows of the renovated old firehouse were still lit up, glowing warmly from within.

There was no sign of Taya's car, but I left the closest parking spot free, just in case she came to see Max. I picked up my bag from the passenger seat and climbed out of the i10. The garage's front door was locked, but I found my key and let myself into the reception area. A stack of Max's business cards leaned in a wire holder and the red *Grand Opening* banner lay folded up neatly on the front counter.

"Max?" I called out.

"In the garage!" came the muffled answer.

I moved through the polished old wooden door into the converted firehouse's huge garage. A radio on one of the workbenches played some 80s-era Motörhead. Rest in peace, Lemmy. I heard humming from beneath the big white SUV before Max pushed against the bumper and slid out into view.

"Hey, Lil," he said.

Max smiled up at me. His dimples were smudged with black grease that made the deep blue of his eyes shine out like fragments of twilight sky. But his hands were covered in grease, too, so Max stood carefully and made his way over to a steel sink in the corner. He squeezed soap out from a dispenser mounted on the wall and even from yards away, the astringent orange scent was powerful enough to make my nose tickle. It takes strong chemicals to keep Max's hands clean.

"Is the truck ready?" I asked. As much as I loved my little i10 – which was hell of a lot – Max's truck was far better equipped for off-roading.

Max glanced up from scrubbing his hands and nodded over his shoulder at me. "All filled up and good to go. I threw a tent and some canteens in the back for you, too."

"Thanks. I didn't even think about extra water," I said. I probably should have, but luckily, Max is always looking out for me. "I'll return the truck in one piece, promise."

"What are you after this time?" Max asked. He rinsed his hands, inspected his fingernails and went back for more soap.

"Unicorn."

Max's thick blond eyebrows shot up. He half turned toward me, spraying soap and water across the concrete floor before he remembered what he was doing and stuck his hands in the sink again.

"Really?" he asked.

"Yeah, really."

"Why would you hunt down a unicorn, Lil? Aren't they... uh... good guys?"

I laughed. "No way. Unicorns are more like goats. Magical goats. They'll eat *anything*. People's gardens, people's cars and, you know, people."

"So no granting wishes."

"Nope," I said cheerfully. "That's djinni. Unless your wish is to get stabbed. Those horns are wicked sharp. Unicorns are territorial and use their horns to kill anyone that wanders onto their patch."

Max winced. "Ouch."

"But I've found this one's territory, so I'm going out there to go pick a fight."

"What about only letting virgins ride them?" Max asked. "Is that part true?"

"Actually, yeah. Last time I got anywhere near a unicorn, it bolted as soon as it saw me. But you know why unicorns like virgins, right?"

"No. Why?"

I smacked my lips. "Tastes like chicken."

"...Uh..."

Max shook his head, then finished washing his hands and dried them on a blue paper towel. When Max was satisfied with his work, he pointed toward the stairs up to his apartment.

"I made you some food, too," he said.

Sweet. Max's food wasn't gourmet, but it's good and he always makes plenty of it.

I followed him out of the garage and up a narrow flight of stairs to his newly rebuilt apartment. The lights were all dark in the living room, but a row of hanging steel lamps glowed over the kitchen counter and illuminated several large paper bags.

"I packed you some burritos, both regular and breakfast," Max said. "There's fruit, too, granola and a bag of beef jerky."

"Homemade?" I asked hopefully.

Max smiled. "Yeah. Nothing fancy, but it'll keep you fed."

"Thanks." I gestured to the counter full of food. "How long do you think I'm going to be gone?"

"I wasn't sure," said Max. "So I packed about five days' worth."

I laughed. "Well, if I can't catch a unicorn in five days, then I deserve to starve."

Max didn't look too certain about that. But he laughed, too, and hugged me tight to his broad, hard chest. I heard his heartbeat speed a little at the closeness and felt it against my cheek.

"Do you need anything else, Lil?" Max asked.

He didn't mean food. I felt the subtle stirring of his cock against me, even through his jeans and mine. There was the warm golden heat of Max's lust for me, too, but the expression on his face was one of concern. My job is dangerous and few people know that as well as Max does.

We've been best friends forever, and best friends with benefits since high school. Max has been my go-to guy for a sexual charge ever since I started bounty hunting for the College. What would you call that? Sex battery, maybe? Well, Max does fuck like a machine. But I shook my head.

"Not unless Taya's hiding around here somewhere," I said. Taya was Max's incredibly hot girlfriend of three months. "Anytime she wants another threesome, I'm all in. But otherwise, she's got sole custody of your cock. Besides, I already filled up."

Filled up. I snickered at my own double entendre and Max released me with an indulgent smile. He stepped behind the steel kitchen counter and nodded toward the coffee maker.

"How about some coffee, then?" he asked. "For the road, since it's late?"

"Sure, thanks."

I sat down on one of the stools that Max had set up along the kitchen counter while he brewed me a cup. I could still hear the radio playing downstairs. Max went to the refrigerator for milk and then to a cupboard for sugar.

"What happens if you *are* out there for more than a day?" Max asked as he poured my coffee into an insulated mug. "Did you get enough sex to hold out that long?"

"He wasn't as good as–" I almost said *you*, but that might make things awkward for Max. "–some guys. He was pretty fired up, but even the biggest charge only lasts about twenty-four hours."

It would have been a lot easier if I just brought Max with me to fuck every day until I caught the unicorn. But I couldn't. Max had Taya now. They seemed happy together and my best friend deserved to be happy. What if they got married? Had I already been with Max for the last time?

"I'm sure it'll be enough power to finish the job," I said.

Max nodded and filled the rest of the coffee cup with tons of cream and sugar, then pushed it across the kitchen counter to me. I wrapped my hands around the mug. It was warm and smelled good.

"You be careful out there, Lil." Max was smiling, but his voice was serious. "I'd help more, if I could."

I caught Max's hand on the counter and squeezed it. "I'm fine. Plenty charged up to run down one magical goat. You've done more than enough. You always do."

Max put his other hand on top of mine. "I promised, didn't I?"

"Yeah," I said. "And you keep that promise every day."

What promise? Well, if you want to know about that, if you *really* want to understand Max and me, then you need to go back nine years now, to our final month of high school...

Chapter
TWO

Nine years ago.

There was a little overlook down in Southport, just off of Pierpoint Road. You know the kind of spot. Every town has one. Maybe a place that has a view or is tucked just out of sight so the police don't stop there too often. Where the ground is littered with empty beer cans and used condoms, but none of that makes it any less beautiful because it's about the memories, about getting drunk with your friends for the first time or losing your virginity, about being young and having your whole life ahead of you.

The spot in Southport was one of those with a view. It wasn't a great view – mostly steep hills covered in the worn gray blocks of old waterside warehouses. But between them lay the dark silver of the bay. This far south, the water was flat and still, throwing back the reflection of the golden half-moon like a dare.

Max and I stretched out across the back of his truck, on a blanket laid over the lumpy metal of the bed. The truck wasn't quite done yet – Max was still working on it in auto shop class – but it was drivable. So when I called, he picked me up at home and drove us out to the overlook.

Now Max propped himself up on one elbow to look at me. He was wearing the same jeans and tight, threadbare old Metallica t-shirt that he had been in class that day. Max had outgrown the shirt at some point during junior year, but it was his favorite and there was no money for a replacement, so he wore it anyway.

"What's up, Lil?" Max asked. "I thought we weren't hanging out tonight. Aren't you supposed to be with Blake? You said he had something planned."

I was still dressed for school, too, but I wasn't supposed to be. Max was right – I had plans and a sweet little red dress to go along with them. But the dress was back at home, along with the plastic bag from the drugstore with coppery eyeshadow chosen to go with my green eyes... and a box of condoms.

"Yeah," I said. "Blake and I had plans."

"What the hell, Lil?" Max protested. "It's your birthday. Your eighteenth birthday! C'mon, this is the big one. What are you doing out here with me?"

I prodded him in the ribs with one elbow. The gesture was met with a lot more taut resistance than it used to be. Max was never one of the scrawny kids, but he had grown a lot in the last couple of years.

"Because you're my best friend, stupid," I said.

"Thanks, Lil. But that's not what I mean. Why did you call me instead of Blake? He's your boyfriend."

I threw an arm across my face. Was that sound my heartbeat pounding in my ears or the tidal crash of the bay against the concrete below? I didn't know. I couldn't think.

"Because I'm turning eighteen," I mumbled from under my arm.

"So?"

With just that one word, Max seemed so much older than me. His eighteenth birthday was only six months before, but my best friend always sounded like an adult while I was still the same stupid, fumbling kid. Was it because he was already so grown up?

Max had practically raised his two little brothers, after all. Or was it only because I was such a fuck-up?

"I'm eighteen." I pulled my arm off my face and looked at Max. "I'm... legal now. Blake has this whole dinner planned for us and I know what he's going to want afterward. He wants to fuck me."

Max's eyes widened and he choked on that, then tried to recover his composure before I could make fun of him. Max flopped down beside me, but he didn't back down from the conversation.

"And... you don't want to?" he asked.

"No, I totally do. That's the messed up part."

Max frowned and scratched his cheek. The whole shaving thing was still new to him and left his face a little pink, like he was always blushing just a bit. Or maybe he was *actually* blushing now?

"Lil, if you want to fuck Blake, then do it," Max told me. "What's wrong? Do you need condoms or something? We can go get some right now. You can wait in the truck, if you're embarrassed."

I groaned. "No, that's not it at all. I'm so horny, Max. Like you wouldn't believe. Like I'm changing panties five times a day horny. If I go out with Blake tonight and he asks me for sex, I'm going to be all over him."

"But... but you don't want to do that?" Max asked slowly. "How come? I thought you and Blake were okay."

"Oh, good. I managed to fool someone, at least."

I sighed and squeezed my legs together. Worried and frustrated as I was, the conversation was still getting me wet. Again.

"I mean, we *should* be okay," I said. "Blake's cute and everything. But I don't know if I want my first time to be with him. I don't even know if I want to keep going out with Blake at all."

"Did he do something creepy? You know I'll stuff his head up his own ass if you need me to."

I shrugged. Not that Max could see it with both of us lying down, shoulder to shoulder as we stared up into the star-studded sky.

"No," I said. My stomach clenched at what I was about to admit. "But I... I never wanted to date Blake in the first place."

"Then what the fuck are you doing with that guy?" Max asked.

"His parents know my parents. My foster parents, I mean. Bill and Sandra. I thought maybe they would be happy if I was dating their friends' kid. That maybe they would let me stay longer. I'm eighteen now, Max."

"Yeah, you keep saying that part."

"Sex isn't the only thing legal for me. Bill and Sandra can kick me out if they want to now. What the hell would I do then?"

My voice cracked at the end and the final words came out raw. Max scooted another inch closer and wrapped one of my shaking hands in his. The pads of his fingers were rough.

"So... you're just dating Blake to stay on your foster parents' good side?" Max asked.

I nodded in the darkness. Most of the overlook's streetlamps had burnt out years ago and none of the city workers bothered to replace them. All we had left was moonlight.

"Yeah," I said. "Which sounds really shitty. And even shittier when I think about sleeping with Blake."

"You don't need to do that, Lil." Max squeezed my hand. "Bill and Sandra won't throw you out."

"I... I'm not so sure." I sniffled and hated the sound of it.

"Well, you can always come crash with me if they do."

"Because it worked so well last time you tried that."

"Hey, we were five years old when the Foresters sent you away," Max pointed out. "But we're eighteen now."

I couldn't help a bitter little laugh at that. "Oh yeah, your parents will be even happier to let a horny teenage girl stay over with their three sons."

"You know Jake and Peter both have crushes on you, right?"

"Yeah, I do. It's kind of cute." I drew a deep, shuddering breath. "This whole thing is shitty, isn't it? Why am I such a fuck-up?"

"It sucks," Max agreed. "But you're not a fuck-up, Lil."

He only wanted to comfort me, but for some reason, I kept arguing with him. If Max was going to defend me against myself, I would make him fight for it.

"Yeah?" I asked. "What else do you call it when I'm so horny that I masturbate in English class? I have no idea what the homework is tonight, Max. I was too busy trying not to moan in the middle of class!"

"God, Lil! Did you really do that?" Max asked. To my pleasure and irritation, he sounded more interested than aghast. "Like, today? I was sitting right next to you!"

"Yes, today. And yes, really! I can't seem to get enough. I may not want to sleep with Blake, but did you know that I've already sucked his cock? When he pulls it out, I can't say *no*. I daydream about fucking him and finger myself off and then feel like a whore because I don't even *like* the guy. And then I just have to get off again because there's a part of me that loves feeling like a slut!"

Max's voice came out choked. "Holy shit. Should you even be telling me this stuff?"

"You're my best friend." I said it like a challenge. "So suck it up. See? Suck. I'm so fucked up that I can't stop talking about sex. Last week, I gave Blake head twice in a row after the game. He came in my mouth and I just kept going."

"Lil..." Max said in a low voice. He shifted uncomfortably, but didn't tell me to stop.

"Blake poured another load down my throat and I still didn't stop. He grabbed my hair and had to pull me away. Away, Max. What guy has to pull his girlfriend *off* his dick?"

"He was probably uh... pretty sensitive after all that," Max protested mildly.

"Yeah," I said with a sigh. "I'm going to end up fucking Blake. I don't even know why I'm trying to keep it from happening. Is there a disease or something that makes you cock-crazy?"

"I don't know, Lil. Maybe you should go see a doctor."

"The doctor I have through the foster agency is kind of hot. I'd just end up–"

I stopped. Max had drawn his legs up, knees pointed to the sky. But it wasn't enough to hide the serious bulge growing in his jeans.

"Oh my god, Max," I said. "Are you hard?"

"What? No!"

Max pushed himself up into a hunched sitting position and the truck rocked on its shitty shocks. His dark blue eyes were wide in the starlight. I laughed, but it wasn't mocking.

"You totally are!" I sat up next to him and stared. "All that stuff about me sucking cock gave you a huge boner, didn't it?"

"I'm uh... sorry, Lil," Max said.

"Don't you *dare* be embarrassed after everything I just told you. You're my best friend."

Max raked his fingers through his hair and sighed. "Yeah, I know. That's the thing... you're my best friend."

"What? Just because I'm your best friend, I can't be hot and give you raging hard-ons?"

I fixed Max with a stern, green-eyed glare. He gulped as my gaze fell to his lap. I just couldn't help myself... It was like his cock was magnetic. I knew that I had to be making Max uncomfortable, but just couldn't seem to look away. He was doing his best to conceal the tent in his jeans, but it was way too big to hide.

The sight stirred something inside me, something difficult to describe but impossible to contain. It was hot enough to burn between my legs, but cold enough to make me shiver; heavy enough to pull insistently inside me, but as light and delicate as butterfly wings.

"Let me see it," I said. Demanded.

Max blinked. "What?"

"Show me your cock. I made you hard and I want to see it."

"No way, Lil," Max said. He shook his head. "I can't do... that!"

"Why not?"

"I've never... No one's ever seen it before! You know, except me," Max admitted, blushing darkly in the dim light.

"It's my birthday!"

Max gulped again and looked down as he folded his hands over his lap, still failing to cover up the tent in his jeans. I sat up on my knees and crawled a little closer. Every inch of my body tingled with heat. I could never remember wanting cock more than at that moment, even when I had Blake's dick in my mouth. Every slight movement made my soaking wet panties slide subtly, maddeningly against me.

"Stop it, Lil." Max's voice was choked and threatened to crack. "You just said you went down on Blake when you didn't want to because you couldn't stop yourself."

My mouth went dry, but my pussy went even wetter. The hot emptiness inside me ached, screaming silently to be filled. I yanked my t-shirt up over my head and tossed it aside. It landed and dangled over the edge of the truck bed.

"What are you doing?" Max asked.

I reached back for the hook of my bra. I tore it off and threw it away – I didn't know where my bra went and gave exactly zero fucks about that. Max stared at my bare breasts for the first time and his expression became one of hopeless desire. But then he forced his eyes shut, pressing his thumb and forefinger against the closed lids.

"Holy shit, Lil," he gasped. "Stop! Don't do something you'll regret."

Max's face was so brightly flushed that it almost glowed and I swore that I could *feel* how much he wanted to open his eyes and look. He was too busy avoiding my half-naked body to hide the rigid length in his jeans anymore. I wanted... no, *needed* to see it, to taste and feel it. I sank down onto my hands and knees and prowled across the blanket.

"Look at them," I said. "Look at *me*, Max!"

His hand shook as he dropped it again. He opened his eyes and stared at me. They were wide, the pupils dilated until the circle of blue iris nearly vanished. Max looked frightened, but the huge bulge in his pants grew even more pronounced as he took in the sight of me.

"Lil, why are you doing this?" Max asked.

"Because I *need* to fuck. I'm not going to be able to say *no* to the next cock I see and I don't want it to be Blake. I don't want to feel like a whore. Help me, Max!"

I crawled closer, practically on top of him. He was still staring at me, not blinking. My nipples were little pink peaks stiff enough to cut glass, but not because it was cold. The summer night was warm and clung to my skin like a caress. My pulse pounded so hard that I could barely hear my own words.

"You're my best friend, Max," I said. "Please fuck me!"

I didn't say *please* to Max – or anyone else – very often. It was downright rare. Almost as rare as Max telling me *no*. His gaze rose up from my breasts to my green eyes. Slowly, he nodded.

"Yes, Lil," he answered in a strained whisper. "What... what do you want me to do?"

"Show me your cock," I said again. My voice was just as quiet and tight with anticipation as his.

Max drew a deep breath and yanked his shirt off over his head. The muscles of his chest and stomach shone silver with sweat in the moonlight. He lay back across the blanket-lined truck bed, un-clenched his hand and shook out the white-knuckled fingers. Max unbuttoned his jeans and then pulled the zipper hesitantly down.

I couldn't breathe. I watched the little metal tab and a shiver followed it down, winding along my spine.

Shaking and nervous, Max hooked his thumbs over the waist of his jeans and the boxers beneath. He lifted his hips and pushed at his clothes and for a moment, his bunched thighs obscured my view as Max struggled to untangle his pants and shoes.

"Damn it," he grunted.

But Max managed to kick his clothes away. He leaned back again and then I could finally see it – my best friend's cock, long and thick and flushed just as deeply as his face. Every inch was smooth but subtly textured, both rock-hard yet somehow delicate-looking despite its size. We had gone swimming up at Mission Beach too many times not to see how Max's shorts clung when they were wet. I knew that he wasn't compensating for anything with the truck, but seeing his dick naked and erect was... amazing.

Something inside me knotted tightly at the sight. Not my stomach. Lower. It was a hot, heavy and somehow primal throb between my legs.

"Lil...?"

I leaned down closer to Max and felt his breath on my lips. I didn't know if Max was asking permission, asking if I was sure or even realized that he had said my name at all. His eyes fell shut, but not to block out the sight of me this time. I closed my eyes, too.

My lips touched Max's and completed some strange, powerful electrical circuit deep within me. Sensations I could barely name and could not contain surged through me and I pressed myself hard against Max, mashing my mouth to his with ravenous passion. He pulled me close to him, meeting my kiss with equal passion and desire. One strong hand cupped the back of my head, fingers twining through my red hair. The other found my breast and slid gently, almost reverently over the soft swell. Max groaned and I drank in the sound.

Something had begun inside me and I needed to feel more. I thrust my tongue further into Max's mouth, tasting him and eliciting another deep sound of pleasure. His hands tightened in my hair, over my breast.

More.

I clawed at my jeans and ripped them open. I tumbled and nearly fell when I desperately stripped off my pants. Max moved clumsily with me as I toppled, holding me, holding our kiss. Our teeth crashed together and one of us yelped in pain. I didn't know who, but we didn't stop. My tongue and Max's twined. We gasped with each other's breath until my vision was dimming around the edges from the lack of air.

Max guided me the rest of the way down to the truck bed. My legs spread instinctively and my racing heartbeat pounded through my body as Max pulled himself between them. The hard heat of his cock slid against my thigh, making my back arch and thrusting my breasts skyward.

More...

"God, you're beautiful, Lil," Max said in a thick voice.

The head of his dick nudged at me, but I was so wet that it slipped up and rubbed a blazing line of sensation across my clit.

"More!" My moan was probably too loud for a public place, but I didn't care.

I pushed Max's hips down with one hand and grabbed his cock. It felt far too long and huge in my hand to possibly fit into my pussy, but I wasn't scared. Maybe I should have been, but there was only heat and lust and wetness and the all-consuming need to have Max inside me. Now.

He hesitated, though, there with his dick pressed between my trembling legs.

"Lil, are you sure?" Max asked. "I... I can still stop if you don't want this."

"I need you, Max."

I pulled him closer, into me. Max's cock spread the slick pink of my pussy open and then in. We both gasped at the strange, glorious new feelings. I had fingered myself before – a lot – but this was something else entirely. My body tensed reflexively at the invasion of hard heat. Max stared at me with worry and wonder in his deep blue eyes.

"Lil?"

"Fuck me!" I said. "Please!"

I wrapped my legs around Max's waist as he sank himself deeper into me. He filled my pussy slowly, inch by inch. Fire raced along my nerves and I dug my heels into Max, pulling him the final distance until his cock was buried to the hilt inside me. Actually *inside* me.

He leaned forward, jaw clenched tightly. Was Max already fighting not to cum? This was his first time, too, I realized. And Max was giving it to *me*.

"Yes!" I cried out. A sharp pain stabbed through my scalp. "Ow!"

"Sorry," Max gasped.

He shifted his weight and lifted his hand off my hair. I raised my head awkwardly and let Max comb it up and out of the way. He held himself up over me on those thick arms and his cock pulsed inside me like a second heartbeat.

"What... what do you want me to do now, Lil?" he asked in a strained voice.

I bit my lip.

"Start... moving," I told him.

I knew that I wanted more, but wasn't entirely sure how to get it. Max nodded, though. A line of sweat ran down from his disheveled blond hair and along his jaw. Max rocked his hips slowly, first out and then easing back into my tightness as gently as he could. Every thrust of his cock into me forced a gasping moan from my lips.

He drove himself deep into me and the wet sound of our bodies coming together rose in tempo and volume, almost drowning out my breathless cries. Max spread me open so wide that it felt like he could see, could feel all the way through me. It wasn't just his size or the increasing speed of his cock moving in and out of me... There was something other than the physical pleasure filling me, flowing somehow from Max and into my body.

What was it? I had cum before... I'd started masturbating years ago. What I felt now was so much brighter than any climax, and so much better. This feeling was glorious, glowing invisibly inside me and somehow golden, like bright sunlight or rich honey. I didn't understand and I didn't care. I just wanted more of it.

I wrapped my arms around Max and ran my fingers along the hard lines of his broad shoulders, exploring my best friend's body in a way I had never even considered it before. And the sensations... I could practically *taste* how badly Max wanted me. Not on his lips as he kissed me, deep and hot and hungry, but in the very air. I couldn't get enough of it.

"More!" I screamed. "Fuck me, Max!"

"Yes, Lil," Max groaned.

He hammered his cock into me, no longer trying to be gentle. We were too far gone for that. I raked my nails down Max's back as he held me against him, making my breasts slide over the hard planes of his muscled chest. His heart pounded like a drumbeat – I could hear it as clearly as I heard my own rough cries.

"I... I need you deeper," I gasped. "Fuck me from behind. Hands and knees."

Max drew back to do as I had just requested, but I grabbed his hips and he lurched to a stop. I didn't want to be empty. Ever. So I pushed Max up to his knees on the blanket and twisted so I could roll over without separating our bodies.

Well, that was the theory. It wasn't like I had a lot of practice. I raised my foot and kicked Max in the head. Just a graze, really, but he reeled like I had punched him in the jaw and his cock was suddenly gone from inside me.

"Oh, shit! I'm so sorry," I said. I put my hands over my face, mortified.

Max shook his head. "It's okay. I'm fine."

He looked a little woozy, but with the sight of me naked before him and wetness streaming from my pussy, he couldn't stay down for long. And staring at the slick, thick length of Max's waiting dick pulled me back in as inexorably as gravity.

I couldn't stop the whimper that escaped my lips. The maddened cock-lust that had me sucking Blake through two loads was just idle curiosity compared to what I felt now. That searing golden sensation was flowing into me again and my every sense was afire with it. I could smell the testosterone surging through Max's body, and feel... fuck, I could feel *everything*. Even the faint summer breeze was an ephemeral caress that set me shuddering in pleasure.

I didn't even have the patience to roll over like I had asked. I just grabbed Max's wrist and yanked him back down against me. His eyes flew wide and he almost fell as we skidded together along the truck's bed. I crushed my lips to his and felt blindly for his cock. But my senses were sharpened to a razor edge and without looking, my fingers unerringly found Max's dick. It was so hot and heavy that I nearly came just from the weight of it in my hand.

Max shoved his hips forward, sinking his cock into me once more. I wound my legs around his waist, pulling him in and in, even deeper than before. Max's steely-hard length slid so far into me that I felt it in the pit of my stomach. Ecstasy exploded through me.

I clung to Max and shook with the feeling of his surging presence inside my body. I may not have been on top, but I pushed myself up against him with every thrust. The whole world was hot golden sensation flooding into me, Max pounding his cock into my very core.

"Oh god, Lil," Max said. "Stop! I... I'm going to cum!"

He tried to pull out, but his dick was searing, swelling inside me. That bright, blazing feeling was peaking, too. I couldn't let Max go – it felt too good. White-hot cum poured into me in long, hard pulses. Max's thrusts became a wild, erratic dance as our pleasure crested and then crashed together. He let out a loud groan and I screamed in harmony. I came harder than I could even describe.

It was too much. My body was a storm of fire and lightning and unbearable sweet ecstasy. I lashed out for something to hold onto. One hand twisted in the blanket, but the other came down on the

truck's wheel well. My fingers closed and the steel crunched beneath them like crushing a tin can. My right leg jerked under the
onslaught of sensation and I kicked the truck's raised tailgate. Metal
screeched and the whole thing went flying off across the overlook.

Max had been pulling away from me, trying to yank his pulsing
cock out of my pussy before he could shoot his load inside me.
When I thrashed, I had released Max and then bucked, heaving my
best friend and first lover off me as though he were no more substantial than a pillow. Max slid back, flailing as he came to the edge
of the bed and then – since the tailgate was no longer attached – fell
out of the truck. Naked, he landed on the gravel-strewn ground
with a grunt.

I sat up slowly. I still wasn't quite in control of my body and little
aftershocks of orgasm made me twitch and gasp. But that feeling of
strength remained, of over-sensitized sight and smell and everything else. And the hot golden glow of Max's lust burned like a
miniature sun. I felt... invincible, like nothing in the world could
hurt me.

Until I looked at Max. He was climbing to his feet and staring at
the broken tailgate a few yards away, then at the wheel well and the
finger-shaped dents I had left in the metal. Max was shaking.

"What... what the fuck was that?" he panted. "What happened?"

The nearly invisible blond hairs stood up along the back of
Max's neck and down his arms, but I saw every one of them. I heard
his heart racing and smelled the sharp tang of his adrenalin, of his
fear.

"Lil..." Max's voice was a hoarse rasp. "Lil, what happened to
your eyes?"

My eyes? I had no idea what he was talking about, but I hated
how Max was looking at me... like I was some kind of monster. I
reached out for Max, but he staggered away from me. He turned on
his heels and ran.

Chapter
THREE

I screamed after Max, but he was already gone. My best friend... I pulled the blanket around me. Or tried to, but the blanket tore in my hands like tissue paper. What the fuck was going on? What was wrong with me? I drew my bare knees up to my chest and squeezed my eyes shut against the sight of the mangled truck, against the tears.

Something vibrated across the truck bed, muffled but still insistent – at least, to my weirdly sharpened senses. My phone! I grabbed my jeans and fished the cell phone out of my pocket. Was it Max? Or maybe my foster parents, calling to tell me how worried they were about me... But when I flipped the phone open, I saw Blake's number. His voice came thin and tinny over the speaker.

"Yo, Lily. Where are you, babe?"

I sobbed and my hand tightened on the phone. The screen shattered and buttons scattered in every direction. With a scream, I dropped the broken pieces and they clattered across the bed. I couldn't stop the tears this time. I curled up in the back of Max's truck and cried until my eyes ached. But after an hour, even the warm summer evening was turning chilly. Now what? What's a girl supposed to do when she discovers she's a monster?

I almost jumped out of my skin at the sound of tires crunching over gravel. I threw my arm across my eyes to protect them from the blinding headlights, but the other cars were still at the bottom of the road. They only sounded closer because my hearing was so inhumanly sharp.

By the time the other two cars reached the overlook, I had managed to carefully pull my clothes back on and scramble down out of the truck. I recognized the two boys and three girls from school. One of the guys grinned and waved at me through the window.

I climbed up into the cab of Max's truck before he could call out an invitation to party with them. What would happen if I said *yes*? A beer, a blowjob... accidentally ripping some poor teenage boy's cock off because I was a fucking freak? No, I had to get out of there.

I had balled up Max's clothes and tossed them into the passenger seat. But now I searched through his pockets until I found the keys, feeling like a thief. I jammed one of them too hard into the ignition and metal squealed. I flinched. The truck was a tough old thing, though, and when I twisted the key, the engine turned over and rumbled like a satisfied lion.

When I reached up to adjust the rearview mirror, I froze. My eyes... That's what Max said just before he ran.

A stranger's eyes stared back at me from the mirror. The irises were still flecked with green, but the rest of the color was a dark gold like some kind of unearthed treasure. Cursed treasure... I put my hands over my face and shuddered, but I had no tears left and when I looked up again, those golden-hazel eyes were still there.

If I could have run away from myself, I would have.

I pushed the mirror down so I couldn't see myself. It snapped off the windshield and bounced into the heap of Max's clothes. I threw the truck into gear and drove away from the overlook.

Every light along the road was as brilliant as the sun, but somehow, none of them blinded me. I heard the radios in other cars playing every kind of music and felt the throb of deep bass like a vibrator. *Sensory overload* was an understatement. By the time I made it back home, I couldn't stand it anymore. I was shivering and panting and flinching away from everything.

I parked Max's truck crookedly on the street, yanked the keys free and fled up the driveway to my house. With a monumental effort of will, I slowed my steps and carefully opened the front door. It was quiet and dark inside, though I heard the television going in Bill and Sandra's bedroom – a late-night comedian talking about politics like someone actually cared.

I crept up the stairs to my room, undressed and collapsed into bed. My pussy was still slick with Max's cum and I smelled him on my skin. I guess I wasn't quite out of tears yet and I cried myself quietly to sleep.

Happy fucking birthday, Lily Quinn.

―――

When I finally came downstairs in the morning, the house was already empty and warm yellow sunlight streamed in through the open windows. I was supposed to be at school and both Bill and Sandra were at work. There was a note on the counter, written in my foster mother's neat handwriting.

> Lily, I know it was your birthday yesterday, but that's no excuse to violate your curfew again. Family meeting tonight.
> - Sandra

I smelled Sandra's perfume and the faint scent of her morning coffee on the paper. Yep, still a monster with inhuman powers.

I read the note again, then crumpled it up and threw it in the trash. I knew perfectly well how *that* meeting would go. I broke too many rules, talked back and swore too much, never showed enough respect... And my latest foster family didn't even know that I was some kind of golden-eyed freak. When they found out, Bill and Sandra would tell me to leave. Then probably call the cops to *make* me leave.

Well, screw that. I wouldn't give them the chance. What the hell did I have to stick around for, anyway? My family didn't want me. My best friend ran off and left me alone. I was a monster. There was nothing for me here.

I grabbed a few boxes of crackers and granola bars out of the pantry, then decided to take the peanut butter and cookies, too. The cookies were gone by the time I made it back upstairs. For some reason, I was *starving*.

I finished off the crumbs and threw the package into the laundry room. It was too light to do any damage, but my fucked-up inhuman strength made the box rebound off the wall with far more force than it should have. I stalked into my bedroom and pulled my schoolbooks out of my backpack. When it was empty, I stuffed the food inside, along with some extra clothes and underwear. There wasn't much money in my wallet, but I didn't know where my foster parents might have kept any more.

I was feeling sorry enough for myself to start crying again. When I wiped my face with a tissue, I caught my reflection in the mirror on top of the dresser. My eyes were still that weird gold-hazel color. If I just didn't look too closely, they could almost pass for human.

But I knew better. I grabbed a pair of sunglasses and jammed them into my pocket, then threw my backpack over my shoulder and headed downstairs again. I didn't look back. I was pretty sure that fucked-up monsters didn't get to be sentimental. And it wasn't like this place had ever really been home.

I opened the front door and just about tripped over my own feet in surprise. My hand tightened convulsively on the doorknob and the brass squashed like putty in my fingers. A woman stood in the doorway, calmly inspecting me. She was dressed simply, in a neat white skirt suit and cream-colored blouse, but she was beautiful enough to make my stomach clench in jealousy. Her hair was ridiculously long, falling past her waist in platinum blonde ringlets. It was wet, too, sparkling with a thousand tiny droplets like diamond beads that didn't drip at all down her clean white clothes. Her skin was nearly as pale as her hair, but the woman's eyes were a shockingly brilliant blue.

I wished like fuck that I had eyes like that.

My mysterious visitor seemed to be somewhere in her thirties, but it was hard to tell. Dress her up in a cheerleader outfit and she could probably pass for the hottest girl on my entire high school squad.

I scowled at the woman. "I'm not buying anything and I don't need to find Jesus. Go away."

"My name is Evaine," she said. "I'm a friend."

The woman's voice was light and musical, with an accent that sounded European – all liquid vowels and smooth consonants that flowed together like water.

"Fuck you," I spat. "I had one friend and he ditched me last night. Leave me alone."

I stepped around the woman and marched down the driveway to Max's truck. My one-time best friend already hated me, so I may as well steal his stupid car, too. I yanked open the door and flung my backpack inside, then climbed up behind the wheel. But when I stuck my hand in my pocket for the key, it was gone.

The lady – Elaine or whatever – stood beside the truck and held up Max's keys pinched between her finger and thumb. I snatched for the keys, but the blonde woman pulled them away and my hand only closed on empty air.

"You're frightened," she said. "Something happened last night, when you were with a young man."

"Fuck you! Were you watching us? Are you some kind of voyeur pervert, lady?"

She gave me a small, strange smile. "No need for titles, Lilith. You can may simply me Evaine. You have much to learn, but I can teach you."

I had no idea what the hell she was talking about or why she knew my real first name. No one called me *Lilith*, not even the teachers at school. I made another grab for the keys, but Evaine stepped back out of reach.

"Give me those!" I shouted.

"I sensed your awakening," Evaine said in a much calmer voice than mine. "Others will discover your existence soon, and few of them are your friends."

"What the fuck do you mean, *awakening*?"

The woman in white turned and made her way up in the direction of the house once more – still holding Max's keys. Unless I wanted to walk or try my hand at hot-wiring the truck, I had to follow her. I jumped out of the truck and kicked the door shut behind me, leaving a sizable dent in the metal and shattering the window. I flinched and hurried after Evaine, back into the house.

"What did you mean by *awakening*?" I asked again as she led me into the living room. "And how the hell do you know my name?"

Evaine turned to face me, but didn't sit. Her expression was so serious, though, that I found myself sinking down onto the couch.

"Lilith, you are a cambion," Evaine announced.

I blinked. "A... camo bean?"

Evaine looked down at me with the faintest expression of exasperation. She shook her head and gave me a wry smile.

"I suppose that term has fallen out of use," she said. "A cambion is the child of a human and a demon of lust. Your father was mortal, but your mother was a succubus. Half of your blood is demonic. Your kind are extremely rare, Lilith. The world has not seen a cambion since Merlin's day."

I wanted to scoff, to laugh or say something suitably sarcastic in the face of this bullshit. Demons? Merlin? This Evaine lady was totally insane... right? Or fucking with me? But I couldn't forget the broken tailgate or the fear in Max's eyes. I knew there was something horribly wrong with me.

Because I was half demon.

I put my face in my hands and wanted to scream. Tears stung my eyes and ran from between my fingers. I really was a monster.

Evaine finally seated herself delicately on the other end of the couch. I didn't look up, but I felt the cushions shift and settle, heard the soft rustle of cloth and smelled the clean scent of her.

"How do you know my name?" I mumbled through my fingers. "Am I on some secret government monster registry now?"

"No. Your government knows nothing of those like you. But I was there when you were born."

I dropped my hands and stared. "Are... are you my mother?"

Evaine laughed. It was a musical sound and didn't seem mocking, but I blushed furiously. My question wasn't funny, was it? My hands curled into fists tight enough to hurt.

"No, Lilith," said Evaine. "I may no longer be human, but I'm no succubus."

"Then how were you there when I was born? Where the hell was that? I don't even know," I admitted. "I've been in foster care pretty much forever."

Evaine reached out and put one of her hands on mine. Slowly, I uncurled my fingers. My nails were edged red with blood, but there was no sign of any cuts on my palms. What the fuck? I pulled my hand from hers, grabbed a frilly throw pillow and clutched it against my knotted stomach.

"Demons are forbidden from the world," Evaine said. "They were sealed away by Merlin so long ago that the truth of their evil has faded into legend. But sometimes young, foolish wizards will summon a succubus or incubus from the Nether for their pleasure. There is nothing quite like the lust demons."

"Wizards?" I asked, bewildered.

"Mortal sorcerers, students of Merlinic magic. Your father was such a man, Lilith – a man of powerful magic and desires. But a succubus does not conceive a child easily. It happens only when they fall in love."

I scowled and gripped the pillow harder. The fabric tore and stuffing puffed out around my fingers like bits of manufactured cloud.

"Wow," I said. "So my dad summoned my mother to be his fuck-toy and she fell in love with him? That's some serious Stockholm's Syndrome shit."

"Your father is an intelligent, powerful and commanding man," Evaine told me gently. "The kind of man that a succubus couldn't resist. She fell in love and became pregnant with his child."

"Me."

Evaine nodded. "Yes, Lilith. Understand that your mother devoured the sexual energies of mortal men. Men like your father. Energies which he provided in abundance."

"So succubusses... succubi? They uh... run on sex?" I asked. That seemed pretty fucking important. Was that what was going on with me?

"Succubae," Evaine corrected. "When your mother – a demoness of lust – fell in love, it so fundamentally changed her that sex could no longer sustain her. What she needed instead, your father could not give."

"So my dad starved my mother to death? Asshole."

Evaine gave me a small, sad smile. "Your father has committed many sins, but that's not one of them. What your mother needed from him was his love. It's not his fault that he did not return her affection. We cannot always control our hearts."

I sighed. I guessed Evaine had a point. "So... what happened?"

"Your father was young, ambitious and frightened. Summoning demons for any reason is strictly forbidden by the laws of his order and he could not risk anyone learning what he had done. So he banished your mother back to the Nether, where he believed that she and the child she carried would die."

"But he was wrong," I said. That much seemed obvious.

"Demons are powerful creatures, in body and in spirit. Your mother did die, I'm afraid, but not before delivering her baby girl on the shores of Avalon."

"Avalon? That place isn't real," I said before I could close my mouth. Half-demon girls didn't get to decide if magical islands were make-believe.

"Merlin's seal stands on Avalon and it was in the stone's shadow that I delivered you. Your mother whispered your name to me as she faded and died."

"I was... born on Avalon?" I asked. "Then what the fuck am I doing here?"

"Avalon is a strange and cold land, Lilith. It is my home and I serve the mystic isle as its steward, but it is no place for a child. There is only one mortal there and he would have been of little use to you as a father. So I carried you back to the human realm and surrendered you to a hospital."

Ditched again. The story of my fucking life. I swiped more tears out of my eyes. Shit, I was tired of crying.

"Your mother named you *Lilith*," Evaine said. "But I gave you the last name *Quinn*."

"Why?" I asked, frowning. "Is that your last name?"

"It means *wisdom*."

What the fuck did that mean? My frown turned into a scowl. "Is it my father's last name? Why didn't you take me to him?"

Evaine regarded me with unwavering aqua eyes. "The Castle and the College – the sect of Merlinic magi to which your father belongs – stand guard against forces from beyond this world. That is why summoning a demon is so grave a crime under their law.

"Your father could not take you, Lilith. He couldn't have protected you from his own order. He didn't even know that you lived until I told him so. And now that your first sexual encounter has awakened your demonic heritage, you are in danger. The College does not tolerate demons or their offspring."

I sat bolt upright, dropping the pillow I had been clutching. My body went taut and cold. "Doesn't tolerate...? What are you saying?"

"There are wizards who work as hunters for the College. They are paid in gold to capture or kill those like you, whom their elders have determined pose a threat to humanity."

"And... and they're coming after me? Shit!"

I leapt to my feet. Was some kind of magical SWAT team about to burst in and kick my ass? Sure, I was the first to admit I was a freak and a monster, but I didn't want to *die* because of it.

"Why didn't you tell me before?" I shouted. "We have to get the hell out of here!"

Evaine remained seated and looked up at me with a delicately amused expression on her face. "I am telling you what you need to know, when you need to know it."

"Don't give me that *I'll tell you when the time is right* bullshit, lady! Am I about to get shot in the face by magical bounty hunters?"

Evaine's expression became grave and she seemed just about to answer when the front door banged open. I screamed and jumped. My foot caught on the corner of the couch and I fell, sprawling across the living room floor. Evaine's demon hunters were going to gun me down on the ground like someone's rabid pet...

But when I looked up, I recognized the guy standing in the open door.

It was Max.

Chapter FOUR

Max ran across the living room. He was dressed for school, but his chest was heaving and the fabric of his t-shirt stuck to his skin with sweat. I still had his truck and we weren't neighbors anymore... Had Max run the entire way from the high school?

"You... you weren't in class today," he panted. "I... looked for you. Why are you on the floor, Lil?"

I hauled myself to my feet and glared at my one-time best friend. "What the fuck do you care?"

Max paled a shade, but he didn't back off. "Lil, I... I'm—"

"You left!" I shouted. "You ran away from me!"

Max crossed the living room and grabbed me into a hug, but I stiffened and shoved him back. He flew through the air and then skidded across the carpet until he thumped against the wall. Max shook his head and looked up at me.

"I'm sorry, Lil," he said. "I was scared. I don't know what's going on with you, but I... I'm your friend. I shouldn't have run."

"*You're* scared?" I pointed to the wall where he had impacted it. "I just threw you across the fucking room. I'm a monster, Max, and there are demon hunters out there who kill things like me!"

Max stood and moved in close again, but more slowly this time. Like he was approaching a dangerous animal. Which wasn't far from the truth, I supposed.

"Lil, you're not a monster," Max told me. He extended one hand. "And I'm going to be right here for... for whatever comes next."

"You don't get it, Max! I'm not kidding. I'm half succubus! I didn't even think they existed a day ago and now... now..."

I didn't even know what to say. Everything was such a mess. How could any of it be real? It was all some horrible nightmare, but I couldn't wake up. Max closed the final distance between us and folded his arms around me again. He felt solid against me. This time, I didn't push Max away.

"I'm so scared," I whispered.

"Me, too," Max said. He squeezed me tight to his chest. "But I'm going to stay here with you through... whatever this is, Lil. I'm scared and I don't understand any of it, but I'll never run again. I promise."

"This is not a good idea."

This came from Evaine, who had remained so quiet through our little reunion that I had nearly forgotten all about the pale-haired woman. Max didn't seem to have noticed her at all and jumped. Evaine rose, frowning, and Max stepped between us.

"Lil, who the hell is this?" he asked.

"Lilith," Evaine said, ignoring Max. "The College is only the first to learn of your awakening. I have convinced them to give me some time, but then there will be a test. A single chance to prove that you are not the monster they fear."

Oh god, that sounded ominous.

"Others will learn of your existence and your life will be one of danger," Evaine told me. "I can teach you the skills that such a life will require, and your cambion heritage will give you the strength and power to survive in the supernatural world. But if you further involve this boy, I cannot guarantee his safety."

Max's eyes widened, but he didn't back off. Evaine's expression softened a little.

"The College can take his memories," she said. "It is a painless process. They can send the boy away. His life will never touch yours again and he will be safe."

"Max... won't remember me at all?" I asked.

"Fuck that!" said Max. "Lil, what is this shit?"

"Maybe I shouldn't tell you. Evaine's right. My life is going to be awful... if this College place doesn't just kill me for failing their test. If we stay friends, you'll be in danger, too. Apparently."

Max rounded on me, fists clenched and shaking. "You want to make me forget you?"

"No," I said. "But I don't want you to get hurt. Thank you for... for coming back. Now it's time for you to go, I guess."

"That's not your decision to make, Lil," Max said. His voice would have been as hard as stone if only it hadn't cracked on my name. "It's mine."

"If you remain by Lilith's side, your life will be strange and dangerous," Evaine told Max, speaking directly to him for the first time since he had blundered into the middle of this. "You must keep her secrets and you must keep them well. If you fail, the College *will* discover it."

Max's face was still pale, but he nodded.

"You don't share the powers of Lilith's blood," said Evaine. "You will be vulnerable, Maxwell. Her enemies may become your enemies, and you're not strong enough to fight them."

"I could... try," Max stammered. "I'm a pretty big guy."

Evaine's smile was both kind and pitying. "There are forces in the world and beyond that no mortal man can fight. Even the wizards who battle them often die in the attempt and you have none of their abilities. Do you still wish to stand by Lilith's side?"

"I already said," Max answered. "Lil, I'm with you to the end. I promise."

I couldn't see through the tears anymore, so I groped blindly until Max grabbed my hand and squeezed. He was so solid and... *there*. Max wasn't just my best friend – he was *the* best friend. Whatever happened now, I didn't have to face it alone.

"Very well," Evaine said. "Then you can at least make yourself useful. Lilith has much to learn, Maxwell. So take off your pants."

Chapter
FIVE

"Lilith, stop," Evaine said.

We were upstairs in my bedroom. It had taken some persuasion to get Max naked, but not much. Between his new promise to me and well... being an eighteen-year-old boy, it wasn't too tough to convince him to ditch school and his clothes.

Now I had my best friend laid out on the narrow bed. I straddled Max's waist and rode him hard. That had taken even less convincing.

The feel of his cock in my pussy filling and stretching me was even better than the night before. It was sweet and hot and touched places deeper inside my body than I ever knew existed. I grabbed the headboard as pleasure seared through me. Wood splintered under my hands. Again.

"Lilith," Evaine said. Her voice was still soft and musical, but there was a firmer note in it now. "Stop."

I moaned and writhed on Max's dick. That sweet, brilliant gold sensation was pouring into me, the feeling that Evaine told us was Max's desire, his sexual energy. I wouldn't starve without it, Evaine assured me, but it was so *good*. I didn't want to feel anything else ever again...

Max groaned. I grabbed his shoulders and held him down on my bed. His chest was covered in red bite-marks and several of them were darkening to purple bruises in mute testament to my excitement. My wetness ran in shining streaks across his stomach.

"Lil," said Max. "Lil, I'm going to cum…"

His voice was thick and rough. The sound of it was better than the best chocolate, especially to my over-sensitive hearing. But I didn't need the warning. I felt it in how Max's already thick cock swelled even bigger inside me, in the tightness of his balls as my ass came down against him over and over. I saw the flutter of his racing pulse under the skin of his throat.

"Lilith, stop!" Evaine said.

"I… I can't," I whispered. "Oh god, more…!"

Evaine grabbed my shoulder and I shoved her away with a breathless growl. She fell back a step before gracefully recovering her balance. I felt a pang of guilt, but I didn't stop. I *couldn't* stop.

I slammed myself down onto Max's cock. His hands were curled around my hips, trying to restrain me. Max was strong, but not stronger than me. Not anymore. His dick turned to molten steel in the wet clasp of my pussy and then gushed into me. If what had come before was orgasm, then I didn't even know what to name this feeling. I felt the creamy heat of Max's load filling me. I felt how bright white it was with the strange mingling and swirling of senses that made me call the sexual energy *golden* and told me that it tasted sweet.

The fullness of Max's cock pumping thick cum into me was too much… I couldn't think anymore. My whole body trembled and tightened with the savage intensity of my pleasure.

"Ah, fuck!" Max cried. "Lil!"

His climax pulsed harder inside me and I wondered if it could shoot me right off the end of his long cock. For a second, I thought that was exactly what happened, until I realized that Evaine had grabbed me again. She yanked me off of Max and held me back as his cum dripped down my trembling thighs.

Max's fists were twisted into the sheets and his cock fell against the sweat-slicked plane of his stomach. A final pale streamer of semen splashed out across his skin. I moaned and strained toward Max, but Evaine pulled me back.

"What the hell are you doing?" I asked. "Why are you stopping me?"

"Because you do not yet have control. Look what you've done."

Evaine pointed down at Max. There were red patches on his hips where my thighs had gripped him, darkening slowly to an ugly purple-black color. More bruises stained Max's ribs and my nails had left not just pink streaks, but bloody lines down his chest. I clapped my hands over my mouth, feeling sick... but I still smelled Max on my skin and my pussy squeezed down on nothing, making his load stream out from between my legs.

"Shit, Max," I said. "Oh, shit. I'm sorry!"

"I... I'm alright, Lil," he groaned.

Max tried to sit up, but then he winced and fell back into the sheets with a low grunt of pain. He gave me a wobbly smile, then gulped and squeezed his eyes shut. Evaine held onto my shoulder. Her hand was cool against the heat surging through me. It occurred to me that I probably should have been embarrassed to be naked and fucking my best friend in front of this strange woman. But I was too worried about Max for that thought to stick for long.

"Succubae are far stronger and faster than any mortal woman," said Evaine. "They are dangerous. The energies you gain from lust and sex give you a measure of their power."

I sank onto the corner of the bed, staring at Max where he lay sweating in the sheets. Evaine knelt beside me and gently prodded at one of Max's bruises. He let out a reluctant groan.

"But a succubus is a demon and cares nothing for the men and women she takes," Evaine explained in a soft voice as she examined

Max's injuries. "They are her victims. You must be better than that, Lilith, if you don't want the College to hunt you down. You must be better than your worst instincts. Do you understand?"

"Yeah. But what about Max?" I asked.

"I'm good," he said. "Don't worry about me, Lil."

Max struggled to sit up, but Evaine put her hand in the center of his chest and pushed him back into the bed.

"You heal swiftly, Lilith. But your human lovers do not," she told me, then looked down at Max. "Lie still."

He nodded. Evaine's hand remained on Max and he looked over her shoulder at me, one eyebrow raised. His still-hard cock twitched against his stomach. Panicked though I was – and it was a lot – I couldn't blame Max one bit. I'd never really had a thing for girls before, but this Evaine lady was *damned* hot. Weird, but hot.

Evaine closed her eyes and opened her mouth. The sound that came from her lips... but I don't know if I could fairly have called it singing. There was definitely a melody, but no words that I could make out. The notes slid and flowed over each other like water. I tried to hum Evaine's song later, but could never quite remember how it went.

The angry red and purple marks all across Max's skin turned pink and then yellow around the edges. As Evaine sang, the terrible bruising – and what had to be fractured bones beneath – healed until all that remained were a few slightly flushed spots along his waist and chest.

Evaine pulled her hand away and sat back. Max whistled.

"Wow," he said.

"Are you okay?" I asked.

"Yeah." Max prodded his torso a couple of times. "Good as new, actually. But Lil... you didn't stop when I came."

"Shit!"

I leapt to my feet. Semen streaked my thighs in pale, gleaming lines. It felt like Max had pumped a gallon or more of the stuff up into me. I cupped my fingers to my streaming pussy and couldn't help a moan as my sex-crazed body tingled at the touch.

"We're *so* fucked," I groaned. "And last night, too! There's no way I'm not getting pregnant."

Evaine smiled and I nearly forgot how hot she was. Did she not think this was a big deal? What would happen now? I guessed the best I could hope for was that this Merlinic College that Evaine kept talking about wouldn't hunt down a pregnant girl. Or would they even care...?

"Lilith," Evaine said. She put her hand on my shoulder. Damn, she was strong. Almost as strong as me. "You must listen. Like your mother, sex is a vital part of your nature, but you cannot contract disease from it. The power that sex gives you will heal any infection before it takes root."

"Yeah, great," I answered absently.

It wasn't disease that I was worried about right now, though I supposed I might be grateful for that later.

"And like your mother," said Evaine, "you cannot conceive a child unless you are in love with the father."

My hammering heart slowed a little and I flopped down onto the edge of my bed again. I pushed the sweaty tangles of my red hair back from my face and let out a long sigh.

"Oh, thank god," I said.

Max was quiet for a moment, eyes turned down to where his cock lay long against his stomach. It was streaked in his cum and mine. I stared at it, too. Suddenly, the feeling of Max's load dripping slowly out of my pussy was delicious. A large, pearly drop leaked from between my legs and rolled down my inner thigh.

"Yeah. Okay. What do we need to do next?" Max asked, looking up at Evaine.

"First and foremost – control," she answered. "If Lilith cannot learn to restrain herself, the results could be devastating."

"How am I supposed to control myself?" I asked. "All I think about is cock. Cock, cock, cock. And maybe... pussy?"

I blushed and looked away out the window, even as the admission made a hot electric thrill run through my body.

"Your demon blood is strong," Evaine said. "You must master the succubus half of your nature, lest it dominate you."

"Dominate?" I asked. There was a demon inside me. A sex demon. Would feeding it make it stronger? "Like... it can take over?"

Max sat up and the blood drained from his face. Not his cock, though, I couldn't help noticing.

"You can and must learn how to balance and control your dual natures," Evaine said. Her voice remained stern, but gentle. "It will require time and patience, but it can be done."

"Have you done this before?" Max asked. "Taught a uh...?"

"Cambion," Evaine answered as she began unbuttoning her pristine white jacket. "Yes. I taught another cambion, long ago. His powers were frightening and burned out of control, too. He sought my wisdom and together we learned how to tame his father's demonic influence."

"Together?" I asked, trying not to sound too hopeful.

Evaine nodded. She shrugged out of her jacket and draped it over my desk chair. Hours had passed since this strange woman appeared at my front door, but beads of water still glittered in her platinum ringlets.

Max's fingers found mine and he held them tightly as Evaine removed her silk blouse. She wasn't wearing anything beneath. I bit my lip, but that didn't stop my quiet whimper at the sight. Evaine's breasts were high and small, tipped in peaked pink nipples that made me think of flower buds.

Okay, I was definitely attracted to women, too. But thoughts of *bisexual* or *lesbian* didn't really cross my mind. I just wanted to feel good, to pleasure and be pleasured. I craved it, needed it like I needed air.

Evaine unzipped her white skirt and pushed it off down her long legs. She wore no underwear at all, apparently. Something about that thought made my heart race. Evaine's pussy was just barely visible between her thighs, soft and a delicate pale rose color that only made me think even more of flowers.

"Wow," I whispered.

Beside me, Max nodded in mute agreement. My mysterious new teacher stood naked in my bedroom, rising like an alabaster statue over us. Like an angel.

Evaine sank gracefully to the floor in front of me and placed a slim hand on each of my knees. She spread my legs open before her, exposing my slicked pussy and the creamy cum dripping out of me. I leaned back against Max, feeling his racing heartbeat echoing my own.

"The sexual energies that empower you will flow freely," Evaine said. "It is nothing so physical as orgasm or a man's seed."

She ran one finger along my inner thigh, tracing a slippery white line of Max's cum where it had oozed from my pussy. I shivered and let out a moan. Evaine held up her finger.

"You do not need to force it, or take it," she told me. "You will be better than that, Lilith. You are beautiful, sensual."

So slowly that I found myself biting my lower lip in anticipation, Evaine sucked her dripping finger into her mouth like it was the most delicious thing she had ever tasted. Her aqua eyes drifted shut, silvery lashes so long that they brushed her cheeks.

When she had licked up every trace of Max's cum and mine from her skin, Evaine ran one wet finger along her lips until they gleamed pink. Watching her, I could barely breathe. Evaine trailed her fingertips delicately along the smooth curves of her side, then to her breasts. She cupped her palms lightly over the hard nipples and then her hands were moving again, higher to rake through her pale white-blonde hair. It fell in moonlight-colored curls across her shoulders and chest.

"Do you feel it?" Evaine asked. "My desire?"

"Yes," I whispered.

Evaine wasn't even touching me, but I did feel it. I felt her lust with senses that were nothing so mundane as touch or smell. And it was good. Evaine's desire was a slow, sweet golden current like pouring honey. I stared up at her and wondered how long until I was begging her to fuck me.

"Don't force or hunt sex, Lilith," Evaine said. "You will inspire lust and passion, make it burn inside your lovers, and warm yourself by those flames."

She bent and trailed her lips along my thigh, tongue swirling through the slick wetness there. I trembled and my breath came in short gasps as Evaine moved up. When her mouth brushed over my pussy, I squeaked and grabbed the sheets. They tore in my hands.

"Restraint," Evaine reminded me.

Her voice was pitched low with desire, even more melodious than before, and I wanted to moan at the lovely sound of it. I wanted to slide my fingers into all those silver-blonde curls and yank Evaine's face down between my legs. I wanted to press my pussy against her beautiful lips until I gushed.

But that wasn't restraint. That was going to get me hunted down and executed by wizards.

"I... I'm trying," I panted.

I made my hands unclench and took a deep breath. I felt the brighter heat of Max's lust pouring from him. His mouth hung open and his cock jutted rock-hard from his lap as he watched Evaine touch her lips to the most sensitive part of me. I wanted to devour them both, cover Max and Evaine both in love bites and drink in their delicious desire until I blazed with the hot golden light.

Evaine kissed my pussy deeply, slowly. Her lips moved over me, wet and delicate, and I ripped another handful of sheets before making myself let go. I trembled with the effort. Evaine's tongue slid into me, licking Max's semen out of my slit. The sound of it was wet and beautiful. Pleasure coiled in my belly and exploded with sweet sensation.

"Ah, fuck...!" I screamed.

If the all neighbors hadn't been away at work, I was pretty sure that they would have called the cops. Not that I cared right then. Evaine's smooth, controlled golden lust filled me as her tongue swirled between my legs and she drank up every creamy drop of Max's load. When his cum was gone, I gushed my own into Evaine's waiting mouth.

"Oh god," Max breathed. "That is so hot."

He had shifted up to kneel beside me on the bed, fist wrapped tightly around his rock-hard dick. I wasn't even sure he knew he was doing it – Max's dark blue eyes were riveted to the sight of Evaine between my legs. His chest was flushed and the slow pumping of his hand up and down his cock made the muscles bunch and release in a rhythmic dance. Each long stroke coaxed another pearly drop of precum from the darkened head and they ran across his knuckles in a pale streak. The sexual energy baked off Max like heat from an oven. Like heat from the fucking sun.

"Come here," I panted.

I grabbed Max's cock from his hand and pulled him closer until I could feed his rigid length into my eager little mouth. I moaned at the taste. Why had I never sucked Max's dick before? Oh yeah, I remembered in a daze: he was still my best friend. That would have been weird. That didn't seem to matter right now, though – just his thick shaft forcing my lips further and further open.

"Lil, yes!" Max panted.

His hand came up hesitantly, then gently cupped the back of my head as I sucked his dick. I was supposed to be in history class right then, not in my bedroom with a cock in my mouth and a tongue buried in my pussy. Evaine's lips caressed my clitoris and I let out a muffled moan of delight.

I wanted more and swallowed Max's cock deeper, but I had underestimated his size and my untrained gag reflex. I choked and saliva ran all down his length – which Max didn't seem to mind, actually – but before I could try again, Evaine sucked the hard little nub of my clit between her lips. My spine arched up off the mattress, pleasure shooting through me like lightning, and Max's dick became a handhold more than anything else.

"Lilith," Evaine warned. "If you care for the boy, be gentle."

The breath of her words slid over my dripping slit and I shivered, both at the sensation and at her reminder. Max's cock was still in my hand and I was squeezing him tightly. My best friend panted hard and fast, his face and chest flushed red, and a ceaseless stream of precum ran from the tip of his dick. I could have hurt him. Badly. Max had literally put the most sensitive part of him in my hand and trusted me with it.

It would have been a crying shame to damage such a magnificent cock. I made myself release Max and went to work licking all up and down his dick. I couldn't hurt him using just my tongue, right? I licked as carefully as I could. It's what Max would have done for me.

Restraint didn't come easy. There was too much pleasure inside me and it seemed to burst from my body in wet gushes that Evaine drank up without missing a beat. I moaned and writhed on my broken bed, matching every stroke of her tongue in me with one along Max's jutting cock. I whimpered at the effort – I wanted him in my mouth, in my pussy. I wanted to jerk Max's dick until he painted my face and tits with every white-hot drop of spunk that he could muster.

But I held back. Restraint.

Evaine sat up, licking her lips. Even her breasts were shiny and wet with my juices. She rose to her feet and nodded down at me as I lapped gently along Max's cock.

"Better," Evaine said. "There may be hope for you yet."

I threw my hands in the air to celebrate my victory and punched Max right in the jaw. He slammed back against the wall and then sagged into the sheets. His dick remained unflaggingly hard, but his eyes were glazed.

"Ah, shit," I said. "Max? Are you okay?"

He fought for a moment to focus his eyes, then flashed me a wobbling thumbs-up. Good. I was nowhere near done. I wasn't sure if that was my succubus half or my teenage girl half talking, but I crawled across the bed toward Max. He gave me a dazed grin and reached out.

Evaine sighed and shook her head, but she didn't get dressed. Hooray for fucking!

Chapter
SIX

*A*fter eight hours and a few more of Evaine's healing songs, Max was the one to hear a car coming up the driveway. My senses were far better, but my attention was entirely consumed by his cock and Evaine's sweet pussy.

"That's Bill and Sandra!" I gasped. I sat bolt upright in the bed and threw Evaine's leg up off of me. "What time is it?"

"Uh, about five o'clock," Max said. "Shit, I was supposed to meet with Mister Harvey after shop class."

"Fuck!"

We collided as we both dove for our clothes. I threw Max's jeans over to him while he was still rubbing his temple. My underwear were missing in action. How the hell did that happen? My room was too tiny for anything to get lost...

Evaine stood beside my desk, already clad once again all in white. She held my panties hooked over one finger.

"You have a great deal yet to learn, Lilith," Evaine said. "Sex is only a part of what I must teach you if you are to survive."

The first thing I had to survive was a family meeting with my foster parents. I had no desire to add a naked boy in my bedroom to the agenda and figured that being dressed was another crucial step. I snatched my underwear from Evaine, but when I opened my hand, I was also holding a business card. The lettering was silver on a white background and I had to turn it to catch the light.

Evaine tapped the business card with one perfect fingernail. "Come to me at this address after school tomorrow and I will teach you more."

"After... school?" I repeated. "I'm supposed to go back to high school after all of this?"

Max hopped across my bedroom as he tried to wrestle his shoes and shirt on at the same time and failing at both. He banged into the wall and the window rattled.

"Many things in your life have changed, Lilith," Evaine said. "But not that. You're still half human and your mortal education remains important."

"But we skipped school today," I protested.

"Had I not intervened today, you would have left the city. The College would surely have interpreted your flight as a signal of guilt and moved against you."

Max finally yanked his shirt down over his tousled blond hair. "Left the city? Lil, were you running away?"

"Uh, yeah," I admitted. I pulled on my panties and jeans, then found Max's keys on my desk and held them out. "These are yours, by the way."

Max closed his hand over mine and didn't immediately take the keys. He gave me a hard, lingering kiss that nearly had me tearing off his clothes again, then finally accepted his keys and stuffed them into his pocket.

"You will learn about the worlds beyond this one, Lilith," said Evaine. "But the mortal realm is still your home and you must be able to live in it."

I combed my fingers hastily through my hair. "Seriously? You expect a half-succubus to focus on algebra?"

"Yes," Evaine said. "I do."

"Shouldn't I be studying for the College's test?"

Max stood at the window and looked down. "Uh, Lil? Sandra and Bill are on their way in."

He was right. I felt the slight tremor through the townhouse as the front door closed downstairs and smelled Bill's aftershave.

"Out the window," I said. "Quick!"

Max's eyes opened wide, but he yanked the window open. He swung over the sill and I grabbed his wrists, lowering my best friend as far as I could. With all my sex-powered strength, he barely seemed to weigh a thing, but my arms were only so long. Max still dangled a good six feet above our postcard-sized front lawn.

"Do not speak to anyone about this, Maxwell," Evaine said conversationally, like I wasn't trying to sneak a boy out my window. "The College will silence you if you cannot silence yourself."

"Got it," Max grunted. "Lil, drop me before your parents get up here!"

"I'll see you tomorrow, right?" I asked.

Max's hands shook in my grasp, but he nodded awkwardly up at me. "Yeah, Lil. I promised not to run, didn't I? Don't you try it again either."

I squeezed Max's hands in mine, nodded and let go. He fell and landed on the grass with a groan. Max darted a glance at the front door, but it didn't open, so he gave me a dimpled grin and then scrambled off down the hill in the direction of his truck.

When I turned back to my bedroom, Evaine was gone. I gulped. There were only two exits from my room – the window and the door. Was she downstairs with Bill and Sandra?

"Oh shit," I hissed under my breath. "Oh shit, oh shit!"

No way were Evaine's calm explanations of demons and wizards going to fly with my practical foster parents. I flung the door open and sprinted down the stairs, taking them two at a time. I had to get to Evaine before she made everything worse...!

"Wait!" I called out as I galloped into the living room. "Don't–!"

I skidded to a stop. Evaine was nowhere to be seen, but Sandra stood beside the dinner table, setting down an armload of brown paper grocery bags. Bill was in the living room, staring at the torn-up throw pillow and then at me.

"Oh, uh... hi," I said.

"Family meeting," Sandra told me. "Right now."

———

I admitted to my foster parents that there was... stuff going on in my life. My whole world was changing and I was learning a lot of new things about myself. I kept the details vague, but broke down into genuine tears. There was a College test coming up, I told them with very real worry, an important one that would determine so much of my future.

I even confessed to dating Blake just to make them happy. That I knew he expected sex, but I didn't want to. Okay, that last bit wasn't *quite* true. But my foster parents seemed to feel bad about it, so Sandra was pretty gentle when she yelled at me about violating curfew on my birthday and breaking my bed in a "fit of rage." And Bill didn't even bring up kicking me out of the house. At least I wouldn't be homeless while I figured out how the hell to manage life as a half sex-demon.

I promised both of them that I'd try to do better. The miracle was that I kind of did.

You know... eventually.

I broke up with Blake two days later and gave him a conciliatory blowjob that had him smirking through the rest of the day. I didn't tell Blake that I had been practicing on Max, though. I could get more than half of my best friend's cock into my mouth and was gunning for full deep-throat by the end of the school year. I only had a couple of weeks left, so I got in as much practice as I could.

The address on Evaine's business card was for a dance studio she rented, though I had no idea if she was staying there or only using it for my lessons. It was a small, two-story building with a mission-style red tiled roof and round-cornered white walls tucked away just a few blocks from my high school.

Evaine insisted that I continue going to class every day and made me finish my homework before answering any of my questions. Max only came with me to the dance studio about half the time, but the same rules applied to him – homework first.

We weren't very good at obeying those rules. Well, I wasn't very good at it and Max wasn't very good at saying *no* to me.

We sat in one corner of the studio, textbooks open while Max and I pretended to pay attention to something about ancient Rome. Evaine stood nearby, turned away from us and speaking softly to the apparently empty air in some language that sounded a bit like rushing water.

I took advantage of her inattention to stick my hand down the back of Max's jeans and grab his ass. He jumped, but knew better than to yelp – that would just get us in trouble. I winked at Max and slid my hand around to the front of his pants to brush along the instantly hard length of his cock. Max's jaw tightened against a groan and I smirked.

"Lilith, you're supposed to be doing your homework," Evaine said.

She was still facing away and I didn't immediately remove my hand from Max's jeans. I stuck out my tongue at her back. Now Evaine turned to look at me.

"How the hell did you see any of that?" I asked. "Magic or something?"

Evaine gestured around the dance studio, at the walls lined in mirrors. I sighed and reluctantly withdrew my hand from Max's jeans. He let out the breath he was holding and Evaine crossed her arms.

"Your restraint remains lacking," she said.

"I didn't hurt Max!" I protested, then glanced at him. "Right?"

Max nodded, though his face was still bright red. Evaine turned her disapproving gaze on Max and he pulled the nearest textbook into his lap.

"There's more to proper discipline than avoiding injury, Lilith," Evaine told me. "You bear the blood of a succubus. Your sexual urges will always be strong, but you must learn to control them."

"Before they control me?" I asked, rolling my eyes. "Is this about my demon half taking over?"

"Come with me. Both of you."

Max closed his history book obediently and rose to his feet. I stood more slowly, sighing. But when Evaine marched us upstairs, my bad mood vanished instantly.

There was an office up above the dance studio, but the desk had been shoved off to one side and replaced with a sturdy four-poster bed. The sheets were perfectly smooth. Did Evaine actually sleep in it? Questions for another time.

Grinning, I bounded toward the waiting bed. Now this was the kind of homework I could get into! But Evaine grabbed my arm in her steely grip. I hadn't fucked Max since yesterday morning – a little quickie behind the gym at school – so I wasn't strong enough to break away.

"Hey!" I protested.

Evaine pulled me back from the bed and pointed to a chair in front of the desk. "Sit."

I sat with a frown and Max stood in the door, looking confused. But as Evaine glided across the room to the bed, I sat up straight in my seat like a preppy girl in the front row of class.

"What do I get to do now?" I asked.

"Watch."

"Just... watch?" I repeated, pouting.

"Watch what?" Max asked.

Evaine hooked her finger at him. "Come to me."

Max's eyes widened. The bulge in his jeans hadn't faded one bit from downstairs and now it strained at the front of his pants. Evaine sat on the edge of the bed. She wore a pale blue sweater that hugged her slim curves and a cream-colored skirt. When Evaine leaned back into the bed and slowly parted her legs, Max and I shared a glance. My teacher still wasn't wearing any panties.

"Uh... Lil?" Max said in a choked voice.

My mouth went dry and I squeezed my thighs together. My pussy flared with wet heat.

"Oh fuck yes," I whispered.

Max walked closer on unsteady legs as Evaine slid her sweater up over her soft, round breasts and removed her skirt. Next, she reached for Max's shirt, sliding the hem up to reveal flushed skin and hard muscles. My mouth went from dry to watering in an instant.

So gradually that both Max and I groaned, Evaine unzipped his jeans and pulled his thick cock free. She curled her fingers around Max, giving his dick a long, sensual stroke. I whimpered. Max looked at me, but Evaine just kept going.

When he went for his belt, Evaine put her hands over Max's and she shook her head. She undressed him slowly, bit by bit until I was squirming in my chair.

"Fuck her, Max," I panted. "Oh god, please fuck her!"

Max gulped, looking back and forth between me and Evaine. She lay across the sheets, curly white-blonde hair fanned out over the pillows and her long legs spread. Max let Evaine pull him onto the bed, then gasped as her hand slipped down his chest to his straining cock.

I sat up straighter in my chair, craning my neck to get a better view as Evaine guided Max's dick to the slick, soft pink of her pussy.

Then she grabbed his taut ass in both hands and pulled Max slowly inside her, inch by inch. I watched his cock vanish into Evaine, biting my lip and gripping the arms of the chair so hard that they creaked.

When Max's entire length was finally buried inside Evaine, she pulled him into a long kiss. Her back arched in the sheets, pressing her slender body up to meet Max's. Her hands slid over his skin and traced the lines of his chest in lingering, unhurried caresses.

There was nothing of the frantic, urgent fucking that I had desperately demanded every day since my awakening. Evaine led Max in a slow, sensual dance and he moved against her with far more restraint than I had ever shown. His bunched muscles trembled, but his hips rolled gracefully between Evaine's spread legs and she smiled up at him.

Fuck, they were beautiful together. I was so wet that it soaked through my jeans, so I yanked open the zipper and thrust one hand down my pants. Evaine let out a soft, musical moan and I echoed her with my own hungry, whorish sound. I cupped my hand over my pussy and felt wetness running between my fingers. My clitoris hardened insistently against my palm.

Max kissed his way down Evaine's throat to her pale chest. His lips left flushed blooms in their wake and Evaine gasped as he sucked one of her swiftly stiffening nipples into his mouth. Or maybe I was the one who gasped.

I rubbed myself frantically beneath my jeans. Not enough... I jammed a finger into my pussy. Still not enough. I inserted another finger and then a third. I whimpered and pumped them in and out between my legs.

Gently, Max bit at the soft flesh of Evaine's breast and looked across her slim body to me. I felt his desire like a bullet between my eyes. Max was sunk to the hilt in Evaine, but even without touching me, his lust burned like a flame. The heat of it exploded inside me and I came hard, my hips rising up off the chair.

Max worked himself into Evaine, still slowly but visibly restraining himself. He hooked her legs over his elbows to spear his cock even deeper into her beautiful pink slit. You couldn't really call the sounds Evaine made moans – they were too musical. She sang out her pleasure in high, clear notes that crescendoed with each wave of climax. Max's breath heaved faster, the sound of it rougher and more primal, but no less intoxicating. It was only with a monumental effort that I kept my fingernails from digging furrows into the desk chair's arm.

Max pulled out of Evaine, making wetness splash from his dripping dick and across her soft skin. My teacher grabbed his flushed length and with just a few gentle strokes, she had Max squeezing his eyes shut and groaning in release. Cum streamed from his cock, pouring across Evaine's smooth stomach like spilled cream and dressing her entirely in white again.

I withdrew my dripping fingers from my jeans and Evaine sat up. Max's load ran down her body in pale streaks.

"Restraint and discipline can be sweet, Lilith," she told me in a slightly breathless voice. "Are you ready to try?"

"Yes!" I said.

I jumped up to my feet before realizing how bad that looked. Blushing, I ducked my head and walked to the bed as slowly as I could manage. Max sat back on his heels, panting. Sweat darkened his blond hair. His cock was still flushed and thick, slick with his cum and Evaine's gushing wetness. He watched me approach the bed and it rose, hard and ready in seconds.

"He lacks nothing in stamina," Evaine noted.

She slid off the bed and stood to make room. Max's cum oozed down her skin and I wanted to pin her down and lick it all up. But if I didn't do exactly what Evaine asked, she might banish me back to the desk chair again. It had been a glorious show, but now I ached with the need to be filled and my fingers just weren't enough.

"Undress," Evaine instructed.

Nodding, I began unbuttoning my shirt. Blood rushed in my ears and my heart pounded a thundering drumbeat in my chest. I dropped my shirt and then bra to the floor, following them with my shoes, socks, jeans and panties. Just the feel of the air against my bare pussy was almost too much.

"Get on the bed," said Evaine.

Trembling, I pulled myself up onto the bed, facing Max. His gaze raked over my naked body and his hands tightened into fists on his thighs.

"What do you want us to do?" Max asked.

Evaine moved around the bed to stand beside me. I looked up at her and gulped. I wasn't sure what she had in mind. Was this another lesson, or punishment for not paying enough attention to my homework?

"Lilith, get onto your hands and knees, facing away from Maxwell," Evaine instructed.

I did as she told me to, brandishing my backside at Max. His breath came faster. So did mine.

Evaine ran two fingers down over her breasts and belly until they were gooey with Max's spunk. She showed them to me and I opened my mouth to lick them clean, but Evaine withdrew her hand again. I moaned. Wetness streamed from between my legs.

Then Evaine pressed her sperm-slicked fingers against my asshole. I tensed and pulled back before I could stop myself. No one had *ever* touched me there. But Evaine put her other hand on my shoulder and held me still. She rubbed warm, slippery circles over my ass.

"Anal sex can be intensely satisfying for both partners," Evaine said. She applied a little pressure and I gasped. "But it is difficult and demands both care and restraint. It will require you to master your self-control, Lilith."

She pushed the tip of one finger slowly into my tight opening and I whimpered, burying my face in the pillows. The sensation of something being inserted up my ass was intrusive, invasive... but good, too.

"Are you okay, Lil?" Max asked. "You don't have to do this, even if she says so."

I smiled into the bed. Not many guys would turn down anal sex, let alone stand up for the girl who wanted to back out.

"I... I want to do it," I said, looking over my shoulder. "I want you to fuck my ass."

Max nodded very seriously and grabbed my butt. He pried and held my pale cheeks spread as Evaine wriggled the tip of one slippery finger harder against the clenched muscle trying to keep her out. It slid just a fraction of an inch deeper into my ass and I whimpered again at the sensation of fullness. My pussy gushed all down my thighs as Evaine worked her finger slowly into me.

"Oh god," I breathed. "Fuck!"

But Evaine withdrew her touch before I could cum, leaving me trembling on the edge. She stroked sweaty red hair back from my face and regarded me with cool blue eyes.

"Do you want this, Lilith?" Evaine asked. "Can you show restraint and patience?"

"Yes," I answered in a shaking, breathless voice.

I hadn't been more excited and scared all at once since my birthday, since I fucked Max for the first time. I inhaled sharply at the feeling of his cock nudging against my ass and flinched away. Max pulled back and gave me a second to recover before pressing forward again.

This time, I held still.

Max forced the hot, blunt weight of his dick against my ass. I knew I should be breathing, trying to relax, to accept him, but I couldn't. My taut little hole spread open and open and it felt like it was never going to stop... Then the crown of Max's cock popped softly through and nestled inside my ass.

"Fuck, Lil," he gasped. "It's so tight. Are you okay?"

I nodded, though my neck felt wobbly. I still didn't have the breath to speak and as Max slowly pushed himself deeper up my ass, it only got harder. There wasn't room in my body for breath – I was too full of cock. Max was astonishingly, impossibly huge inside me. If you asked me to draw the size of his dick from the sensation, I would have shown you a picture of a telephone pole.

Max eased back, letting me suck down a mouthful of air.

"No," I whimpered. "More...!"

He bent himself over me, wrapping his strong arms around my waist.

"Yes," Max said. His voice was rough in my ear. "More."

His body moved against mine, feeding another thick inch of un-yielding hardness up into me. My arms shook and collapsed beneath me, dropping my face and shoulders into the pillows. But my ass remained thrust in the air, impaled on Max's cock.

Evaine scooped up more of his slick load from her stomach and rubbed it over my tautly stretched hole, making it wet and slippery. Max slid another inch into my ass and I quivered in the sheets. He was so huge inside me that I felt the hot pressure of him in my pussy, too, pressing through my own flesh from deeper within than I ever could have imagined. It was like being fucked in both places at the same time. I was still trembling, but for every nerve regis-tering pain, a thousand more screamed with pleasure.

At last, Max's hips came to rest against my ass. It must have taken ten minutes of patient thrusting and waiting, giving me the chance to adjust and relax as I took a cock up my butt for the first time. But now he was buried balls-deep in my ass.

"He's all the way inside you," said Evaine. Delicately, her finger traced the sensitive pink ring of my anus stretched around Max's dick. "Do you like it, Lilith? Was it worth the work and wait?"

I don't know if an ear-splitting shriek of pure ecstasy was quite the answer Evaine expected, but it's the one she got. Pleasure ex-ploded from deep inside me, blasting through my entire body and obliterating all thought. I reacted on instinct, rocking forward and then back to spear my ass on Max's cock again. He grunted and grabbed my hips, moving with me.

I felt Evaine's smaller hand at the base of my spine. She applied gentle pressure, pacing me as I writhed on Max's dick. I wondered if she was doing the same for him, but if anyone has the restraint to ass-fuck a girl without hurting her, it was Max.

Evaine guided us into an even rhythm that smoothed out the dizzying but jagged peaks of my climax and kept it going until my voice went hoarse from screaming. Max's hips rolled fluidly, his cock sliding without cease in and out of my ass. He churned the load of cum Evaine had spread over his dick inside me until I was full to bursting.

Under my teacher's careful direction, Max played me like a musician did his favorite instrument. I couldn't stop cumming and Evaine held me in place while he fucked my ass. Max's desire and his cock surged into me, consumed me. I was so tight around Max that every slight change in angle or pressure was monumental. When his dick began to swell, I felt it overstuffing my ass with heat and hardness. Evaine's hand slid up my spine to brush my cheek.

"Oh fuck, Max," I gasped. They were my first coherent words in what felt like forever. "Cum in my ass!"

Max's fingers tightened around my waist and he slammed himself deep into me, but Evaine didn't tell him to stop. Not anymore. I had shown restraint and now it was time for my reward.

"Lil...!" Max groaned.

He filled me with steel and then with cream. His cock pulsed inside me and flooded me. I was drowning in slick, blazing sensation, consumed by the feeling of Max pumping my ass full of cum. Each liquid geyser was as hot as magma, searing my nerves. There was too much – Max's cock had barely fit up my ass and his load was far too massive. It spurted and leaked from my overtaxed hole to soak the sheets as my vision went gray and hazy.

When I came back to my senses, I lay curled on my side in the bed beside Max. He leaned against the headboard, stroking my damp hair. Evaine sat naked on my other side, inching her fingers down my body toward my spunk-filled ass.

"Good lesson," I murmured.

Chapter
SEVEN

The next week in English, I actually had a finished essay to hand in. I didn't even flip the teacher off at the end of class. It was way too late in the school year to make a good impression, but there was no need to worsen a bad one.

Feeling pretty damned grown up, I stuffed my notebook and ratty school copy of *The Once and Future King* into my backpack as the bell rang. I followed the rest of my class out the door and fell into step beside Max. He smiled at me.

"What do you want to bet that I get a better grade than you?" I asked.

Max laughed. "Just because you managed to turn in a paper on time for once doesn't mean you're going to get a good grade."

"And you are?"

"Maybe," Max said, flashing me some dimple. He checked his watch. "I need to pick up sugar for Miss Dean before Home Ec tomorrow and get Peter's baseball stuff out to him for practice. He forgot his bag this morning."

English was our final class of the day and I wasn't supposed to report to Evaine for another hour, so I walked with Max toward the parking lot. Some of the other students waved to us on the way out.

Mostly to Max. You might have noticed that I have kind of an attitude problem and Evaine's efforts to smooth my jagged edges were relatively recent.

"Want a ride to the studio?" Max asked.

"Nah," I said. "You've got a lot of shit to take care of and I was thinking of hitting the library for a bit."

Max whistled, impressed, and held open the gate that led out past the football field to the student parking lot. When the chain-link banged shut, I grabbed Max's wrist and began hauling him off the sidewalk.

"Um," he said. "The truck's over there."

He pointed off across the gravel lot, strewn with a hundred other old beater cars. None of the kids at Southport High School got Corvettes for their sixteenth birthday. The only time we saw nice cars at Southport High was when one of the fancy Northbay schools was having an away game on our end of town.

I led Max in the direction of the football field, to a stand of redwood trees that hadn't so much been planted there as just grew up against the back row of bleachers like massive weeds. By the time the janitors got around to dealing with them, the trees were too big to pull out without hiring a landscaping crew to do the job. The Southport PTA had been trying to raise the money for that since my freshman year.

Under the tangled redwood branches, the sun shone in broken mosaic patterns across bare earth and discarded cigarette butts. I could still hear other kids talking about their weekend plans and complaining about homework assignments so close to summer vacation, but the parking lot was hidden from view. We were alone under the red pillars of the trees. I released Max and stepped back a few feet – I couldn't get much further away without bumping into a tree trunk or stumbling out into the parking lot again.

"Get your cock out," I said.

Max sighed, but he was smiling and his rising blush colored the dimples in his cheeks.

"I've got those errands to run, you know," he protested even as he dropped his backpack against the base of a tree. "And then I need to get home and make dinner."

"You can always walk away from me," I said.

Max didn't answer. He just unbuttoned his jeans and slowly drew the zipper down. I wanted to dive in there and grab his dick, but as I had learned, some things were worth waiting for. Max reached down into his boxers, flushed and darted a look around the redwood grove, then pulled his cock out. It was already half hard and lay long across Max's palm.

"Mmm, yeah," I said. "Now jerk off for me."

Max blinked. "I... uh... what?"

"Evaine says I can collect sexual energy even when no one's touching me. That it's about desire, not actual contact. Remember when you were fucking Evaine at the studio last week?"

Max's cock thickened and grew longer in his hand. "Oh... yeah, I remember."

"I felt it. I felt it when you wanted me, even though you were balls-deep in Evaine's hot little pink pussy."

Another inch. Max's fingers closed almost convulsively around his rising cock.

"I want to try it," I said. "I just want to watch you touch yourself."

"And see if you uh... charge up off it?" Max asked.

I nodded, but had to admit to myself that it wasn't the only reason. I had never seen a guy masturbate except on the internet, and grainy video shoved through a shitty modem didn't count.

Max's fist tightened around his dick. He leaned back against one of the redwood trees and let out a deep sigh. His hand moved up, fingers circled under the big blunt head. Silky skin slid over the hardening flesh beneath, then grew taut as Max's cock lengthened.

He tugged down to the base, just above his balls and a liquid pearl of precum beaded at the tip. Max squeezed with another sigh and it dripped down his flushed length. When Max pumped his fist up again, the oozing wetness left his dick gleaming. I wanted to jump him *so* badly. But I waited. I was getting pretty good at this patience stuff.

Max's blush seemed just about permanently seared into his cheeks, but he jerked his cock in swift, smooth strokes without faltering. I felt that golden energy building slowly. It wasn't the same as when Max was fucking me, but it was just as sweet.

I watched closely, memorizing how my best friend liked to be touched. Yesterday, Evaine had donned a shiny blue strap-on and instructed me through trying some things that Max confirmed felt amazing, but this was different. This was what Max did for himself and I wanted to be able to do it, too.

"Damn, that's sexy," I said in a low voice.

"Really?"

Max's hand slowed and then stopped. I almost punched him for that, but Max was holding his hard cock out for me to look at. I bit my lip against a moan and felt another searing jolt of Max's lust.

"You uh… like watching?" he asked. His voice was far less steady than his hand.

"You have no idea," I said. "Will you cum for me? I want to see it. I want to watch you blow a huge load for me."

Max's fingers closed once more into a fist and his head fell back against the tree's rust-red bark. His grip was so tight around his dick that it forced another big, pale pearl of precum from the end. Max pumped his cock faster.

"Fuck, Lil. That's sexy," he panted, echoing my earlier words.

"What? Saying how much I like your dick? How much I want to see it shoot?"

I stepped closer and Max's breath came in short gasps. When I went down to my knees on the ground, he groaned aloud.

"You think I'm hot, right?" I asked.

I knew he did. I drank in the bright gold glow of his desire for me with every stroke along his cock, but I still wanted to hear it.

"God yes," Max said in a breathless, husky voice. "So beautiful, Lil. I..."

His knuckles were a line of white dots. Even in June, it didn't get very hot on the coast, but sweat ran down Max's skin. My senses were sharp enough now to smell the warm, musky scent of his arousal. I breathed it in with a satisfied sigh that only seemed to inflame Max more. His free hand came up, shoving his shirt out of the way to rake his fingernails over his hard stomach, down toward his cock and leaving flushing streaks across his skin.

"Do you always shoot so much cum?" I asked in a low purr. "Or is that just for me? I love knowing *I* did that. That *I* made you cum. It's *my* cum, Max, and I want it!"

Max's whole body went tight. I could have watched him like that all day. I'd like to say that it was by merit of my hard-won self-restraint that I didn't stuff my hand down my pants, but that would be a lie. The urge to finger myself off was strong, but drowned out by the single-minded desire to make Max cum all over my face. I wanted him helpless in the throes of his pleasure. Needed it. My heart raced as fast as Max's hand moved.

"Yes, Lil. Yes..." he breathed. "All yours, as much as you want..."

I leaned forward, staring, and Max came. Hot white spunk splashed my face and ran slowly down my skin. Max loosed one huge torrent after another for me, all over me. So much cum, just like I had asked.

Max sagged against the redwood tree and looked down at me, blushing even harder as he took in the sight of my face covered in his load. I basked in the glow of his desire for a long moment before I grabbed the hand that Max offered and stood up.

I licked my lips, tasting, and then ran my fingers through the thick cum on my cheeks. I flicked it out across the packed earth and trees, pale against dark soil and red bark. Marking my territory, I thought with a grin, claiming it all as my fuckspot.

"Mmm. Thanks, Max," I said.

"You're thanking me?" he asked. "You're uh... welcome. I made a pretty big mess, though."

"Well, that's what I asked for."

Still blushing, Max stuffed his cock back into his jeans and carefully zipped them up again. Damn, that was a sexy sight. If Max didn't have other shit to do, I probably would have torn his clothes off and fucked him right there.

He shouldered his backpack. "Sure you don't want a ride?"

"Yeah," I said. "Go on, get out of here before I jump you."

Max didn't look like he would mind that, but he nodded and headed off through the trees in the direction of the parking lot.

When he was gone, I picked my way through the trees toward the gym. I wiped most of Max's cum off my face, but a lot of it had soaked into my shirt. I needed to clean up and change before making the walk out to Evaine's studio. The idea of spending the afternoon in my gym clothes was unappealing, but they were the only spares I had at school. If this kind of stuff was really going to be the rest of my life, I had to start carrying around extra clothes. Or at least dress in layers.

Southport High School usually emptied swiftly after the final bell. Our sports teams weren't very well funded and there certainly wasn't much money left over for any other after-school programs. So when I emerged from the overgrown thatch of redwoods, I should have been alone.

I wasn't.

A huge black dog crouched in the parking lot. No, not a dog. No dog was that big, that black or that... wrong.

The monster stared at me with eyes the color of blood. Another pair of eyes opened along the hound's muzzle. And then another and another – rows of otherworldly red eyes, all fixed on me.

The massive dog growled deep in its throat and hunkered down, shoulders knotting up to pounce. Dark claws like oversized onyx fishhooks dug inch-deep furrows into the ground. I grabbed a fallen redwood branch and held it out.

"Good dog," I said in a cracking voice. "Fetch!"

I hurled the stick off across the parking lot. Not even one of the hellhound's multitude of eyes flicked toward it.

"Yeah..." I said. "Didn't think that was going to work."

The monstrous black dog leapt at me. I shrieked like a girl half my age and ran. My feet kicked up sprays of gravel and then I was moving.

And holy shit, how I was moving. I could always run a pretty respectable mile in PE, but now my body was flush with the energy of watching Max and the parking lot blurred past as I ran. Between me and a car moving at highway speeds, it would have been a photo finish.

I laughed and the wind whipped the sound away. There was no way that freaky black dog could keep up... Until I crashed face-first into the chain-link fence. Metal screeched and the links distended, but then they threw me back down to my ass in the dirt.

Right. Note to self: pay attention to where you're running.

I rolled back up to my feet and whirled. The dog was right on my heels – it was slower than me, but not by much. A dozen eyes burned like coals along its malformed head. I looked at the fence again. If I was strong enough to snap a headboard, maybe I was strong enough to–

There wasn't time to complete the thought. I bunched my legs beneath me and jumped. I sailed up, nearly caught my jeans on the top of the fence and then thumped down to the ground on the other side. The hellhound lurched to a stop where I had just been and its huge jaws snapped shut on empty air.

"Ha!" I said, patting the dust off my ass. "Not so tough now, are you?"

The monster dog snarled again and threw itself into the distended fence. It bit and steel strained, then sheared between the hellhound's long teeth. Before my heart could do much more than stutter, the beast had bitten a me-sized hole right through the fence.

"Oh shit," I said.

I spun away and kept running. Not so fast that I couldn't see what was coming this time – slamming myself into a concrete wall at seventy miles per hour would probably kill me as surely as the big, mangy monster nipping at my heels – but fast enough. At least, I hoped so.

Bounding up the stairs that led to the English building, my mind worked just as quickly through what the hell I was supposed to do next. Call the police? I had broken my cell phone on my birthday and my foster parents wouldn't buy me a new one yet. Campus security? What exactly could they do against an eleven-foot-long wolf-dog from hell? Taser it? Maybe give it detention?

My feet pounded on the cracked concrete path that ran from the math building to science. I spotted a couple of silhouettes in the darkened window of my biology classroom. I couldn't tell if they were students or teachers. Either one might have been sharing a joint after class. I considered shouting at them or maybe crashing straight through the glass, but then all I could see was the looming black reflection of the hellhound. It was close enough to feel the heat of its breath on my neck. No one at school could help now...

Evaine! I had to get to Evaine. She would know what to do.

I risked face-planting against a row of lockers and poured on a little more speed. I pulled ahead of the hellhound again, but we were almost at the front gate of the high school and there was another seven-foot wall of chain-link suddenly looming up ahead. I planted my heel, felt the hot golden rush of inhuman power burning through my muscles and jumped. I landed on the other side, right next to a mother and her freshman daughter exiting the administration office. They shrieked and grabbed one another.

"Get the fuck out of here!" I shouted. "Go!"

Mother and daughter gasped and fled back into the front office. I wasn't sure if they were doing what I told them or just trying to get away from me, but I didn't stick around to ask. Behind me, the hell-hound didn't even slow down – it charged right into the fence, snapping and snarling and tearing its way through the chain-link again.

Which way was Evaine's dance studio? I sprinted across the upper parking lot – the one for teachers and visiting parents – and out onto the sidewalk. What street was I on? Pierpoint? Yes!

The hellhound burst through the fence behind me and bounded across the parking lot in long, loping strides. I think I left some shoe rubber on the ground in my haste to pull ahead.

Along the straightaway of the Pierpoint Road sidewalk, I had the advantage. There wasn't much to smash into and I could really let loose. Car horns honked, but I didn't know if those were at me or the huge black blur chasing after me. Would someone call the police? I wasn't sure whether to hope for that or not.

I reached the intersection of Pierpoint and South Carver Street. The crosswalk light was red and cars wove their way through the road in front of me. In the afternoon traffic, they moved a lot slower than my crack-cheetah sprint. If I just timed it right, I should be able to slip between the cars...

I had to slow down for my opening. My hesitation was only a fraction of a second, but it was enough for the hellhound to close the distance between us. I heard its thunder-rumble growl and spun toward it, staring into crooked rows of glowing red eyes. I smelled the beast's breath, like cold stone.

Shit, I was dead. But if I was going to die, it wasn't going to be like this, eaten by a fucking monster. I threw myself backward, right into the road. I raised my middle finger, flipping off the hellhound as I fell.

Gleaming obsidian fangs snapped shut on my shirt and yanked me back, momentarily arresting my fall. But then the cloth tore and

I kept tumbling, leaving the hound with nothing but my shredded t-shirt clenched in its teeth.

Well, at least my cumstain problem was solved.

I fell out into traffic. Tires screeched and horns honked. I caught just a glimpse of tinted windshield and wide eyes, then the car slammed into me. Glass and bones shattered and someone was screaming. I flew across the pavement, my mouth full of blood. I smashed down into the asphalt and everything exploded in pain...

But I wasn't dead. The sexual energy Max had given me burned with a fire that would have been blinding if it were something you could see. It poured through me, impossibly pulling my broken bones back into place.

I leapt up to my feet again. Blood spattered my bra and my whole body hurt like hell, but I was alive. I got hit by a car and survived! Traffic had lurched to a complete standstill, though, as everyone stared at the topless girl in the road. Somebody whistled... I think. My ears were ringing like the final bell of the school day.

The car that had hit me had come to rest in the middle of the intersection. Its driver jumped out and ran toward me. I recognized him from my math class – I was pretty sure his name was James. He must have just left the high school.

"Oh my god!" James shouted, waving his arms. "Are you okay?"

"Yeah, I'm fine," I said.

I turned this way and that, searching for the hellhound. There, stalking through the shadows between the stopped cars. It moved with eerie speed even with its belly pressed low to the ground.

James was still running toward me with his arms outstretched. "Do you need CPR?"

"No!" I cried. "Get back in your car!"

"Are you *sure* you don't need mouth-to-mouth?"

The hellhound was closing in. So was James.

"Yeah!" I shouted. "Get the fuck out of here!"

"...Please?" James asked.

The monster leapt at me. I shoved James to the side hard enough to bounce him off the door of the nearest car and slam it shut on the driver, who had been about to climb out. James' eyes went glassy with the impact, but he hit the ground as the huge black hound landed where he had just been. Its claws raked sparks up along the surface of the road.

I darted between the cars. Voices bellowed and horns honked, but I was more worried about the deep snarl coming from right behind me. I dodged around a blue minivan and then I was on the far side of the intersection, back on the sidewalk. Only four more blocks to Evaine! Just across the Pierpoint bridge and then a left down Bayview...!

The hellhound chased down the sidewalk after me, its long black claws leaving gouges in the concrete. What would they do to my flesh if it caught up? Would I be able to heal from that?

My chest burned and my legs ached. What the hell? I'd felt fine through the whole sprint across the high school. Scared as fuck, but no panting or cramps... But now I could barely catch my breath. And even more frightening, I was slowing down.

Evaine had told me that the power I got from sex was finite. It only lasted for about a day after I got it. What if I could burn through it, too? How much had it taken to heal my body when James just about turned me into a hood ornament? Enough that I was running on fumes now.

Sweat streamed down my face and the back of my neck. The hellhound devoured the yards between us. If I were lucky, I'd make it out onto the bridge before the hound was on me. I ran for all I was worth, but I was moving no faster than your average topless girl in a horror movie.

For the second time in five minutes, I was sure I was about to die. Or worse.

Cold air raised the hairs across my bare, sweaty skin as I staggered out onto Pierpoint bridge. The wind always blew up off the distant water, the long finger tributary of the bay. Every year, some dumb-ass kid climbed over the railing and dove off the bridge, underestimating the strong, icy tides even during the summer. Dark seawater churned and hissed fifty feet below, loud enough to still be audible over the unceasing grumble of cars.

It was the howl, though, that made goosebumps break out all across my skin. I turned back toward the sound. Maybe I could at least die on my feet, fighting the hellhound... Who the hell was I kidding? I didn't know how to fight, but I was damned well going to try.

The hellhound crouched at the end of the bridge. Its fur bristled like great porcupine quills and the rows of red eyes remained fixed on me... but it didn't follow me over the water. The monster paced across the sidewalk, staring at me. It let out another blood-chilling howl and then vanished. Just... vanished, like it had never been there at all.

My legs turned to rubber and I sagged against the railing. A couple of freshman boys that had been walking home ahead of me came jogging back, eyes wide.

"Wow, what happened?" one of them asked, looking me up and down.

"Did... didn't you see the big-ass dog thing?" I gasped, pointing the way I had come, where the hellhound had just been.

The freshmen shook their heads and I felt the hot, youthful burn of their lust. Yeah, of course they hadn't seen the hound. Not when there was a girl running down the road in jeans and her bra. I shoved past the boys and staggered across the bridge in the direction of Evaine's studio.

Chapter EIGHT

I ran as best I could the rest of the distance to the dance studio. When I came wheezing and stumbling through the door, Evaine was waiting for me.

"You're late," she said.

"Huge... dog..." I panted. "Fuck-ton of eyes... chased me..."

"Rest for a moment, Lilith. Then tell me precisely what happened. Where is your shirt?"

Evaine led me over to the stairs and I sank down onto the bottom step. I gulped down a few breaths and stared up at her. Evaine was dressed for a workout of some kind. She wore a pair of blue leggings and a white sports bra. Her pale hair was pulled back into a braid that fell all the way to her waist.

"There was this... massive black hellhound-looking thing at the school," I told Evaine. "It chased me and I ran. It didn't seem to give a crap about anyone else, though. I got hit by a car, but I healed."

One of Evaine's silvery eyebrows shot up. "Where did you get the sexual energy to do that?"

"I had Max jerk off for me."

"And he gave you the energy to regenerate from major wounds?" Evaine asked, brow still raised.

I nodded.

"I see," she said. "Did any of the humans witness you using your powers?"

"Uh, a couple of people. Kind of. There was a lot going on and I was shirtless when James tried to run me over." I gestured to my bare midriff. "But I couldn't move so fast after that. I think putting my bones back together took a lot out of me."

"Where is the beast now?"

"Don't know. When I hit the Pierpoint bridge, it howled and stopped following me. Then it disappeared."

Evaine had crouched down next to me, but now she stood and put her hands on her hips. She regarded the studio's front door with a hard expression.

"What the fuck was that thing?" I asked.

"What you faced today was a grim," she answered. "A demon-hound. They live on the fringes of the Nether and serve the demons there."

"I uh... what now? Demon-hound?" My voice squeaked a little. "What did it want with me?"

"I am not yet certain. Grims are not true demons and so not bound by the Seal of Avalon. They are one of the few things that – with difficulty – can pass from the Nether and into this world."

Evaine gestured for me to stand. I rose on shaking legs and followed her into the practice room. She had set out padded mats along the wooden floor. Evaine picked up a duffel bag from the corner and tossed it to me. It was light enough to catch easily.

"There are clothes inside," she said. "Put them on and wait here for me."

"Wait? What?" I cried. "Where are you going?"

"Grims cannot cross running water, even over a bridge, which is what saved you today. But they are hunting dogs and now this one will try to return to its master in the Nether and report. I must find the grim before it can do so."

I looked down at the duffel bag in my arms. Evaine was... going to find the grim? While I waited here? My mysterious teacher was self-possessed and beautiful, but that demon-hound was a fucking monster. A perfect ass wasn't going to stop the hellhound.

I knew. I'd already tried.

But when I looked up to convince Evaine not to go, she was gone. I ran to the front door and yanked it open, searching wildly up and down the road outside. There was no sign of Evaine.

I closed the door and locked it, just in case, then went to change into the clothes Evaine had given me. There were a pair of light mesh shorts, a snug sports bra and a tank top to go over that. When I was finished dressing and splashing some water on my face, I was feeling a bit calmer. Enough to start getting curious and restless, at least.

I walked across the wooden floor to the mats and prodded at one with my toe. They seemed a lot like the ones stacked in the corner of the high school gym. What were they for? There was a perfectly good bed upstairs. I stepped onto the mat, feeling it compress slightly under my weight. Come to think of it, why did Evaine have the dance studio at all? Max and I could have done our homework at any library and fucked Evaine in a motel room. What did we need all of this space for?

"You forgot this at school," said a voice from behind me.

I jumped and turned. Evaine stood in the middle of the studio, holding my backpack. I guess I'd left it in the trees after making Max put on his show. A few curling strands of platinum blonde hair had come loose from Evaine's braid, but she seemed otherwise unperturbed.

"Holy fucking shitballs!" I cried. "You just about gave me a heart attack! Did... did you find the grim?"

Evaine nodded. She deposited my backpack against one of the mirrored walls.

"What happened?" I asked.

"I dealt with it," Evaine answered. She stepped onto the mat and looked at me with hard aquamarine eyes. "Come here."

"Am I in trouble? I mean... what about my homework?"

I gestured toward my backpack, but Evaine shook her head.

"Later," she told me. "It's time for you to learn how to use your body, Lilith."

"Isn't that what we've been doing for weeks?"

"You must learn how to defend yourself," Evaine explained. "And given what occurred today, it is past time for those lessons to begin."

"What? Fight? You... you think I could fight something like that huge demon-bear?"

"Demon-hound."

"Whatever," I said. "Do you really think I can fight a monster like that?"

"You may have to. There are many supernatural creatures in this world, Lilith. The grim is only one and not even among the most dangerous."

"What the hell could be worse than that thing?" I asked.

"Vampires and werewolves stalk humans through the night. There are Unseelie fae always ready to take advantage of an unwary mortal. Dragons and wyverns, yeti and ogres, living shadows and elementals of fire. That is why the College and the Castle have their hunters."

"Wait," I protested. "You told me there was a test! And if I pass, those bounty hunters aren't going to come after me, right?"

Evaine inclined her head. "That is more or less true."

That was... a strange answer. But I was more interested in what Evaine was offering: the chance to learn how to fight, how to defend myself if something like that demon-hound ever cornered me again. I closed my hands into fists and threw a few punches at the empty air.

"Alright, then," I said. "Teach me how to fight."

Evaine smiled gently and put her hands over mine, pushing them down. "Let's start with some basic stances."

———

I spent a lot of the next week on my back, but mostly because Evaine had thrown me down there. When I was all juiced up on sex, the bruises healed quickly, but there were a lot of long days of being tossed around, kicked and smacked.

Max still helped me with the sex and my homework. He had gotten a better grade on the English essay and offered to work with me on the next one. And after hearing about the grim, he insisted on giving me a ride to the dance studio every day, no matter what else was going on.

I don't know how many times we fucked in his truck, but let's just say that having reliable transportation didn't prevent me from being late to Evaine's lessons. On those days, combat training was extra fun. I punched my way right through three heavy bags and even smashed a chunk out of the concrete wall behind it. When I looked close, I could see the indentations left by each one of my knuckles.

A week before the end of the school year, Max dropped me off at the studio with a promise to bring dinner if I had to stay late. Which was happening a lot – Bill and Sandra barely saw me anymore, which suited everyone just fine.

I waved to Max and went inside. I was already dressed for more ass-kicking and the mats were still laid out across the dance studio. But today, Evaine stood at a folding table set up in front of one mirrored wall. A large duffel bag sat open on the top.

I approached cautiously, watching her in the mirror. My teacher wasn't above distracting me so she could catch me unaware, or hitting me when my guard was down. She said it was to teach me alertness. Evaine didn't seem the kind of woman who would beat me just to be cruel or prove her own superiority, so I was forced to take her seriously.

Sometimes Evaine scared the shit out of me.

"How was school today, Lilith?" she asked, not turning around or even looking at me in the mirror.

"Good," I said. "Looks like I'm actually going to graduate. Barely, but still."

"You've been working hard. I'm pleased."

I grinned, but before I could feel too proud of myself, Evaine was speaking again.

"But your greatest test is yet to come. Are you ready?" she asked.

"The College one? How can I be ready? You haven't told me anything about it!"

"The time is coming soon."

I badly wanted to follow up on that – Evaine turned being mysterious into a fucking art form – but then I forgot all about tests as she started covering the table in the contents of her duffel bag: pocket knives, big buck knives, and one huge curved blade as long as my forearm. There were brass knuckles, too, and something with spikes and a rattling steel chain.

"Uh... what are we doing today?" I asked.

And then Evaine began pulling out the big guns. Literally. From her death bag, Evaine withdrew revolvers and automatics, each larger than the last, until she held up – I shit you not – an Uzi.

"You are strong, Lilith," said Evaine. "But your power has limits. It can run out."

"Like with the grim."

Evaine nodded. She examined the cylinder of a massive .44 magnum.

"Precisely. And you are but one of many supernatural creatures that make their home in this realm. Few are as strong or fast as you are, Lilith. But those of demonic blood or taint – like vampires and werewolves – are most likely to take an interest in you and be able to match your power. In those contests, it is not your strength which will decide victory. You must be smarter and better prepared than your enemies."

"Do you really think I'll need to know this stuff?" I asked.

"Yes."

"Why? Is it going to be on the College's test? Am I going to have to duel a wizard or something?"

Evaine didn't answer that. She turned to me, holding a broadsword in one hand and the magnum in the other.

"Where do you wish to begin?" she asked.

Chapter
NINE

Graduation was almost uneventful. Bill and Sandra came. They sat next to Evaine and kept staring at her. I don't think she ever did introduce herself to them.

Max's parents were working that day, but Jake and Peter cheered like little lunatics when their big brother got up on stage. And they cheered just as loud for me. I seriously considered flashing them in thanks, but not everyone in the audience deserved that view. So I just waved and then winked at the principal as he handed over my diploma. He blushed and stammered his way through the rest of the ceremony.

Afterward, Bill smiled at me and Sandra gave me a hug that actually felt genuine.

"Congratulations, Lily," said my foster father. "You really pulled your act together. We're impressed."

Sandra nodded. "You're welcome to stay with us as long as you like, of course. But you're a young woman now and I'm sure you'll be wanting to strike out on your own soon."

I was still trying to figure exactly how to answer that when Max pushed his way through the crowd of shouting, laughing graduates and picked me up into a tight hug. He spun me in a circle before putting me down.

"Hey, we did it," he said, grinning. "We finished high school!"

"Yeah, it was pretty touch and go for me at the end. I couldn't have managed it without you, Max."

Evaine didn't need to push or shove her way to my side. She was simply there, wearing her white suit again. I wasn't sure if it was the one from when we first met or another just like it. Evaine put a hand on my shoulder and gave me a soft kiss on the cheek.

"You've done well, Lilith," she said. "There's only one last thing to finish."

"...The test?" I asked.

Evaine nodded. Her hand remained on my shoulder. "It's time."

My stomach knotted and I turned to Max, who was talking to Bill and Sandra. Something Bill said made my best friend blush a bright scarlet.

"Hey," I called to them. "I have to take care of something. I'll meet you guys at the house."

"I've been working on my lasagna in Home Ec all year," said Max. "I think I've finally got it down. Will you be back in time for dinner?"

My mouth went dry. "I... really hope so."

Max flashed me his dimples and a thumbs-up. I drew a deep breath and then looked at Evaine again.

"Okay," I said. "Let's go."

Evaine led me out to the parking lot and to a sleek silver convertible. It was a dead sexy machine, but I was too nervous to tell Evaine so. Max would have killed to get his hands on that car... Or at least given some epic puppy-dog eyes.

I climbed into the white leather passenger seat and Evaine started the car. The crush of traffic leaving the high school hadn't begun yet and we slid smoothly out onto Pierpoint Road. While Evaine drove us, I unzipped my green polyester graduation gown.

Underneath, I wore the knee-length black skirt and button-up silk blouse that she had given me. Now I understood why.

I caught my reflection in the rear-view mirror and gulped. I wasn't pulling off the good girl look very well.

Evaine took the freeway north and then west, out toward the edge of the city, almost up into the coastal mountains. We followed a twisting, single-lane road out to a long gravel driveway flanked on either side by vast, ancient oak trees. A substantial iron gate barred the way, but swung open as Evaine's car approached. A pair of big, fierce-looking gargoyle sculptures crouched on top of the tall gate-posts.

"Friendly," I said.

Evaine glanced at the gargoyles as we drove past. "The College is unknown to most humans and does not entertain many visitors. Not here, at least."

"Then why am I here?"

"You're a special case, Lilith."

Yay... I tried not to fidget.

Beyond the high stone walls stretched huge lawns and gardens that looked like a cross between an actual college and a massive arboretum. The buildings were old and impressive, all red brick cloaked in dark green ivy. The air was still and secretive.

I clasped my hands in my lap and willed them to stop sweating as Evaine parked under one of the oak trees. She got out of the car and after a moment of frozen terror, I did the same. We were in front of the largest building, a mansion bigger than any house I had ever seen.

"You still haven't told me what kind of test they're giving me," I said. My voice was tight and squeaky. "Are... are there hunters here already? Will they kill me if I fail? Like, immediately? Did you bring any of those guns? Can I have one?"

Evaine shook her head and gave me a lovely, gentle smile, but she didn't say anything. That only made me more nervous.

My knees were water and I was sure I was about to fall right over as Evaine took my arm and guided me across one of the manicured green lawns. The last month of training and teaching suddenly felt more like playing, like I was practicing to audition for *Buffy the Vampire Slayer*. Maybe the porn parody... But now, it was all too real. I was really at the College and the wizards here really would kill me if I didn't pass a test I knew nothing about.

Evaine escorted me not to the large mansion, but around the side to a small flat silver pond. It looked normal enough... except for the seven dark-clad figures gathered a few yards away from the water's edge. There were four men and three women, all at least twice my age and dressed in long robes, like judges.

Or like wizards. Holy shit, real wizards!

The ring of College sorcerers had been talking, but they fell silent at our approach and bowed to Evaine. I glanced sidelong at her. Was she some kind of foreign royalty? Was I having crazy sex with an obscure British princess? I sort of hoped so. If I was about to be gunned or wanded down by a bounty-hunting wizard, I would like to have done something awesome before my untimely demise.

But when I returned my attention to the circle of robed men and women, there was more than respect in their expressions. I saw worry there, too, and suspicion.

"It has been... some time since you last honored us with a visit, Lady," said the tallest of the wizards. He had a long, stern face and back-swept auburn hair just beginning to go gray at the temples. "Now you bring a cambion before us and ask us not to destroy such a creature."

I tensed and balled my hands into fists. They really did want to kill me. I wasn't going to make it easy. Evaine had taught me how to fight for a reason, even if she wouldn't give me a gun. How much good would a few weeks of martial arts do against magic, though? Well, I'd go down swinging, at least.

"She's dangerous," said the wizard.

"Dangerous to whom exactly, Vincent Myrdon?" Evaine asked in a smooth voice.

"To our entire world," answered the tall man, Vincent. "To all worlds."

"Merlin was a cambion," Evaine pointed out.

Wait, what? I knew that Merlin founded this group of wizards, but had he really been a cambion like me? Was he the one that Evaine talked about training? Fuck, how old *was* she? I really wanted to ask, but Vincent scowled so hard at us that I flinched back. Only Evaine's hand on my arm held me steady.

"Merlin's power – and this girl's – comes from demon blood," Vincent said. "And it was Merlin himself who sealed the demons away in the Nether to keep our world safe from them."

Evaine glided forward, pulling me into the ring of mages. A raven-haired woman cleared her throat and spoke.

"At your request, Lady," she said to Evaine, "we waited before dispatching our hunters to destroy this cambion. We charmed the memories of those who witnessed her powers in use. But now we can delay no longer. The girl must prove herself."

The wizard standing to her right was shorter than the others. He had a fuzzy white beard and peered at me over the rims of his thick glasses.

"She's just a child. This doesn't seem fair," he said.

"Even children can be dangerous," Vincent argued.

The black-haired sorceress nodded and pointed into the middle of the circle where Evaine and I stood.

"How old was Arthur when he took up Excalibur?" she asked. "Younger than this girl."

"Arthur was tested," said Evaine. "And Lilith deserves the same chance."

Vincent Myrdon bowed his head for a moment, then took a step toward me. His hand emerged from one voluminous black sleeve and I tensed, ready to run or fight.

The wizard brandished a simple bronze... cup? Goblet? It had a stem like a wineglass, but short and stocky. There was no design on the plain metal and it seemed old, like something from a museum.

Vincent held the cup out to me and, lacking any better ideas, I took it. It was heavier than it looked, but didn't zap me to ashes or anything. The wizards all stared at me.

"Uh..." I said. "Now what?"

"Go to the pond and fill the cup," Vincent answered.

"What? That's it?" I blurted. "I thought this was a test. I'm not a waitress!"

"Fill the cup."

Vincent's voice was hard and cold. If this was part of the test, then I was already fucking it up royally.

I walked through the ring of wizards and across the grass toward the pond, clutching the cup in both hands. Evaine watched me from just behind Vincent, neither smiling nor frowning. Not a lot of help there.

At the water's edge, I knelt and made sure I had a secure grip on the cup – I didn't think it would look very good if I had to jump in and fish it out. I waited for a tense moment, but nothing leapt from the pond at me, so I scooped up some water and stood again. After I checked that there was no mud or duckweed inside, I carried the full bronze cup back to the waiting wizards and offered it out to Vincent Myrdon.

My hands shook so hard that the water rippled and sloshed. Vincent took the cup and regarded me with an unreadable expression on his hard-lined face, then poured the water out into the grass at his feet.

"The test is complete," Vincent said.

I stared at the ground and then up at the tall, auburn-haired wizard. "What? You're not even going to drink it?"

"Of course not."

"That was your test? Can I carry some water? But that was easy!" I protested.

"Percival didn't find it so."

Max may have gotten a better grade on his *Once and Future King* book report, but I still recognized the name.

"Percival...? Like King Arthur's knight?" I asked.

Vincent ignored my question and raised the bronze cup.

"Her heart is as pure as any human's," he announced.

The other wizards nodded. The short one with the glasses even smiled at me. Vincent wasn't done, though.

"The Grail judges her heart only here and now," he said, pinning me with an unyielding stare. "You are not a monster... yet."

"Wow, thanks," I muttered.

"We will be watching you," said Vincent. "Should you ever become a danger to humanity, Lilith, then you will be hunted down without mercy and even the Lady cannot countermand that final order."

Evaine dipped her chin once in acknowledgement. With that, Vincent turned his back on me and walked away through the grass. The short little bespectacled wizard came to shake my hand and congratulate me, but then followed the rest out across the College grounds.

"Am I supposed to go with them?" I asked.

"No," said Evaine. "This is a place for the wizards, not for you. Unless you would like to follow in Merlin's footsteps and study their magic?"

I shook my head. "Did you see the way that Vincent guy was looking at me? No way do I want to attend a school where he's the principal."

"He's the High Magus. Vincent Myrdon has recently been elevated to the seat."

"Whatever," I said. "The point is, I really don't want to get sent to that guy's office for not following the dress code."

Evaine laughed and we began walking back across the green grass in the direction of her car.

"You have passed the College's test," she said. "Your whole life lies ahead of you. What will you do now?"

"I'm not sure. I guess I could go to college and become a vet or marketing rep or something... But that seems like kind of a waste. I mean, anyone can do that stuff."

Evaine gave me a sidelong glance. "Are you saying that you feel some obligation to use your unique abilities for the betterment of your world?"

"Hey, I've watched *Spider-Man*. With great power—"

"Comes great responsibility," Evaine finished.

"You know *Spider-Man* quotes?" I asked.

"The saying has been around for much longer than that, Lilith."

That wasn't a *no*. Evaine smiled mysteriously and I laughed.

"You can just call me *Lily*," I said. "If you want."

"Very well... Lily."

We walked a little further in silence while Evaine let me think.

"Hey, those hunters," I said at last. "The ones that the College would have sent after me if they thought I was dangerous... They're all wizards, right? You told Max something like that."

Evaine nodded.

"They hunt the monsters that hurt people," I said. "Things that humans can't fight."

Evaine nodded again.

"Do you think they would ever let someone like me become a hunter?" I asked slowly. "I mean, as long as I can get laid, I'm faster and stronger than any human. That's got to be useful for a monster hunter, right?"

Evaine stopped and turned to look at me.

"The life of a hunter is a perilous one," she told me in a serious voice. "Even for a woman of your considerable power. Is this truly the path you choose, Lily?"

"...Yeah. I think it is."

Evaine resumed walking and I fell into step beside her.

"You will need more training," she said. "What I have showed you are only the basics. If you wish to become a College bounty hunter, you will face the worst and most dangerous creatures in all the worlds. You have much more to learn, Lily."

I grinned at Evaine and picked up the pace. I couldn't wait to get started.

Chapter
TEN

Present day.

My cell phone buzzed in my pocket, wrenching me back out of my memories. I took my hand from Max's and pulled out my phone. The call was from Doyle, one of the other bounty hunters. I hit the green *accept* button.

"I heard you were after the unicorn, too," he said as soon as I picked up.

"Yes. And also, hello," I said.

Asshole.

Doyle ignored me. "Well, the hunt is over. I caught the unicorn and teleported it back to its own forest. It won't be eating any more mountain bikes. Or mountain bikers."

It was almost courteous of Doyle to let me know that the job was done. Now I didn't have to spend all weekend driving around the hills and shouting *Here unicorn, unicorn, unicorn!* like an idiot.

Almost courteous. Doyle was one of the youngest hunters and still felt the need to gloat whenever he managed to bag a bounty.

"Thanks, Doyle," I said. "Have fun spending your gold. Maybe you can even buy some friends."

I ended the call while the wizard was spluttering and pocketed my phone, then picked up my coffee again.

"Too late?" Max asked.

"Yeah," I said with a shrug.

Max sighed and ran a big hand through his hair. "Maybe you would have been there first if you hadn't stopped to chat with me."

"I'm pretty sure five minutes wouldn't have made a difference."

"Still, I'm sorry you lost this one, Lil. I know how important your job is to you," Max said. He regarded the counter full of suddenly extra food. "Do you want to take any of this home?"

"Hell yeah. I never turn down your cooking. I ate my entire birthday cake last week in fifteen minutes flat."

"I remember." Max made a mock-horrified face. "The carnage was terrible."

I laughed. "Hey, if Kalen's still locked up in the Tower, do you think I could bring you a special ingredient for next year's birthday cake?"

"Umm... yeah? It's your birthday, Lil. You can have anything you want."

Max helped me carry the food downstairs – which wasn't necessary when I was charged up, but I appreciated the gesture – and out to the parking lot. When it was all loaded into the trunk of my car, I stood up on my toes to kiss Max on the cheek. He wrapped his arms around me and held me tightly to him.

I shut my eyes and inhaled the scent of him. It was just the same as that first night together, when we discovered what I was. Max's body was hard against mine and growing harder.

"Thank you, Max," I murmured into his chest.

"For what?"

"You really did it, you know. You've stuck with me through all of the crazy shit."

"Always, Lil. Whatever happens, I'll always be here for you."

"I know," I told him.

I made myself release Max before either of us could get too caught up in the moment... but it was hard to let him go.

I climbed into my car and started the engine. Max stood in the parking lot and I waved to him. He waved back, but waited and watched as I pulled out into the road. Finally, Max turned around and headed back into his garage. What now?

I could probably track Derek – Darren – down again and pick up where we had left off. But I shrugged and turned right onto Valley Road, heading north toward the College. I might have missed the unicorn, but there were always other jobs.

For more stories by
Natalie and Eric Severine,
visit us at **LLStories.com**

LOOSE LEAF
STORIES